MW00390394

Unmending
THE VEIL

LISA HEATON

This is a work of fiction. Names, characters, places, and themes are the product of the author's imagination or are used fictitiously. Any resemblance to actual events or persons, living or dead, is coincidental.

Published by: Faith Forward Press
Mt. Juliet, TN

Copyright © 2012 Lisa Heaton

All rights reserved. No part of this book may be reproduced or transmitted in any form or by any means, electronic or mechanical, including photocopying, recording, or by any information storage and retrieval system, without permission in writing from the publisher.

ISBN: 978-1-7320068-0-5

Scripture taken from the HOLY BIBLE, NEW INTERNATIONAL VERSION Copyright © 1973, 1978, 1984, by International Bible Society. All rights reserved.

KING JAMES VERSION, SLIMLINE™ REFERENCE EDITION. NASHVILLE: THOMAS NELSON, INC., 1989

DEDICATION

"But by the grace of God I am what I am, and His grace to me was not without effect."
(1 Corinthians 15:10)

For Jesus, the Author and Perfecter of my faith.
I am no longer a mess because of You.

TITLES BY LISA:

On 4/19
Beyond 4/20
Deceiver
A Thousand Blessings
Room to Grow

Nonfiction:
You. Are. Loved. Live the Love Song

PROLOGUE

The Dream

Robin knelt in the thick mud, trembling, listening for Mike. Crouched beneath a row of dense brush, she feared she was still exposed. It was after midnight, a time she should have been hidden by darkness, but the moon was full and cast a telling glow over her white nightgown. Every labored breath burned deep into her lungs, and a piercing sensation ripped through her right side. Likely, her ribs were broken again. When she heard Mike sloshing through the mud in the not-so-far-off distance, she covered her mouth, hoping to muffle the sound of her raspy breathing. His footsteps grew only louder until Robin quit breathing altogether. He came to a stop just a few feet from where she hid. Through the openings of the spindly brush, she could see his ankles, and with no hope of escape, she watched as he took those final steps toward her.

"I told you not to run!"

Mike grabbed hold of her arms and snatched her from her hiding place, her bare feet dangling in mid-air as he held her face-to-face with him.

He staggered in his drunkenness, his eyes so heavy that when he blinked for too long, he swayed as if he might fall over. Like it did most often these days, his breath reeked of whiskey and made her nauseous. Robin searched his eyes, hoping for some sign of the old Mike. This night, he was a stranger who treated her as if he had never loved her at all.

Robin sobbed and pleaded with him. "Mike, you love me. Please stop this."

Unfazed, he slung her to the ground.

She skidded several feet before colliding with a protruding tree root, her face taking the brunt of the blow. It left a peculiar taste of blood mingled with dirt in her mouth, so she began to gag and spit. Mike was doubled over with his hands on his knees for support, heaving. Often the sickness would be the end of the violence, but unsure this night, she pulled herself up onto her knees and began to crawl away.

When she felt his hands wrap around her ankles, she began to kick and struggle, but with ease Mike flipped her over and reached down to pick her up. He was crying at this point.

"I won't let you leave me," he said in nearly a whisper as he tossed her over his shoulder and stomped back through the mud the way they had come.

PART ONE

ONE

Robin sat atop the steep stone steps, ones crafted with painstaking precision and embedded into the earth over a century before. In June, while the days were warm and sunny in New Hampshire, early morning at sunrise was still cool and crisp. Crisp enough, in fact, that when she breathed in, the air stung her nose. While it was refreshing, there was something about it that took her back, made her remember running and the sting of chilly air burning her nose and lungs.

She had run the night before in her sleep, looking for a place to hide. What she was experiencing, more often in the past weeks than in many years, was reliving the end of things. It was the night that put an end to who she was and where she belonged. In the wake of it, she had become a misplaced object.

In an effort to chase away the memory, Robin stood and started down the steps, ready to get a start on her day. Small fishing boats began to appear out of the mist that often blanketed the lake. A boater waved. She waved in return, thankful to see signs of life and summer as Lake Winnipesaukee exploded with color and vacationers flooded the area inns, cabins, and summer homes. Within the hour the grounds and water would come alive as more people began to stir about.

She glanced back at the charming old mansion, her home year-round. With soft yellow clapboard siding, it appeared to be the sun itself sitting on the hillside as it glowed in the early morning light. Robin had long since decided if she must be misplaced, there was no lovelier place to be. While others had to wait for summer vacation to enjoy the scenery, she lived out her life with breathtaking views in her backyard. If there was a possibility of being near to God anywhere, it was here.

Robin stopped when she reached the steps leading to the porch of the Willow and turned back to watch as the morning sun danced and twinkled along the water. This was her favorite cabin since it had the finest view at the inn. There were plenty of shade trees surrounding the small cabin, yet there was a nice clearing leading directly to the lakeshore.

Once inside, she went into each of the two bedrooms. Just as she was leaving the second, the front door swung open and a man tossed a duffle bag through the doorway.

The man froze. "Oh, I'm sorry. I must have the wrong cabin." He reached for his bag.

"No, wait." Robin moved toward the door. "You have the right cabin. I was just checking things out to make sure it was ready for you."

This was the school teacher. For some reason she had expected a bald man wearing horn-rimmed glasses. This man was like no teacher she had in school, with his tattered jeans, old t-shirt, and bare feet.

When she realized she was staring at him, Robin laughed. "Well, everything's fine here. I'll be going. Enjoy your stay."

"Chris Wheeler." He dropped the bag again and held out his hand.

Robin took his hand and nodded. "I know. I spoke with you on the phone."

"Yeah, about the reservation for the other cabin, I won't need it after all. I will pay whatever cancellation fee you need to charge. But I still want this one for the summer."

"No worries. It will rent out soon enough."

For a few seconds Chris stood there staring at her. Then, after blinking a few times, said, "Well, I'll run back to the car and get the rest of my gear."

In an effort to lessen the awkwardness of the moment, Robin smiled and said, "Do you need any help?"

"Sure, thanks."

Chris led the way to his car. Once there, he grabbed the smallest of his bags from the trunk and handed it to her. "I appreciate your help."

She grabbed another of the larger bags. "No problem."

"Hey, that's pretty heavy."

"I've got it."

When she lifted the bag with little effort, he whistled. "Wow, a real mountain woman."

She laughed out loud at that since she considered herself on the girly side.

While they walked back to the cabin, Chris tried to make small talk, about the weather and the lake. Robin didn't say much in return. He seemed nice enough, but by the time she reached the porch, she couldn't get away from him fast enough. It was something about the way he looked at her. Or maybe it was the dimples that formed when he smiled at her.

Chris took his bag from her and tossed it on the porch. "I can get the rest later."

"If you'd like." With that Robin turned to go, saying over her shoulder, "See you around."

***

Chris stood on the porch and watched the woman move toward the main house, realizing she had never mentioned her name. Now, thinking about it, it seemed intentional. She was kind, yet impersonal, since she never made eye contact. Her voice was sweet, though, and with her subtle accent, he supposed she wasn't originally from the region.

He smiled at his reaction to her, how he had stumbled in the conversation. What he had first noticed were her eyes – they were dark, velvety brown and obviously capable of causing a chemical meltdown in his brain. Still baffled by the awkwardness of their encounter, he grabbed his bags from the porch and headed into the cabin.

The photos online did not do the place justice. The main living area was warm and inviting with a stone fireplace on the opposing wall from the front door. A sofa faced the fireplace and two oversized armchairs flanked it. All was in good order and updated.

Chris threw a bag onto the bed and sat, stifling a yawn. It was early, but he hadn't slept more than three hours the night before in anticipation of the trip. Lately, even when he did sleep well, fatigue still plagued him. This was new for him. A slower pace was not a lifestyle he knew how to navigate.

Now surrounded by utter quietness, a nonexistent luxury in his condo back in Boston, his mind jumped to Vanessa and he replayed their last conversation. She was supposed to come with him for the first week but at the last minute decided she wasn't camping material. It had been her idea to tag along, even though he had all but said he wanted time alone. Her words, that she wasn't up for ten days of self-analysis and life introspection, aggravated him still and sounded like something she had gotten from Dr. Phil.

By the time he had left her place, though, he could only feel sorry for her. This wasn't what she had signed up for, being with him through all that was ahead. He could hardly blame her for bailing out. She said it was too much for her to handle. It was too much for anyone to handle, especially in a new relationship.

Chris looked around the small cabin and got a sense that this was exactly where he needed to be. If Vanessa had come, he would have spent his time catering to her emotions rather than doing what he felt most led to do, spending the time he had left with God.

***

On her way back to the main house, Robin tried to focus on anything but Mike. After her encounter with Chris it began again. With every blink she saw Mike's face, not his angry face but the one of shock, disbelief, and finally fear. She stopped before reaching the dock and rubbed her eyes, trying to force the scene from her mind, but her stomach began to churn like usual. No matter how many times she tried to convince herself it was over and done, there was a small part of her that wondered if it would ever be. For years she had lived her life as if something large and looming teetered overhead. Especially over the past few weeks, she sensed a storm was brewing, one she could never face and survive.

A guest stopped her near the shore and asked about area attractions. She just stood there looking at him, her mind blank. Information that she typically knew off the top of her head was simply gone.

"Come with me, and I'll get some brochures for you," Robin said, trying to play off her lapse in memory.

They walked and made small talk along the way. Even then, Robin found her mind wandering. Once she got Mr. Tucker squared away, she went to find Emma.

Robin pushed through the swinging door and moved into the large sunny kitchen. She had to grin at the sight before her. Emma, the inn's owner and her best friend, was standing there with a muffin hanging from her mouth, stirring a large bowl of pancake batter. Since she had known her all her life, Robin often wasn't as aware of Emma's loveliness as she was at that moment. In her early fifties, Emma was more stunning than most women twenty years her junior, Robin included.

Robin sat on a stool nearby. "Do you need any help?"

"Not so much," Emma drawled, her Southern accent more pronounced than usual, "but you can get the sausage out."

Robin went to the refrigerator, stopping on the way to plant a kiss on Emma's cheek and adjust her hair clip, a little butterfly glued to the end of a brown bobby pin. Emma liked all things winged and colorful, so most days her auburn hair was adorned with some sort of flying creature.

In an attempt to sound more chipper than she felt, Robin said, "How did you sleep?"

"Like a log. How 'bout you?"

Robin looked away. "I've had better nights." Still, the fog of a fitful night was heavy upon her. Her eyes burned from interrupted sleep and her mouth was dry.

"Are you okay? I heard you call out."

With a nod Robin moved to the sink.

Emma stopped stirring and looked at her. "Are you sure you're all right?"

"Yes." Then Robin said with more honesty, "It shakes me up for a while, but by midday it usually goes away." That wasn't at all true. It never completely went away.

While Robin washed up at the kitchen sink, Emma moved in close behind her. "Did you see him?"

She played innocent. "See who?"

"The blond-haired cutie in the Willow."

"His name is Chris, and yes, I saw him."

"I'm thinking summer romance," Emma said and sipped her coffee, looking at Robin over her cup with mischief in her eyes.

Robin dried her hands and shook her head. "No offense, but he may be a little young for you."

"Watch it!" Emma was smiling still. "You know what I mean – you."

"And you know better."

"He was too early for check in, but who am I to turn him away?" Emma whistled and waved her dish towel. "If I were a few years younger, why, he'd be in trouble."

"Oh, right! Listen to you. If he paid you any attention at all, you would run and jump in the lake."

Robin laughed at the thought of Emma pursuing any man. She rarely dated. With sultry brown eyes and an hourglass figure, every unattached man in the surrounding county had made a play for her at one time or another. The only man she could ever remember Emma showing interest in was Stan Cooper, the vet in a nearby town, but even he had never won Emma's heart. Robin had to believe no man ever would.

Emma laughed along with Robin. "I wouldn't go so far as to jump in the lake, but you're right, I would run."

She popped Robin with her dish towel. "Food is on the sideboard. Go eat, sassy girl."

The buffet was loaded with every breakfast food imaginable, all presented on extravagant serving dishes and platters. Since breakfast was the only meal provided at the inn, Emma insisted on pulling out all the stops. The guests who stayed in the cabins were invited as well, so on any given morning during the summer months, the dining room was full of chatter and excitement over the day to come.

Robin sat alone at a table near the window and watched as Chris walked toward the inn. He disappeared from sight for just a few seconds before he walked into the dining room and toward the buffet. It was then she noticed he still wore no shoes. With his messy hair and bare feet, she had a sense he was a man who drifted with the wind and envied him that.

His back was to her as he piled his plate high, especially with bacon. She would have to let Emma know to plan on making more. Then he turned to look at her, catching her staring at him as he had on the porch before. She only nodded and turned her attention back to her food as she stabbed a piece of sausage and twirled it around in her syrup. Just as she poked it into her mouth and a dribble of syrup ran down her chin, he walked up to her table.

"Is this seat taken?"

She wiped her face and scanned the room. There were a dozen tables in the room, five of them empty.

"Uh, no."

"May I sit with you?"

"Sure. I'm just about done, though." Robin began to squirm.

Chris sat across from her and pointed to her plate. "You've barely touched your food."

"I have other guests checking in soon."

"I've counted six cabins. How many rooms are here in the main house?"

"We only rent out four on the second floor."

"It's even better than the photos online. This room is magnificent." He glanced up at the lofty ceiling. "Hard to imagine that people once lived here, lived like this."

"A bit too ornate for my taste, but guests seem to like it."

"I guess you live like this." He grinned and looked out the wall of windows. "You get this spectacular view all the time."

"It is beautiful. I'm fortunate." She stood and picked up her plate. "Well, I hope you enjoy your breakfast."

Without waiting for his response, Robin moved away from the table.

Robin set her plate in the sink, closed her eyes, and drew in a deep breath. Chris was handsome, and she had been alone for so long now. A man like that could only cause problems. Never once in all the years she had worked at the inn, had she been attracted to a guest. In this case it wasn't just a weekend ahead to try to avoid him; it was the entire summer.

"What's wrong with you?" Becky said.

"Nothing." Robin pushed thoughts of the teacher out of her mind. "Where've you been?"

"I went to the station with Tommy. He wanted to gas up the boat and get bait to take a group out fishing."

"I came up to your room, assuming you were still asleep. But then I guess I forgot how much you like going to get gas and bait." Robin scowled. "I suppose you were looking for Brad?"

"Not exactly." Becky looked away.

"He was a jerk last summer. I can't imagine that will be any different this year." When Becky only shrugged at that, Robin patted her arm. "Be careful. I just don't want to see you get hurt."

With the change in her appearance, Robin suspected that if Becky did run into Brad, he would regret letting her go. She had dropped a few pounds and highlighted her already blond hair. Even before the changes, though, she was beautiful, inside and out. This year, however, there was something more sophisticated about her; she seemed less a girl and more a woman.

"Have you seen the guy from the Willow?" Emma said to Becky as she stepped in from the dining room.

"No. Who is it?"

Robin wanted nothing to do with the conversation. "While you two old hens gossip, I'm going to work. Is Tommy outside?"

Becky shook her head and rolled her eyes. "Yes. He's out on the dock and in a mood."

Robin found Tommy working on an inboard motor, his long and lanky body stretched across the back of the boat. The last thing she needed was one of the boats to be out of commission. "Is something wrong?"

He glanced up at her and then back at his task. "Nope, I'm just replacing the spark plugs. I filled her up this morning and got some bait. Does the old couple still want to go out?"

"Yes. I told them you would be ready at eight." She paused and waited as he was banging things around. "Are you okay?"

"Not really." He stopped what he was doing long enough to look up at Robin. "So, who's the guy Becky is looking for?"

Robin hid a grin. The way Tommy stammered when Becky talked to him was almost comical, yet sweet, too.

"Just a guy from last year."

This was Tommy's first summer working at the inn, so they were all just getting to know him. Though quiet at times, he was witty and always seemed to have some comeback. Not today.

When Tommy didn't speak again, Robin said, "I'll send the couple down in a while."

Tommy only nodded.

On the walk back up to the main house, Robin met Chris on the stairs. It was obvious he was trying to be friendly, but she still couldn't bring herself to talk to him with ease.

He pointed toward the dock. "Do those boats belong to the inn?"

"Two of them. As a matter of fact, Tommy is about to take the larger one out fishing if you're interested."

"No. I'm not much on fishing. I'd like to go out and do some painting."

"Do you know enough about boats to take one out alone?"

"My dad was a fisherman. I ought to."

"But you don't like fishing?"

"No, never did." After a few quiet seconds, he said, "So is there another boat I can take?"

"Sure, see Tommy. He should have the keys."

"Thanks." Before she turned to leave, he said, "You're Robin, right?"

"Right."

"Nice to meet you formally, Robin."

"You, too," she said as she turned to go.

Back on the porch Robin turned and watched Chris as he made his way to the dock, his hair ruffled by the breeze. Even after he disappeared into the boathouse, she stood watching still. She couldn't figure out what made her so uncomfortable around him, other than how attractive he was. Usually, she was so unaffected by men that even the most handsome ones didn't appeal to her. With Chris, however, she felt a small flicker of something. Not willing to explore the thought any further, Robin just shook her head and moved on.

TWO

Unable to sleep, Chris made his way out to the water's edge and sat on the bank watching the full moon reflect off the water, the brightest night in the week that he had been there.

Occasionally, he would see the slight ripple of a fish popping to the surface, but soon the water would again become still. It reminded him of his dad. When he was a boy, for hours on end he would sit with his father, staring at the water, just waiting for something to grab onto the line and cause a ripple. Always, he had hated that silent waiting. But if given the opportunity again to sit and fish with his dad, he would wait with new appreciation for the kind and gentle man his father had been.

Close to midnight, Chris stood and turned to go, but when he noticed someone running toward the water, he froze and watched as the female figure touched her first foot onto the wooden planks of the dock. She was running still and continued on until she reached the end of the structure, where she stopped and teetered on the edge. With the blanket of moonlight overhead, even from so far away, he could tell it was Robin. She stood still, gazing out into the dark water. Though he should have turned to go, Chris found he couldn't take his eyes off of her.

A brisk wind swept in from the lake, blowing her nightgown, silhouetting her small frame. It was like watching a haunting scene from a movie. He stood paralyzed in anticipation of what she might do next. Then, when she lifted her arms overhead and sprang off into the water, Chris ran toward the dock. When he reached the end of the pier, he stood helpless, watching her swim farther from the shore. What would possess her to do such a dangerous thing as to swim at midnight alone?

On the walk back to his cabin, he was glad he had fought the urge to call out to her. If he had, he was certain it would have been an invasion of some private moment. He couldn't help but wonder what caused her to remain so leery of him. Skittish was the term that came to mind, like a pup you might get from a shelter. He shrugged. Maybe it was just her personality.

Each time he had studied her, he found a distinct sadness in her eyes that spoke of distant pain. This night he wondered if he had caught a glimpse of her therapy. People were known to do stranger things when running from sorrow. It was in that moment he understood: that vacant look in her eyes was deep and debilitating sorrow. Robin was broken.

Because he often found himself butting into other people's lives, he was tempted to try with Robin, to see what made her tick. She was intriguing, to be sure, but this trip wasn't about helping others. It was about trying to reconcile himself to his future, or lack thereof.

***

Robin found Emma on the porch waiting for her with a towel. She was shivering and thankful for how well Emma cared for her.

"You know it terrifies me when you do this?" Emma said.

"I know." Robin never looked at her. "I don't mean to scare you."

"This isn't about how I feel. I just can't imagine anything happening to you. I don't want to lose you."

"You won't lose me."

Emma stood and wrapped her arm around Robin's shoulder. "Let's get you in and warm."

They walked together through the gathering room and toward the stairs. Robin stopped there. "Was I loud?"

"Just a little."

"I'm sorry. Maybe I should go."

"No way." Emma pulled Robin into her arms. "I will cancel upcoming reservations until we figure this out."

"I can't let you do that again."

"You matter more to me than renting rooms in this inn." Emma moved Robin back to look at her. "Do you hear me?"

She nodded. "I just keep thinking about him and…" Robin couldn't finish the thought.

"I know. It makes sense that you are. It's been five years, so it's almost time."

"Let's not talk about it now."

Emma took Robin's hand. "We won't. Let's get you up to bed."

Behind the counter in the lobby, Robin braced herself for a confrontation as Mr. Jenkins stormed toward her. The look on his face was already a declaration of war. He and his wife had checked in just a few days before, and so far he had complained about everything from the soap to the fishing.

"Good morning, Mr. Jenkins. What can I do for you?"

He only scowled in return. "I would like to be moved to another room."

"Is there a problem with the room you're in now?"

"Yes, I'd say. Last night in the middle of the night, someone began screaming at the top of their lungs. Even when it stopped, I lay awake for hours."

The blood drained from her face, and Robin was prepared to apologize, but the man wouldn't let her get a word in.

"It was either someone playing a horrible joke or...well, I'm not sure what, but I refuse to go through that again. I mean, waking from a dead sleep like that could give an old man a heart attack."

For the first time she saw what seemed to be a trace of vulnerability in the crotchety old man.

Emma rounded the corner in time to hear much of Robin's exchange with Mr. Jenkins.

"Mr. Jenkins, I apologize, but that was –"

Emma said, "Robin, can you see to Mr. Wheeler? He's on the back porch and has a question about the shore tour. I told him you would be right out."

Emma turned to Mr. Jenkins and gave him her best smile as she looped her arm through his. "Why, Mr. Jenkins, you're looking quite dapper this morning."

Robin slammed through the door and stepped out onto the back porch looking for Chris. He wasn't there. She peeked back inside before starting toward the steps, trying to figure out where he might have gone.

"I just wanted to get you away from Mr. Jenkins." Emma said.

Emma walked through the screen door and grabbed Robin into her arms. "I'm so sorry, sweetie."

After a moment Robin stepped back. "I was thinking maybe I should move to the Birchwood. Last time I did this, you couldn't rent out rooms for an entire summer. I won't do that to you again. I can stay there until someone rents it." She walked to the edge of the porch and crossed her arms over her chest. "I think I could use the time alone anyway."

"Hummingbird, I've told you, you are welcome to stay in one of the cabins, for good if you want."

A couple stepped out onto the porch making their way to the lake, so Emma took Robin's hand and led her through the porch entrance to the kitchen.

Once alone again, Robin said, "Or maybe it's best that I leave. He will be up for parole any time now. You know he'll come."

"I do know." Tears filled Emma's eyes. "I saw what he did to you before. I know what he's capable of." She straightened and choked back tears. "When our guests leave, we will cancel upcoming reservations and hire someone, security to stay here in the main house."

13

"I can't let you do that."

Emma took Robin by the shoulders. "You can't stop me. I will do whatever it takes to protect you."

"Why would you do that for me?"

"Because I love you." Tears came again, this time tumbling over her lashes. "You're the daughter I will never have."

Robin stepped into Emma's arms. "I love you, too." She smiled. "Every girl should have a second mom."

When Emma would finally let her go, Robin stepped back and said, "For now, I'll move to the cabin. We will see how things go."

Emma nodded, her eyes filled with concern. "I don't want to see you turn out like me. There's so much more to life. I hate to see you live like this. Maybe you should talk to someone."

"To turn out like you wouldn't be all that bad."

"You know what I mean. Don't stop living, Robin. Look at the years I've wasted because of a broken heart."

"I don't think you can call what I have a broken heart." She looked away, wanting to believe her own words. Emma was hanging on to lost love, while Robin was trying to escape it.

"I know. You have a broken spirit, and I think maybe that's worse." Emma reached out and rubbed her cheek. "We're damaged goods, you and I. I just want more for you. You're all I have in this world, you and your mom."

Robin put her arms around Emma again, deliberating her words, damaged goods. Though Emma had used the term for herself, this was the first time she had ever included her in that, but it was true. And she had to wonder if she would ever be mended again.

***

On his way to the main house, Chris watched Robin and Tommy leave the porch, each with boxes in hand. Since that first day, Robin had seemed to dodge him whenever possible, so he didn't intend to do any more than give a quick nod in their direction.

"Hi, Chris." Robin slowed.

When she actually acknowledged him, he said, "Do you need any help with that?" He stopped, which forced her to do the same.

"There are some things on the back porch. If you want to grab a load, that would be great."

"Sure."

Chris headed for the house with a smile on his face. Maybe she was finally warming up to him. While his only motive was simply to be friends with her, he struggled to understand why she shied away from him. Maybe that was changing now. He grabbed an armload and headed back toward the cabins, then realized he had no idea where he was taking his load.

He met up with her on her return trip. "So where exactly am I taking this stuff?"

Robin smiled. "The Birchwood, just down from you."

Knocked off balance by her smile, just as she passed by, he stumbled over a large rock. Red-faced, he joked, "I meant to do that."

She laughed and kept moving. "Oh, obviously."

Chris took his load into the cabin and looked around, wondering who was going to be staying there and why nothing was in suitcases. When Robin returned, he took one of the boxes she was carrying.

"Who's going to be staying here? Is it a family?"

"No, I've decided to stay down here for a while."

Though tempted to ask more, he didn't. Whatever distance she maintained was possibly closing, so he wasn't going to push his luck. After a week of near silence, he would ease into getting to know her. The night before was a sure clue: Robin was much more fragile than she appeared. His mountain woman was not at all what she seemed to be.

Chris left Robin and went back to his cabin instead of up to the main house as he had intended. He sat and looked at his easel and the scene that should contain Robin. Hours after seeing her the night before, he had worked on the painting. With his eyes closed even now, he pictured Robin standing there under the moonlight. Her image was burned into his mind still, down to the whipping of the wind against her gown and hair.

He was able to draw the dock and the water and even the moonlight in detail, but he could never capture Robin's delicate silhouette. It was as if she didn't belong in the scene staring back at him from his canvas.

***

The day after moving to the cabin, when Robin entered the dining room for breakfast, she found Chris there. The room was nearly full, but even if not she would have made it a point to speak to him. After filling her plate she approached his table in an attempt to seem less rude than she had been.

"Do you mind if I sit here?"

"Not at all."

Robin sat across from Chris and began to eat. For a moment neither spoke, until finally, she said. "Thanks for your help yesterday."

"No problem." Chris smiled at her. "Happy to help."

"Look, I know I haven't been exactly friendly, and I just wanted to say that I'm sorry about that. It's not you."

"No, that's all right. You were fine."

She grinned at him. "Liar."

"Okay, maybe a little." He was quiet for a moment, then said, "Look, if I ever gave you the impression that I was coming on to you, I didn't mean it that way. I was just being friendly."

"I didn't think that." She looked away. "I'm just a bit stand-offish, more so than I should be in my line of work."

"And I'm probably too in-your-face. I've always been like that, never met a stranger." He chuckled. "Gets me into trouble from time to time."

His laugh made her smile. She liked his easy-going nature. On more than one occasion, she had seen him by the water's edge, reading what appeared to be a Bible. It didn't surprise her in the least since it fit his gentle disposition.

She looked out at the water. "Will you paint again today?"

"I will. This has been relaxing, a slower change of pace."

"Nothing like Boston," Robin said.

Chris chuckled. "No, nothing like Boston. So, I have to ask. What's it like living here year-round?"

"In the summer, hectic like Boston." She paused and nearly shivered at the thought of it. "Laid back and freezing in the winter."

"I bet the lake is beautiful in the fall."

"Spectacular," she said. "I can't imagine a more beautiful place."

Robin sighed at the ease of their conversation. This was a turning point. Finally, she saw her summer as something more than maintaining a strategy to avoid him. That had become tiring, and honestly, she didn't have the energy to keep it up.

THREE

Like most mornings, Robin sat on the steps awaiting the sun's next appearance. In five years, other than during the miserable cold season, rarely had she missed a morning. There was something healing about witnessing the sun rise from behind the trees and the beginning of a new day. The Sunday before, just before getting ready for church, Robin had sat in this very same spot and had an unusual encounter. When the glow of the sun peeked from across the lake, there was a shadow cast across the water that looked like a cross. It only lasted a few seconds, but during that time she found her heart beat a little faster and she unconsciously whispered the name of Jesus.

While the sun had not yet come up today, there was enough light already to make out a figure walking toward the stairs. It was Chris coming to join her, something she didn't mind at all. Now that they were neighbors, they ran into each other often. She smiled as he drew nearer. Obviously, he hadn't been awake for long. His hair was standing on end, reminding her of a little boy up early to watch Saturday morning cartoons. Without a word he took a seat next to her.

"In the past two weeks, I've never seen you out so early. What are you doing up this time of morning?"

Chris yawned. "I got up early yesterday to paint the sunrise and realized what I've been missing all my life. After all these years, I figured out what God does first thing each morning. It's worth losing sleep over, so I set my clock for this morning, too."

Robin sighed. "I think this may be where God lives. He's most real to me when I'm here. There's something in the combination of the sun and water."

It unlocked a door within her which had been closed off for nearly six years. All other times, even when looking at the very same sight from the very same step, her heart was securely fastened shut against God.

Chris nodded. "I get that, the draw of the water."

She offered him her coffee cup, and surprisingly, he took it. "Are you officially a morning person now?"

"Maybe not officially."

After sipping the coffee he handed it back to Robin and rubbed his temples. "So, how long have you been here?"

"About half an hour, I guess."

He chuckled as he said, "I mean at the inn."

"Oh." She laughed with him. "Almost five years now."

"For some reason I thought you may have grown up here."

"No, I was raised in North Carolina, but I did spend many of my summers here."

"I can hear that – a slight Southern drawl." He grinned at her. "Nothing like Emma's."

Chris took her coffee again and sipped. "I used to come here when I was a kid."

"Really? How old were you?"

"We were here at the lake every summer until I was twelve. My dad died just a month after we got home that year. Things were never the same after that, and we never came back."

The change in his expression moved her. She understood the difficulty of loss and the fact that life is somehow supposed to go on in spite of it.

"I'm sorry. That must have been hard, losing your dad at such a young age."

With a shrug he looked out at the water. "It was tough, but I guess we survived – barely." He paused a moment. "That's what I'm here for, looking for that feeling from back then, when life was still okay."

"I hope you find it."

He nodded and was quiet a moment. Then he said, "So, I've been wondering, are you and Emma related?"

"Not really, but as close as you can get, I suppose. Emma and my mom grew up together in Raleigh. That's near where I grew up, in Whitley."

"How did you two end up here?"

"Emma moved here before I was born."

Robin slid the band from her ponytail and let her hair tumble over her shoulders.

"Her great aunt lived here with her late husband until he passed. Years after he died, she opened it up as an inn and had the cabins built – just to give her something to keep her occupied. When she died, she left the place to Emma. Since then, Emma has opened the place up for the summer and fall."

"What made you decide to move here? I mean, I guess it's totally understandable. This place is amazing."

"I was in a bad place in my life. At the time I only came here to get away for a while." She sighed, remembering how lost she had felt then. "But then I just never went back. My parents moved out West – so there was nothing to draw me back to North Carolina. This is just where I landed – with Emma."

"She seems like a wonderful lady. You know who she reminds me of? Sophia Loren or Ann Margret, one of those legendary big screen stars. Like, her presence in the room charges the air or something."

"I know what you mean. The way she dresses and carries herself, it's like she brings a 1940s air to the place. I've always wanted to be as elegant as her." Robin's heart sank a little. "She's had a rough way to go, though. Back in her twenties she was a nurse in the Army and engaged to a soldier. Right before they were to be married, he was killed in an accident."

"So she never married?"

"No, never. She barely even dated. She just kind of shut down that side of her."

Robin could relate to Emma's story and now regretted how personal the conversation had become. She reached for her coffee cup and stood.

"Well, I better get up there. I'm sure she's cooking breakfast. I should see if she needs any help. See you later, Chris."

"Robin."

"Yeah?"

"Thanks for talking to me this morning. I'm sorry if I invaded your quiet time."

"No invasion. I enjoyed it."

***

With Robin gone, Chris remained on the steps for some time more, his headache only now fading. The fresh morning air seemed to have helped. He genuinely wasn't a morning person, but the morning before he had been out early and seen Robin sitting where he now sat. This morning, he had made it a point to get up early to see if he would find her here once again.

He felt drawn to her. Without a doubt, she was pretty, but it was more than physical attraction. Maybe it was the soothing way she said his name. It sounded soft on her lips, and he caught the most distinctive hint of her Southern accent in her two-syllable pronunciation. While he would never consider her fragile, there was something particularly delicate beneath her surface. It was more of something he sensed rather than actually saw. Whatever it was about her, he liked being with her.

Over the past weeks, he had been on an emotional rollercoaster. He needed something – or maybe someone to focus on besides himself. The fact that he had talked about his parents before didn't help. Maybe coming back to the last place he ever saw his mom sober wasn't the best idea after all. It only served to remind him how much his life had fallen apart after his dad's death.

Chris stood to go up for breakfast knowing there was a plate of bacon in his future. What dying man wouldn't eat his weight in bacon?

***

Robin walked into the kitchen to find Emma sitting at the island, drinking her coffee, her view through the window ensuring she had seen her with Chris.

"Good morning." Robin waited, knowing Emma was about to grill her.

Emma smiled. "Good morning. I see you were talking to Chris."

"Yes, I was talking to Chris." Robin threw her arms in the air with feigned excitement. "Good news! We're getting married this afternoon. I hope that's not too short a notice for you to make the cake."

Emma only shook her head. "You know, he really seems like a nice man. It wouldn't hurt to get to know him."

"I know. You've said that. And I am getting to know him. I'm just not planning on any kind of relationship, that's all."

"What do you know so far?"

"He's an art teacher, so his passion is painting. He spent his summers here at the lake when he was a kid. I've learned all kinds of things about him."

"Good. It sounds like you know enough to marry him."

When Emma became quiet, Robin said, "What?"

"How did you sleep?"

"Better. No bad dreams all week. No need to worry."

"I don't like the idea of you being so far away."

"I know, but for now, this is what I need."

Tommy pushed through the door and walked without a word to the refrigerator.

"Good morning," Emma said.

"Morning." Tommy unscrewed the cap to his soda and took a drink.

Robin glanced at Emma and grinned then looked at Tommy. "Late night?"

Tommy said, "Yeah, pretty late. Have you seen Becky yet?"

"No. I imagine she's still asleep." Becky was always difficult for Robin to get up and around. It was the same the summer before.

Tommy reached for an apple. "Did she sleep here?"

Robin hesitated. "I assume so. Why?"

"We were in town last night, and she hooked up with that Brad guy." He looked away.

"Tommy…" Robin trailed off, knowing it was best to leave it alone. No sooner than she stopped speaking, they all watched as Becky climbed the back porch steps, sandals in hand.

Robin looked back at Tommy. "Becky's home."

"Yeah, thanks," he said and left the kitchen.

Emma shook her head as she stood. "I told you this would happen."

"What, about Becky and Brad?"

"No, Becky and Tommy. They are both too cute for something not to happen between them. Plus, they go to school near each other, both business majors. Sweet kids – it's a perfect match."

"After Becky's walk of shame, I don't think this is about Becky and Tommy."

"You'll see." Emma chuckled. "I know these things."

Robin and Emma both froze when they heard Tommy raise his voice in the other room.

"Should I go say something?" Robin said.

"No, give them a minute. I want to hear."

Tommy said, "You deserve whatever you get from that guy."

"I didn't go home with him if that's what you think. I know he's a jerk." She paused for a few seconds. "I got stranded across the lake and had to wait for a fisherman to bring me back."

"I'm supposed to believe that?"

"Believe whatever you want. I didn't stay with Brad."

Becky slammed through the kitchen door and stopped when she saw Emma and Robin there. "Morning."

"Good morning," Emma said as she passed Becky and headed into the dining room carrying biscuits.

Becky stood staring at Robin. "I suppose you were listening in?"

Robin shrugged. "How could we not?"

"It's not what everyone thinks." Becky sat on a stool and dropped her sandals on the floor beside her.

"It's not our business. You're nineteen years old."

"Still, I want you to know. I slept on a bench at the marina."

"Why would you do that?"

"Brad dropped me in the middle of nowhere when I said I wasn't going to spend the night with him. I didn't want to call Tommy."

"Why didn't you call me?"

"You warned me."

"So what! You could have called me. I would've come." Robin moved to stand closer to Becky. "Anything could have happened to you out there alone." Robin shook her head. A whole lot of drinking went on out on the lake and at that marina.

Becky looked out the window and watched Tommy walking toward the dock. "I like him."

"Who?"

"Tommy. He's cute and sweet."

"Uhhh, not sure leaving with Brad was the best way to tell him."

"I know it was stupid. I didn't know how much I liked Tommy until last night. The way he looked at me when he left was…" She sighed and looked back at Robin. "I don't know. I just know that overnight, I kept wondering what he was thinking of me."

"It's not too late. Tommy seems crazy about you. Go and talk to him."

"Maybe after a shower." Becky stood and reached for an apple and then her shoes.

Emma entered the kitchen just after Becky left. "Told you so. Maybe next it'll be you and Chris."

Robin rolled her eyes. "On that note, I'm heading in to breakfast."

***

Chris entered the dining room and headed toward the buffet. At that exact moment, Robin backed through the swinging door just as Chris was passing by. Their collision caused her to stumble.

"Oh, sorry," Chris said and reached for her.

"No, I'm sorry. I just came barreling through. I'm surprised I haven't done that before."

There was finally a moment where he realized he had held on too long, so he grinned and released her. He sniffed the air. "Is that bacon I smell?"

She chuckled at that. "Yes, Emma will be out with it in a minute. Since you've been here, she's been making extra."

"A man's got to eat." He went to the buffet and began loading his plate. "Good grief! Don't talk to Tommy this morning."

Robin grabbed a plate and followed Chris through the line. She chuckled. "Teenagers, am I right?"

"Absolutely right. I'm around them five days a week ten months out of the year."

Emma entered and placed the bacon in the warmer. "First round for you, Chris."

"Much appreciated," he said and started with six pieces. "Will you join us for breakfast?"

"I've got muffins in the oven, so I better get back in there." Emma caught Robin's eye and winked. "You two enjoy your breakfast." Her words were nearly a song.

Robin smiled at her and with obvious sarcasm, said, "Thanks Emma, we sure will."

Chris approached the table. "What was all that about?"

"Nothing, just Emma being Emma."

Chris sat with Robin at a table near the window. While he tried not to stare at her, he did notice how the sunlight streamed through the window and glistened through her dark hair. And those eyes – it was happening again, that melting down of brain cells as he had experienced the first day he met her. He had to force himself to focus on his food to keep from morphing into a drooling, blabbering mess.

In an attempt to divert his mind, he said, "Is there anything to do around here at night? I'm getting a little stir crazy sitting around the cabin."

"I don't go out enough to know, but I'm sure there are a few places you might enjoy. I know Tommy and Becky go to a place over in Wolfeboro."

"I wasn't thinking about a bar, if that's what you mean. I meant more of a restaurant or something."

"Well," she paused as she thought, "there are a lot of great restaurants. What do you want? Seafood? Steak?"

"I was kind of hoping you would go with me. I mean, nothing serious or anything, just grab a bite to eat."

Chris could see her mind was whirling and found that he was holding his breath as he waited for her response.

"Well, I uh…well, I guess that would be all right. I mean, you said nothing serious."

"How about tonight?" He couldn't help but smile at the cuteness of her response.

"Tonight?"

Her expression was priceless. She had no idea how adorable she was, looking at him with those big doe eyes.

"Yes, tonight. You know, that time period between today and bedtime."

"I guess I could go tonight." She blinked and blinked again, then said, "I'd better let you know later. I have several things –"

"Great, tonight it is. I'll pick you up at seven."

Without finishing his meal Chris stood and left the dining room before she could change her mind.

***

Once alone, Robin could hardly believe what had just happened. She had agreed to a date – the last thing she wanted. Why hadn't she just said no? She groaned aloud as she slapped her forehead with her palm.

"Humph, looks like I'm on a roll." Emma was beaming as she plopped down in the chair across from Robin.

"I guess you were spying on us?"

"Of course. Did you expect any less?" Emma leaned in. "I'm thrilled beyond anything I've known in eons."

"What am I going to do?" Robin said.

"What do you mean?"

Robin drew in a sharp breath and then exhaled again. "I can't do this."

"Why not? He seems like a great guy."

"I know, but I'm in no position to date anyone." Robin thought about Chris's smile; he had such a kind smile. "He said it was nothing serious. Maybe he just wants some company."

"You mean, maybe it's not a date?" Emma chuckled as she waited to hear Robin's response.

"Yeah, maybe it's not."

"Okay, and I'll be seeing Santa Claus in a little while. I'll ask his opinion."

Emma reached out and patted Robin's hand. "Sweetie, just go and have fun. You deserve a wonderful night out with a nice guy. Just do it."

Robin shook her head. "I'm not going. I will catch him in a while and let him know."

Emma leaned in closer. "Robin, you need to live again."

"How can I?" She sat looking at Emma. "Of all people, you should understand."

"Understand what, that you're scared or that you're still holding on?"

"Both." Robin's eyes filled with tears. "I don't know if I want to live again."

"One dinner, please. Just go out and have a good time with a nice guy."

Robin groaned. "What would I wear?"

"I have plenty of dresses." Emma glanced out toward the dock. "Well, look at that."

When Robin turned, she saw Becky on the dock with Tommy. Then when Tommy spread his arms, Becky stepped into them. Robin nodded. "You were right."

"Get used to saying that," Emma said, her voice once again singing a song.

Robin followed Emma into her room and to her closet. Though Emma seldom went out, when she did, she always looked spectacular. Surely, they could come up with something from the dozens of dresses there before them.

She sat on the bed, feet dangling and swinging as Emma pulled one dress after another out of the closet. Robin turned up her nose at the first few, but finally there was one she liked.

"Oh, I love that one."

After removing it from the plastic cover, Robin held the dress up to herself. It was long, almost reaching to her ankles. The color could only be described as a buttery yellow, Emma's favorite color, and the fabric was soft, smooth cotton. She liked that it had a vintage air about it.

"I don't know if yellow is a good color for me," Robin said as she pulled the dress over her head.

"Honey, with your looks, any color is your color."

"I don't think I've ever seen you wear this before. Where did you get it?"

Emma said, "Oh, I've had that dress a hundred years, at least. And no, you've never seen me wear it."

"Do you really like it?"

"You look gorgeous, like it was made just for you."

Since she had spent the past five years in jeans and shorts, Robin now felt awkward wearing a dress.

"I couldn't imagine anything more perfect." Tears spilled over Emma's lashes.

"Why are you crying?"

"I don't know, sweetie. I guess I'm just glad to see you live a little. Hummingbird, you have to let it go."

Robin looked down at her bare feet sticking out from beneath the yellow fabric. "I don't know if I can ever let it go. What if that's part of who I am now?"

"No. It's not part of who you are. You're still who you were before it happened." Emma took Robin's face in her hands. "The real you is just hiding somewhere in there. Let her come out tonight."

"Should she go with no shoes?" Robin wiggled her toes as Emma looked down.

"You're cute and all, but I don't think you can carry off that look the way Chris can."

Emma went to get a pair of matching yellow shoes.

Robin grimaced. "They may be a little much. Do you have anything a little simpler?"

"What about these? They will go nicely with a barefoot man."

With a grin, Robin did stop to wonder if Chris would wear shoes. Not once had she seen him wear them since he arrived.

She slipped on the white sandals. "Okay, so now I have an outfit, what about my hair?"

***

Once alone, Emma felt herself glowing as if a lamp had been switched on deep in her soul. In many years she hadn't seen Robin so excited. Well, maybe excited was a bit of an overstatement, but Robin was smiling a genuine smile at least. The light in the lamp grew brighter at the possibility of a new chapter in life for Robin. Chris may not be the answer, but at least he was the beginning of Robin's daring to question again.

For five years Emma had been trying to reach out to her, to help Robin heal after the end of her marriage. Because of their circumstances, Emma often found herself too ashamed to say much at all. Her truest desire was to comfort Robin as her mother, but she had given up that right when she placed her newborn baby in her best friend's arms all those years ago. Emma would never have the luxury of such a connection with Robin.

While the events leading to her arrival were horrid, Robin's decision to come to the inn and ultimately to stay on full-time was the most significant event to happen in Emma's life in the past thirty years. It was her secret do-over, a means of finally getting to know the daughter she had given away. Even though it remained a secret, in her heart she was Robin's mama. She found the greatest love she had ever known in her life – even beyond that of Robin's father, the one love she once believed she could never live without.

Maybe that's why she couldn't help but cry as Robin had tried on the dress. Emma had planned to be married in it to Robin's father. How poetic that Robin had stood there before her with that particular dress on. The fact that Robin reminded her so much of Rob, her hair rich and dark like a strong cup of coffee, made tears inevitable. He was quick-witted like Robin. If only she could know how much like him she was.

Emma sighed and considered Robin's confession from before, that she may never be able to let go of the past. That was the most she had ever spoken of her time with Mike. It was a subject that was off limits. Of course she understood Robin's reluctance. She had escaped a living nightmare. Before her life took such an abrupt turn, Robin had been so full of life. Sadly, that part of her was shrouded now, the real her hidden. Blanketed by a funeral pall for years on end, Robin seemed to be no longer among the living. How familiar that trait was to a woman who had responded precisely the same to death and loss. *Two peas in empty pods – that's us*, Emma thought.

Tears sprang to her eyes, so she covered her face and tried to shake the horrible image. When Robin had arrived five years before, she was barely recognizable after Mike had beaten her that last time, her face so swollen and battered that it had taken over a month for the swelling and deep purple bruising to fade completely. Even still, her wounds inside were far from mended. Emma's own heartbreak of some thirty years before paled in comparison to Robin's.

FOUR

Robin stood at the counter in the lobby, working on the list of reservations for the following week – at least as much as her mind would allow. Her dinner with Chris was later that night, so that kept her distracted. *Why had she even agreed to it?* She had to wonder as she tossed a stack of papers onto the counter. After leaving Emma, Robin had taken the dress to her cabin. Since then, she waffled between canceling and not. For the moment she was thinking not. She grinned to herself knowing that would change within five minutes.

Only one guest was in the gathering area of the lobby, sitting on the large leather sofa reading the paper, an accountant if Robin remembered correctly. Robin had offered to get her a coffee but the woman declined.

All of the rooms and cabins were full and there were no more guests expected, so when a woman walked in, Robin wondered if maybe she was lost. She appeared to be since she was wearing stiletto heels and carrying a purse the size of a small automobile.

"Hi, may I help you?"

"Yes, I'm looking for Chris Wheeler. He is staying in a cabin here."

For the briefest moment Robin was unable to speak. Becky was standing nearby and gave her a wide-eyed look. She knew about the date since Emma had been running her mouth.

Robin said, "Yes, he's a guest here."

"I know he's a guest here." With eyebrows raised the woman blinked in rapid bursts. "Can you tell me where I might find him?" Each word was deliberate as if Robin might be slow to understand. Then smiling, she said, "I was supposed to be here with him but was unable to come at the last minute. I'm here to surprise him."

"Oh, I'm sure he'll be surprised all right." Robin moved from behind the counter. "Come on, I'll show you to his cabin. I can't wait to see the look on his face."

"What do you mean?"

Robin looked at Becky and rolled her eyes but never turned back to the woman. "Oh, I just love being part of a surprise. That's all."

Chris had asked her out, not knowing his girlfriend would show up. It would be humorous to watch him squirm – worth whatever offense she might have felt, not to mention the woman walking down all the steps and through the grass in heels would give Robin a chuckle. She deserved it after her condescension before.

They approached Chris's cabin and found he was sitting on the front porch. Already his expression was hilarious. Robin smiled at him, and with her best *Price Is Right* gesture, said, "And here he is."

With eyes wide Chris jumped from his rocking chair and headed toward the stairs. "Vanessa, what are you doing here?"

She threw her arms around his neck. "I wanted to surprise you. Are you surprised?"

Over Vanessa's shoulder Chris looked at Robin, his eyes apologizing.

With the girlfriend's back to her, Robin mouthed to Chris, "Surprise!" then turned and walked away, once again shaking her head.

***

Inside the cabin Chris and Vanessa sat at the small table.

"I'm so sorry about what happened. I guess I just freaked," Vanessa said.

Chris sat, looking at her with a blank expression. Of all the times for her to have a change of heart, it had to be the same day he had asked Robin out. Although Vanessa was talking, trying to explain, he had a difficult time concentrating on what she was saying. He kept picturing Robin saying, "Surprise!"

"What I said about not being with you through this –"

With his hand out to stop her, he said, "You were right."

"No, I wasn't."

Chris reached for her hand. "I have to be honest with you. I don't think we should be together either. I know you feel lousy about the timing, but I think we both knew it wasn't working out between us even before." He looked down and sighed before looking back at her. "Neither one of us would admit it, though."

He leaned in, trying to make this easier for her. "Sweetheart, you can't allow guilt to keep you with me anymore than I can be with you just because I'm in a bad place in my life." He touched her cheek. "I care for you, but I'm not in love with you."

Vanessa withdrew her hand and sat back. "So why did you invite me here in the first place?"

Chris was about to remind her that he hadn't invited her but chose the high road instead. "At the time it seemed like a good idea. Since I've been here, though, I've had time to think more about us."

There was an awkward moment of silence, one Chris was tempted to fill, but he was at a loss. This was so unexpected and his mind was still filled with Robin being the one to bring Vanessa to his cabin, that he found himself with little to say.

Finally, Vanessa stood and moved to where her purse sat on the counter. "So you mean I've driven two hours for you to break up with me?"

"For the record, that morning at your place seemed like a break up to me. That's how I took it. And you could have called."

"I wanted to surprise you. I hated how things ended." She shook her head. "It doesn't matter now," she said as she reached for her lipstick. "Truth is you're right. This wasn't working anyway. You're a nice guy – maybe a little too nice, bordering on dull."

Because he knew she was reacting out of hurt feelings, Chris just sat, choosing to say nothing in response to her biting comment.

"I should go."

Chris stood with her. "Look, Vanessa, we've had some great times together, and nothing will ever change that. I would rather us end this on a happy note."

For a second she stood looking at him and then said, "I want that, too."

"Want me to walk with you?"

She leaned over to remove her right shoe. "No, I'm good." Then, taking off the other and placing them both in her purse, she sighed. "Call me when you get back to Boston."

"I will. Drive safely." Chris watched as she picked up her purse and walked out the door.

Now, he just had to talk to Robin. She had agreed to go out with him so reluctantly, Chris supposed he had lost the opportunity. Just in case, he decided to shower and dress for dinner, hoping she would give him another chance.

***

Hours later, Robin sat on the edge of her bed, foot propped up on the corner, painting her toenails. She had taken a shower and was now letting her hair air dry. The yellow dress hanging on the closet door seemed to be mocking her. With a smile, she reminded herself that she had at least had the courage to accept a date. The fact that it fell through this time was beside the point. What was most notable was that in the process she discovered there was still a tiny flicker of life left inside her, something she would have sworn didn't exist any longer. That was promising. Next time, given the opportunity, she might really go. Such a possibility caused her stomach to churn in dread. In truth, she knew she was far from ready to date. Still, though, the flicker was revealed.

She thought about Chris, and for just a split second the hair on the back of her neck prickled in semi-jealousy. The woman was so beautiful, so cover-of-a-magazine sophisticated that it was easy to see why he was with her. In his defense he had said "nothing serious" when he asked her to dinner. So he had a girlfriend; it wasn't the end of the world. Robin was determined that when she saw him next, she wouldn't make a big deal about the whole thing.

With toenails wet, Robin walked on her heels through the living room. Just as she passed by the door, someone knocked. A quick peek at the clock in the kitchen showed exactly seven o'clock.

"Surely not!" she whispered aloud.

When Robin answered the door, Chris stood there, hands thrust deep into his pockets. "Hi," he said with a sheepish grin.

She opened the door a little wider. "What are you doing here?"

"I'm sorry. I thought we agreed on seven?"

It took her a while to respond. "Well, I just assumed your girlfriend would have a problem with you going out to a 'nothing serious or anything' dinner with another woman."

His face took on a soft expression. "She's not my girlfriend. She's gone now." He took a step closer and said, "Please go to dinner with me. I'll explain it all then."

Robin stood looking at him for a few seconds, his pleading expression melting her resolve. He looked so handsome in his khaki pants and blue shirt, a shirt nearly the exact shade of his eyes. It was the first time she noticed what an unusual shade they were, deep blue with pale gold streaks running through them. She blinked, holding her eyes shut longer than necessary. Part of her wanted to go, but the last thing she wanted was to get in the middle of some on again off again relationship.

"Maybe we shouldn't," she finally said. It was then that she looked down and saw that he was wearing loafers, a sight that made a smile tug at her lips.

"Please, Robin, just dinner." With a feigned sigh he leaned against the door jamb. "I'm all dressed up with nowhere to go."

"Can we agree this isn't a date?"

He shrugged. "Sure. Just two pals having dinner."

"Pals?" The way he said it made her grin.

"Buddies, friends, compadres, whatever you want to call us. How about two hungry people eating dinner together at the same place at the same time? Are you hungry?"

"Yes." She swung the door open wider. "But as you see, I'm not exactly dressed."

"I have all the time in the world." His expression fell and he said, "I'll sit out here and wait."

Seated at a table on the deck of one of the marina restaurants, Chris and Robin had decided on seafood, and this place was one of her favorites. On the drive over she had supposed she would feel uncomfortable, but she hadn't. From the moment she had gotten into his car, Chris kept the conversation light and fun. Already, it was shaping up to be an enjoyable evening.

"So, Robin, what did you do before coming to Lake Winnipesaukee?"

She glanced down into her water glass and thought of Mike. "Oh, not much really."

"Independently wealthy?"

"No, nothing like that. Actually, I was married."

He grimaced. "I hope I didn't bring up a painful subject." With a smile he clapped his hands. "I tell you what, let's change the subject entirely."

"That sounds good. Now, you tell me about being a teacher. Do you like it?"

His smile broadened. "Oh, I love teaching, and as you've probably noticed, I also love to paint. But more than anything, it means so much to me to be able to make a difference in these kids' lives. Being a Christian teacher in a public school has its challenges, but I do what I can to show God's love to them."

Chris gazed out at the still water for a moment. "I was on a bad road when I was young, until one of my teachers in high school saw something in me that I never saw in myself. Her belief in me changed my life. That's what made me want to be a teacher. She invited me to church – of course, you could do that back then."

"Tell me about her."

"Her name was Gloria Nelson, my music teacher my freshman year. I had just moved in with my aunt and changed schools, so it was a really tough time for me. If anyone ever needed Jesus, I did then."

Reminded of when they talked on the stairs about the summer his dad died, Robin noticed his eyes became cloudy, as they had that day. For a moment she wondered if eyes could be overcast like weather then determined his could. She had heard the eyes are the windows to the soul, and for the first time she could visualize it. His eyes were more than just beautiful blue eyes; they revealed secrets about him, and she wondered if he knew that about himself.

Out of consideration, she said, "Should we change the subject again?"

"No, I'm fine. It's just that when I think of that time, it's still painful for me. I suppose it always will be. My mom began drinking after my father died." He shrugged. "I don't know, maybe she drank before and I was just kept away from it. Every year she got a little worse, until finally I went to live with my aunt when I was fifteen."

Robin looked away. "Alcohol is a destructive thing," she said with too much understanding. "My husband began to drink. That changed every-thing."

Like a flash of lightning from out of the blue, her mind was struck with memories of his rage and loss of control. Though normally able to push such memories away, she found they were so fresh and real in that moment that she was overtaken by them.

For a brief time they were both silent. They had found common ground that only people who had lived it could understand.

Robin tried to refocus on this moment rather than what once was. She shoved it away like usual, pretending it was indeed over and done.

Chris leaned in closer. "Changing the subject, thanks for coming tonight. It's getting pretty lonely sitting in that cabin every night."

She grinned. "Well, you did have company today." Robin had resisted the urge to bring it up so far, but this was a perfect opportunity.

"That was Vanessa. We dated for six months. It went on for about three months too long, but neither of us wanted to be the one to initiate the split. I guess she was feeling a little guilty and wanted to set things right."

"Guilty? You mean she broke it off?"

"Yes, in a way. She was supposed to come out for the first week and a half but at the last minute decided not to come. It was just a symptom of a bigger problem, and I knew it."

Robin watched him for a second, noticing that he didn't seem too concerned over the break-up. "Do you mind me asking what happened today?"

"Not at all. I told her I wasn't in love with her."

"And are you?"

"No, not at all. Don't get me wrong, she's a fine person, and we've had a good time together, but when…" Chris trailed off and looked away.

When he stopped midsentence, Robin decided not to question him further. "You know, for two pals having dinner, we have gone way too deep. Let's go back to the surface."

"You're right. What's your sign?"

She chuckled. "Okay, a little deeper than that."

"When's your birthday?"

"March 3. I just turned thirty," she said. "Yours?"

"July 23. I'll be thirty-eight."

"Hey, you'll be here for your birthday. We will celebrate with you. Emma loves any reason to throw a party."

"A party sounds terrific." Chris hesitated and then grinned. "You know what I like?"

The expression on his face and mischief in his eyes gave her reason to grin too. "What?"

"How your eyes sparkle in the candlelight and how you suddenly seem present and in the moment. You're not always like that. Often you seem miles away."

"I know. I'm working on that," Robin said.

"Like coffee at sunrise, you're present then."

"Yeah, I suppose I am. I feel like a different person there."

"I noticed that. You're good company there." Chris said with a soft smile.

"Just so you know, most nights, we usually meet out under the gazebo. I mean, Emma, Tommy, and Becky. You're welcome to join us there anytime." Robin leaned in closer and whispered with mock pity, "I hate to think of you sitting there in that lonesome ol' cabin all by yourself."

He smiled. "I'll take you up on that."

After leaving the restaurant Chris asked Robin if she would like to take a walk around the marina.

"It's too nice of a night not to," Chris said.

"Agreed."

They strolled around and talked. He was kind and funny, a man any woman would be grateful to go out with. Robin sighed a little as she glanced his way. Any woman but her. If she were honest with herself, she knew there could never be anything romantic between them. It was more than not being ready to be involved with someone at that moment. Robin was certain she wouldn't be ready for an exceptionally long period of time. By the time she was healthy enough emotionally, she would be way too late for a summer romance with Chris.

Finally, having covered every corner of the marina, they stopped at the end of the last pier. Robin leaned against a wooden post, sensing it was the moment to try to explain to him that for them it was simply poor timing. She gazed for a moment at the boats lined one after another, them swaying with the movement of the water in a hypnotic and soothing way.

When she turned back toward Chris, she found his hand raised and close to her face, and for an instant she had anticipated a strike to her cheek. Out of instinct she threw an arm up over her head and tried to move away.

Chris grabbed her arms to prevent her from going over the edge and into the water. "Robin, I was just reaching to move a strand of hair from your face. I'm sorry. I shouldn't have." He stood there frozen. Finally, he said, "Did you think I was going to hit you?"

Unable to look at him, Robin instead fixed her eyes on the worn wood of the dock. After a few awkward seconds, she whispered, "I'm sorry." She pushed past him. "Maybe we should go."

Chris jogged to catch up and matched his pace with hers as they walked along to the car in silence. Once inside, he started the car and backed from the parking place. After putting the car into drive, he casually moved his hand to hold hers until she eventually moved it away. They rode in near silence all the way back to the inn.

When Robin reached the bottom step of her cabin, Chris touched her shoulder. "Robin?"

Without turning to look at him, she whispered, "I'm sorry about what happened back there. I feel ridiculous." Tears burned her eyes, so she blinked them away.

"Don't be sorry. You know I would never –"

"I know, Chris."

Even in the moment, she hadn't actually believed he would hit her, so why did she flinch that way? She supposed it was because Mike had been so constantly on her mind. Her fear of him, even after all those years apart, was as fresh still as it had been during their final year together. The constant uneasiness of doing or saying something that might set him off – even the thought of it at that very moment set her hands to trembling.

For several seconds he stood there with his hand resting on her shoulder.

With a quick glance and a forced smile, she said, "Thank you for dinner. I had a lovely time."

He moved his hand from her shoulder and nodded. "Thank you for going with me."

Robin stepped through the doorway and closed the door, fighting the urge to cry. She hated to cry. Too much time had been spent on tears, and what had it produced? Nothing.

She went into the spare bedroom and began shifting boxes around. When she came to the box her favorite hiking boots had come in, she removed the lid and sorted through the stack of papers until she found the ones she was looking for, her divorce papers. With a heavy sigh, she unfolded them and stared at the names at the top of the page. *Robin McGarrett vs. Michael McGarrett.* On the last page she studied his signature. It was precise and legible, not his usual scratching signature. She always wondered why he had signed them without a fight. It was totally out of character for him. Still, he had. Why did that surprise her after all that had transpired that final night?

Now, looking at his signature, it caused a different reaction than when she had first received the papers from her attorney. Mostly, she felt numb. All those years before, she had felt something akin to hatred for him, though she knew she could never hate him in the truest sense of the word. She hated what he had become. She hated that he had destroyed their lives. She hated the memory of his blood all over her and the way he looked to her for comfort. How could he expect comfort from her? And where did her ability to give it come from?

FIVE

Chris sat on the porch of his cabin thinking of Robin and how pitiful she had seemed as she flinched from him earlier in the evening. At that moment, the pieces had fallen into place. She had run from an abusive husband; that was what had brought her to the lake. And the distant pain he found in her eyes was both emotional and physical in nature. She was even more wounded than he realized.

Up until that moment, the evening had gone so well. Occasionally Robin had giggled, and when she did the entire room had lit up. Even the candle on the table seemed to flicker more brightly because of it. In rare moments when he could pull his mind away from how pretty she looked or how her eyes caused his stomach to flutter, he acknowledged the injustice of it all. There was no time to get to know her fully or to become known.

There was that one moment when he had come close to telling her that he was sick, but the words had hung in his throat. It was as if saying them out loud would make the diagnosis all the more real. So far, it was still like a bad dream, one he knew would be over soon enough. The evening had been too fantastic to ruin with such an admission.

In hopes that Robin would be there, Chris headed down to the gazebo where he found Emma talking with Tommy and Becky. He stayed for some time in case she eventually showed up. By about ten, though, he was ready to give up and go back to his cabin.

He stood. "Well, I guess I'll see you guys in the morning."

"Chris, why don't you stay a minute?" Emma nodded at the young people. "I'll see you two in the morning."

He sat back on the wicker swing. Once alone, Emma moved to sit next to him and patted his leg.

"Am I to assume the date didn't go so well?"

Chris smiled a half-smile and shrugged his shoulders. "I had a wonderful time. But it wasn't a date."

"Humph! Seemed like a date to me."

"She said we couldn't call it that."

Emma grinned. "I can see her saying that." When Chris remained quiet, she said, "You're obviously here looking for her."

"Yeah, I'm not exactly sure what happened." He leaned his head on the chain of the swing. "I mean, I know, but maybe you can tell me how I might make it better."

He blinked and for a split second could see Robin flinching again. "He hurt her didn't he, her husband?"

Emma simply nodded.

"I reached out, just to move her hair from her face. She flinched as if I might hit her." Chris paused. "How could he hurt someone so sweet?"

"I don't know. He wasn't always like that, but there at the end he became a monster. It was the drinking. He terrorized her and…" Emma hesitated. "Things got really ugly."

"Where is he now?"

"He's still in North Carolina."

Chris stood and paced, unable to comprehend how any man could raise his hand to a woman. Robin's face was so delicate, her frame so small, how could he hurt her that way?

"I would never hurt her." He blinked again, imagining her flinching away. Everything was getting muddled. He hardly knew her yet felt drawn into her story already.

Emma had moved to stand beside Chris. "I know. Just be easy with her. She has a delicate spirit right now. It's not that she won't eventually heal; she will. She's a strong woman, stronger than I could ever be."

He shook his head, knowing he couldn't allow himself to get involved in this; it was just too much. The thought no more crossed his mind when Vanessa's words came back to him. Those were the exact words she had used – it was too much for her. He needed to think and pray through this.

"I'm going on to my cabin, but thank you for talking to me."

"Chris?"

"Yeah?"

She smiled up at him. "I'm glad you had a nice time."

"Thanks," he said, smiling at her long drawn out words.

Back at his cabin, instead of going inside, Chris sat on the top step, kicked off his shoes, and just looked out at the water. To his left was Robin's cabin, less than two hundred yards away. To his right were the stone steps leading to the lake. On one side she lay sleeping and on the other was the image of her sitting there at daylight. Straight ahead was the small dock where she had once stood, facing the wind just before diving into the chilly water. He was surrounded by her and had to believe it was more than a coincidence he was there.

In truth, it wasn't too much for him, and he knew it. He wanted to help her heal. God had given him a particular insight into her, which in past experience usually meant he was being invited in. With that in mind, as he prayed and pondered, he began to sense he had been brought to New Hampshire for a reason other than his own. Clearly, he was encountering God's hand at work. God had one final mission for him.

***

Robin drifted off into a fitful sleep and immediately began to dream. It began the same way it usually did. She was running barefoot, dressed only in her nightgown, the chilly drizzle making her shiver as she raced down the driveway. Mike was screaming her name from the porch. She had never considered running before, but this night she was more frightened of him than ever. To run was her only hope. Already, he had pushed her into the bathtub, and she feared her ribs were broken. With each step she took, her chest cried out in pain. After yanking her out of the tub, he had hit her several times, the first backhand by far the worst. Her teeth ached still, and her cheek felt on fire. When Mike threw her on the bed and began loosening his belt, she believed him to be unsteady enough to topple. That was when she made the decision to run. With both feet she shoved him as hard as she could, scrambled off the bed, and began running. Now, she realized she had nowhere to go.

Drenched in sweat, Robin bolted upright in bed, kicking at the covers tangled about her feet. For a moment she wasn't sure where she was. The sights and sounds around her seemed foreign. Then suddenly it dawned on her: she was home at Emma's where she could run.

***

Chris had been sitting in the silence for over an hour, so when that was interrupted, it took a few seconds for his brain to respond to what his eyes were witnessing. Robin passed by his cabin at full speed, barefoot and wearing only her nightgown. Immediately, he knew where she was going.

He resisted calling out to her; instead, he jumped from the porch and followed her to the dock, where she stopped at the very end. Just as that first night, the moonlight allowed him to watch the events unfold. She was gasping for air, breathless from her sprint to the lake, but still she lifted her arms preparing to dive.

Chris stepped onto the dock. "Don't do it, Robin." His words were soft, intentionally reassuring.

She froze but didn't turn to face him. "I have to." With that, Robin dove in and began to swim.

Chris walked to the end of the dock and sat, determined to wait for her. This time he was close enough to hear her as she stroked through the water until she swam so far out the sound faded.

He had no way of knowing how much time had passed, but it seemed like an eternity as he waited. It was different from when he had seen her do this that first week. Then, she was a stranger to him. This time, she was someone whose story had captivated him and drawn him in. Clearly disoriented and out of breath already, Robin was far out in deep, dark waters. If she didn't return, he had no means of rescuing her, a thought that made his heart pound only harder.

When she did make it back, Chris held out his hand, offering to lift her out of the water. She took his hand.

Robin sat on the dock, draped her hair over one shoulder, and began to wring out the water.

Chris's heartbeat was only now beginning to steady. "One night, something tragic could happen. You may not make it back."

She allowed his words to sink in. "Honestly, I don't know if that would be such a bad thing."

"Robin…" Unsure of what to say, only partially understanding what was driving her, he finally said, "What makes you do this?"

With a shiver she wrapped her arms around her knees and gazed out at the water. "Some nights, I relive the end."

He began to unbutton his shirt. "You know, I saw you here on the dock when I first got here."

She took the shirt he offered without looking at him.

"You were standing there and then suddenly you dove in. I guess I thought you were… I don't know, trying to hurt yourself or maybe that you were crazy." He paused and wondered. "Are you trying to hurt yourself?"

"No. It seems to be the only thing that makes it better, though. After I swim, when I come back I feel stronger. I may not be able to run away, but I can swim away."

Robin stood and turned to leave. "I'll see you tomorrow."

She had closed the door on further questions, so he dared not ask any more.

"It is tomorrow." He smiled at her. "Can I at least walk back with you?"

"Sure."

They walked along together without speaking, and when they reached his cabin, Chris continued on with her. Once they reached hers, she slipped the shirt from around her shoulders and handed it to him.

Unsure of what to do, he said, "Do you want me to come in?"

"I'll be okay. Thanks, though."

"You should talk to someone. You don't have to live this way."

"It's all I know anymore."

Her hopeless expression gripped his heart since it was a feeling he knew all too well these days. He watched her as she moved up the stairs and toward the door, knowing he had to do something.

"See you for coffee?"

She never turned. "Sure, I'll see you then."

***

Early the following morning, just moments after the sun peered from behind the familiar tree line, Robin was sitting on the steps, looking out at the water. Out of the corner of her eye, she saw Chris approaching. Her cheeks flushed at the memory of what had happened the night before, both at the marina and when he had followed her to the dock. What could she say? There was no way to explain it to him. She barely understood what drove her actions.

Chris climbed the stairs and sat beside her. When he noticed the second coffee cup sitting beside her, he smiled, took the cup, and nudged his shoulder into hers. "Great service here." Then, after taking a sip, he said, "I know someone who can help, someone you can talk to about this."

She had not gone back to sleep after their encounter the night before. For hours she had been thinking about the things he said. When he suggested the possibility of something tragic happening and she found it wasn't something that sounded so bad – that was the point when she truly comprehended how far she had fallen into despair. The truth was, she didn't want to live the remainder of her life this way.

"You've seen my days around here. I don't have a whole lot of free time."

"He'll speak with you here."

"I could never afford that."

"He's really cheap. As a matter of fact, he does free counseling at my church."

With eyebrows raised, she said, "He would drive two hours? Why would he do that for someone he doesn't even know? What's the catch?"

"As a favor to me and no catch."

Chris outmaneuvered her every attempt to avoid counseling.

"One session, that's all you have to do. If you think it helps, great. If not, then at least you gave it a try."

"Let me think about it." Robin was only trying to buy some time. The more she thought about talking to someone about her past, the less she liked the idea.

"Sure. Just let me know."

They sat for a moment more until Chris said, "I think I'll take a boat out again today."

"What do you paint while you're out there?"

"Anything. Everything. Often I just sketch. My time is running out, and I want to capture everything I can while I can."

"You're here for another month and a half."

"I know. It seems to be flying by, though."

"Summer is like that."

"Yeah. Time flies by," he said.

Robin observed Chris's expression and wondered. There was something there that concerned her when he spoke and the way he wouldn't maintain eye contact.

Robin walked up the steps and found Emma watching out the window. By the time she made it inside, Emma had poured herself a cup of coffee and was leaning against the counter, trying to act casual.

"Morning." Robin anticipated the questions that would come.

Emma wasn't smiling. "You look sleepy."

"Rough night," Robin said as she went to pour another cup of coffee.

"I figured. Chris was looking for you last night."

"I'm just not ready."

"Then I'll never pressure you about dating again." Emma reached for Robin's hand. "I'm sorry I did."

Robin shrugged. "It's okay. I know you have my best at heart."

"More than you could ever know." Emma crossed the kitchen and peeked into the oven at her biscuits. "He is a nice guy, though, right?"

"He's a great guy, and I had a good time with him, but you know how complicated things are. I need more time."

Emma nodded. "Of course. You take all the time you need."

When Robin moved into Emma's outstretched arms, they stood for a quiet moment. *I thought it was getting better, but the turmoil inside seems to be getting worse.*

"What if he comes?" Robin said.

"Then we'll be ready."

In the shape she was in, Robin knew she would hardly have the strength to fight him.

Robin moved through the remainder of the morning as if in a fog. For much too long she had spent days like this. The nightmares would come, and she would spend the final hours of the night fighting sleep, terrified the dream would pick up right where it left off. Only once did she make it all the way to the end, and that was undoubtedly worse than the continual chase, much worse.

By early afternoon she was exhausted and went to her cabin to rest. After only half an hour of napping, Robin moved to sit on the side of her bed. For the first time in many years, she prayed her first heartfelt prayer. "I don't want to live this way anymore. Show me You're there, God."

***

Chris had been out on the lake for the past three hours. While painting and praying, his constant thoughts had been of Robin. She needed help. Her eyes that morning were tired and sad, full of pain, not distant pain as they usually were, but pain terribly present at that moment. It was evident to him, she was as low as she could possibly be, but wasn't that the best place for the Lord to begin a mighty work?

He had to admit, he was attracted to her still. If he hadn't been in the first place, he would have never asked her out to dinner. So the attraction was something to be thankful for, but avoided. He felt certain God had brought him there specifically to reach out to her, and that was accomplished by the initial attraction. God was funny like that. Had Chris not been drawn to her, he would have remained within himself, concentrating on his own end.

Chris considered another example of the genius of God. In order to keep him totally dependent upon Himself and his mind off his growing feelings for Robin, it would require Chris to cling to God and die to self in a way he had never known. God was still choosing to grow him spiritually even so close to death. Chris knew, in order to separate his own feelings and thoughts from what was best for Robin, it would take dependence on the Holy Spirit each and every moment he was with her. How could he not marvel at the strategic wisdom of God?

Chris stayed for nearly half an hour more before heading back. When he did make it back, he found Robin sitting on his porch, rocking. He dumped his paint supplies, along with two canvases of not-so-great work and joined her in the other chair.

Without looking at him, she said, "Do you really think he can help?"

"I don't know about him, but I do know he'll lead you to the one place you can find some peace."

"Where?"

"God. I know him well enough to guarantee that's where he'll take you and your broken spirit. I can also tell you that healing can be found no other place. If you'll go to Jesus, it'll get better. Maybe slowly, but it will eventually."

"Have you talked to him?"

"Yes. He can be here tomorrow. Is there any particular time that's best for you?"

"Lunchtime, I suppose. That way I won't feel the need to explain my absence."

"You mean to Emma?"

"No. I'll tell Emma, but I would rather not discuss it with anyone else."

"You shouldn't have to. This is between you and God and whatever you decide to tell the counselor."

"Chris..." She sat for a moment trying to collect her thoughts. "I don't know the way to God anymore. I used to, but I haven't in a very long time." After a brief pause, she said, "I've been a tremendous pretender."

Chris nodded. "I know that."

He had anticipated this conversation and knew his observations about her would likely swell up a defensiveness in her that might prevent any further openness.

"At the risk of offending you, I'll tell you the way I see it. Since I've been here, you've left for church on two Sundays, and it seems less productive than if you were going to the grocery store. At least from the store, you would bring back a sack of food, something of value, something to nourish you. Instead, you're practicing religious routines. You leave and come home empty handed."

She remained silent. When he had the boldness to continue, he went on. "Have you always gone to church?"

"Yes."

"Has it always been as it is now?"

"No."

"There is routine and there's relationship. The reason I know yours is routine is simple, really. When I watched you jump in the water and swim, witnessing your apathy about your own safety, I understood the hidden meaning behind it: you want relief even if it's in the form of death. These things witness to your routine. You can't be in a close and intimate relationship with

Jesus Christ and remain so tormented. I say this because I've experienced the same thing in varying degrees."

He paused for a second and wondered if he could possibly express his thoughts in a way that might make sense to anyone but him.

"I've never articulated this, so cut me some slack in my presentation."

Her smile prompted him to continue. "There's no such thing as darkness. In actuality, darkness is the absence of light. Make sense?"

She nodded, indicating it did.

"Similarly, chaos and torment – what you're experiencing now, are the absence of peace. The absence of peace means you've somehow stepped away from God. Make no mistake, He will never leave you or forsake you, so absence means you have moved, if you are a believer, that is."

When he dared to glance at her, the way she looked back caused him to momentarily stumble with the words, so he tried to ignore what her eyes did to him and went on. "God is not the author of confusion. So anytime you feel that kind of commotion in your mind or in your heart, you have to determine what steps you took away. He came to set the prisoners free. When you are in a close relationship with Jesus, you are free from that kind of turmoil. And you, Robin, are anything but free."

Robin sat with her mouth hanging open. Finally, she nodded and said, "Here, at noon?"

"Yep."

She stood. "I'll be here then."

SIX

To her surprise Robin had a restful night of sleep. Since she would soon be churning up muddy waters, she had anticipated a difficult night, but it was, thankfully, a night of rest. She sat on the stairs that morning, wondering if Chris would come again. She had brought coffee for him just in case. Within seconds of that thought, she saw him appear from behind the small row of trees leading from the cabins.

When he sat beside her, he thanked her for the coffee. After a minute of awkwardness, he said, "After the things I said yesterday, I wasn't so sure I would be welcome this morning. I'm sure I came off as preachy." He took a sip of his coffee. "I didn't mean it that way."

"You were right in everything you said."

His shoulders relaxed. A moment later, he said, "I thought about this all last night. You know what I've come up with?"

"What?"

"You've mended the veil."

She studied that for a moment then finally said, "What does that mean?"

"When Christ died on the cross, the Temple veil was torn. So when you asked Him to come into your life and forgive you, from that point forward, you have had complete access to God. He died to offer you that. When you pray, you don't have to toss words up into the air and hope He catches them. You can sit right here with Him and simply talk." Chris patted the stone beside him. "Here, every morning, He will sit with you." He pointed. "Standing out on that dock, He stands with you. Talk as you would to Emma or to me.

"This morning for example, I said, 'Lord, Robin is in a mess, and I need the words to lead her to You.' I didn't use a whole bunch of religious terms, like, thee and thou. I just talked to Him. Or, maybe I'll say, 'What do You think about this or that?' Then I wait and listen for Him to answer. Mostly, He responds through His Word. Sometimes, He speaks into my heart, but always, always He answers, even when it's not what I want to hear. Honestly, a lot of times it's not what I want to hear. But still, He speaks."

This concept was foreign to her. Never, even before turning from God, had she prayed in such a way. If she had to explain what she experienced when praying, it was more like slipping words into a balloon, filling it with helium, and releasing it into the atmosphere in the hopes it would reach the right destination. The times it mattered most, her balloon had obviously missed heaven.

"I've never prayed like that, never felt close enough that He would hear me."

"He wants to be that close, Robin." Chris turned to her and gave her a sympathetic look. "It makes sense that you don't feel close. When you've been hurt the way you have, it's easy to build a wall between yourself and God. That's what I mean by the mended veil. Stitch by stitch, you've recreated the veil in your own heart, which gives you the sense that He's far away."

She nodded. "I can see that."

With his words she grasped a truth that she could have never identified on her own. What he said was an accurate description of what had happened to her over the past years. More than six years had passed since she was willing to look at God. That exact moment was still so vivid in her mind and so engraved into her heart, she could feel the weight of it in her chest still. God didn't help when she called, so she had intentionally stepped away from Him.

"You've run from His presence rather than run into it."

"I've never heard anything like this."

"This is something I've pondered for years."

"Obviously!"

His thinking was so profound she could hardly imagine how she had missed his depth before. Then again, she had made it such a point of keeping him at arm's length that a conversation at this level was all but impossible.

Chris continued. "In my case, I realized that I couldn't reconcile what I read of the God of the Bible with what I was seeing in the world and experiencing in my life. From that, I concluded He wasn't active in the lives of everyday people like me, so I installed a zipper, closed the veil, and went through the religious motions. That got me nowhere but miserable and defeated. Eventually, I realized I was seeing other people with what seemed to be a real relationship with Jesus, and I wanted that, to be a real deal person."

"What you said about stitch by stitch, that was probably more my case."

"That's what you need to talk about then, your stitches. Once you expose them, that will begin the process of unraveling them. Until that veil is unmended, you can never be close and intimate with Jesus. Until you choose to move back into Him, you'll never know the peace and freedom He offers."

"I'm scared to talk about it. It terrifies me to relive it."

"There's a verse that comes to mind; it's about God being a candle shining a light into darkness. I'll have to look that up for you. Basically, what I get from it is that you have to allow those things into the light, and He'll show you the way. He can heal them then, but if you keep them hidden, you'll keep swimming in dark waters." He grinned at his pun.

"I don't want to swim there anymore."

"I know, and you're doing something about it. You've agreed to get help. You are choosing to move back where you belong, into His presence."

Robin nodded. "It's time."

For a moment they were quiet. Then she said, "While we're here and things are still quiet, I want to tell you something. I was going to tell you the other night, but then I acted so weird." Her cheeks flushed at the memory, so she looked back out at the water.

"What?"

"I'm not in a good place to date anyone right now. I think you're a great guy, but I'm just not ready for that."

"I get that." He gulped down the last of his coffee. "Honestly, I'm not either."

"Vanessa?"

"No, other things. I'll save them for some other time."

"Agreed."

The following day, with a few minutes to spare, Robin was nearing Chris's cabin. She had nearly backed out, but after talking it over with Emma, decided to press on. Emma had been pleased to hear she would be talking to a counselor. Though Emma didn't grasp the Christian aspect of the healing Robin needed, still she encouraged her to talk openly. The things of God were not something Emma was ever open to. In the years that Robin had been there, she had been going to church alone. Emma had no interest and had even asked Robin to stop inviting her. When looking back, how much good had it done her? No wonder Emma didn't see a benefit since she had modeled none.

When Robin arrived at the cabin, she was disappointed to see there was no other car there, only Chris's. Certain she hadn't seen anyone come in through the entrance of the inn, she feared the man wasn't coming. It had taken everything in her to agree to this, and now she was ready to get started.

Even as she was still tapping on the door, she heard Chris invite her in.

"Hey." She opened the door and peeked in.

"I'm here. Come on in."

Chris was sitting in one of the club chairs by the fireplace.

"He's not coming?" She grimaced.

"He's here, Robin. Have a seat." Chris pointed to the chair across from him.

48

"It's you." It was a statement rather than a question. For some reason the possibility that Chris was the counselor had never even crossed her mind, but now as she thought about it, it made perfect sense.

"Does it bother you?"

"No." She pondered a moment. "I don't think so."

"Why would it bother you?"

"I suppose it doesn't matter."

Just two nights before they were out on a non-date – maybe that was why this seemed awkward. For the briefest moment she had considered the possibility of beginning something with him. She didn't know what to call it other than what Emma had: a summer romance. Whatever the case, he was willing and free, so she had nothing to lose by talking to him at least once.

"I have experience if that's what makes you hesitate. I got my counseling certification a few years ago and have been volunteering at my church since. I'm no pro, but I'm willing to listen, to try and help."

"No hesitation. Just tell me how to begin."

"I will start with prayer."

Robin nodded.

"Our Father, we need Your presence today. Guide my words and heal Robin's heart. Only You can be what we need, the Wonderful Counselor. It's in Jesus name we pray. Amen."

Chris looked at her and smiled. "Tell me your story. Help me know you more."

"Like childhood, that far back?"

"Sure. You can go as far back as you want. Give me the highlights."

A slight smile tugged at her lips. "I had a happy childhood, wonderful parents. They loved each other and loved me."

"Brothers or sisters?"

"No, just me."

"Milestones?"

For a quiet moment she tried to come up with a milestone but could think of nothing before her early teens. Childhood had been fairly uneventful.

"I kind of felt invisible for most of my early life. Not at home, of course, but at school. I had several good friends, but I wasn't wildly popular. Then one summer, I kind of blossomed. I grew a little taller and wore my hair a little differently. When I went back to school things were different."

"You became more popular?"

"No, I didn't mean it that way. I guess I stopped feeling so invisible."

"Boyfriends?"

"One."

"What was his name?"

One, that word echoed around in her heart. There had always been only one. With a soft smile, she chewed on her thumbnail, considering the early days.

After another moment of hesitation, she whispered, "His name was Mike."

It suddenly struck her that she hadn't spoken his name aloud in many years. While it felt strange saying it to Chris, the sound of Mike's name was just as familiar as her own.

"How old were you?"

"Thirteen, we both were. It was middle school, seventh grade."

"Tell me what it was like to become visible," Chris said.

***

Robin sat alone on an overturned log, holding a stick with a marshmallow dangling on its point. In order to get it just right, she allowed it to catch fire and then pulled it to her mouth to blow it out. When she looked up, she found him staring at her. Mike, the guy she had been secretly watching since the beginning of the school year when two separate elementary schools merged into the larger middle school building. This was a big deal to all the girls, since it afforded a brand new crop of boys to whisper about.

Robin noticed him the first day of school, and as unlikely as it seemed to her, he noticed her too. Often, she caught him looking at her during social studies. That was their only class together and suddenly her favorite of the day. His seat was over near the windows and behind hers, so that rarely allowed a chance for her to peek at him. She soon discovered that every time she dared a glance, he was looking her way. Then again, Shelly Masters sat in front of her. Who could help staring at her with her new figure? No girl but Shelly seemed to mature as much over the summer. Not only the new boys from West Elementary, but the boys from her school noticed her transformation as well.

He was tall but not freakishly so. That came a few years later. Still, he was tall enough that she could see him over the other heads in the hallway between classes. His hair was brown, a shade or two lighter than hers, and his eyes were dark blue and smiled when he did. She liked that most about him. Because he was a jock and so cute, most of the girls were talking about him. From what she had heard, he had no girlfriend.

So there she sat, marshmallow ablaze, and Mike was smiling at her. It was then that he began to walk her way. Before making it to her side of the campfire, someone announced they were going to play Seven Minutes in Heaven. He halted his movements at that point. Robin looked around wondering what the game was, but since it kept her from talking to Mike, she already disliked it.

Couples were paired up and sent behind a small group of trees for seven minutes, and she suspected they might be kissing but had no way to be sure. This was, after all, her first boy/girl party. Her parents had allowed her to go only with the assurance that everyone would be outdoors with adults present. After the third couple was sent off behind the trees, Shelly walked up to Mike and whispered something in his ear. Then she giggled, and Robin's heart sank. It shouldn't have surprised her. With Shelly's summer makeover, of course he would want to go with her. Robin watched him shake his head, though. Then he continued what she thought was his earlier trek over to where she sat.

When he reached where she was sitting, someone teased, "Mike and Robin," meaning they should be the next to pair up and go behind the tree line. Suddenly, many voices chimed in and only grew louder.

Where were the adults? Robin wondered. *Where was the way out?* She didn't know what to do or how to react. If she ran toward the house, everyone would laugh at her, but to go behind the trees with Mike could be a fate worse than embarrassment.

He squatted down before her and placed his hands on her knees. "We don't have to go if you don't want to."

On his face and in his eyes was a look of tenderness she would have never expected from a jock. Of course she had daydreamed about this moment, but in her version there was an air of arrogance about him. This Mike, however, this huge football player, wasn't arrogant at all. Actually, he was surprisingly sweet.

Robin looked at him, and without conscious thought of it, her head began to nod. *What was wrong with her head? Did it not know her dad would kill her for an affirmative nod?*

He held out his hand and grinned. "Let's just do it to shut 'em up."

They walked hand in hand to the small clearing and for a moment just stood there. He was holding a flashlight, so it wasn't entirely dark, but it was still dark enough to be creepy.

Mike was the first to break the silence. "I've been trying to get up the nerve to talk to you since the beginning of the year."

"Really?" she said in awe of the moment.

Her heart was pounding and her hands trembled; her entire body shook. It was cool out but not enough for the convulsions she was experiencing. *Did*

51

he notice? Her mind was wandering, and all she could do was shake and grin like an idiot. He said something, but she missed it due to her crazy, wandering mind.

"Huh?"

"I said I don't know exactly what we're supposed to do back here."

She chewed her thumbnail and whispered, "Me neither."

What happened next was something that would cause them to roll with laughter for years to come.

He shrugged. "So, wanna be my girlfriend?"

"Sure." What else could she say?

"Can I give you a kiss?"

This time, "sure" wouldn't even come out of her mouth, so her rebellious head began to nod again.

Mike leaned down and kissed her on the cheek.

***

That moment, when viewed through Robin's history, was when her life truly began. Mike became her everything.

Chris smiled. "That was a nice story. Did you date for long?"

After recounting the night they met, Robin realized how long it had been since she had allowed herself to think back on such fond memories. For so long she had feared recalling the good times but found it less painful than she had anticipated it would be.

"We weren't actually allowed to date until I was sixteen. Even then it was with serious restrictions." She grinned. "My dad was crazy overprotective."

"You were together for some time then?"

"We married when we were eighteen."

Chris nodded. "Oh, so when you said one, you really meant only one?"

"Yes," Robin said. "I was only ever with Mike."

"What was he like back then?"

With Mike's image still dancing around her memory, Robin gazed into the fireplace, wishing it was cold enough to have a fire going. That thought led her to remember she had agreed to take some firewood down to another cabin that afternoon. They were having a bonfire after dark.

"Robin?"

Robin glanced at Chris, unsure of what he had just asked. Without warning, she felt flush and unable to breathe, so she jumped to her feet.

"I should go. I don't think I can do this anymore."

Chris stood and hurried to stand between her and the door. "If you're uncomfortable, we can stop. I believe it was a good start, though."

"Thanks for talking with me. I'm sure it'll help." Robin stepped around him and rushed toward the door.

He followed her out and onto the porch. "Tomorrow at noon?" he said as she bolted down the steps.

"I don't think I can," and without another word, she left him standing there.

The remainder of the day, Robin tried to stay away from the others as much as possible. Though not upset exactly, she instead felt far away. Memory after memory flooded her mind, and for the most part, she simply wanted to wade in them alone. From the moment they met at the bonfire, all the way through school, she and Mike were inseparable. When she said she was no longer invisible, it was true. Everyone knew and loved Mike, and because she belonged to him, she oftentimes felt she lived on center stage with him. From sweethearts to marriage it remained ideal until their lives were shattered by loss and grief. Those were the memories that threatened to drown her.

She questioned whether she could go and speak with Chris again the next day. Sure, she could tell him sweet stories of middle school and high school. Even those first few years of marriage, though occasioned by separation, were beautiful and full of real and genuine love. It was the next chapter she feared.

Later that evening, Robin sat with Emma on the swing under the gazebo. Becky and Tommy had just headed back up to the house, leaving them alone for the first time. She had encountered Emma several times throughout the day, but each time, someone was around, preventing her from talking about her time with Chris. Robin knew Emma well enough to know she was dying to know.

"So how did it go today?"

"Surprising. Come to find out, Chris is the counselor. I'm not sure why I didn't figure that out before." She shrugged. "But it was good, I think."

"That's all I get?" She patted Robin's leg.

"Today wasn't so hard. I know it'll get more difficult, though."

"But you'll stick with it, right?"

"I don't know if I can."

"Did you talk about Mike?"

"A little."

Emma was quiet for a while, then said, "I can't imagine how difficult it must be, but you have to." She stopped and sighed. "What you experienced with Mike, you need to let it out."

"I know." Robin leaned up and rested her forearms on her legs. "That wasn't even Mike, not that man at the end. Today, I didn't think of him or talk of him."

"Robin, we have to discuss what's coming. This will be the first place he looks for you."

"Not tonight. I just can't."

"Okay, sweetie." Emma rubbed Robin's back. "Are you sleeping well?"

"Last night, yes."

Chris was walking toward them, so both became quiet.

"Mind if I join you?"

Emma stood. "I was just heading in. You two enjoy the stars."

"You don't have to go on my account," Chris said.

"Early mornings, you know." Emma patted his cheek. "Have a good night, sweet thing."

She looked back at Robin. "See you in the morning, Hummingbird."

"I'll come up early for coffee."

Both remained quiet for a moment after Emma left until finally Chris said, "Hummingbird?"

"She's been calling me that since I was a little girl. It's a play on my name. She loves birds and butterflies."

"I see."

"Sorry to take off today. I guess I felt some things I wasn't ready for."

Chris took the seat next to her and turned to face her. "There is no required amount of time. We will simply talk as you feel you can. No more, no less."

"I appreciate that."

They stayed away from any hint of the past and chatted until nearly midnight about senseless things. From weather to what outdoor activities they each liked, they kept the conversation in nonthreatening places.

Because she had to get up so early, Robin eventually said, "It's getting late. I should go soon."

"I know." Chris paused. "I'm sorry to keep you out so late."

"No need to be sorry. I enjoyed it."

"About tomorrow, I think talking more will do you some good. You barely got started today. Please consider coming back."

"I will." She smiled. "I'm truly grateful that you care."

"I do care, Robin. Just keep an open mind."

***

54

At the end of the night as he walked back with her to her cabin, Chris was let down. It was one of those perfect nights, one you hate to see end. Without question he wanted to help her, but the truth was, he simply liked hanging out with her. Because he had no hidden agenda, simply being friends with her would be easy to do. He sensed she was good for him and helped to keep his mind off impending things. For as long as she was willing to be friends, he would seek her out.

With her guard down, Chris found Robin a delight to be around. She was funny and sweet and sarcastic. It wasn't lost on him how much they had in common – except football, and on that, they violently agreed to disagree. He hated the Panthers and she hated the Patriots.

When they reached her cabin, Chris said, "Sunrise and coffee?"

"Sounds good to me. I'll bring the coffee."

Chris headed back to his cabin knowing, if things were different, he would pursue her to the ends of the earth. The sad thing was, by the time she was saved from such a vulnerable place, he wouldn't be around to witness it.

SEVEN

Robin sat in Chris's cabin ready to begin again. The night before was unusual in that she dreamed of Mike, but not the end-times Mike. Instead, she dreamed of good times, times when she was her happiest. That was a gift.

"We had a good marriage. No, we had a great marriage."

"No signs at all of violence early on? Or even when you were dating?"

"No, not at all." She hesitated. "I can only think of one time he was even angry. In a way he became violent then, but he didn't physically hurt me."

"Tell me about it."

"It was our junior year. Something happened that really upset me, so I broke things off with him. He didn't take it well at all."

"What did he do?"

"He hit a locker a few times, nothing else."

"Were you standing near the locker?"

"Yes, but he wasn't angry at me. I think he was angrier with himself and maybe a little jealous."

"Was he often jealous?"

"Back then? No, not really. I suppose I had never given him reason to be."

"And this time?"

"I wasn't trying to make him jealous. This guy was talking to me, and Mike flipped out."

"Tell me what happened."

"Mike had gone to a party one night without me. As far as I know, it was the first time he ever drank. He came to my house later that night and told me that something had happened, he had kissed another girl." Robin had been devastated; especially considering it was Shelly, the one girl most guys hit on. "He kept apologizing and promising me that nothing like that would ever happen again."

"What did you do?"

"Nothing. I was too hurt to do or say anything. I just went inside. The next morning, I caught a ride to school with my dad instead of Mike."

***

When Robin reached the steps on the east side of the building, she saw Mike pull in and park where he usually did. Across the expanse of lawn she could see that he was watching her and was certain he had gone by her house to pick her up. At even the sight of him, her eyes filled with tears, so she hurried into the building and through the hallway to her locker. Along the way she realized that people were watching her and whispering. Surely she wasn't imagining it. The question was settled when her closest friends grabbed her and dragged her into the restroom.

"He's such a pig!" Emily said.

Rachel nodded her agreement. "I'm so sorry. I wasn't even in the same room, but I heard about it."

The two began to discuss the details between them, who saw what, who should have said what.

"I've gotta go," Robin said to her friends, who were much too engrossed in the details of the night before to notice she left.

She tried again to make it to her locker. At that point it became clear; it wasn't her imagination at all. All eyes remained on her throughout the morning. Plus, she heard several eyewitness accounts that painted a more disturbing picture than Mike's version of, "She kissed me, and I guess I kissed her back." Apparently, they were groping all over each other right in front of everyone.

By lunchtime she had heard all she wanted to hear. Whenever anyone approached, she threw up her hand and told them she knew. Mike had tried to talk to her on several occasions, but each time she hurried off, too heartbroken even to hear what he had to say.

At the lunch table with Emily and Rachel, Robin watched him as he approached. By this point, with all she had heard, her mind was made up. Humiliated by the stories and hurt to her core by his desire for someone else, she was determined to end things with him. She felt she had no choice; it was his doing, not hers.

Mike straddled the bench next to her and moved in close. For a minute he just sat there, looking at her. Robin noticed that others around gawked in curiosity and seemed to enjoy her pain. It was the juiciest piece of gossip the school had known all year, and ironically, those who had gladly put them on a pedestal were just as delighted to watch them topple over.

"Please talk to me," Mike said.

Robin turned to face him. "It was more than a simple kiss." She lowered her voice. "Do you know how many people were watching you?"

He nodded. "It was stupid, and I can't do anything but tell you how sorry I am. Baby, I love you." He moved his hand to the back of her neck and pulled her to him. "Please forgive me, please." Then he rested his forehead on hers. "I have nothing but you; you know that."

Mike was so close she could feel his breath on her face. His eyes revealed his desperation, but his eyes were not all she could think of. Everyone was still staring, watching this private encounter to see what she would do. With cheeks burning, she whispered, "I think we need some time apart."

Even as she spoke, she knew it would never be as easy as she made it sound. After being together for four years, she was so wrapped up in Mike that she wasn't sure who she was apart from him. Still, even after all she had heard about how he had touched Shelly and how she had touched him, Mike was all she wanted. Her weakness for him made her feel needy and pathetic.

"No. Don't say that." He held her to him. "I'll do anything to make this up to you, anything."

"There's nothing you can do."

Robin pulled away from him, took her tray, food untouched, and dumped it into the barrel trashcan. With feigned strength and holding her head high, she left the lunchroom. Once alone in the hallway, though, she ran all the way to the restroom, locked herself in a stall, and began to cry. While sitting there on the toilet, she went through half a roll of tissue before the end of lunch bell sounded.

After school during cheerleading practice, Robin was near to where Mike practiced football. On several occasions, she heard his coach yell at him, "Where's your head, McGarrett?"

Robin tried not to look, but when she did, she found Mike staring at her. Clearly, he was a mess, and it broke her heart for him. Once, when she had taken a fall during one of the stunts, she saw him begin to run toward her. Again, the coach yelled.

When her practice was over, she caught a ride home and waited for him to call. She knew he would. While they spoke on the phone, he begged and pleaded, but she refused to give in. After their third conversation, her dad insisted Mike not call again.

At school the next morning, Robin was at her locker before first period when a boy named Jeff approached her. He was a guy Mike didn't like, so Jeff was only talking to her to spite Mike.

When Mike caught sight of him there with her, he slammed his locker door and stormed toward them. The look of fury on his face sent Jeff scrambling.

Mike spun her around to face him. "I know you better than this. You would never go out with him just to hurt me."

She only sighed. He was right; she would never do that to him. Even though the hallway had gone virtually silent with onlookers watching their exchange, she no longer felt embarrassed as she had the day before. Instead, she wanted the whole thing to be over, the argument, not the relationship. She loved him and had come to conclude during the sleepless hours of the night that she would forgive him anything.

Mike grasped her by the shoulders, pressed her against the bank of lockers, and moved his face nearer to hers. "I swear to you, if he touches you, I will kill him!" With that, he slammed his fist into the locker next to hers multiple times.

Robin jumped at the sound of the pounding next to her ear but never once considered he might hit her. He stood there, towering over her, breathing hard and swearing under his breath. While she had never seen him so angry before, still, she felt no fear of him.

She reached for his hand. "Look what you've done. Your knuckles are bloody."

He never looked at his hand. Instead, his eyes were trained on hers. "I don't care. I don't care about anything else, only you. What happened with her will never, ever happen again. Please don't leave me, Rob."

His voice was loud and his eyes moist with tears even with all their friends looking on. Yet he was unafraid to fight for her or plead with her, right there in front of them. He loved her enough to make a fool of himself, and she loved him even more for that. At that realization she slipped her arms around his waist and rested her head on his chest. "I could never leave you."

***

Robin sat with Chris, reliving the moment even then. She could hear Mike as he whispered in her ear, "Never again. Do you hear me? No one but you."

From then on, that was the way it remained.

"Tell me about your marriage."

She sat there, biting at her lip, trying to muddle through the onslaught of memories. This part, going back to the good times was like a journey home after being away for so many years.

"Mike enlisted in the Marine Corps right out of high school, so we married before he left for basic training. I stayed with my parents and started classes at a community college nearby. Immediately after, he was deployed to Afghanistan for a year. It was tough, but we got through it."

"And then?"

"When he came back, he was sent to Camp Pendleton, California. Things were great between us. It was really our beginning as a married couple. We had never been away from home, but somehow, being so far away from family caused us to grow even closer."

She closed her eyes and envisioned their dumpy little studio apartment. It never bothered her as long as she was with Mike. He was all she had ever wanted, and at the time she truly believed she was living out her happily-ever-after. Nothing could have ever prepared her for what was to come.

"Then he was deployed again for another year. That year was much more difficult. I was all alone there in California. It was too expensive to fly home often and too far to drive. I got a job and continued taking classes, which helped somewhat.

"Once he returned home, he had only another six months left and decided not to reenlist. We moved back to North Carolina after that."

"What was he like when he came home the second time?"

"Different from the first time. He wasn't sleeping well and often seemed agitated."

For some reason, even after all that had happened, she felt the need to defend him. "He was never unkind to me. He just wasn't like that. You would have to have known him then to understand."

She sighed over what was lost. "He treated me as if I were his whole world. That's how it always was." His image filled her mind. "He cried a lot when he came back. That wasn't like him. Sometimes he would just hang on to me and cry. When I would ask him why, he would say he couldn't imagine ever losing me."

Robin stopped for a moment, lost in the memory of how much he loved her. He did love her.

"Are you okay? Do you need a break?"

"A break would be nice. Actually, can we pick back up tomorrow?"

Something was stirring in her chest, something she needed time alone to process. A tidal wave of emotions washed over her, causing her to long for those days. No such longing had occurred in many years, and she was unsure how to filter out the good from the bad, the happy from the sad.

"Your rules, remember?"

"Again, sorry about yesterday. I shouldn't have taken off like that. Thanks for not giving up on me."

He smiled and nodded. "Oh, I imagine it won't be the only time you try to run. I'm patient, though."

"Thank you so much. I wonder how I could ever repay you for this."

"You don't have to repay." He paused as if thinking then changed his reply. "Who knows, maybe I'll think of some way. I'll let you know."

"You do that… anything you say."

***

Chris was left alone with his thoughts of Robin's story. The look on her face when she spoke of Mike had told the story of her love for him, even if she hadn't spoken a word. He was surprised at how much more open she was, almost animated. Her eyes sparkled, danced even, while she recounted stories of their early years together. Only in rare moments, as if she suddenly remembered the love story she recounted no longer existed, her eyes would cloud over with that reality.

After hearing of her relationship with Mike, Chris felt a peculiar sense of jealousy. He had never known a love like the one she had described and grieved the absence of it. Though he had been in what he would call love, it was never the deep and lasting kind of love he had hoped for. There was a reason he was still unmarried at thirty-seven.

Obviously in her case, it was no more lasting than his had been. So having heard stories of their early relationship and how good things were, he had to wonder how things had taken such a drastic turn, leaving them divorced and her so damaged.

He stood and went out to sit on the porch. Joe, the old guy in a cabin nearby, waved and spoke as he passed by with his grandkids. Chris waved in return. This was a great location to be, right on the path leading to the dock and main house. Because of the number of other guests, Chris didn't feel as if he was traveling alone. Funny that he saw the benefit in that considering he had made the trip specifically to be alone. God had a different plan.

His mind traveled back to Robin's story. Based on the fact that Mike had served a couple of tours in the Gulf, post-traumatic stress disorder was the likely reason for his behavior. For a man to transform from what she had described of Mike to a violent abuser, some event or series of them had to trigger it. War would do it. Whatever it was, Chris was determined to get to the root of it. The only way Robin would ever be able to live again after all she had endured was to place her past before the throne of God. If she would allow him, Chris would help her do just that.

***

While cleaning one of the second-story guest rooms, Robin was left alone to think. Her mind traveled from place to place back in time. With a semi-smile she thought about the donuts. After all those years donuts and her wedding night still made her heart warm and break all at the same time.

***

Robin sat on the side of the bed and looked up at Mike. He was standing there before her, grinning an awkward grin.

"You know what this reminds me of?" He sat beside her as he spoke.

"What?"

"Seven Minutes in Heaven. Remember how we didn't know what to do?"

"Are you saying you don't know what to do?" she said with a smile.

They had waited to be married before being together. After what had happened with Shelly their junior year, Robin was able to trust Mike again. Something changed between them then. Out of his regret and her heartbreak, there developed a deeper level of intimacy, a greater sense of commitment than ever before. Now, on their wedding night, it was finally okay to make love, and there they sat, both fidgeting, not sure what to do or how to please the other.

"I think I'll figure it out," he said as his grin broadened. He moved in to kiss her, whispering, "I've waited years for this. You better believe I'll figure it out."

It was sweet and beautiful, at times even funny. They giggled in the darkness as they explored each other and all that was finally open to them. It was worth the wait, something so much more than either anticipated. They shared something few people ever find, and both were aware of that fact. His love for her ran deep and wide, and she was certain nothing would ever change it.

The next morning she woke up alone and suspected he had gone out to get them something to eat. Mike never missed a meal. She wrapped herself in the sheet and plopped down in the middle of the bed and turned on the TV. Within a few minutes she heard the key slip into the lock, and Mike walked in carrying donuts and two jugs of milk. It was their first breakfast together as a married couple.

***

When Mike returned home from overseas the first time, Robin picked him up at the bus station. Because she was living at her parents' and wanted privacy for his first night back, she had booked a room at the same hotel. On the way there he pulled into the parking lot of the donut shop, smiling as he put the car into park. "So we don't have to get out in the morning."

Alone in their room, he knelt before her. "I want to tell you something. Married guys were hooking up with some of the women there. It happened all the time, but I never did. I would never do that to you. There isn't another woman in the entire world for me."

Robin slid her arms around her husband's neck. "Promise me."

"I promise – no one but you. For all my life – no one but you."

He kissed her with such intensity that tears came to her eyes. Nothing could ever take that kind of love away; she was sure of it.

The next morning, they sat in bed and polished off an entire dozen donuts.

***

Robin sat on the bed she had just made, tears springing to her eyes. It became their thing, donuts. Because of it, she hadn't eaten one in years.

EIGHT

Robin knocked on Chris's door, and when he didn't answer, after another minute she turned to leave. They had agreed to meet, so she was surprised to find him gone. On the way back to the house, she saw him heading up from the dock.

He raised his hand and shouted, "Hey, sorry, I lost track of time."

In that moment she became aware of something she should have recognized before. He was there on vacation, paying handsomely for the cabin rental, and here she was taking up his time with free counseling. He was rushed from his morning out on the water to get back to meet with her. She was being selfish.

Robin met him halfway between the cabins and the dock. "I just realized how I've monopolized your time. I'm so sorry I haven't seen it before now."

"Monopolized my time? What are you talking about?"

"You felt rushed to be back here to meet with me when you should have no schedule to keep. I'm so sorry."

He chuckled. "You have to be kidding me." He just passed by her. "Come on."

She fell in behind him. "Are you sure?"

When they reached the cabin, he dropped his backpack on the porch and moved to sit in one of the rockers. He pointed to the other chair. "Sit."

She did so. For a moment she was quiet, still concerned that she was invading his vacation. How could someone, a virtual stranger to her, give so much of his time to a woman he barely knew? "Have you always been this way, so giving?"

He smiled and looked down. "I don't know that I would call myself giving."

"I would."

Chris waved her off. "Enough of that. Let's talk."

"So, where shall we begin today?" she said.

"Are you ready to tell me about the hard times?"

"Maybe." Robin squirmed in her seat at the thought of it.

"When was the first time he hit you?"

She looked out at the water, not at all prepared to talk about it, but knowing there would be no relief over the end without taking him through the beginning; she had to power through.

"I went to work for a car dealership as a receptionist. One night after closing up, my car wouldn't start. Of course I tried to call Mike, but he never answered. He had been going out after work drinking with the guys. At first it was just occasionally, but before long, he went out a few nights a week. I imagine he was ignoring my calls because he didn't want me asking when he might come home. I did that a lot.

"I wasn't sure what to do. One of the sales guys offered to drop me off, and I thought it was no big deal."

She was quiet for a minute. The memory of that night, the beginning of the end, brought with it an indescribable ache deep inside. It reached a hidden place she was certain had become numb. In that moment, however, the stabbing pain of disappointment and loss pierced her heart, assuring her she was anything but numb.

"Even after I got home I tried to call, but he still never answered. When he came in a little while later and heard I had accepted a ride home, he went off the deep end. It was like nothing I had ever seen in him before. He began accusing me of cheating and threatened the guy. I didn't understand what was happening. I kept trying to explain, but it seemed the more I did, the angrier he got."

A shiver ran along her spine at the recollection it.

"He reeked of stale beer and cigarette smoke from the bar, and at one point, he grabbed me and tried to kiss me. I was so disgusted by him in that moment, I shoved him away."

She paused and let out a long breath, recalling how he had looked at her after she pushed him. It was the very first time she saw his anger directed toward her. Up until then, he was simply angry at everything. Burnt toast might cause him to throw the toaster. Lost keys would result in upside down furniture and slammed doors. In those moments she would rush in and try to help diffuse his anger. That night, though, she was the target of his rage, and no one was there to help her.

"After I pushed him, he slung me across the kitchen and into the counter. I think maybe I cracked a rib. The bruising and pain lasted for weeks."

She stopped, unable to go on. That night, from there on, things only got worse. He never hit her or pushed her around again, but it was the first of many times he forced himself on her. Not in a violent way, but as some means of trying to make up with her, he began kissing her, telling her how sorry he was and how much he loved her. Even while she tried to stop him, he held her firmly in his grasp and continued kissing her until finally she gave in to him.

Afterward, and all throughout the next day, she had lived in stunned silence, hoping the entire thing had been a terrible dream. No matter how much she tried to push the memory away, the bruises on her wrists where he had held her down were evidence of its reality. Even worse was the memory of how she responded to him, desiring him as much as he had her.

Chris watched her as she sat lost in her memories. Finally, he said, "That night, was there anymore violence?"

"No," she lied as she looked back out at the water. Some things were too humiliating to discuss.

"What happened afterward?"

"He was so drunk, but eventually he realized what he had done. He cried and told me how much he loved me. I became the typical stand-by-your-man woman."

Robin snorted at her own stupidity. In truth, she had believed him when he said he would never hurt her again. Of course she believed him. He had never lifted a finger to harm her before. How could she ever anticipate what was to come? For nearly a year it happened, not every day or even weekly but enough to make life so completely miserable that even when he was stable and not drinking, she lived in fear that he would snap or that something she said might set him off.

"Did he hit you only when he was drinking?"

"Yes."

"How long did it go on?"

"Nearly a year."

Chris stopped rocking, leaned up, and clasped his hands together. "I'm glad you got out when you did. Many women stay for years. Some never make it out."

"That last night left me no choice, or I would have never left him on my own."

"What happened that night?"

All she could do was shake her head to try to ward off the bloody memories of it. "I can't, not yet."

"Okay, I understand. No pressure." He leaned in closer. "After that first night, how long before it happened again?"

"A few months later. Honestly, I'm surprised it didn't happen sooner than it did. He was becoming more and more volatile. Everything upset him. Even sober, he had this incredibly short fuse. I never knew what might set him off and felt as if I was walking on eggshells constantly. I became nervous and jumpy, knowing something was terribly wrong. Then one night it happened again. The next morning, I was pretty beat up."

Robin shook her head and took a deep breath. In some ways is seemed like a lifetime ago, but in others it seemed like just yesterday.

"We were at a movie one night when a guy I had gone to school with while Mike was on his first deployment approached us. I barely knew him really. I don't even remember his name. When he was about to walk away, he said it was good to see me again and leaned in and hugged me. I just stood there frozen, looking up at Mike. He was furious and grabbed hold of the guy and shoved him. The guy apologized but Mike took a swing at him anyway and knocked him into a wall.

"The entire way home Mike screamed at me, asking if I had gone out with him, if I had slept with him. I cried and tried to reassure him, but he just wouldn't listen. Once we got home, Mike ranted and raved then finally stormed out. When he came back later, he dragged me out of bed and the whole thing began again. It was different than the first round. He was so drunk and angry that he began to shove me. Then he began to hit me. Until that final night, it was the worst of all the times.

"Did you call the police?"

She sat for a moment looking at Chris. Finally, she said, "He was the police. He got on at the sheriff's department just after we returned from Pendleton. The friends he drank with were all deputies. Even if not, I never would have called and risked getting him into trouble. His job was everything to him. After losing so much, I couldn't take that from him too."

"What do you mean he lost so much?"

Robin couldn't face Chris or answer right away. Eventually, she said, "Who he was before the war."

"Did you tell anyone?"

"No."

"Were you scared to?"

"I don't know, maybe." That wasn't exactly true, so she clarified. "Not scared. It wasn't as if he threatened me if I did. I just didn't want anyone to know."

"Why do you think that is?"

She only shook her head and shrugged. By the time the abuse began, they had been married over five years. In all those years, she and everyone else believed them to be the happiest of couples. Was that what kept her silent, her embarrassment?

"So, Mike never saw anyone for PTSD? I'm no professional, but it's pretty obvious that he was suffering from it."

"No."

"Did you try to get him to?"

"No."

Chris sat for a few seconds looking at her. "Robin, something kept you quiet. What do you think that was? If you had to guess?"

Tears filled her eyes and she looked away. "I couldn't imagine anyone knowing how broken he was, how broken we both were." She turned back to look at him. "Was that just pride on my part? Did I allow it all to continue because of what others might think?"

"I don't think so," Chris said. "In the middle of the storm, you couldn't see the clear way out. I don't know much about PTSD since I've never directly counseled anyone with it." He paused. "Until now." When she looked at him with eyes wide, he said, "Maybe you have a form of PTSD yourself. The abuse you suffered, the life you lived constantly on the edge, you very well could be suffering from it, too. Your dreams and the way you have avoided your past, it's something to consider."

"But I'm feeling better. My dreams have stopped."

"I'm not saying yours is at the level of Mike's, but you likely have it to a degree."

Robin considered it. "Maybe I do."

"If your nightmares come back, or if you don't see some improvement over the next few weeks, it would be wise to continue on with counseling, to find someone who specializes in PTSD after I'm gone."

"I'd like to see how this goes first."

"I agree. Let's cover a little more today."

She nodded.

"Did anyone at work notice?"

"I never went back to work after that first night. From then on he was insanely jealous, so I simply stayed home. It was easier than the accusations and fights that arose when I did go out. I never understood why, but he lived in fear that I would leave him." Robin looked at Chris. "Never, not once did I threaten or even consider leaving him." She sighed. "I was willing to suffer the abuse as long as I was with Mike."

"Did you go to church then?"

"Yes." She stood and moved to the railing. "But not when I had bruises."

Chris walked to where she stood. She was gripping the railing, so he placed his hand over hers. "I'm sorry you had to live that way."

"Me, too. I was so sorry things became what they did." She closed her eyes. "I loved him so much." When she looked back at Chris, hoping to convince him of something she was certain of, she said, "He loved me, too. I never doubted that. From what I've told you, I know it doesn't sound like it, but he did. I should have gotten him some help. It all would have been different if I had."

"You can't blame yourself. You did the best you could with what you had at the time. We all look back at our past and make sound judgments of what we could have done differently. Then we spend way too much time beating ourselves up over what we didn't do."

"How can I not? He was sick. I knew he needed help, but I did nothing. Of course I'm to blame."

"This isn't about blame. It's about healing. Remember that. That may be one of the most important lessons you learn from me. We aren't looking back to cast blame but to bring your pain into the light so that God can heal you."

Chris looked down at his hand, still on Robin's, and moved enough to put a little distance between them.

Something came to Robin's mind. "You know what?"

He swallowed hard as she looked up at him. "What?"

"Looking back, I can see it happening. Every strike was like another stitch in the veil that you talked about, until finally, I could see nothing of God at all anymore."

The power Mike had over her mentally, emotionally, and especially physically was so traumatic, she lost the desire to even get out of bed most mornings. Early on, she would wonder if God was looking on, watching what was happening in their home. At some point, though she wasn't sure when it finally happened, she stopped caring if God was watching, convinced He didn't care at all. It was then that she became numb to life altogether.

"Hindsight gives you great insight. It will also help you heal. You can see what caused you to turn from God, and in knowing that, you know what barriers have to be removed."

He rubbed his temples and sat. "I may have to call it a day."

"Are you okay?" She went to him and squatted down. "Can I get you something?"

"I think maybe I'm coming down with something. I'll go in and sleep it off."

She only stared at him for a few seconds. "Please let me know if you need anything. Can I leave you my number?"

"Sure."

Chris went inside to the table and pointed to a pad of paper. "Just write it there."

Without another word he went into the bedroom and closed the door.

Robin stood there in the middle of the room, staring at the closed door, wondering what had just happened. Was he suddenly that ill? He was fine one moment and practically staggered to the bedroom the next.

***

Chris flopped onto the bed and covered his head with his pillow, hoping to sleep off the raging headache and nausea. More than anything he wanted to get Robin's words out of his head. He could nearly envision her being pushed and struck. The image in his mind was tormenting. Millions of women lived that life every day, but Chris's deepening feelings for Robin brought the reality of it painfully close to his heart.

There was that moment when he had placed his hand on hers as an innocent gesture of concern, but soon enough he had realized he was allowing it to remain there simply to be touching her. Clearly, the lines were getting blurred, and he would never do anything to jeopardize her trust in him. Based on his deepening feelings for her, he realized how careful he would have to be moving forward. This was new territory to navigate. His commitment as he drifted off to sleep was to ensure that Robin never know how easily he was falling for her.

Later that afternoon, after Chris woke from his nap, Robin stopped by to check in on him.

"You had me worried."

He tried to laugh it off. "Sorry about that. It came out of nowhere, but I'm better now."

"Would you like to come up for dinner? Emma's cooking, and she wanted me to invite you."

"I feel privileged. If it's anything like her breakfast, consider me in."

"Great. Come up in about half an hour."

"I'll be there."

When Robin left, Chris sat on the sofa. He should have told her then that he was dying or at least that he was sick. Many times he considered how he might tell her, but every time, he acknowledged it would likely derail her progress. Out of concern for his condition, she would feel the need to give him his space, or something to that effect. Because of that, he wasn't so sure he would tell her at all.

NINE

In her room alone, Emma sat on the bed with her phone in hand. She had just hung up with the sheriff after talking to him about Mike. He had agreed to call and find out when Mike would be up for parole, promising to get back with her when he knew. Even with the sheriff's assurance that everything would be okay, Emma knew better. Mike could be at the inn long enough to do serious damage before a patrol car would arrive. He was a massive man, strong and determined. Because he was so consumed by Robin, his intention would be to take her away. How could any of them stop that?

Emma walked down to the lobby, hoping to catch Robin alone and at least let her know she had placed the call. Instead, Tommy and Becky were behind the counter, Tommy working on Robin's computer.

"Where's Robin?"

"I'm not sure. I think she's with Chris."

Once in the kitchen, Emma sat on a stool and looked out through the large picture window. She could see them out on the dock talking. They had been meeting for a few weeks, and there were some signs of restoration in Robin. Emma was incredibly thankful for the progress she was seeing and for Robin's willingness to seek help. There seemed to be something brighter in her outlook and attitude.

Chris had begun going to church with Robin the past few Sundays, and Emma had even agreed to go with them the next week. She had always believed in God and gone to church as a girl, but it had been many years since she thought of such things. Recently, witnessing the miracle that was happening in Robin's life, Emma sensed she was catching a glimpse of God in action. Something about that gave her hope for her own heart and almost a willingness to seek God for some restoration of her own.

"Emma, there's a call for you." Becky was peeking around the kitchen door.

"Thanks, sweetie."

She stood and followed Becky to the lobby, thinking of Robin again. Several times she had tried to talk to Robin about what they would do if Mike were to show up, but each time Robin would not-so-subtly changed the subject. Emma could hardly blame her. Whether or not Robin was prepared to face what Mike's release might mean, Emma was surely not going to sit idly by and let him surprise them. Her plan was to take a proactive approach. She had been serious about hiring a full-time security guard. Robin meant that much to her, and she would pay any price to keep her safe.

"Emma, this is Jerry. I tried your cell, but I must have copied the number down wrong."

"You've heard back already?"

"Yeah, and not good news. The guy is up for parole next week."

Emma burst into tears.

Becky and Tommy were exchanging looks and began to walk from behind the counter to give her privacy. Emma shook her head, indicating that they stay.

"Now, listen, we will keep an eye on things. I'll touch base with the parole board on Monday. If he gets out, I'll add your place to our regular patrol. If he does show up, you can call us."

"Thanks for getting back with me so quickly." Emma sat the phone on the counter and wiped her eyes with her handkerchief.

Becky's eyes were wide. "What is it?"

A couple sitting in the wingback chairs stood and made their way to the stairs. Once they were gone and the lobby was empty, Emma said, "Robin's ex-husband might be out of prison as early as next week."

"Oh, no!"

Although it was Robin's personal business, Emma realized it would affect them all. "He'll show up here. I have no doubt."

"Prison?" Tommy said.

Emma nodded.

Tommy looked back and forth between Becky and Emma. "What can we do?"

"I'll kill him!" Emma said without hesitation.

He shook his head. "Emma, you can't –"

"Oh, yes, I can!"

Tommy tried to reassure her. "Look, we'll just watch out for him. If he comes we will stay with her until the police get here."

Emma knew Tommy had good intentions, but he had no way of understanding the man they were dealing with.

"I have to talk to Robin." Without another word Emma rushed away to find her.

When Emma saw that Chris was alone on the dock, she went straight to Robin's cabin and waited for her in the living room until the sound of the shower stopped.

"I'm out here. We need to talk."

Robin came into the room, hair dripping wet and tying her robe. "What's wrong?"

"I want you to move back up to the main house. Immediately!"

"Why?" Even as she spoke, Robin closed her eyes and exhaled.

"He's up for parole next week."

Robin sat on the sofa beside Emma and stared straight ahead for a moment. She shook her head. "Maybe I should leave. I don't want to put you in danger."

Emma burst into tears. "Please don't leave. I hate to imagine life here without you. You're all I have."

Robin wrapped her arms around Emma. "I'll stay. I just don't want to cause any problems for you since I honestly don't know what he might do."

Emma took Robin's face in her hands. "This is your home. I won't allow him to drive you away."

***

After dinner Chris spotted Robin standing alone on the dock. With her back to him, he could see she had her arms wrapped around herself, her shoulders downcast.

For just a moment he hesitated, wondering if he should invade her solitude. He seemed to do that a lot. With all the old memories she was dredging up and having to process so much, he knew that time alone with God was where her real healing would begin. Not with him.

He hung his head and wondered what he was thinking, allowing himself to feel this way for the troubled woman standing out there on that pier? As if life away from this place had no sting of reality, he had allowed himself to become consumed by her and her story.

Chris walked out onto the pier and came to stand quietly beside her, hands dug deep into his pockets. She smiled up at him, acknowledging his presence, but remained silent.

"Do you want to talk," Chris said. "If not, I can –"

"Don't leave."

When she leaned her head against his shoulder and sighed, it felt unusually intimate. He slipped his arm around her and rested his hand on her shoulder.

"It looks like my past is about to catch up with me."

"What do you mean?"

"Mike."

"You think he's coming here?"

She nodded. "I know he will come looking for me. I've never doubted it for a minute."

"Emma was looking for you earlier. I could tell she was upset."

"He's in prison, but she found out he's up for parole next week."

"Prison?"

In all the weeks they had spoken, she had never mentioned Mike being incarcerated. Chris had assumed she had left him. So far, she had talked about many things but never the last night.

"The last time…" She raised her hand to tuck her hair behind her ear. With her eyes cast down at her feet, she said, "The last time, he went to prison for what he did to me."

Chris turned her to face him and touched her cheek with his fingertips. "I can't imagine how anyone could hurt you that way."

When she glanced up at him, those big brown eyes filled with fear, his heart beat faster. After what he had heard so far, she had reason to be alarmed.

"Do you really think he'll come here?"

Robin turned to face the water. "I'm sure of it."

Monday morning, Robin was working behind the counter in the lobby. When she heard a familiar sound, a distinct grinding and squeaking, and then a hard slam, she froze. In that moment she was taken back to her former life. Her stomach sank and bile rose up into her throat. For a moment she stood there paralyzed, looking toward the front door, waiting to see Mike's face. Just as she knew would happen someday, his large frame filled the doorway. Her knees buckled beneath her, so she grabbed for the counter trying to steady herself, and she staggered sideways toward the back door. She watched in horror as he pulled the screen door open and stepped inside.

She looked down, realizing she had no control over her legs. In her head were echoes of her brain shouting, "*Run!*" But all she could do was stumble. This scene unfolded in slow motion, as Robin's mind was spinning, and then it all came back to her – her plan. Different from being at his mercy that final night, she could run. With that in mind her legs carried her clumsily toward the door where she might find help. Just as she pushed through the door, she heard Mike call after her, but her own screams drowned out his words. Haunted for years by this possibility, Robin had meticulously planned her escape down to every detail. Hour after hour, she had pushed herself to swim farther and faster. Now the time had come, so if only she could reach the water, she could get away from him.

Robin slammed through the door leading from the back porch and sprang into mid-air as she jumped over the back steps. Secretly, when no one was around, she had practiced this jump, recognizing it might mean living or dying. She landed with precision as practiced and never missed a step while she continued across the lawn and toward the stone stairway. Over the years, having considered and experimented with the quickest route, she had discovered she could slide down the hill next to the steps faster than she could run.

***

Chris was passing the edge of the tree line when he heard faint screams off in the distance. He had a sinking feeling and moved as fast as he could toward the main house. It was like watching a movie play out in slow motion as he witnessed Robin sliding down the steep hillside, nearing the bottom. His first thought was that she must have fallen until something else caught his eye. Midway down the steps was a massive man jogging down at a rapid pace. Suddenly, it dawned on him; it was Mike chasing her.

After all he had heard about the guy, Chris knew this wouldn't end well. With Mike's size Chris knew he couldn't do much without a weapon. Still he moved in their direction, hoping to slow him down long enough for Robin to escape. With adrenaline pumping and his heart pounding, he was prepared to do whatever it took to save her. He had nothing to lose.

Though running as fast as his legs would carry him, he watched helplessly as Mike closed the distance between them. There was no way Chris could get to her first. Robin was so close, the dock merely inches from her, when Mike reached for her. Chris considered her path of escape, and her late night swims came more into focus. The water was her getaway plan, probably had been for as long as she swam alone.

A family was close by and stopped to watch, along with a man on the dock holding a fishing pole. All were fascinated by the sight.

Chris witnessed the most unsettling sight of his life unfold. From afar he watched Robin crumple to the ground, vulnerable and exposed to Mike. When Chris drew nearer, though still not close enough to be of help, he saw Mike simply stop and stand over her. Without saying a word he sank to his knees before her and began to weep.

***

At Mike's touch Robin dropped to the ground and hunkered down with both arms covering her head.

"I'm not here to hurt you, baby. I had to tell you how sorry I am. Please forgive me," he whispered and stroked her back with soft circular motions. Again, he broke out into loud sobs.

When she dared to look up at him, the sight of him crying brought tears to her eyes. Large tears rolled down his cheeks, reminding her of the countless times he had clung to her and begged her not to leave him. His words when he spoke were tender and his touch on her back familiar. She could still see Mike there, but this wasn't the man she knew before. He had aged well beyond five years, a sprinkling of silver now mixed within his dark hair.

Movement behind him caught her attention, and she could see what Mike couldn't. Emma was standing directly behind him holding a rifle. The look on her face was determined; she was prepared to fire. Chris had just arrived and was standing next to Emma.

Robin whispered, "No, Emma."

"I'll kill you for what you've done," Emma said.

Mike only glanced at Emma, then turned back and stared at Robin with a vacant look. "It doesn't matter. Let her do it if it brings you peace."

"I'm asking you to please put the gun down," Robin said, knowing what it felt like to carry Mike's blood on her own hands. It was something she wished on no one else, especially Emma.

"I want you to stand up and slowly move away from her," Emma said with a steady voice.

Mike ignored all that was around him. "All I wanted was a chance to talk to you. I had no idea that I would frighten you like this." He paused as he looked away. "I should have known, and now I see what a mistake this was. Never, even to say I'm sorry, would I have come if I thought it would hurt you like this." His face wrinkled as he fought back more tears. "I can't explain how or why I did all that, but I'm begging you to forgive me. Not a day has gone by that I've not thought about you or about what I put you through. I needed you to know, I found Jesus, just like you said."

He stopped and sighed. "I don't know how we got here, Rob. I just know it was all my fault."

When Mike spoke the name of Jesus, it took Robin back to that last night and the look of fear in his eyes as he lay on the floor, blood gushing from his abdomen with every beat of his heart. It was all she knew to speak to him at that point, her only hope for him, his only hope.

Now, looking into his eyes, seeing how desperate he was for her to hear him, she sighed a long overdue sigh after waiting for the worst for so many years.

She lowered her eyes and noticed his hands resting on his knees. At the sight of them, something happened in her mind like a deafening roar of thunder. In that moment there was no one there but the two of them. With hesitation she reached out to touch his hands, but with a flash a scene came to her mind. She withdrew her hand. It was those same hands as they had once lifted her lifeless baby from her arms and handed him over to the paramedic. That day all those years ago, with her arms empty, knowing she would never feel the warmth of Michael in them again, she had let out a cry and with it the very breath of life from within. From that moment on, she too had ceased living.

While looking at his hands, Robin realized that Mike had begun the process of dying on that same day. She had withdrawn into herself and away from him. Without her he had died by drowning himself in a bottle.

This was it, the moment she had dreaded for the past five years. It wasn't retaliation or revenge on his part that frightened her. Deep inside, she had feared facing the tremendous emptiness of her arms since the loss of her child. She feared having to see Mike again and relive it over and over. She feared that someday she would have to go back to that house and face the one moment of her life that she had tucked away safely in some deep recess of her heart.

Mike held his breath as Robin reached for him, but when she withdrew her hand he exhaled and his shoulders slumped even lower. He began to cry again, so he wiped his nose with the back of his hand and stood. "I'm so sorry I've bothered you."

When he turned to go, Mike stopped and nodded at Chris. "Just take better care of her than I did."

Robin looked at Emma, and said, "I'm okay," and then watched Mike as he started up the stairs. His shoulders hung low, so low in fact he hardly looked like a tall man at all. The way he grasped the railing as he ascended the stairs, it was clear he had little strength to make it to the top.

"Mike," she said. "I'll walk with you."

Robin walked in step with him. All along the way up, she thought back to a time when she loved Mike, a time when she couldn't imagine living without him – before the drinking and violence. Maybe he could be that man again. Without question it was too late for them, but hopefully he could start fresh, with someone new. She wanted that for him, to begin again.

Both remained quiet. Oddly, it wasn't at all awkward. He was the one person who inhabited the planet that she knew better than anyone else, and he knew her that way. Two people who shared a common history that no one else could enter. That recognition made her heart burn with regret, and she was certain there could never be another living soul who would know her that way.

At his truck he stopped and turned to face her. She finally spoke. "I hope you stay away from the booze, Mike."

This wasn't a moment she had ever prepared for. When she had played out the scene in her head, it was always the worst possible scenario. After all that had happened, she thought it could never come to this, a simple good-bye. Well, not quite so simple. The tearing she felt in her heart was anything but simple.

"I will." He shook his head. "I know how hollow that may sound, but I truly mean it. That night so drastically altered the course of my life…" He trailed off. "Rob, whatever was going on in my head, all that chaos and confusion, it's gone now. I imagine you will always see me as that man, but I'm not him anymore. I never will be again."

"I believe you, Mike. That man was never the real you." She took a deep breath, the weight of her inaction heavy upon her. "I should have gotten you some help. I'm so sorry that I didn't."

"Nothing, absolutely nothing that happened between us was your fault. I can never say I'm sorry enough."

"I'm just glad you're better now."

He leaned against the truck and covered his face. For a moment he stood there, rubbing his stubbly cheeks. Finally, he said, "I know there's no way to undo it or make up for any of it, but Robin, I just need you to know, since the very beginning, I've loved you more than anything in this world. Still do."

She looked away. "Don't."

At his words the pain searing through her chest became even more unbearable. For so many years she had loved him just as he described. There was nothing she placed above him, but in the end their love was never enough. Now, standing so close to him, even after so many years apart and all that had happened between them, her instinct was to move into him. She knew what it felt like to be wrapped in his strong arms, to be molded against his body. If she allowed herself, she could feel the sensation of it on her skin. How could such love still linger?

"I'm not asking for anything. I know it's too late for us. I just had to see you, to tell you how sorry I am. That's all."

Before this day Mike's memory brought with it fear and torment, but finally, standing there with him, all that remained was sadness so real and palpable it caused her mouth to go dry.

Barely able to talk, she whispered, "I'm glad you came. I think we both needed this – some closure."

"About the house. Trevor is moving out next week. I can't afford to buy you out just yet, but I'll come up with the money as soon as I can."

She held up her hand. "No. I don't want any part of it."

"It's half yours."

"It's yours now, Mike. I won't ever come back there."

When she said those words, declaring the end of them, he began to cry again and stepped in to draw her into his arms. "I'll always love you, Rob, and I'll always be there waiting just in case." Tears streamed down his face and tumbled onto her shirt. "Words can never tell you how sorry I am or how thankful I am to have once called you mine."

He held to her, his grip so tight that Robin could barely breathe, yet strangely, she had no desire to pull away. For the first time in many years she didn't feel so misplaced. It was a sense of belonging that lasted for only a split second, but in that second she felt less empty. From out of the blue, though, roaring to the forefront of her memory, violent scenes flashed across her mind, causing her to pull away.

Mike took a step back. "I promise you; I won't bother you again."

Without another word he moved to his truck and slid behind the wheel.

Robin went back, stood on the porch, and watched his taillights bounce down the gravel drive. Tears poured down her cheeks as she whispered, "Goodbye, Mike."

TEN

A few miles down the road, barely able to see to drive, Mike pulled over to the shoulder and put his truck into park. All he could picture was how terrified Robin had been of him in those first few minutes – and rightly so. He remembered little of the violence, but what he was able to recall made him cry out in sheer agony for her sake.

There by the lake, for a split second there was a glimmer of Robin veiled behind the blank expression on her face. He had caught a glimpse of her, not the Robin he had always known but the grieving mother who eventually became a stranger to him. When she had reached out to touch him but then withdrew her hand, he found all hope pouring from his heart like the draining of a bathtub. He had felt it swirl round and round until finally all hope was gone and all that remained was the gurgling sound of the last drops escaping him. During the long journey to see her, his mind had been certain all was lost, but still, deep inside, in a place where he had no control, hope floated around wondering, "What if?" That moment with her had ended that foolish question.

When she had called out saying she would walk with him, he noticed that her expression was altered. No longer was there a look of alarm as in the beginning or the emptiness of a grieving mother, but rather something closer to tenderness, similar to the look she had worn when she had once given him a second chance he didn't deserve.

Finally, standing with him beside the truck, the expression in her eyes nearly caused his knees to buckle, large dark eyes conveying such deep emotion and boundless grief. For twelve years when she had looked at him, he found nothing but love and devotion, but this day, only sorrow remained.

When he had held her, she felt so tiny in his arms. How could he have hurt her the way he had, nearly killing her? That was the same girl he had danced with at every prom, holding her in his arms that very same way, the girl who had knelt over him on the football field, crying when he blew out his shoulder, ruining all hope of a scholarship. She was the same girl he saw that first day of school, wanting so much to make her his, and the woman he married and planned to spend the rest of his life with, the mother of his only son. How could he have destroyed what they once shared? Mike shook his head at the reality of it. He became his father after all.

No more remained of their life together other than their home. Everywhere he turned, she was there. Their son was born there and died there, and every memory that mattered was in that house.

He thought back to that moment when he had found out he would be a free man. When his hearing had been moved up a few days, and things went as well as they did for his release, he had believed that going home would fill the void he had known over the past years.

***

Mike left the prison that afternoon with his brother, Trevor. The drive home held such promise. Once home, though, reality settled upon him and brought with it a glimpse of what life would hold without Robin. Years had passed and life went on for everyone else, but for him time had stood still. The hope of home proved to be a cruel deception and certainly no better than the prison he had just left. Unprepared for the onslaught of emotions he would experience in Robin's absence, soon after arriving home, Mike had to get out of the house.

He stood at the bottom of the steps leading to his mother's house and recalled how growing up, all he had ever wanted was to get out. Now, he was back, tail tucked between his legs. When he had married and left home, he remembered thinking with a sense of confidence, or more correctly arrogance, that he would never live the way she did. His mother's poor decisions and inconsistency had driven him crazy all his life. Yet there he stood, newly released from prison, with the hope she would at least be glad to see him.

His mom was standing inside, arms crossed, looking at him through the screen door. Without much in the way of enthusiasm, she said, "Hey. I thought you got out next week."

Mike hesitated a moment before continuing up the steps. No matter the difficulty of their relationship, he had missed her and was glad to see her. She looked exactly as she had the last time he saw her, a pretty woman still. Young to have a son thirty years old, she had barely turned seventeen when she had him. Her hair was the same dyed-blond shade she had worn for years. Now, though, her roots were revealing her natural color of brown, his color. Her blue eyes were lighter than his, and for the first time he noticed how much her age was showing around them.

"They moved the hearing up to today. Trevor came to pick me up." He paused at the door. "I just wanted to stop by and say hi and thanks for all the cards and letters."

Though she hadn't visited him once, she was faithful about staying in touch.

"I figured you would make it by."

She pushed the screen door open for him and patted his arm as he passed by. "I have some dinner on the stove if you're hungry?"

He sat at the table waiting for his mother to join him, realizing just how much he had missed sitting at a real table with real food and family. Though he hadn't lived at home in many years, and no matter how glad he had been to be away from her, she was still his mother, his family. After he married, Robin was all the family he thought he needed. How time changed things.

"You going by the feed store? I talked to your uncle, and he said he would put you to work."

Mike followed her eyes, noticing how she watched his hand shake as he ate. He hadn't had enough to eat in five years. Now, tonight at his mama's house, he found he could hardly even eat in front of her. He was sure she only saw his dad when she looked at him since he was what she had always called the spittin' image of his father. That thought caused him to rest his fork on the side of his plate.

"I'll call him first of next week."

"Why not tomorrow?"

Mike looked down at his plate. "I have something to do first."

She dropped her fork, the sound of it startling them both.

"You can't be planning to go find Robin."

"Yes, ma'am, I am."

Kathy stood without saying another word and left the room.

Mike sat, looking at his plate, unable to eat another bite. After a minute he stood and followed her. When he got to the screen door, he stopped and stood inside. "It's not what you think, Mama."

"Don't ya think you've done enough?" She turned and glared at him. "She should have killed you. Then at least she wouldn't have to worry about you comin' after her."

He stepped out onto the porch. "I would never do anything to hurt her. Not again."

She stormed toward him, wagging her finger. "That's what you said the day you married her, remember? You promised me you'd never do what your daddy did."

Mike swallowed hard. That last year, it became a common occurrence to wake up after tying one on to find bruises on her face and arms and things broken around the house. No matter how many times he swore it would never happen again, it did.

"I don't know how it all started."

"It's the drinkin'! I told you never to start that."

"I know, Mama."

"She never came back, and I don't blame her." Kathy looked away. "I was the one to clean up the mess you made, splatters and puddles of blood all over the house. Hard telling whose blood was whose."

Mike looked away. On many occasions he had tried to piece together the fuzzy details of that last night. He mostly drew a blank before the moment he laid there on the kitchen floor, with her holding his head in her lap, and he remembered the ambulance ride. He remembered calling out to Jesus. No other pieces ever came together.

She spun back around. "After all that, do you think she will welcome you?"

"No."

"I think ya ought to leave well enough alone." She sighed in resignation. "Are you even allowed to leave town?"

"No, ma'am, but it doesn't matter. I plan to go and come right back. If I get caught, it'll be worth seeing her."

"If you get caught, you'll land right back in prison."

"I know, Mama."

***

Mike sat in his truck on the side of the highway, cried out for the moment. The fact that he had left his wife behind seemed unreal and wrong in every way. It was what she needed, though, to be done with him. He deserved losing her.

With all that mattered behind him and little before, he reached for the gearshift and pulled it down into drive. He would head home and figure out how to walk through this life without his family. Certainly, only God could carry him through that.

ELEVEN

After Mike was gone, Robin found Emma alone in the kitchen.

"Hey," Robin said.

Emma stood and held her arms out.

When Robin stepped into Emma's arms, she let out a long deep sigh. "It wasn't at all what I expected."

"Honestly, me either. I've never been so relieved." Emma moved back and reached for Robin's hair and moved it from her face.

"He was hurting." Robin said and looked out the window to where she had knelt with him. Tears filled her eyes.

"And well he should be hurting."

"Please don't. No matter what happened…" She broke down.

That moment of goodbye had crushed her. His final look of resignation and loss was caught up in her mind, bouncing back and forth until she could do nothing but cry.

Emma said, "I'm sorry. I can't imagine what today was like for you."

"It was the end of life as I've known it since I was thirteen."

"I know, sweetie. After today, though, you can begin again, without the past hovering over you." Emma smiled at her. "You are making such progress with Chris. Now, you can really begin to look toward the future."

Robin nodded. "Have I ever told you that being here saved me? I would have never made it through the past five years without you."

Emma took Robin's face in her hands. "I will always be here for you, always." She moved her head to rest on Robin's. "Have I ever told you that you being here has saved me?"

Robin grinned. "You didn't need saving."

"I did. I needed a family, Robin. That's what you are to me. Don't ever forget that."

Robin talked with Emma for more than an hour and then made her way to Chris's cabin. After tapping lightly on his door, she turned to face the lake. The sun was just setting, and the sky shimmered with a brilliant orange glow. It was as if the outer edges of the earth were ablaze, and in that moment, she wished she could capture the memory and keep it forever. Suddenly, all things were new. No longer would she anticipate or dread an inevitable encounter with Mike. What she had feared most was behind her, and up ahead of her was a new life to be lived. Somehow, somewhere along the way, hope had crept up inside her and the implications of it seemed limitless.

"I'm glad to see you're all right," Chris said.

She turned to face him, nodded, and smiled halfheartedly. "Yes, I'm all right." Cheeks burning, she looked down. "I guess I overreacted."

Without returning the smile, he said. "I don't think it was an overreaction. Based on your history, I think it was perfectly normal."

A small sigh escaped her. "Now there's nothing to worry about, not anymore."

He looked over her shoulder rather than in the eye. "So what does that mean?"

She thought she caught a trace of coolness in his tone, something she hadn't heard from him before.

"What are you asking?"

"Are you going back to him? It's pretty easy to see you're still in love with him."

"Are you serious?" She took a step toward him. "How could you think that?"

"I don't know." He shook his head. "I don't know anything anymore."

Robin was at a loss for what to say. Finally, she said, "Are you saying I should go back?"

Even with the pain and regret she felt when Mike was driving away, never once had she considered going back.

"No, not at all. That's something you have to decide."

"I'm not even considering it."

Something was going on, though she wasn't at all sure what. He seemed unusually pale and distant in a way she hadn't seen before.

"Do you think we need to stop counseling now?" Robin said.

"No, absolutely not."

He sat in a rocker and began to move back and forth. "You still haven't told me how you got to where you are today, either of you."

No doubt, she had been avoiding the most difficult revelations. Yes, she had shared how Mike had changed when he began drinking and how the violence began, but she had yet to find herself strong enough to tell him about Michael and the moment that sealed their fate.

"There is something I haven't told you yet. I've been thinking about it a lot, and I believe it was the very first stitch."

He stood and nodded toward the door. "Tell me now."

Robin followed him in and took her usual seat. When Chris was seated across from her and after he prayed, she began. "When we moved back from California, I was pregnant, three months along. We were so excited and could hardly wait to be settled and begin our family. My parents were overjoyed at the thought of their first grandchild. They helped us pay for our house so I wouldn't have to work."

Robin sat for several minutes, unable to go on. When this happened, he was patient with her and waited for her to begin again. Chris never pressed her.

Finally, she whispered, "His name was Michael, and he was the sweetest little baby you've ever seen. Big," she said with a soft smile, "he was really big even when he was born." Robin became quiet again.

Chris broke the long silence. "Tell me how he died."

"SIDS."

She gripped the arms of the chair and closed her eyes, seeing Michael so clearly.

"He was nearly ten months old. When I approached his crib that afternoon, he was just lying there, cold and not breathing. I picked him up and held him to me. There was this sound, this loud and shrill sound, and I kept wondering what could make such a horrific noise." She opened her eyes and looked at Chris. "It was me. I screamed and screamed until nothing came out anymore."

Enveloped by the memory, Robin pulled her knees up to her chin, wrapped her arms around her legs, and buried her face in them. In her mind she could see every aspect of Michael's room. She could feel the soft material of his terrycloth pajamas on her hands and smell the distinct scent of baby powder.

The sights and smells and sounds of that day were so real in the moment that she began to breathe in short rapid breaths. This penetrating and excruciating pain was what she had been avoiding for years. She jumped to her feet and held out her hand toward Chris. "I can't do this. I can't do this," she said, shaking her head.

In her mind she could see Michael's lifeless face. There was no smile of recognition, as there normally was when she lifted him from his crib. His eyes were closed as if he were sleeping peacefully, but he wasn't sleeping. He was dead, and she was screaming.

Robin dropped to her knees and began to sob. With a loud cry, she doubled over and rested her face in her hands on the floor. "I was sleeping. Why was I sleeping?"

Her words came between racking sobs and at times were indistinguishable from her cries. Chris knelt beside her and placed his hand on her back.

"I'm so sorry." His voice was soft and low. "What more can I say but that I'm grieving with you?"

For several minutes she rocked and cried. Finally, unable to look back at that day any longer, she rose up and looked at Chris. Out of breath and nearly in as much pain as she was the day it happened, Robin said, "My baby died while I was sleeping." Tears fell from her face and onto the floor. "I never, ever took naps, no matter what. Why was I sleeping that day? If I had been awake, I could have saved him."

Chris wrapped his arms around her and held her close. "No, there was nothing you could have done."

"I prayed and begged God to give him back to me."

The anger she felt toward God was as fresh in the moment as it was the day she watched the first scoop of dirt land on that tiny silver casket.

"God wasn't there," Robin said.

"Yes, He was. He has promised to never leave us or forsake us. No matter what your eyes saw or your heart felt, He was there. Look back and tell me what you see in that room."

"It was just Michael and I."

Chris moved in and whispered near her ear, "The Psalmist said, 'The LORD is close to the brokenhearted and saves those who are crushed in spirit.' He was there, Robin. No matter what it felt like, He was there."

He prayed aloud, "Father, give her eyes to see You when You seemed to be hidden. Mend her heart and draw her near to You. May she know the peace that passes all understanding as You bring her comfort that only You can."

The peace of that prayer washed over her. In all those years, not once had anyone prayed over her that way. Robin wiped her tear-streaked face with the back of her hands.

Her voice was low. "I've looked back for years now, and all I see is me sitting in that rocking chair holding my dead baby. There was no one else."

"God never left. He simply didn't answer the way you wanted."

Chris reached out and wiped her cheek.

"I don't know of any more valid question than why God would allow a baby to die while his mother begged for his life. I don't know why. But I know He was there with you. You were never alone."

"If He was there, I would have my little boy."

Contrary to what Chris believed, she knew God had turned a deaf ear to her. Year after year, she had relived the anguish of that day, and each time she was alone. From that very moment she never asked God for another thing, ever. She stopped talking to Him altogether. Later on when Mike would come home drunk and violent, she never prayed for God to help her. What good would it do since He would just let her down?

Why she continued to go to church, she could never fully understand. Maybe because it was expected or because that was all she knew. How she felt had been her secret. During and after Michael's funeral, when someone would try to console her with Bible verses and words of encouragement, she would nod while tuning them out. She despised them for trivializing her son's death that way. Michael's death was a zipper, not a stitch. From then on she refused to look at a God who had the power to save and yet refused.

"All I can say is that we've entered holy ground here, Robin. His ways are not our ways, and His thoughts are not our thoughts. There's no way I can explain this to you. I can't answer for God. But I do know this: He sent me here for you. He loves you and wants you back with Him."

"He left me!"

Chris remained calm and insistent. "No, He's right here, and He wants you to see Him."

Unable to receive Chris's words or believe what he said to be true, Robin whispered, "I don't want to see Him – ever!"

With that she stood and left the cabin.

***

When the door slammed shut, Chris sat looking at it, stunned by all that had just happened. From the moment he had found her on his porch, he had been unsettled, even more so than the uneasiness he already felt since watching her walk away with Mike. There was something about her long history with him that troubled Chris. Hidden in the way they had looked at one another was a deep level of intimacy. The way they had walked in unison – it was an old familiarity that he didn't have with her – and never would.

Up until they had come inside, that was all he could think of, Robin possibly returning to Mike and what that would mean for him. His feelings for her were blurring his judgment and possibly his advice. Should she go back? Chris sat quietly, acknowledging he was crossing a line he should never cross – his heart was anyway. No matter how he felt for her, he would never undermine her trust in him by exposing his feelings.

Once they had begun to talk inside and she told him of her son, Chris was better able to remove himself from his own feelings and focus on her story. While she poured out her grief, he had never felt more helpless to help or more burdened by another's pain. Her history was truly tragic. Like Job, little by little, she had lost all that mattered to her, leaving her as broken as anyone he had ever encountered. If he thought he had what it would take to bring her some relief, he would put his own feelings aside and walk through this with her. Instead, he was now well aware of how much deeper her trauma was than what he had the wisdom or power to overcome.

"Lord," he prayed, "do something. I'm in way over my head."

***

Later that night, once it was dark, Robin went out to the water's edge and stood looking at the moon reflecting off the water. She lifted her eyes to the heavens and found she faced the twinkling of a million stars. It was like an explosion of fireworks set off to get her attention. Something about the sight caused her to sense God's presence in a way she hadn't in many years. It wasn't comforting at all and only caused her to ask, "Where were You?"

Alone in bed hours later, a sense came over her and made her know, not just suspect, that God had indeed sent Chris to help her. Then something else happened, something like the tinkling of a familiar song playing off in the distance where you can almost remember the words but not quite. God's presence felt almost familiar, as if she had never turned away from Him. It didn't last long, but it was present long enough to stir up a yearning she didn't realize existed inside her anymore.

TWELVE

The following morning, Chris went to see if he might find Robin on the steps. When he didn't, he walked down to the boathouse and grabbed a fishing pole. For a moment he stood and looked at it, smiling at the memory of his dad's constant reminder. "Son, you just have to wait and be patient. A fish will come if you're in the right spot." If he ever had been, Chris knew he was now in the right spot. God had made sure of it.

Back out on the dock with a small tub of grub worms, Chris cast his line and began to wait.

He thought of Robin and how inadequate he was to counsel her. All he had was some minor training but not the experience she needed. Talking with people, getting them to open up, was his gift, and he often used it to help God's people, but in Robin's case, more than informal counseling was needed. Surely, someone with experience could reach her. When he returned to Boston, he would call around and find someone local to help her. He would pay any price. All he knew how to do was to point her back to Jesus. Spiritually, that was what she needed, and no matter what she believed or felt, God was there with her and for her. But how could she break through the pain long enough to see Him? It was beyond him.

With the wind coming in off the lake, his bobber floated in close, so Chris reeled in and cast again. It was mindless effort, exactly what he needed at the moment.

The night before had been torturous for him, and the few hours he did sleep were fitful. He came to realize that somewhere along the way he had fallen desperately in love with Robin. What he had considered love in other relationships was nothing like what he felt for her. He had never felt less for self and more for the other as he did now. Still, no matter his love for her, his motives remained pure. Since they could have no future together, for her to ever know his true feelings would be pointless.

With a small smile, he thought back to their first session together and recalled how jealous he had been of her love story since he never had one of his own. Now he did. It was more than his attraction to her. It was who she was that drew him in. She was strong and courageous, even when she considered herself so weak.

The more he thought of it, the more he determined that loving her wasn't pointless. It was a gift, something God gave him there in the final months of his life. He deeply regretted not having the opportunity to share a lifetime with her, but he realized for him, it would be the remainder of his lifetime. In his heart he knew if given a miracle and more time, he would pursue her and do everything imaginable to make her fall in love with him. Under the circumstances, though, he would take the gift of love over the certainty of death. Love would be his focus and the fact that his Savior cared so much about him that He would allow him to experience it in this way. Love would be the last and greatest emotion he would know, the greatest of all things to cling to.

***

Robin found Chris sitting on the dock fishing rather than the steps as usual and decided to join him. She wanted to talk to him about what she had experienced the night before.

Robin handed Chris his coffee. "I'll grab a pole."

He nodded and took a sip.

When she returned and once she cast her line, she said, "Yesterday was tough, more than I expected."

"I can't even imagine how painful that was for you." He turned to look at her. "I'm feeling completely inadequate. I wish I knew how to help you more. Honestly, I'm afraid I'm in over my head."

"I disagree. The mere fact that I've talked about this at all means something. I wouldn't have opened up to anyone else. I'm grateful for you."

She smiled at him and then looked back out at her line. "I wish I could explain it better, but for now all I can say is that I feel something within me coming back to life – some small sense that God is near. That's only because you're helping me."

Chris looked away. "I'm humbled that you would even say that."

"I mean it. This has only begun because of you."

For some time they sat saying nothing. Finally, he glanced at her. "Have you ever played 'Would You Rather'?"

"I don't think so."

"It's a game where you get two options, and you have to choose one."

"I didn't know it was an official game, but I suppose I have."

"Just before you came down, I was thinking about what I should cling to in this season of my life, and it brought me to a question for you. This is something serious. Are you in the mood for that?"

"Maybe."

He looked at her with sympathy. "Would you rather have ten months of loving Michael with the pain of losing him or not to have known him at all?"

Robin drew in a sharp breath and without hesitating, whispered, "Ten months with the pain of losing him."

"I have a new way to frame this for you. I'm not sure it'll help, but I'll try it." He placed his pole in one of the holes for support, wanting to give her his full attention.

"Stop holding on to Michael's death, Robin. That's your entire focus: that day, that moment. Instead, hold on to the love you have for him. Hold on to his life." Chris hesitated then continued on. "I didn't even know about him until yesterday. Somewhere between you moving home with Mike and the joy of your new house you could have told me, but you intentionally left it out. You are so busy trying to somehow comprehend the incomprehensible, wondering why God didn't save him, that you've stopped remembering him or his life. You need to share his life with others.

"This may be an odd comparison, but the Lord brought it to my mind last night, so I feel it's worth sharing. Think about Job: he lost all his children, plus everything else, but I imagine the loss of his children was his truest grief. If you were to ask him now if the sorrows of this world pale in comparison to eternity, you know his answer would be yes. If you asked him if the millions of people over the years who have benefited by his story was worth all he suffered, he would say yes.

"Don't get me wrong. I'm not comparing you with Job, but rather Job with Michael. If you were to ask Michael now if his limited time here on earth was worth the mighty works God would do in his mother and father, he would tell you yes. Robin, with his current, eternal perspective, he would tell you yes."

He held his hand up before she could speak. "I'm not saying God caused Michael's death. The simple fact is that we live in a fallen world. There was some genetic abnormality in his little body that caused him to stop breathing while he slept. God wasn't the cause, but the effect was that He will use the tragedy and pain of it to show Himself to you. Even then, you didn't know God. If you had, you would have turned to Him for comfort. When you know Him, you know that He's your only place to run. Only He has the arms that can heal such a broken spirit, but you turned away, testifying that you never knew Him at all."

Robin sat without speaking, the things Chris said turning over and over in her head. He was right; she never truly knew God before. She knew some facts. She believed Jesus was God. She believed He saved, but she never knew Him, and she still didn't. Finally, she was willing. If that was the place of healing, she wanted to go there, to get to know Him.

Her face held no expression.

"Say something. Have I hurt you?"

"No, I'm not hurt." She placed her pole in the holder and turned to him. "Again, you're right. I don't want to keep holding on to Michael's death. Tell me, then, how can I cling to that love?" She held one hand out to him and tapped it with her finger. "Put something in my hand that helps me do that. I need something, an action to help me get started."

"Go talk to Emma," he said. "Tell her all the funny, sweet, and silly things you can think of about Michael. Describe his laugh and his personality. Remember his life. Share his life. Thank God for every day of those ten months. Then thank Him for the things He will do in and through you because of knowing Michael. After that, each and every day, find a way to hold on to his life, if only on the inside."

"I can do that."

"Sure you can."

She sat for a moment more until finally she leaned in and wrapped her arms around his neck. "Even as I speak the words thank you, they fall short. I can never express my gratitude for how you are investing in me, in my future.

Chris squeezed her a little. "You never, ever have to thank me. I'm the winner here."

She moved back and tilted her head. "How's that?"

He only shook his head. "Just glad to have a front row seat to watch what God is doing."

Later in the afternoon, after lunch, Robin found Emma in the kitchen cleaning. It was where she spent most of her time. She had remodeled the room two years before and now considered it her resting place. That seemed odd with the flurry of work that went on there, but for Emma, it was her place.

"Do you have a minute?" Robin said.

"For you, bunches of them."

"I would like to tell you about Michael." Robin poured them each a cup of coffee and she took a deep breath, praying for strength.

With eyes wide, Emma dropped a cookie sheet into the sink and moved to sit on a stool. "I would love to hear anything you want to share."

Robin began and went on for more than an hour, trying to recount every memory she had of Michael. From his smile and giggles to his temper when he was hungry, she shared all she could remember. It was, in a sense, like pouring cool water on a burned hand, painful, yet soothing at the same time, the sweetest therapy for her wounded soul.

Afterward, Robin experienced something akin to laying down a heavy load. It was more than emotional relief; it was physical as well. Suddenly, she felt less alone. For years she had kept Michael hidden in her heart, but this day, it was as if he filled the air around her. She pondered how this particular therapy could be so effective and determined that love is sweetest when expressed, and that was what she had done that day. She expressed her love for Michael, something she would continue to do from that point forward.

After dinner Robin sat alone in her cabin and opened up her Bible for the first time in many years. On Sundays she would turn to whatever passage the pastor directed her to, but she never read along. She went through the motions, just as she was taught to do as a little girl: bowing when they said bow, opening her Bible just as everyone else did, but it was like being a little child again since she stayed in her own world, thinking of other things. With her mind closed off to God, she had kept the veil securely mended.

Prior to Michael's death, she had thought herself so faithful. If the doors of her church were open, Robin was there. Still, what Chris said about her not knowing God before Michael's death was accurate, and she knew it back then. She served and worked but recognized something was missing. It was most obvious around particular women, those who had a passion for Jesus that she didn't. It was clear to her when they spoke of their love for the Lord that somehow she was lacking something they had attained.

Within the past two days, Robin had seen Mike and had openly spoken of the loss of her son. The extremes of her emotions and the turmoil she felt inside could have easily overtaken her. Instead of running this time, she would take them to God.

In the book of Job, she looked up a verse Chris had given her. Even before he began to counsel with her, he had mentioned it. Her version was different from what he had written out for her. His was from the King James Version.

> *"Oh that I were as in months past, as in the days when God preserved me; When his candle shined upon my head, and when by his light I walked through darkness; as I was in the days of my youth, when the secret of God was upon my tabernacle."*

Hers read:

> *"How I long for the months gone by, for the days when God watched over me, when his lamp shone on my head and by his light I walked through darkness! Oh, for the days when I was in my prime, when God's intimate friendship blessed my house." Job 29:2-3*

Chris's version called it a candle, hers a lamp. Both were beautiful images and made her hear that sound again, that familiar tinkling in her head. There was a momentary lightness in her heart, and for an instant she felt less burdened. Any given moment before, heavy of heart would have best described her. At long last she yearned for the days when she didn't feel so far away from God and finally believed there may be a way back.

THIRTEEN

Another week passed, and all that remained of Chris's vacation was one week. He had rented the cabin through the end of July, which was fast approaching. His progress with Robin was nothing short of miraculous. Over the past week she had been so open with him and for the first time willing to take steps toward God. She asked questions and spent several days telling him about her son. He could see it happening, the veil being unmended, stitch by stitch, now that she was open to the Lord's removing the stitches she had sewn. Still, she had far to go, but to see any progress at all was proof of God's handiwork in her life.

When he wasn't with Robin, Chris was praying. He had spent more time in prayer during that summer than he ever had. Strangely, he caught glimpses of God like never before. Not only was God actively working in Robin's life, He was working in his own. At a time when any man would question and fear, Chris felt a closeness and intimacy with Jesus that he had never known. Though at the beginning of the summer he would have considered himself a man who walked with God, by the end of it he was prepared to declare himself a man who lived in God's presence. The Lord had shown up in nature as he painted, in His work with Robin, in settling Chris's apprehension over the end, so much so that Chris considered the possibility that God lived full-time at Lake Winnipesaukee.

Finally, he didn't fear death or even dwell on it, for that matter, for he knew what was to come and was at peace with it. Only once had he even reconsidered another opinion or chemo or radiation, and that thought, or more correctly momentary sense of optimism, was in hopes of adding more time to his life so that he might spend it with Robin. He finally settled the matter in his heart not to seek any of those alternatives. He had been diagnosed by one of the best oncologists in Boston, and a second opinion was given by another who was highly recommended. To pursue treatments would only postpone the inevitable. Without question the brain tumor was inoperable, his death certain. Somehow, assuredly divinely bestowed, he was at peace in his spirit.

Recently, his symptoms were becoming more problematic. His head hurt so horribly at times, that he would begin to vomit. He had yet to have seizures, as he was warned he might, but he knew his illness was progressing quickly. So far, he had not yet decided if he would tell Robin and wavered back and forth from day to day. The place he stood for the moment was not to tell her.

Her progress was such that if she heard something that disturbing, she could be right back where she began, wondering why God wouldn't save him. It was a possibility, and he wasn't prepared to be the reason she questioned Him again. Chris knew that God had a plan, even when it wasn't evident. Actually, in his case, the plan was becoming amazingly clear. Without the illness, Chris would never have come to the lake. Without his attraction to Robin, he would never have gotten to know her. Without getting to know her, he would never have recognized her wounded spirit. Every step was in order, beginning with his impending death. God was not One to figure out, merely One to stand in awe of when encountering His providence.

Just an hour before, he had taken pain medication so that he would be able to meet with Robin. The day before, he had to cancel, and in doing so he again aroused her concerns about taking up his vacation with her problems. He smiled to himself, appreciating what a thoughtful woman she was, so concerned with others that she had left herself out for many years. Finally, in God's all-knowing manner, having recognized Robin would never put herself first, He intervened in her life and was bringing her freedom.

***

Robin tapped on the door as she turned the knob. "Are you ready?"

"I am. Come on in."

With reluctance she moved toward the chair across from Chris and sat at the edge of her seat. "I'm running out of time, I know. It's time to get it over with."

Chris nodded for her to try again.

She had tried on several occasions to tell him of her last night with Mike. Not once was she able to get more than a sentence or two out. All she had been able to get out so far was that she was washing her face before bed when it all began.

She took a deep breath and started again. "Usually, I would hear his truck. I guess with the water running, I missed it that night. Normally, when I would hear him pull in, I would try to prepare myself for who might walk through the door. I never knew what to expect. That night, I didn't see it coming until it was too late.

"He grabbed me around the waist and threw me into the bathtub. I was tangled up in the shower curtain, and the rod fell and hit me in the face. Blood began to pour from my nose and all over my nightgown. At that point he wasn't even looking at me. Instead, he was hitting walls and even crashed his hand into the mirror over the sink. Glass was everywhere and his hands were bleeding. I had no idea what had set him off and was too stunned to even speak.

"When he finally turned his attention back to me, he reached down and grabbed my wrist. He yanked me out of the tub and dragged me into the kitchen. There, he pushed me down into a chair, and that's when I saw them, a pack of birth control pills on the table in front of me.

"I'm not certain how he got them. All I can think is that he must have been at the drug store and the pharmacist thought he was doing me a favor."

"You were on the pill and Mike didn't know?"

She nodded. "I didn't want another child, not after losing Mikey."

Her heart sank when she recalled the many months Mike was so hopeful that she might be pregnant. Each time, she knew better and still allowed him to hope. Even before the violence began, she had secretly gone to the doctor to get the prescription.

"He smashed them with his fist and began screaming at me. The things he said were terrible and true."

She held her finger up, indicating she needed a minute. Robin leaned back in her chair and recounted Mike's words, ones that had resounded in her heart for years.

"He said all he had ever asked for was another baby, and I had refused him that. Then he slammed the pills again. He kept screaming at me, that I was sleeping while our son died."

Tears poured down Robin's cheeks. "He began to weep, and with his tears came an explosive sort of anger that I had never witnessed before.

"He flipped the table over and pulled me out of the chair. Once he dragged me into the bedroom, he threw me on the bed, and he…" She closed her eyes and drew in a deep breath. "He hit me in the face a few times.

"I had never run from him before. This time, though, he was different. I had a feeling if I didn't get away, he would kill me. He began taking off his belt, and I knew what he was about to do."

A knot formed in her stomach.

"So I took both feet and pushed him into the wall. He was drunk enough that it seemed to stun him for a minute. It was my chance to run.

"At the front door, I grabbed my purse and kept running. I dug around, but my keys weren't in there. Most likely, he had taken them; he had done that before. I heard him come outside as I was running down the driveway, but he wasn't chasing me yet. He just stood on the porch screaming my name."

She stopped for a moment and sat, gripping the arms of the chair until her knuckles turned white. Even at the memory of it, her heart was pounding, and she could feel the chill of the night air and the jagged rocks beneath her bare feet. She shivered.

"I was barely dressed, and it was drizzling out. It was cold, and I was shaking so badly I could barely keep running. When I ran out onto the road, I knew I was out of his sight for a moment. I made it to a large group of trees and into some thick brush. It was muddy out, and I could see I was leaving a trail, but there was simply nowhere else to go. The moon was bright, and I was too visible. He found me easily enough.

"Back inside the house he took me to the bedroom and forced himself on me."

She gazed into the fireplace and avoided making eye contact with Chris, not wanting to see the expression on his face at her admission.

"He raped you?" When she nodded, he said, "Your way of expressing what Mike did is, in a sense, lessening the significance of it. It was rape."

"It wasn't the first time, but that night was nothing like before." She paused, not wanting to tell the whole truth. "The times before, I gave in to him, responded to him even." She hesitated and shook her head. "I know how that must sound."

Chris wiped his eyes then leaned forward in his chair and rested his elbows on his knees. "What do you think it sounds like?"

She regretted telling him about it at all. At the memory of it, her breathing became labored, and she could nearly smell stale alcohol in the air. Mike would whisper in her ear, telling her how much he loved her. Always, he would say, "Baby, please love me." Even the recollection of it made the hairs on the back of her neck stand on end and her heart thud like a drum.

"He would change, become like the real Mike again. He would tell me how much he loved me and how he couldn't stand the thought of losing me. Then it would turn from something ugly to what it used to be."

"Do you feel ashamed that you responded to him?"

She nodded.

"He was your husband, Robin, the man you loved. If your heart or even your body responded to him once he became tender and loving toward you, it wouldn't seem so out of place to me. Maybe you wanted what you once had with him so desperately that you were willing to reach for it in that moment." He shifted in his seat and moved in closer to her. "Shame is something that keeps people in darkness, especially women. Your body responded how it had always responded to your husband. Determine this very moment that you have nothing to be ashamed of."

She nodded again, grasping his words as some new means of looking back on what had always caused her such shame. "All I ever wanted was our old life back. When I could catch a glimpse of it or of the old him, I clung to it."

"This night was different, though?"

"Yes. The tenderness never came. The way he looked at me, it was as if he didn't see me at all, as if he were looking at a stranger. At one point he told me since I would no longer be on the pill, he would do that to me every night until I got pregnant."

She closed her eyes and placed her hand over her mouth, recalling how that had terrified her. For a moment she was unable go on. Finally, she whispered, "When he was finished, I said something really foolish. I knew better." Sweat broke out on her forehead at the memory of it, and her breathing quickened.

"What?"

"I told him he had become his father. There was no crueler thing I could have said. When he was a little boy, his father used to beat his mother, Mike, and his little brother. He totally snapped when I said that. The look on his face was like nothing I had ever seen before. He wrapped his hands around my throat and began choking me, screaming at me to take it back. Then he lifted me from the bed and held me against the wall with my feet dangling above the floor."

Robin stopped and looked at Chris. The memories felt so real in the moment, every detail so vivid that it caused her airway to actually feel constricted. "You wanna know what I was thinking?"

He nodded.

"I kept thinking, I hope I die, so I won't have to live this way anymore."

When Chris looked down, Robin suspected he was crying. His feelings for her were never more obvious than at this moment. Maybe that was what allowed her to go on when all she wanted was to run away from the memories of what happened next.

"Something happened." Robin sighed, still trying to figure out how things took such an abrupt turn. "I don't know. All of a sudden, he let go of me and jumped back as if he had been scalded. For some reason he rushed from the bedroom. When I fell to the floor, I lay there gasping, trying to catch my breath. I could hear him in the kitchen throwing things, and I figured he would come back. But everything got really quiet." She paused, remembering the sight of it. "That's when I looked over and saw his holster on the dresser.

"I could barely stand, but somehow I got up and went over to the gun. I took it out and turned off the safety. I hardly remember walking into the kitchen, but next thing I knew, I was standing there watching him bent over the sink vomiting. I waited until he stood up, and when he turned around to face me, he didn't seem at all surprised. I was holding the gun out, and it was shaking so badly I could barely aim. I guess I never realized how heavy it was. He just stood there, looking at me. He never even made a move to stop me. There was something different in his eyes by that point, maybe resignation or regret; I'm not sure what.

"Finally, I pulled the trigger, and the sound of the blast was deafening. After the first shot, he looked down at his stomach and then back at me. So I kept pulling the trigger. I know I hit him at least twice – maybe more. By that point it was as if we both were moving in slow motion. He put his hand over his stomach and slumped to the floor. I dropped the gun and went for the phone. While we waited for the ambulance, I sat with him, and he kept telling me how much he loved me. He just kept saying, 'I love you, baby. I'm so sorry.'" Even after all that had happened, she knew he meant it.

Robin looked Chris in the eye. "I did it on purpose. He wasn't coming after me again. I meant to kill him."

She allowed the wicked truth to linger in the air between them. Self-defense was the term the police had used, so did her parents and Emma, but the real truth was that she sought him out to kill him. Just before pulling the trigger, she could hear his words ringing in her head that he would get her pregnant. He was consumed by the idea of having another baby, but it was the one thing she would never allow.

"Once we were taken to the hospital, I never saw him again – until he showed up here."

Robin closed her eyes and pictured Mike as he had wept before her that day by the lake. He was no longer the monster she had come to fear. He was Mike – her Mike, the man she had loved since she was thirteen years old. Even now it was surprising how difficult it had been to watch him drive away that day. Robin sighed, the sight of his taillights flashing in her mind still.

"Can we stop now?" She stood. "It's in the light now."

Chris stood, too, and placed his hands on her shoulders. "Yes, Robin. It's in the light. Now, you've given God something to work with."

"I'm glad it's out. I've told that to no one other than the investigator who came to my hospital room."

"How does it feel?"

"I'm not exactly sure yet. Can we talk about that next time?"

"Sure. Whenever you're ready."

Robin said, "I'll see you in the morning for coffee?"
"Sounds good."

***

Even before Robin closed the door, Chris rushed to the bathroom. For several minutes he hovered over the toilet until the bout of nausea subsided. Once he was able to get to his bed, he sat on the edge and sighed, his mind filled with the things she had told him.

Most of the time, Robin had spoken as if she were in a trance. There were no tears, and she seemed unusually disconnected from the story. The only time he had ever seen her cry was when she spoke of Michael. He found it unusual under the circumstances. A few times, he was sure he saw tears well up in her eyes, but each time she was able to blink them away.

There came a moment in her story when he nearly lost it. Up until that point, he had been holding back a rising tide of emotions. At her admission, though, that Mike had raped her, he could hardly stop the tears from coming. That was the woman he loved who spoke those words and carried that shame, not some stranger – the woman he would carve out a future with if God would only give him a miracle.

Now, knowing Robin had shot Mike, it made sense that she thought Mike was coming to kill her. After hearing the story he could view their encounter by the lake with new perspective. Of course she was hysterical, having waited years for his retaliation. Instead, Mike was broken, remorseful for the terrible things he had done to her. Even Emma's actions now took on a new dimension. She was prepared to kill Mike. Had Chris known the gruesome details, he might have felt the same way.

He spent the remainder of the night in his cabin. Tommy stopped by to invite him up for dinner, but he declined. With the way he was feeling, Chris was beginning to wonder if he would even last the final week without Robin finding out the truth. All he could do was pray for enough time to make it through.

FOURTEEN

Over the past few days, Emma had been making plans for a birthday celebration. Since she felt as if she owed her very life to Chris, it was the least she could do to show her appreciation for how he had helped Robin. Recently, something miraculous was beginning to happen. The change in Robin was evident.

Since her nightmares had ended, Emma had hoped Robin would move back to the main house, but she chose to stay in her cabin where she said she was seeking God.

Emma was beginning to see something of God in her. A concept she had considered "her parents' kind of thing" was beginning to find some basis of reality in her daughter. Never one to believe God was active in ordinary and everyday lives, Emma was witnessing proof that something powerful existed. If it could work for Robin, this journey back to God, then it might possibly work for her, too. She had gone to church a couple of times with them and was considering going more often.

The day of the party, while busy in the kitchen cutting veggies for a veggie tray, Robin told Emma, "I had the hardest time keeping the secret this morning. I thought I was better at keeping secrets, but every time I opened my mouth, I almost blurted out, 'We're throwing you a party.'"

"I never knew you were so bad at keeping secrets either. I'll remember that."

Emma finished icing the cake and put the cover over it. All was about finished. "I'll run to the market later for a few things, but for the most part, we're set."

"Great. Let me know if there's anything I can do to help," Robin said.

Emma could tell that Robin had something on her mind. "What's wrong? Anything you want to talk about?"

"I may be a little concerned about Chris. This morning, he was quieter than usual." She shrugged. "By the time he left, he was much more his normal self, but not early on. Something seems off. He's acting differently, like something's wrong."

"Have you asked him?"

"No. I don't know. There's nothing I can put my finger on, just a sense I get."

"I'll watch him tonight and see if I notice anything amiss."

Robin stopped what she was doing and grimaced at Emma. "If he comes that is. Since he turned down dinner last night that has me wondering. What if he doesn't show up for his own party?"

"If not we'll celebrate without him. I made him my favorite cake."

"I noticed that." Robin giggled at her.

"Not knowing what his favorite is, I had to pick something."

White cake with white icing, though some may call it plain, was Emma's favorite. Not just any white cake would do, only her Aunt Birdie's recipe.

***

Robin walked to Chris's cabin and found him sitting on the front porch. He smiled and raised his hand. At first glance he appeared better than he had that morning, but when she reached the porch, she thought he still seemed pale. She sat next to him. "Do you mind if I ask you a question?"

"No, not at all."

"Are you okay?"

He hesitated an extra second. "Sure, why do you ask?"

"I don't know. You seem a little different."

"I'm okay. Question is, how are you? Yesterday was a tough one."

"It was. I don't know why I waited so long. Afterward, I felt lighter somehow."

"I can understand that."

"What's next?" she said, ready to take any step necessary toward healing.

"I've thought of a few things, such as how you felt afterward."

He never let her rest. His questions were like picking at a scab. She would think it was over, but then he would pick at the wound, causing it to open again and begin to hemorrhage.

"If I had to describe it in one word, it would be disappointment. I was disappointed about life, every aspect of it. Mike had let me down. God had let me down." She stopped and smiled at Chris. "Maybe my mind is changing about that. Time will tell." She paused. "I even felt as if my town had let me down. There was nothing left, absolutely nothing."

She stopped rocking and pondered a moment. "Truth is, I had thought I had life figured out. I never saw any different future than being with Mike. Suddenly, there I was in the hospital, well, both of us in the hospital. We had nearly killed each other, our marriage was over, and I was left stunned. After that night I didn't know who I was anymore. I guess I've felt like that all these years afterwards, too." She began to rock again. "That was who I was. Here, in this life, I feel that I'm pretending. This isn't who I am. I lost me along the way."

"Maybe this is the new you. Not necessarily the you that you had planned on but you under new circumstances. You seem to have a great life here. Emma loves you. Someday, I imagine you'll find romantic love again." He looked away as he spoke those last words.

Robin mulled over his words, and then thought about him and how, early on, she had wondered if they might start a relationship. It didn't take long to know that wouldn't be the case. Not only was she not ready, but ultimately, she wasn't prepared to give her heart to another man. She may never be ready for that. It was similar to her feelings about having another baby. To bring another child into her life would be like saying Michael never mattered or existed. It was the same with Mike. Their family was real at one time. She could never pretend otherwise.

"Maybe this is the new me." She looked at him thoughtfully. "Have you ever been somewhere and just had a sense you don't belong?"

"I think we all feel that at one time or another."

"At times, I feel like I belong here, especially since I've been here for several years now, but more often than not, I feel like I'm out of place, like a misplaced object."

"Have you considered moving back to North Carolina?"

"No, never."

"Maybe it's not a physical out-of-place you're experiencing. Maybe it's spiritual."

"How do you fix that?"

"Keep doing what you're doing. Keep seeking God. Keep reading your Bible. Keep going to church. Find your faith again."

Chris leaned in a little. "Something just occurred to me. Tell me, when you look back to that final night with Mike, can you see God?"

With eyes wide, she said, "Of course not," her tone more abrupt than she intended.

"You said something happened and he let go of you as if he had been scalded. Could that have been the hand of God?"

She gasped and threw her hand over her mouth. A hollow or swollen feeling, she couldn't distinguish which, rose in her chest, and she feared her heart might collapse or burst at any moment.

"Could it have been?" she said.

With her eyes closed, she tried to look back on the scene. Mike's eyes while he choked her were filled with rage, but then there was a softening, a spark of recognition as if he was suddenly seeing her. After that, a look of panic registered in them. He then released her.

Chris said, "I believe it was. I believe God has a plan for you. He saved you that night. God was there."

Robin jumped to her feet. "Then why didn't He stop all of it?"

He shook his head. "Here we go again. I can't answer for God, but I say again, we live in a fallen world. Mike was damaged and out of control, but God spared your life." It then occurred to him. "Like Job, I suppose. Remember, the Lord allowed the circumstances, but He determined that Job's life would be spared."

"I just read that."

"And?"

"I don't know." She sat back down for a second, trying to comprehend it all. Finally, she said, "I'm confused."

"That's understandable. This isn't easy, and you have a lot to sort through. There's a season of healing ahead of you, one that will be between you and God. Just don't hesitate to ask the difficult questions. He doesn't cringe at our tough questions; neither does He apologize for who He is or His plan for mankind. Even when we can't comprehend it, we're each a smaller part of a bigger whole. In the days, weeks, even months to come, take every single feeling and emotion before Him. Hold nothing back. If you're angry, tell Him. If you have doubt, say so. Ask Him questions and then watch and wait for an answer. Will you promise me that?"

Robin nodded, knowing she was in for a long and difficult journey. After years of running, though, it was one she knew she had to take.

Chris looked at her. "I know one thing; the place you must begin is forgiveness."

She allowed his words to sink in for a moment. Then, like watching a movie in her mind of when he came to the lake, she could see Mike crying, begging her for forgiveness. Unable to extend it that day, neither could she do so at the moment. Not only did he destroy their marriage, he nearly killed her. How do you forgive such things?

"How could I possibly forgive him? How can I just forget?"

"Forgiving is not forgetting. The memories will come. They always do. The difference is in how you respond. Forgiveness doesn't mean you are saying what he did isn't wrong. What he did was wrong. Forgiveness isn't a feeling. You may not feel like forgiving. Still, for your sake you have to."

"For my sake?"

"It will release you, Robin. What happened is now between him and God, but as for you, you'll find freedom in forgiveness." He paused a moment, then continued. "I know this one by experience since I had to deal with it concerning my mom. For years I was incredibly angry at her for how she messed up our lives. She stopped being my mom because my dad died. I felt like I lost both parents at almost the same time. Forgiveness didn't come easily."

"How did you do it?" Before Chris's admission, forgiveness seemed impossible, but considering what he had gone through, if he could forgive, then maybe she could, too.

"It took longer than necessary simply because I didn't know how. For me, when I finally got to a point where I could empathize with my mom, that was a first step. I tried to put myself in her position, what she was feeling and all she had lost, and that broke my heart for her. She was so in love with and dependent on my dad. His death destroyed her. With that in mind I started praying for her regularly. Something about that gave me tremendous freedom. From there, I don't know, it became a choice to forgive her. I chose it. So when an ugly memory would surface, instead of allowing anger to control me, I chose to recall how damaged she was, I prayed for her, and I reminded myself that I forgave her. After some time it became part of how I dealt with bad memories. I did this over and over until it eventually became so automatic that I didn't even have to think through it. I went from ugly memory to automatically recalling I had forgiven her."

"How long did it take?"

"For me, over a year. Like I said, I didn't understand the process I just explained to you. I was going through it without the benefit of this hindsight I'm sharing. For you, I hope it takes less time than it took me. Will the same approach work for everyone? I'm not sure, but it worked for me. Now, I can see my mom, and trust me, she's in really bad shape, and I'm able to love her."

"I don't want to ever love him again."

"I'm not saying you have to, not in the way you once did, but you still have to forgive him. Oddly enough, you will love him again, but it'll be God's love, not something you're capable of on your own. Remember, this is for your freedom, not for Mike in any way." Chris sighed. "Before you get to that point, I think you have an even bigger issue."

"What's that?"

"You have to forgive God for disappointing you."

She had no reply, mainly because she wasn't sure how she felt about it. Now, suspecting God may have saved her after all, she realized she would need to go back and look for Him with Michael. It would be a process, one she wasn't sure she knew how to navigate.

"You'll be gone soon."

He nodded. "I know."

"How will I do this without you?"

"I know of another counselor, someone local."

"I'm glad to hear that. I don't think I can do this alone."

"You won't have to." He jumped up. "Hold on. I'll write it down for you."

He went in and when he returned handed her a piece of paper. "Here's my recommendation."

Robin glanced at the paper and then back up at him. "Are you sure?"

"Positive."

"I trust you." How could she not?

"It's not me you should trust."

Robin was sitting on her bed with her Bible in her lap. It was not long before dinner and Chris's party. Something she might almost call hope was fluttering around in her heart as she turned to the book of Isaiah as Chris's note directed her. It read:

> *"For to us a child is born, to us a son is given, and the government will be on his shoulders. And he will be called Wonderful Counselor, Mighty God, Everlasting Father, Prince of Peace."* (Isaiah 9:6)

She reached for the note Chris had given her. His version of the verse was different, and she decided she liked his better.

> *"For unto us a child is born, unto us a son is given: and the government shall be upon his shoulder: and his name shall be called Wonderful, Counsellor, The mighty God, The everlasting Father, The Prince of Peace."*

It reminded her of being a small girl. Every Christmas, these were the words she heard, yet she missed the significance of them then. In all her life Robin had never known God in any of those ways, not one. Below the verse Chris had made a note which read:

> *You will see him as Counselor first. Then, the other ways will come. Eventually, you'll know Him. Once you do, you'll never be shaken again. I promise.*

Robin believed him.

Later that night, the table was set and Chris was on the way. Tommy had gone to get him. At least Robin and Emma hoped he was on the way. With the dining room decorated and the place full, they were having a party regardless. They had spread the word to the other guests inviting them, so providing the guest of honor arrived, it promised to be a great surprise.

***

Chris followed Tommy up the stairs, looking forward to a good meal. He had more energy than he had in a couple of days, so getting out of his cabin felt good. When he noticed that the lights were out in the dining hall as they approached the house, he said, "Looks like they don't know we're coming."

Tommy smiled in the dim light and said, "We ate in the kitchen last night. I suppose we will tonight, too."

There was something off about Tommy. Chris had spent more time with him lately, so for him to be so quiet wasn't normal.

Chris stopped before reaching the porch. "Is something going on with you and Becky?"

When Tommy realized Chris had stopped, he stopped too and turned back. "No, why?"

He shook his head. "You just act different."

"No, we're fine." Tommy shrugged. "More than fine."

"And when you both go back, think you'll keep seeing each other?"

"No question about it." Tommy looked away and grinned. "I can see a future with her."

"That's good to know. Glad things are working out."

"So, uh, they are probably waiting for us," Tommy said.

Chris followed Tommy, still wondering about his behavior. Because he was such a student of people, he knew better, especially with Tommy. They had begun fishing together early mornings when Chris was up to it. Tommy didn't live so far from Chris's aunt, so they had agreed to get together once he returned to the city. Chris knew he would have to have the conversation with Tommy about his illness soon. After he talked to Robin, he would.

They walked into the main lobby area and Chris thought he heard whispers. Just as he rounded the corner toward the dining room, the lights flashed on, stopping him in his tracks, and a crowd of mostly strangers began to sing, "Happy Birthday."

With cheeks burning he looked around for Robin. The night they had eaten at the marina, he mentioned his birthday. He walked over to her and hugged her, holding on for longer than he knew was wise.

"I can't believe you did this," he whispered.

"I can't believe you didn't think I would."

When he stepped back she handed him a box.

Inside he found the best gift a man could ever receive, chocolate covered bacon. He smiled and looked at Emma. "I suppose you made this?"

"You better believe I did. I'm not sure that I've ever given a gift I was so confident of. Never seen a man with your love of bacon."

Chris went to Emma and Becky and hugged them. When he got to Tommy, they settled for a knuckle-bump.

There was a long banquet table in the middle of the room with BBQ and every side imaginable. On the buffet was his birthday cake, his favorite, white. He shook his head and prayed, "Lord, You thought of everything."

Tears sprang to his eyes at the realization that this would be his last birthday. These people had no way of knowing that, yet here he was, his last birthday filled with people and food. He scanned the crowd until he caught Robin's eye. The fact that he would be spending it with her lessened the tragedy of it in a surprising way. It felt like another in a long line of gifts from God.

Since late afternoon, he had been feeling better. The night before, there was no way he could have attended; the headache was too severe. For the moment, however, he felt perfectly normal. To his surprise, thanks to his time in the sun, he wasn't as pale as he would have expected, considering. Other than the dark circles around his eyes, he hardly looked sick. So moments like this, when he felt as well as he did, he could sometimes forget what his future held. There was no way of knowing how long he would feel this way, but he would take it while he could get it. With only a few days remaining at the lake, he wanted to enjoy every last moment of it and linger in his unexpected love story.

***

After dinner Robin was at the table with Chris, Becky, and Tommy when Chris turned to her.

"Take a walk with me?"

"Sure."

Robin noticed how quiet Chris had become, the exact thing that had concerned her lately. During the party he had seemed more like himself, open and social, but now he seemed faraway. There was something he was keeping from her and had been for some time.

They walked out onto the dock and Chris sat. When she did the same, he said, "You remember when I said I would tell you something later, why the timing wasn't right for a relationship for me either?"

"Yes."

"I guess it's about time." He kept his eyes trained on the water. "I'm sick. That's why I came out here for the summer."

"Oh," was all she could say.

"I'm dying."

Her breath escaped her as if she had been kicked in the stomach. That wasn't at all what she expected. She reached for his hand. "How long do you have?"

"A few months, maybe more."

"And there's nothing they can do?" She turned to face him. "I'm sorry. Was that a dumb question?"

"No." He smiled at her. "Radiation or chemo would only prolong it but not stop it." He gave her hand a gentle squeeze. "I don't want to live my last days here on earth fried from radiation or throwing up from chemo. I just want to die peacefully. That's the way it'll likely happen."

"Is it a brain tumor?"

"Yes."

"You have headaches. I've seen you rub your temples and pinch at the bridge of your nose. I just thought it was regular headaches."

"They've been pretty bad lately."

Robin leaned her head over and rested it on Chris's shoulder. "Thank you for trusting me with this. I've known something was wrong."

"I wasn't sure I should tell you. Once I left, though, I knew you would never hear from me again. I couldn't stand the thought of your thinking I don't care about you. I do."

"I know you do. I would have never thought that."

He sat for a moment, still holding her hand. "You are going to be okay, aren't you?"

"Yes. I won't let you down."

"Let me down?"

"We've begun a good work," she said.

"That's scripture, you know. 'He who began a good work –'"

"I know. That's why I said it. We have: God, you, and me. I'll keep seeking Him."

"That's what I wanted to hear."

"Where will you go now?"

"To my aunt's house. I sold my condo." He laughed a sort of sarcastic laugh. "Funny how at the end of it all, you realize things really do mean little. All the junk I had accumulated over the years, I just gave it away. Why sell it? What would I use the money for?" He turned to face her. "The end is simpler than I thought it would be."

"How so?"

"Well, I took the summer and had the best time of my life doing things I would never normally do. I rested, painted, watched the sun come up," he leaned into her and grinned, "had coffee with you, and went barefoot when I could."

She laughed at that. "I wondered why you showed up barefoot."

"You noticed that, huh?"

"I did." She chuckled. "We all did. It's been a topic of conversation."

"I was on my way here, and my shoes felt uncomfortable, restrictive in a way I had never noticed before, so I leaned down, pulled them off, and threw them in the back seat. I've hardly worn any since."

"You did to dinner that night."

"Special occasion."

"Very special occasion," she said. "That's the night this all began."

He nodded but made no comment.

The memory of that night brought Vanessa to mind. "Before we had dinner, Vanessa – she broke it off with you and you're dying?"

"We had only been seeing each other for three months when I was diagnosed, and even those three months were not the greatest. At that point, in her position, can you imagine breaking it off right away? I was confused and a little scared then. It was simply easier to keep things as they were. I don't blame her. If she had loved me, she would have wanted to be with me no matter what was ahead. Same with me.

"I realize now, if we had stayed together, I would never have met you. Well, we would have met but never have gotten this close."

"That's true. I'm glad she dumped you."

"She didn't exactly dump me," Chris said.

"Oh, you got dumped all right, and I really am glad you did." She paused. "Do you realize what you've meant in my life?"

"Honestly, yes. I see something happening in you, and I know God brought me here to help get it started. He will finish it, but He allowed me the privilege of the beginning. You know, I was thinking about this the other day, I've felt more purpose in my life this summer with you than I have in my entire life."

Robin considered his words. "In a way I'm jealous of that. I don't know that I have ever felt I served a purpose. Well, maybe when I had Michael, but since then I haven't. For your sake, what a gift."

"That's exactly what I was thinking. It's been a gift. I'm not saying my only purpose on earth was you, but my final one was."

He looked at her. "Wanna play 'Would You Rather'?"

"Sure."

"Would you rather have a short life with great purpose or a long life with little purpose?"

"Short life, no doubt."

"Me too. Maybe that's why I'm okay with the end."

Tears filled Robin's eyes. "Will you be there waiting for me?"

"In heaven, you bet."

"Are you scared?"

"Maybe of the pain but not of dying."

She thought for a few seconds. "So, you have never seen the fall colors here at the lake?"

He turned to her and smiled. "No, I never have."

"Stay for a while longer."

"I don't know. I fear things will progress quickly now. I'm having some bad days, and I don't want to put you through that."

"Let me be here for you the way you've been here for me."

He smiled. "I can think of nothing better to do with my time than to spend it with you."

FIFTEEN

Robin had been watching Chris from the kitchen window as he painted on the dock. The wind was whipping in off the lake, causing him to grab for his canvas many times. Still, he painted. Her hope, while headed his way, was to talk him in to taking some time to rest. He needed it. The closer she got to him, the more she could see how tired he was, the dark circles beneath his blue eyes telling the tale.

Over these past months, since extending his stay, Chris had good days and bad days, but for the most part the good days were more prevalent. His coordination was failing, so Robin tried to help when she could, mindful though to allow him his dignity and independence. He wasn't a child, and she forced herself not to treat him like one. Early on, after learning of his illness, she was much too worried, hen-peckish even. When he eventually called her on it, she swore off mothering him. So far she had kept that promise. She helped him as needed but allowed him space.

"That's your best one yet," she said when she came to stand by Chris's side.

He smiled at her. "You say that about all of them."

"You're getting better every day then. I think it's spectacular."

"I wouldn't say spectacular."

"Marvelous?"

"I can live with marvelous."

When she handed him his coffee, he thanked her and took a sip. "I should probably go in now."

"You've been out for a long time. Are you hurting?"

"Yes, and feeling a little sick."

"Let me help you gather your things." Robin grabbed his backpack and slung it over her shoulder.

He reached for her arm. "Just lay it down on the dock for now. Can we sit for a minute and drink our joe?"

"Sure we can."

Robin took his cup and waited until he was seated. The sight of him struggling to maintain his balance caused her to look away momentarily, his decline more obvious every day. This was no longer some stranger who was ill but now one of her closest friends.

She looked over at his painting. The fall colors were spectacular this year, a masterpiece by the Master, so Chris had spent as much time outdoors as possible.

"How many times will you paint this view?"

"Until I get it right."

"You must see something I don't. It looks right to me."

"I see something with my heart that I can't see with my eyes. That's what I'm trying to capture."

"What do you mean?"

"I don't know; there's a feeling I get here that I want to be able to take away with me."

Her heart sank. "Take away?"

"It's time for me to go back to Boston."

"Oh." She looked away, out across the lake. Her eyes were stinging, so she blinked rapidly to chase away the tears.

"Don't be hurt, please."

Prepared to say she wasn't, she stopped herself. He had become such a vital part of her life, of course it hurt. From June through October he had been part of her every day. Suddenly, he would leave, and that would be that.

"I need you to understand. I have some goodbyes there, too. It has nothing to do with wanting to leave you. Honestly, I've put it off far too long."

"Are you going to your aunt's?"

"Yes." He paused a moment. "I called my mom. She'll be coming to stay for a while."

"That's a good thing."

He nodded. "Being here with you and Emma has been one of God's greatest gifts to me. These past months, reading together, studying together, and just watching you grow with the Lord, Robin, I'm humbled and grateful to have been a part of that. But they need me, too."

"I'm sorry," she whispered as she looked away and wiped her eyes.

He reached for her chin and turned her back to face him. "For what?"

"For being so selfish."

Chris chuckled at that. "You're anything but selfish. The way you've taken care of me when..." He didn't have to finish. "You're like an angel."

She giggled, mocking him. "An angel, really?"

"Pretty corny?"

"Pretty corny. But I like corny sometimes."

"How 'bout now?" he said.

"Yeah, definitely now."

Robin took Chris's hand. The moment was so strikingly similar to the evening he had told her of his illness, it was slightly disturbing. In the brief time she had known him, she had come to love him deeply. Emma had once asked her if she was in love with him, and the honest answer was no, but she loved him with the same intensity she loved her family and Emma. It was simple love. He was the least complicated thing in her life, and she liked that.

"I'll drive you back."

He had had one seizure not long before and from that point on was no longer permitted to drive. At the emergency room he was warned it could happen at any time.

Without room for discussion, Robin said, "I'll call Tommy. He has already offered when the time comes. I will drive your car and he can bring me back from Boston."

***

Back in his cabin, Chris didn't even bother to put his paint supplies away but simply dumped them on the table. He dropped onto his chair by the fire, the one where he sat while they counseled, and considered his conversation with Robin. At first, finding it nearly impossible to tell her he was leaving, he had finally blurted out his intentions more abruptly than intended. When she had come so close to crying, he nearly changed his mind. To know he was hurting her was nearly unbearable. His decision to return to Boston was the most difficult decision of his life. With every fiber of his being, he wanted to stay, but for her sake, he was leaving. Lately, there was a sense the downhill slide was fast approaching. He felt it deep in his spirit, like the Lord was giving him fair warning. The end would be the worst of him, something from which he wanted to spare the woman he loved.

He closed his eyes and pictured her. Early in the summer, he was attracted, midway through, smitten, and by the end, captivated and completely hers. So by the time fall arrived, he was so helplessly in love with Robin that he felt as if she were a part of him, as if she always had been. Maybe that was the feeling he wanted to capture when he painted, his love for her. It was the purest love he had ever known, the love of a lifetime. There in his final months, he had found his very own love story. She was an astonishing last gift.

After that day, Chris remained only two days more while packing up and preparing his heart to leave her. She was quiet about his departure, hurting because of it. He was certain she loved him, though he was just as certain her love differed from his, and that was okay. In truth, if her love reflected his own, then his death would be much more painful for her. God spared her that.

The morning they loaded his car it was raining, befitting of his mood as they drove away from the cabin and passed by the inn. By the time they reached the highway, the rain had cleared out, and the sun rose high and bright overhead. The mood in the car changed with the weather. All the way, they laughed and reminisced about the summer. It seemed as if they had known each other for years and years, just like family. Like a family on the way home from a vacation might do, they listed the highlights and mentioned even the worst moments of their time together. The two-hour trip flew by. Every moment of it Chris lived in anticipation of the time when Robin would leave him. He knew this was it, the last of them.

***

They arrived at Chris's aunt's house after a brief stop for lunch. When meeting Tina for the first time, Robin was surprised by how young she was, only ten years older than Chris. She had been a mere twenty-five when she had taken him in to live with her. What an unusually selfless act for someone of that age.

"So tell me more about Chris. I can't imagine he gave you too much trouble."

Tina smiled at that. "It was a bit rocky early on. I had no idea what I was doing, and Chris wasn't much on taking orders." She winked at Chris. "We got our bearings eventually.

"I wasn't married then, so with it just being the two of us, we found some common interests and began spending more time together. We started going to church. That changed Chris entirely. Even in his late teens, he was the godliest man I've ever known."

When Chris rolled his eyes and gave Tina a look, she grinned at him and shrugged. "Robin asked. I'm just answering."

"I'm sure she isn't interested in all that."

"Of course I am," Robin said. "Tell me all you want."

"Since we hadn't spent much time together while Chris was growing up, we had to find our footing as family. One common interest we found was art. I'm not as good as Chris, but I love to paint. That was a good outlet for us. We took a class together. It helped us to get to know each other better."

"Chris has done little else but paint over the past few months," Robin said. "I've kept a few and plan to use them in some of the cabins." She turned to Chris and patted his leg. "My favorite is over the fireplace in the main house. It's placed directly across from where I often work. I'll never look at it that I won't think of him." She teared up.

"Don't," Chris whispered as he leaned in close.

A knock at the door got Tina moving, leaving Robin and Chris alone for a moment.

"I'm sorry."

"It's okay. I feel the same." Chris moved in even closer and pressed his forehead to hers. "This is hard."

She only nodded.

When Tina returned with Tommy following behind, Chris moved back in his seat, and as he did, Robin heard him sigh. The look on his face made her turn away.

"Sorry I'm so early," Tommy said. "I wasn't far from here after meeting a friend."

Robin watched as Chris and Tommy embraced. It was a sweet moment as the two reconnected. Their friendship had been unexpected but one Chris valued. Tommy had lost his dad at an early age, so the two found common ground.

They all sat and chatted for a few minutes more until Robin sensed Tommy wanted to get a start on the drive. For him it would be four hours roundtrip.

Tina was asking Tommy a question, so Robin whispered to Chris, "I guess I should go. I don't want to keep Tommy waiting much longer."

Chris grasped her hand and squeezed. "I'll walk you out."

When they reached the car, Chris and Tommy agreed to get together soon. After Tommy got into the car, Chris walked to where Robin stood by the passenger side door. He pulled her to him and held her for several quiet minutes. He was crying, which made her cry. Neither said a word but just sobbed and held on, knowing this was possibly the last time they would see each other on this side of heaven. Finally, he pulled himself away, kissed her on the cheek, and went back into the house. He didn't turn back to look at her. Robin waited, but he never did. Like ripping away a bandage rather than pulling it slowly, he left her standing there, dazed and longing for more of him.

Robin watched until he closed the door before getting into the car. Bewildered at first that he would walk away like that, she knew his intention was to protect both their hearts. He didn't want to let her go any more than she did him. While it would be painful either way, he obviously believed the rip and run approach to be his only option. She knew he loved her.

For the first half of the trip back, Robin said little. All she could do was think about Chris and the empty space that she would know in his absence. With ease he had found a place in her heart that would always be held for him. It was the first time she truly saw God in someone else. Now, thinking back to how he walked away, the bandage analogy, she smiled to herself. He was God's bandage in her life. Though unaware herself, she had been hemorrhaging on the inside. God knew, and He sent Chris to help her begin to heal.

When Chris had said that God had sent him to help her, at the time, she was distraught and couldn't process the implications of that fact, but later, his words permeated her heart and her mind. The realization that God actually handpicked a man like Chris to bring comfort to her proved His love for her; His active, I'm-in-the-middle-of-your-business kind of love. The stitches in the veil had begun to unravel the very moment of that revelation.

Still, there was a journey ahead, but one she looked forward to with much less fear. The few times while reading her Bible when she actually felt God was speaking to her intimately and personally caused an intense longing for more. From those times on, she had opened His Word with great anticipation. She not only read, she studied and poured over the Scriptures, watching for God at every turn.

They had left Boston an hour before, and already, they were stopping for gas. Tommy was pumping while she sat lost in thought, wondering how things were going with Chris and Tina. At the door, Tina had promised to keep in touch. Robin understood her meaning: when Chris was unable to for himself. Robin speculated when his mother might come. Her prayer was that she would come. "Please, Lord, give her enough presence of mind to see her son." From what Tina suggested, it wasn't at all likely. His mother was that sick.

"We're set. Sorry, I should have filled up before picking you up."

"Don't worry about it."

Tommy had been quiet, she supposed, to give her time to reel in her emotions. That was appreciated, but now she would rather talk than think. "So Becky says school is going well for you both."

He only nodded.

Again there was a long silence. Now that she thought about it, Tommy wasn't acting himself and hadn't been since he arrived at Tina's.

"Anything you want to talk about?"

He glanced at Robin. "What? Has Becky said something?"

"No, nothing. You just seem quiet. I'm not picking you for information or anything."

He drove in silence for a minute more. "I think we're having problems."

"You and Becky?"

"Yeah."

"You think?"

"She's pulling away. I can feel it."

"I'm sorry, Tommy." She was, and she was surprised, too. When Becky called, she acted as if things were great between them.

"Why do you think she's pulling away?"

Tommy shook his head. "I don't know if pulling away is the right way to describe it, but there's something going on. When we're together, she acts standoffish. There's some hesitation I don't understand." He paused and scratched his head. "I wonder if she thinks about that guy."

Uh oh, Robin thought. *Why did I ask if he wanted to talk?*

"Not this summer of course, but last year, they…um, they were together. You know?"

In case he was fishing to see if she knew anything, Robin remained silent. She was Switzerland, neutral as neutral could be. She didn't nod; she didn't move her head just in case it appeared to be a nod.

When Robin gave no reply, Tommy said, "Anyway, what if she wants to be with him? How can I fight that, with him being her first love?"

"Tommy, all I know is that every time I talk to Becky, she only seems more in love with you. I wouldn't tell you that if it wasn't true. I think you're borrowing trouble."

"So why is she pulling away? Seems we should be getting closer, but instead, she doesn't want to be around me as much, always has an excuse."

"You need to talk to her. That's my suggestion."

When it came to mind, it made a little more sense to her. The last time Becky had called, she talked about Brad and how she regretted being with him that first year. Now that she was with Tommy and things were becoming more serious, Becky had baggage to bring into the relationship. That wasn't likely easy to carry now that she had fallen in love with Tommy.

Once the conversation started, Tommy didn't take a breath. Instead, he kept on and on with his observations for nearly the final hour of the trip. Robin simply let him talk. His ramblings were sweet and crazy and as full of love as Robin had seen in a young man for many years.

At the notion of silly love, Mike's image came to mind. It was a moment she hadn't thought of in many years, a memory she believed had long since faded, one she cupped in her hands and peered into. It took her back to the day Mike had asked her to marry him and how he had rambled on and on.

It was young, sweet love, just as Tommy and Becky were now experiencing. The remainder of the drive, even while Tommy listed every pro and con of his relationship with Becky, Robin found herself wading in puddles and reflections of the early days, times when life held more promise than pain. Her heart was filled with "if onlys," and she wished more than anything she could go back and live that life differently.

Back at home, life would never be the same, and Robin knew it. She and Emma both grieved the loss of Chris's presence. Since their lasts guests were gone and the inn wouldn't re-open until the following spring, they had too much time on their hands to try to fill. They played games, chatted, read, and tried every other activity they could think of, but his absence screamed loudly in the quiet house.

Robin talked to Chris often, but in the past week, he hadn't called. She tried calling on two occasions, but he didn't answer. Tina called once in between the two calls saying he was sleeping more than before, but she would have him call soon.

Three days after Thanksgiving, Robin found that she had missed a call from Tina. When she called back, she dialed with a sense that this call wasn't good news.

"Hey, Tina, sorry I missed you."

"Hi, Robin."

When Tina remained quiet for a moment, Robin's heart sank. "He's gone?"

"No, but we've moved him to hospice care."

"I'll be there in two hours."

"You don't have to come. I'm not sure he will even know that you're here."

"I promised him I would."

"I don't think it will be much longer. I don't see how it can be."

At Chris's bedside Robin wasn't sure if she would be able to talk to him at all before he passed. He was sleeping around the clock. The next step, she was told, would be a coma. Her time with him was surreal. This sleeping form wasn't the man she had come to know, the one she laughed with and cried with. Chris was already gone.

Mostly alone since Tina worked during the day, Robin read aloud to him, especially from his Bible. She would flip through and find verses he had circled and read them to him. Many of them, he had read to her while he was still with her at the lake. Tucked inside were folded sheets of paper, but she was careful not to open them. Because she assumed they were his personal study notes, she moved them to the back of the book.

Once, he woke up long enough to smile at her but then drifted off again. Hour after hour she waited for another waking moment, but one never came. To pass the time, she talked to him. She poured out her heart, from the serious to the silly. One morning, she was thinking about Becky and wished she could ask his advice. He would know how to handle things.

"There's something going on with Becky. When Tommy took me home he said things weren't going so well, but when I talk to her, she seems so in love with him. I think this has to do with some decisions she's made in the past." She waved her hand. "That's a whole other story, but if that is the case, how do I help her?"

She leaned in and said, "I want to help her the way you've helped me. I want to help people like you did." With a smile, she thought about Emma. "You know, I think I've been helping Emma, at least some. There's something different in her lately. She's finally open to hearing about Jesus and how much He loves her. Trust me; that's such a big deal for her.

"I keep thinking about what you said one day, how you felt more purpose over the summer than you had before. That's what I want, to know my purpose. So far, I really don't think I have one. How sad is that?

"Becky plans to come back and work next summer. When she does, I want to reach out to her. Or maybe I'll try to get her to open up on the phone. Seems she will only say so much for now." Robin smiled and reached for his hand. "I miss you. I wish you could give me some direction here."

During her third day there, Robin sat quietly reading a book that Tina had brought her the night before. When she heard a distinct "psst," she looked up. Chris was grinning as much as his condition would allow.

"Hi," he whispered.

Robin leaned in and grinned. "Well, hi there, sleepyhead."

He seemed so weak, but the moment he saw her there by his bed, she could nearly see his strength return, like he was prepared to fight to spend time with her. When they had last spoken, he said that was his one wish, that he might see her once more before he died. That very moment she had offered to make the drive to Boston, but he asked her to wait.

"I want you to take that." He was pointing to his Bible on the bedside table.

"It'll be my prized possession."

"I know. That's why I want you to have it." He drifted off momentarily.

She stayed close by and waited, hoping he would open his eyes again.

When he did, he smiled at her. "I think I fell asleep."

"Just for a second. It's okay. I'm not going anywhere. Sleep all you need to."

He shook his head and motioned for her to come nearer. When she did, he reached his hand up and placed it behind her head, drawing her even closer. "It's time to pay up."

"What do you mean?"

"You said you could never repay me. I said I would think of something."

She smiled, remembering well. "You're right, and I said anything."

"Anything?"

"Anything."

"Forgive all things, Robin."

"I'm trying." A lump formed in her throat even as she said it. The counselor was back, and he brought with him tough matters.

"Forgive Mike. Remember empathy. Forgive God for taking Michael too soon. 'For in Him we live, and move, and have our being.' Look that up." He pointed to his Bible. "I think I wrote it down, but I don't remember."

Robin began to cry and tried to move back from him, but he held to her.

"Finally, forgive yourself for taking that nap and for pulling that trigger."

Her tears began to drop onto his face as he pulled her the rest of the way to him and kissed her. She didn't try to pull away. For the first time in her life, she kissed a man besides Mike.

"I love you, Robin. What better gift could God give me than you here at the end?"

"I love you, too." Robin stroked his cheek. "He sent you for me."

"I've never doubted that." He blinked long and hard. "Please don't leave me," he whispered near her ear. "I want you to be here with me when I go."

"I won't leave you. I'm right here."

Robin moved onto the bed and lay there with him. The hand holding her head loosened its grip and fell limp. He was asleep again. For over an hour she laid with him and prayed for mercy. She prayed for the Lord to take him home so he would finally be healed. How different this prayer was than the day she held Michael. Finally, trusting God's plan, she prayed His will be done above all else.

Later that evening, Chris slipped into a coma and never regained consciousness. The next day he was gone. Robin was lying next to him when he went to be with Jesus.

At Tina's house the following day, Robin was thumbing through Chris's Bible. Since Chris had intended to give her his Bible, she had to assume the pages she had moved to the back were for her. They were. He had been making notes since leaving the lake. In that moment with her emotions so raw, she was unable to read them. Even in his own death his concern had been for her. "Lord," she whispered, "how could any man be so selfless?"

She hugged Chris's Bible to her chest. Once she returned home, she would read every word he left for her. For the time being, though, she would do her best to be a comfort for Tina and possibly his mother if she showed up for the funeral. Just as Tina had predicted, she never made it to see Chris. He died without having seen his mother at all.

SIXTEEN

After the funeral, Robin arrived home with a heavy heart. The journey ahead of her had felt less intimidating while Chris was alive. He had become such a close friend in such a short span of time that it truly felt as if she had lost a close family member. Emma had driven up for the funeral, and Tommy and Becky had come, too. At dinner the night after the funeral, they had just sat and eaten in stunned silence. He was too young to have been taken. None of them could grasp the harsh reality of it. It didn't even seem real until they had lowered his casket into the ground. At that moment it became all too real.

What was evident that day was that Chris had purpose that spanned well beyond his understanding. The church was filled with hundreds of people, so many, in fact, it became standing room only. Many were students whose lives he had touched. Members from his church were a large part as well. He was loved, as he had loved well.

On a personal level Robin considered her own impact on people and the world around her. Had that been her coffin and her funeral, other than her parents, Emma, Tommy, and Becky, who would attend? At church she sneaked in and out, mindful not to make connections. Her existence was inconsequential for the most part. How can one person make such a great impact and another mean so little? It was a choice he made. She was fully aware of that. Consciously, he chose to look outside of himself, even to the very end, while she lived life looking inward and backward. No wonder she had no idea where she was going since she never looked at the road ahead or the possibilities God placed before her.

The day after returning from the funeral Becky called Robin. They spoke for several minutes before Robin understood the reason for Becky's call.

Robin said, "Something's up; I can tell. If you've called to talk, let's talk."

"I love Tommy."

"That's pretty easy to see." Robin had never mentioned to Becky that Tommy was concerned.

"I don't want to take things to the next level, but I'm afraid if I don't I will lose him."

"Is he pressuring you?"

"No, but I know that's the next logical step."

"That's not true. You're both Christians. That shouldn't be the next logical step."

Becky remained quiet.

"Listen to me. No matter what decisions you may have made in your past, you don't have to make the same ones now. You have a right to say no."

"He knows I was with Brad. I told him. Now, if I don't want to be with him, he will be hurt." She began to cry.

"I know this for a fact: Tommy loves you. But you can't expect him to understand what you're going through. You have to talk to him, explain that you regret making that decision and that it's not what you want for your relationship with him." Robin paused. "I assume that's what this is about."

"Yes," Becky said, sniffling. "I should have never…" She began to cry harder. "Now I can't take it back."

"No, sweetie." Robin smiled to herself at how much she sounded like Emma when she said that. "You can't take it back, but you can make sure you don't make the same mistake again."

They spoke for some time more. Because Robin knew both of them, she was able to reassure Becky, Tommy loved her enough to wait. That day in the car, Robin saw true love, the kind that waits. She knew what that kind of love looked like.

For several days Robin tried to get back into the groove of daily life. It was impossible. Nothing would ever be the same. Both she and Emma sensed it. It was early December, and the usual excitement of the holidays seemed unbefitting. Her parents weren't coming, so it would only be the two of them. At a time when they would usually begin to decorate, neither had the heart for it. This would be a sad Christmas. They both felt it.

One rainy afternoon they sat in the kitchen together and shared a piece of pie, both unusually quiet.

"What now?" Emma sighed and rested her fork on the plate.

"I think I'll go back to school."

Robin had been thinking of taking classes and finishing her degree. She had finished one year while Mike was on his first tour. Then while in California, she had completed a second year.

"School for what?"

"I'm not exactly sure. I have two years behind me, and I might as well do something about finishing."

Chris's contribution into the lives of others had made a lasting impression on her and now urged her on to do the same. She was certain, though, there was a long road ahead for her own healing. Still, there had to be a beginning point, a point at which she set a course to discover her own purpose – her way of helping others.

"I think that's a great idea. Will you begin in January?"

"If possible, after I get back from my parents'. I've been checking into some schools that offer classes online. I may be too late to begin by this semester, but if not, I think I'll try it that way and see how I do. I may be a bit rusty by now."

Emma reached over the counter and took Robin's face into her hands. "Hummingbird, if anyone can do it, you can. I believe in you."

Robin smiled as much as possible with her cheeks squeezed in Emma's grasp. "Really?"

"Really. You can do this, and I'll pay for it."

The argument over who would pay continued until Robin registered. All through Christmas, even up to the point of writing a check, the battle raged. Emma won out and paid for her classes and books. Robin was taking only two to begin with, but she quickly learned that two was enough for someone so out of study practice. School was the best decision she could have made since it turned the normally dreary and boring winter months into something challenging.

New England weather in the earliest part of the year was dreadful. Robin stayed in so much, she was certain that when the spring thaw occurred, she would have forgotten how to interact with people. Other than trips out for groceries and going to church, she and Emma both hibernated. The one and only thing that could draw Robin out of the warm house was her treks to Chris's cabin. Once or twice a week, she went there for counseling sessions, and just as she had done with Chris, she sat in her chair. At the onset his empty chair caused such grief she could hardly pray or make progress, but eventually, she found the Wonderful Counselor had taken Chris's place. In meeting with her new Counselor, Robin envisioned Jesus seated in the chair across from her. Just as Chris had suggested, she talked as she would to him or Emma. She asked the tough questions and often unfurled the ugliness that was trapped in her heart, the bitterness, anger, and disappointment. One thing she observed in how the Lord dealt with years' worth of pain was that all matters were not to be dealt with at once. He would take her through seasons: a season for bitterness, a season for anger. It progressed that way from the very beginning.

One day, she read a verse about not conferring with flesh and blood. The Lord used that verse to hammer a truth deep into her heart: He was her source of healing, and finding another human counselor wasn't her answer.

Jesus Himself, inside of her, was to counsel and guide. Once that concept was revealed to her, she never looked back again. She would use Chris's study notes and ponder all the things he suggested, but her main source of counsel would be the Spirit and the Word. Whether or not she made it to the cabin, each and every day she sought God through her Bible, and His Word soon began to come alive to her.

Robin was bundled up, about to head down to the cabin when Emma came out of the kitchen holding a thermos.

"My gift for you." Emma smiled as she handed her the thermos.

"I can't imagine a better gift on a day like today." Robin looked out the window at the light snow falling.

"You know, I will give you privacy here if you don't want to brave the cold."

"I'll be fine. I'll start a fire." Robin paused. "There's something about being there. At first it was because I felt Chris's presence. Now, all I can say is that God shows up every day when I'm there." She grinned. "Of course He shows up here, too, but there, I often feel as if I'm sitting in his physical presence. That's the only way to explain it."

"Go then. Sit and talk to God."

When Robin turned, Emma reached for her arm. "I want to feel that someday."

Robin stood looking at her, eyes fluttering. "You can. You will. Should we talk about that now?"

"Not now. Soon, though."

"Soon." Robin walked through the door feeling so warm inside that the bitter cold couldn't possibly touch her. She had no doubt that Emma would come to know Jesus. Little things she had said and done were proof that the Spirit was in all-out pursuit of her.

Once settled in and with a fire going, Robin prayed for Emma for several minutes and then opened her Bible. Each day she would begin by reading at whatever place she had left off the day before. To keep a normal flow of reading was the key. If she had questions, she learned that looking for the answer could lead to frustration. It was too precarious to find a verse that seemed to be the answer to a question or concern she faced and try to apply it to her circumstance. Instead, she found that if she simply placed her question or care before the Lord in prayer, then read in her usual manner, the answer would come. While it may not be that day or even within several days, an answer always came. It was the anticipation, the excitement that kept her reading and studying His Word daily. He always showed up, and to her that was one of the first real and significant truths she learned about the character of her God. He is faithful.

She had begun reading Chris's notes just before Christmastime. They were so personal and intimate in knowledge of her heart that she found them at first to be intensely sorrowful. They brought her more grief than gain in the beginning, but eventually, through the strength of the Spirit, she was able to study them. Over time, the Lord used what Chris wrote to lead her through treacherous waters. While navigating along, she would sometimes imagine Chris sitting quietly with the Lord, asking Him how to best advise her. It was a sweet and comforting image to contemplate. He cared so much for her, and because he chose to put so much effort into her, she was becoming well.

His first lesson recorded a verse he had spoken to her in the hospital. He had said, "For in Him, we live, and move, and have our being." On the study page he had taken the many verses that preceded it and dissected it for her. It was from Acts 17. Toward the goal of her healing over Michael's death, his point was that God determined the begin date and end date of his life on earth – He determined the bounds of his habitation. He gives all things breath, and it's His right to determine such things.

> "That they should seek the Lord, if haply they might feel after him, and find him, though he be not far from every one of us…" (27)

His notes expounded the most on this verse, and his assurance again was that God was present in the moment of her greatest pain. No matter what her eyes saw or her heart felt, Jesus was there. Her heart was trying to believe, but her mind couldn't grasp it so far. She held on to hope that it would come. Of all that lay ahead of her, she knew this was the one area that would require God Himself to open up her understanding and plant that belief in her heart. Her emotions over Michael were still as raw and tender as the day she had begun talking about him. It was the longest road ahead.

Another of Chris's notes dealt with Mike and forgiveness. He suggested that in order to have a reference point for empathizing with him, and in doing so, traveling the road of forgiveness, she research post-traumatic stress disorder. It wasn't something to be used as an excuse for his behavior, but it might help her to better appreciate what he had experienced when he came home. In his notes Chris reminded her that Mike had also lost his son right there in the midst of tremendous mental trauma that was already dragging him under.

That day, sitting before the blazing fire, Robin felt a tugging within and Chris's words stung her heart. This all gave her a reason to pause and reconsider their last year together. At the time, when Michael had first died, she had no way of knowing that Mike was struggling. Up until then he had hidden it well. Or if he did display any signs while she was pregnant or while Michael was alive, she chose to ignore them: the sleepless nights and his occasional short fuse. He was so easily startled and jumpy and overly emotional. That wasn't like him. Now that she had researched common PTSD symptoms, it all seemed so clear. Even his drinking made more sense as it was a way of quieting the storm he had brewing within.

Just the night before, while reading through heartbreaking stories on a message board, Robin had run across the location of a local support group for families of those who suffer with PTSD. The church where the group met was less than five miles from her church. It never crossed her mind while looking at the website that she might want to go. Now, she felt as if she had to. She wanted to put faces to so many troubling stories. Maybe in some way, she needed to see that she wasn't alone.

SEVENTEEN

The following night, Robin entered the church where the support group met hoping to not be noticed. Coffee and donuts were on a table by the entrance, a fact Robin tried her best to ignore. Someone was already speaking, a man, about his wife's behavior since she had returned from the Gulf. For some reason that surprised Robin, but it made perfect sense with so many women there on the front lines now. She sat and listened with interest as he talked about the nightmares and sleepless nights.

Next, a woman got up and began to tell about her son. The poor woman had no idea where her son was and hadn't seen him in over six months. Story after story was shared, some – many – reminded her of Mike and helped her to see that he was barely hanging on before Mikey died.

These men and women were sympathetic and understanding of what their husbands, wives, and sons were going through. One thought continually ran through Robin's mind. Why hadn't she reached out for help for them both? Why hadn't she been more honest with herself?

The woman sitting next to Robin leaned over and whispered, "I'm Tracy. Is this your first time here?"

Robin nodded.

"There are a great group of people here, super supportive."

Robin only smiled and nodded again. The woman who was currently talking was telling about her own PTSD after being abused by her returning vet husband. At that point Robin got up and left. It was all too much, especially the guilt of remaining silent when she should have spoken up.

More than two weeks passed before Robin could return to another of the meetings. She hadn't intended to ever go back, but that same urging that caused her to go in the first place continued until she gave in and went. The second time she arrived earlier while people were still milling around and chatting. Robin did as before and went in and took a seat.

Tracy sat next to her and handed her a cup of coffee. "The first time is the toughest. It's sometimes like you are hearing others tell your story."

"Yeah, something like that."

"So is your guy a Gulf vet?"

"Yes." Robin paused a moment and sighed. "We didn't make it. I guess now, all these years later, I'm just trying to understand what I didn't then."

"I'm sorry you didn't make it. But it's good that you're here now."

"I'm Robin, by the way."

"Nice to meet you, Robin, and I'm sincerely glad you came. If you have any questions, I'm free to talk anytime."

More people arrived and soon began to take their seats. This time, Robin was a little more prepared for what to expect. Just as last time, person after person shared fragments of their story. Each was different and sad. All had the common theme of shattered lives and the fear that life might never be normal again. Only one spoke from a positive perspective, Tracy. Her husband had responded well to treatment and was currently working with other PTSD sufferers.

When Tracy sat again and while there was a small break, Robin turned to her. "May I ask you a personal question?"

Tracy smiled. "Certainly."

"Was your husband ever abusive?"

"A few times. We got help."

Filled with the same sense of regret, Robin turned away. Someone approached Tracy and they began to talk, leaving Robin steeping in memories of how Mike wept night after night after Mikey died. When he thought she was sleeping, he would leave their bed and go out onto the porch. A few times, she had watched him through the window, in too much pain herself to try to comfort him. From the day of Michael's death, Robin had so shut down that Mike was left out on his own to try and grieve. He couldn't find his way out of it. Already so broken psychologically, how could anything else come of it other than what did?

"Are you okay?" Tracy said.

"Not really."

"Would you like to talk sometime?"

"Maybe in time. For now I think this is what I need, to see that so many others came home like Mike did, so messed up. I'm working on forgiving him for who he became in the wake of war." She paused. "And I'm working on forgiving myself for not getting him the help he needed."

"Robin, you can't carry that. Hindsight is twenty/twenty, but in the midst of the storm, it's nearly impossible to see daylight."

Robin smiled. "A friend said something similar."

"Listen to that friend. This isn't about what was done then. It's about what you do now. You forgive and learn to live again." Tracy reached for Robin's hand. "Are you a believer in Jesus?"

"I am. That's what this journey is about, restoring my relationship with God and reconciling my past with my husband."

"Then you have Who you need to take your next steps." She smiled. "But if you need a sympathetic ear, I'm here."

Over the next few weeks, Robin attended several more group meetings and continued to read more online. Ultimately, forgiveness, something Robin was positive she would never grasp, arrived and remained. More than able to forgive her husband; she began to pray for him that his mind would remain restored and that he would never again turn to alcohol. More than any other thing, she prayed his heart would heal over losing their son. Just as she still grieved Michael's loss, she knew Mike did as well. It was in praying for him that she found her truest freedom. No longer was she haunted by the end of their marriage; rather, she could look back on those times with a new level of compassion for him.

Hour after hour she reflected upon how much he had lost, too: his sanity, his son, his wife, and his freedom. Even though he was released from prison, she had no doubt that their final year kept him just as bound as it had her. She prayed that he might somehow learn to forgive himself. Memories of the pain and sorrow she saw in his eyes when he came to see her often stole sleep from her. The sound of his weeping was still trapped in her head. Never had she seen a man more broken.

In a continuation of the season of forgiveness, she felt the Lord leading her toward empathy for the woman who had pulled that trigger. In doing so she was better able to grasp the truth, the hidden motive behind her actions that night. When Mike threatened that he would get her pregnant again, she had snapped. It was more than the unbearable thought of bringing another child into such an abusive and chaotic home; it was the idea of another child altogether. After Michael's death she never wanted another child. The thought of it was terrifying. That fear arose long before Mike had begun drinking and was one she had acted on in such a deceptive way that its revelation nearly killed them both.

Robin had to forgive herself for her deception with the birth control pills, as well as for picking up a loaded gun and intentionally trying to kill the man she loved. Able to now consider her actions through hindsight, she discovered empathy came relatively easy for her, too. Just as Mike was out of his mind, being chased by his own demons, she too was bound by oppressive fear and grief. When looking back, she felt such sympathy for both of them that her heart remained heavy and her prayers were ones filled with tears and pity. They were a young, lost couple, trying to wade through a sea of grief and misery. Both were drowning and neither had the means of helping the other.

The only Life Preserver was out of reach for them both. She had turned her face from God, having mended the veil in her distrust and disapproval of His ways. Mike had no such option, for he knew Him not at all.

Her season of healing was beautiful and painful and undoubtedly worthwhile. The moments she spent with her Lord were like surgery at times when there was a cutting away of what deserved no place in her heart, such as fear and unbelief. At other times it was comparable to sitting in soothing waters, warm and comforting, when Jesus simply tended to her wounds. Then there were moments when grief and loss covered her in darkness, and it was during those times that she saw God as most mighty. When all seemed dark and she couldn't see Him clearly, she was secure in the knowledge that it was then that she was resting in the shadow of His wings. To see Him would have meant moving from His embrace. Certain times required the dimness and sanctuary of His encirclement. He was wrapped around her so securely that she felt no need to see Him. He was in her and with her, no matter what her eyes saw or how her mind tried to deceive her. Her spirit knew. "Remain in the shadow of My wings," was what she often heard, and that was what she did.

One day in particular, she considered Chris's words before they had even begun counseling. He said, "And you, Robin, are anything but free." Back then, she knew she was wounded. She knew she was damaged. She even knew she had a broken spirit. What she didn't know was how utterly bound she was. Indeed, she was anything but free. Just the day before this reflection of her lack of freedom, she had read a verse.

> *"But whenever anyone turns to the Lord, the veil is taken away. Now the Lord is the Spirit, and where the Spirit of the Lord is, there is freedom." (2 Corinthians 3:16-17)*

After so many years turning away from Him, finally, by the simple act of turning back, she had found freedom. While she would have never considered it of herself, the truth was, she had been the Prodigal all along. Typically, the image of the Prodigal is of one who falls into a life of outward sinfulness. In her case, turning away from God and closing Him out of her life, she was every bit the same, just as far away as if she had traveled to a foreign land to spend her inheritance.

There was something about this revelation that made her love Jesus more than ever before. Never once had she had the mental image of God waiting for her with outstretched arms. Ever after, though, it would be what she saw of Him when she looked back to the days of her brokenness. He was her Father, calling her to back to Him. Because she had been so far away, so unwilling to listen, He had sent Chris to find her and guide her home. That illustration of His love for her caused her to fall into Him in such a way that she knew she would never be the same.

Winter had finally faded and the cold ground thawed – another New England winter behind her. Life was becoming new at the inn. Robin was new.

One afternoon, not necessarily warm enough yet to be outdoors, Robin sat with Emma under the gazebo. Only the afternoon sun made it possible to remain for long.

"I have some news you might like," Emma said.

"I would love to hear some good news."

"I had a conversation with Jesus this morning."

Robin didn't speak. She knew what Emma was referring to and had seen it coming, but still she sat staring at her, a smile plastered on her face. Finally, she nodded and said, "I've been praying for that."

"I know you have, and I'm thankful you love me enough to keep after me."

"I do love you. To me, you're my family."

Tears filled Emma's eyes. "You're family to me, too."

Robin leaned in and hugged Emma. When she moved back in her seat, she said, "What did you say to Jesus?"

"I asked Him to forgive me for the things I've done. Honestly, I've asked before, but today I believed forgiveness was possible. I still have a long road ahead." Emma glanced out at the lake. "I still have so much to work through."

"At least now you are at the right place to work through it. You have the Wonderful Counselor. That's a game changer."

The following morning, Robin could think of little else but her conversation with Emma. She marveled that the Lord had used her to touch Emma's life, to help lead her toward Jesus. For the first time in many years, Robin felt she had made an impact on the kingdom, something that only spurred her on to do more.

Her classes were winding down, and because she had been so challenged and energized by them, she decided to take more than two in the upcoming fall. Her final math course was completed, a relief since that was her worst subject; and English was done. She was working toward a goal, a future for herself. This time the year before, Robin had still been stuck in the nightmare of her past. Now, she was indeed free to pursue a future, whatever the Lord intended. She was prepared to follow, one small step after another.

By late spring, reservations began pouring in, and in late May Tommy and Becky returned. Cabins filled and the guest rooms were booked for most of the summer. Chris's cabin, however, was never rented. Instead, when the weather was warm enough, Robin moved her things there to stay. No more was it about disturbing guests with her screams. Rather, it had become her shelter and sanctuary. Out of a sense of propriety, she slept in the other room, not Chris's. It felt wrong somehow to sleep where he had slept, intimate in a way she had never thought of him. In that place he was everywhere: his memory was there in his chair, his wisdom on the porch. God continued to use the things he had said and the questions he had asked to draw her near to Him.

The summer was the best she had known in many years, certainly more years than she had been at the lake. Before this transformation she had felt as if she were a part of the periphery of life, no longer involved in it. This year, though, there was an openness, a willingness to engage and invest in the lives of others.

Late one afternoon while Tommy was in town picking up fishing gear, Becky asked Robin if they could talk. They had spoken often on the phone while Becky was at school, so Robin knew that all was well with her and Tommy. You couldn't watch the two together and not see it. Tommy was so openly caring for Becky, that at times Robin was reminded of her own story of first love. Becky could hardly look at Tommy and not smile. They glowed together.

Robin was waiting on her cabin porch when Becky arrived to talk.

"Let's sit here and rock," Robin said, thinking of Chris and how this was where and how it all began for her.

Becky sat. "I'm still struggling. Not with Tommy, with me. I've given something away that I can never get back."

"You gave your virginity away, but not your purity." Robin stopped rocking. "I've thought about this since we talked last, Beck. You are pure only because of what Jesus has done for you, not because of the decisions you've made. You made a mistake and you regret it. Your mistake is forgiven. Now, you just have to learn how to forgive yourself. Forgive that girl who was reaching out in the wrong way for love."

Becky nodded. "I can look back to that summer and now see what I couldn't then. I just wanted to be loved. My closest friends all had great boyfriends. When Brad pretended to like me so much, I guess I just wanted to make sure I didn't lose him." She grinned. "Now that I see what I would have missed out on if things would have worked out with Brad, I'm so thankful for that horrible summer. I wouldn't miss out on this relationship with Tommy for the world."

"I thank God with you. What you have with Tommy is beautiful."

Becky didn't stay much longer, but after she was gone, Robin sensed that maybe she was catching an inkling of her purpose. Though not clear enough to pursue, there was something distant on the horizon, God's plan for her. Somehow, she would help people like Chris did. Nothing could give Robin more pleasure than that thought.

One afternoon, while sitting by the empty fireplace in the cabin, Robin was praying for Becky. In the past week she and Becky had talked on a few occasions. Becky was praying about her need to forgive herself and making progress. They had discussed how Becky's true desire was not for human love or one that any man could offer; her truest desire was to know the love of Jesus with such certainty that human love would forever pale in comparison.

Floodgates opened in Robin's own heart, bringing her face to face with a truth that took her back to seventh grade. Most precisely that was the moment she had sewn the very first stitch in the veil, separating herself from God. Mike became that stitch when she allowed him to be her god. She had called him her rock when Jesus should have been her Rock, deemed him her first love when Christ was to be first in her heart and in her choices. He had been her hero, when only One could ever truly save. How had she missed it all those years?

One morning in her normal course of reading and in the exact providential way of God's dealings with her, she read:

> "For although they knew God, they neither glorified him as God nor gave thanks to him, but their thinking became futile and their foolish hearts were darkened." (Romans 1:21)

Her thinking futile and her heart foolish – there was no better description of her for all those years. She had known God, or at least at a tender young age was growing to know Him, when Mike came into her life and stole all desire of knowing God more. In thinking back she recalled the difference in herself even at church. When Mike began going with her, her entire focus was on him, never what was being taught. If it wasn't on Mike, it was on what others thought of him. The envy of every girl she knew, Robin recalled how she reveled in being his the way they wished they were. Mike was her god. That realization rang over and over in her head until it became a pounding conviction she could hardly bear.

There came a day when the simplicity of the solution became apparent. Robin slid out of her healing chair, knelt, and made a commitment before the

Lord. Aloud, she prayed, "I will have no god before You." It was something so intense and personal that she spoke it over and over. Even when she finished saying it out loud, it chimed in her head and in her heart for hours to come. Something new happened that day. It was nothing she could identify externally, but internally there was a shift. Her heart suddenly belonged to Jesus in totality. *My Beloved is mine and I am His*, became the song of her heart.

By the end of July, nearing Chris's birthday, they all decided to have a huge celebration in his honor. The event was held outside and rivaled any Fourth of July party. It was not only an appropriate commemoration of his life, it was a way to bring all the guests together and share with them who Chris was. At the end of the party, Emma, Robin, Tommy, and Becky walked to his cabin, Tommy carrying a ladder. Each cabin had a wooden plaque over the porch with its name engraved into it. Tommy got up on the ladder to take the name *Willow* down and replaced it with *Chris's Cabin*. It was officially his, a gift from Emma. Robin was merely a guest there for the summer.

Once the summer season was officially over, life became slower for a time. When fall colors ramped up, so would the reservations again, but for the time being, it was a time to breathe and rest. Both Robin and Emma needed the break. The heat that year had been oppressive, so the slightly cooler temperatures drew them outdoors more often. While sitting on the covered porch drinking coffee together one September morning, Robin said, "There's something I've been sensing. I believe I should say it aloud just to hear how it sounds."

"By all means, say it aloud."

"I've forgiven Mike, of that there's no doubt. I've realized, though, that never telling him has been a mistake. The Lord has laid it on my heart that he needs to hear it. He needs it to finish healing."

"Will you call him?"

"I've tried. Several times, I've actually held the phone in my hand to call him, but I can never dial."

Emma hesitated, her eyes narrowing once she did speak. "What will you do then?"

"I'm supposed to go and see him face-to-face. I know it."

Beyond all shadow of a doubt, the Lord was moving her in that direction, and the mere thought of it caused her heart to beat clear up into her throat.

PART TWO

EIGHTEEN

After shifting into park, for a moment Robin sat looking at her former home. Pale yellow with white trim, the house looked like a little dollhouse, her mini version of the inn. She had chosen the color since the inn had been her favorite place growing up. They had put so much hard work into the house, making it their own, that even now the sight of it stirred up a sense of accomplishment mixed with a deeper sense of regret.

Nestled in a little valley between two hills with tall trees, the rear of the property was edged by farmland. There was a long gravel driveway that led from the two-lane highway up to the house, and she noticed on the drive up how well maintained the yard was.

With a sigh she gripped the steering wheel and prayed, "Lord, I don't know if I can go through with this," but she knew she would, no matter how difficult. Along with the sight before her came a flood of memories, good memories, ones that made her want to go back in time when they were so in love. Tears pooled in her eyes as she recalled walking up that set of steps with Mike, his holding Michael and shielding his eyes from the sun when they brought him home from the hospital. All the best things in her life had happened in this place – and all the worst.

Robin stepped from the car and walked up the stairs to knock on the door before she lost her nerve altogether. Though there was no answer, Mike's old blue truck was in the drive and she smelled burgers on the grill, so naturally, she moved down the stairs and toward the left side of the house. Not having an official back door, theirs was instead a side door. At the side of the house, she hesitated. There he was, standing over the grill flipping burgers. It was like old times. He wore a white t-shirt and jeans, and something about the sight made her want to turn and run. Instead, she moved closer.

"Knock, knock."

When Mike looked up and found Robin standing on the other side of the fence, his hand went limp and he dropped his spatula on the ground. For several seconds he just stood staring. Finally, he said, "Robin?"

"Hi." She walked nearer, stopping at the gate. After fumbling with and finally unhooking the latch, she continued on to the patio, where he stood staring at her. The look of surprise on his face made her smile.

"I was hoping to talk to you for a few minutes." When she noticed several burgers on the grill, she said, "But if you're expecting company, I can come back another time."

He stammered. "No, no. I was just making enough for the next few days. Are you hungry?" Mike looked at the grill. "The burgers are almost done." He bent and reached for the spatula. "Hold on a sec," he said and ran into the house.

***

Once inside, Mike tossed the dirty spatula in the sink and reached for another. Before turning to go back outside, he bent at the waist, grabbed his knees, and drew in a deep, steady breath and then let it out. This was the last thing he ever expected. He whispered, "God, how I still love her."

Dazed still by how cute she looked in her ratty old Panthers t-shirt and jeans, all he could think of was the year he had given her the shirt for her birthday. They were still in California then, and he had asked her dad to send it to him to replace the one she had spilled bleach on. Tears sprang to his eyes. That moment, when she had first slipped the shirt on, she was already pregnant with Mikey, but it was too early for them to know.

He swallowed hard and tried to collect himself enough to get back outside, praying, "Please forgive me for how I let You down, for how I let her down."

***

Mike was gone longer than Robin expected, so she had to wonder if it was a bad time. Maybe someone was inside waiting for him, a thought that caused mixed emotions to stir within her. When he stepped back outside, she said, "I don't want to keep you if you have company."

Mike looked back at the house and then at Robin. "No one's here." He smiled as he moved burgers onto the plate. "Will you join me?"

"I don't think so." Even as she said it her stomach grumbled. The smell of charcoal in the air reminded her that she hadn't eaten since breakfast, and it was well after one o'clock.

"Well, maybe one."

142

"That's better." Mike smiled at her and motioned toward the house. "I have everything ready inside."

Upon entering Robin scanned the room. It was her little home that she had made ready for her husband and her son. She looked around the kitchen and found it wasn't filled with bad memories of their final year as she would have expected. Instead, she was reminded of the joy they shared there. Bittersweet – that was what was stirring in her heart.

The cabinets were painted white and the floor was hardwood, original to the home. She noticed that Mike had installed a dishwasher. In her mind she could still envision what it looked like to have pots and pans and baby bottles drying on the counter, a memory that nearly sent her over the edge.

Robin turned and looked across the kitchen toward the hallway leading to the bedrooms. From where she stood she could see the outer edge of Michael's door. It was closed as it had been since the day they had packed away his things.

She tried to change her train of thought and took two plates from the cabinet. With them in hand she stood there staring at them, again spiraling down some deep hole of regret and missing what she once had. A million miles away, she traced her fingers along the edge of one and sighed. They were a wedding gift from Emma, as were most of her dishes.

Mike took a step closer. "You can have them if you want."

"No." She slid the plates back into the cabinet and blinked long and hard as she said, "Do you have paper plates? Then you won't have to clean up a mess."

"Right here." He handed her one.

Of course she noticed that he pulled them from the same cabinet she had originally chosen for paper plates. Why did something so trivial make tears sting her eyes?

Once they filled their plates, they moved outside to eat on the patio. There, she found she was able to recover from the onslaught of memories.

Small talk was easy for them. They knew so many people in common, and that seemed to be a safe enough topic. He caught her up on his family and she on hers.

"I got my old job back. I would have never dreamed it possible, but the sheriff fought for me. I had to go before the town council for a vote – the most unnerving thing I've ever done."

"I bet it was unanimous," she said with a soft smile. Mike was everyone's hero.

"How did you know?"

"Everyone loves you here, Mike."

Finished with half a burger remaining, Robin leaned back in her chair. "That was wonderful. Thank you."

When he pointed to the second half and arched his eyebrows, she knew what he wanted. "Go ahead. I'm full."

He had already eaten two burgers plus her half. She was astounded when he ate another with no bun. "You'll be sick."

Mike chuckled. "I still eat like a horse."

She smiled at that and watched him eat. It was hard not to notice how much bigger he was than when she saw him the year before. His chest was so broad that his t-shirt fit snugly, more so than she had ever seen in past years. Once, when he reached across the table for the mustard, his sleeve slid up over his massive bicep, exposing the bottom of the letters of his tattoo. It was her name, and she wondered what it must feel like to look at it every day now that they weren't together. Even just seeing the tip of it caused a knot to form in her stomach. From that point on she could hardly help but wonder what his new life was like, the one where she had no place.

He wore his ring still, something that truly surprised her. Once, while they were eating, she noticed how he looked at her left hand, his eyes lingering there for a few seconds. His expression caused her to nearly cry since all she could envision was his grin when he had slid her ring on her finger in the first place.

When Robin became quiet, Mike said, "If you're here about the house, I told you before, it's yours to sell or whatever you want to do with it. If you'll give me a little time, I'll check into a loan. Or if you want it back –"

She held her hand up to stop him. "No, I told you I'll never move back here. You keep the house. I'm glad you've been able to start a new life here and thankful that Trevor stepped in and took over the way he did."

"He was able to save up a down payment for his own house while he was here. I know he's really thankful for that. He's getting married in a few months to a great lady. She has a little girl from a previous marriage. He's crazy about them."

"Tell him I wish him the best."

"I will."

The moment had finally come, and no matter how difficult it seemed, she headed straight into it. "Look, Mike, the reason I came is that I wanted to tell you something. When you came to see me that day, you asked me to forgive you, and I never responded to that."

Mike leaned up in his chair, propped his elbows on his knees, and looked at her. "You don't owe me anything, and you sure didn't have to come all this way to say it."

"This is for me," she said. "I need to say this. I need you to know that I forgive you. It has taken a lot of soul searching and a whole lot of time with the Lord, but I do forgive you."

Tears filled his eyes, so he rubbed them and looked away.

"You were sick. I was broken. We never stood a chance." When he dropped his head and began to cry, she said, "I also need to ask you to forgive me for shooting you."

Her words brought with them vivid memories of the sight of him lying there, blood soaking through his shirt and pouring out onto the floor. At the recollection of it, she began to weep. "I still can't believe I did it. It's like some nightmare movie I watched. Your gun was just there, and the next thing I know I was pulling the trigger."

Mike moved from his chair and knelt before her. He hesitated at first, reaching for her and then withdrawing his hands, but then he reached again and took her face in his hands. "Don't you ever blame yourself. I nearly killed you that night." He began to cry even harder. "Baby, I saw the photos of what I did to you. Saying I'm sorry could never be enough. But as for you, don't ever regret it. That's the night Jesus finally got hold of me. I've never been the same since." He sat for a few seconds. "I'll never be the same."

"That night, I was so scared of dying." He stopped and shook his head. "Not as much of dying as I was of going to hell – which I knew I would, and I knew that wasn't where you would be. I think that's what scared me most."

With his hands still holding her face, he moved his thumbs to wipe the tears from beneath her eyes. "I have to tell you, and somehow I just know this deep down, if I hadn't called on Jesus that night, He would've let me die. I certainly deserved it."

His words completed the unraveling of a stitch. Memories of picking up that gun and walking into the kitchen haunted her as much as the beating that came before it. It was forgiveness that she needed. She had already been forgiven by God, and she had even learned to forgive herself, but ultimately, she longed for Mike's forgiveness. Able to look back with great pity on the girl who was so broken and filled with fear that she could be driven to such an act, this day would be her final release.

Though she hadn't planned to tell him, and it was something she never revealed, even to Chris, she felt led to say more. "After I shot you, I planned to turn the gun on myself. I remember thinking there was nothing left. After Michael and then what happened between us, I had nothing left to live for."

He wept as he had the day he knelt with her at the lake, loud racking sobs that made her only cry harder.

"But there you were, blood pouring out onto the kitchen floor, and I knew I couldn't let you die. So I called an ambulance and came back to you…"

She covered her face and for a moment was unable to go on.

"You don't have to do this," he whispered.

Reminiscent of the day they had buried Mikey, he wrapped his arms around her while they both sobbed. With her head resting on his shoulder and his cheek pressed against her hair, he stroked the back of her head.

Eventually, she raised her head, knowing she had to continue on. "I don't know how much you remember, but you were conscious, just barely. I kneeled down beside you and lifted your head into my lap. You kept telling me that you loved me and asked me not to leave you. I realized then I had to stay with you until help arrived. I could never leave you alone and so frightened.

"Next thing I knew, there were police and paramedics. People were shouting and it all became a blur. Once they put us into separate ambulances, no one would tell me anything about you. For the longest time I thought you must be dead."

Mike rested his head on her lap and continued to cry.

Robin stroked the back of Mike's head just as he had done hers, trying to comfort him. His hair was thick and coarse and reminded her she knew every inch of this man. This was her husband.

Several minutes passed until finally he stood and moved back to his chair. He wiped his face with a napkin and sat looking at her.

She whispered, "I'm so sorry that things turned out this way."

"I'm sorry too, Rob." He leaned in. "I destroyed us. There are no words to express how I regret all that I did to you."

For a minute they just sat looking at one another. This was what she needed, closure. That's what today was, a final period at the end of their story.

With a sense of new purpose, Robin said, "I should go now."

He stood and walked with her to the car. When he opened the car door, he said, "Have you gone to see Mikey yet?"

"No. That's where I'm headed now."

"Do you want me to drive you? I know it'll be difficult."

"I think I should go alone."

"I understand. So, where are you staying?"

"The Ramada."

"All the way in Raleigh?"

"Yes."

"Be careful on the drive back then."

He stood there shifting back and forth from foot to foot. Robin sensed he was deliberating if he should lean in to hug her. She considered it too but thought better of it. Her emotions were too raw still. If she did lean into him, she feared it would be too much for them both.

When she sat in the car, he squatted beside her.

"You okay?" she said as she reached out and stroked her hand along his unshaven cheek.

Mike only nodded. Finally, after swallowing hard to choke back his tears, he said, "I'm so grateful you came. This means everything."

"Thanks for letting me come and clear the air."

"You're welcome here anytime."

When she made no further comment, he sighed. "Take care."

"You, too, Mike."

NINETEEN

Mike stood and watched as Robin started the engine, made a loop around the tall oak near the driveway, and rolled away. That moment compared to the day they lowered Mikey's casket into the ground, the feeling of a forever goodbye. His chest felt hollow.

From the moment she had arrived until he closed the door of her car, Mike felt whole again, something he hadn't known since their son had died. The woman he now watched driving away was the one he had married, not the woman he knew in the aftermath of the death of their child. He was himself again, or more accurately, his new self. Both in their right minds and as healed as parents who lose a child can ever be, they almost reminded him of the early days before life crushed them.

He looked down at his ring. He had spent many an hour wondering about the man who ran to Robin's side that day at the lake and if she had married him. She wore no ring today, which gave him little comfort. She deserved to find happiness again. Mike was sure, too, that she noticed he still wore his. It was in with his personal belongings when he was released from prison. Since slipping it back on that day, he hadn't taken it off and had no intention to.

Not a day went by that he didn't think of Robin. He prayed for her, regretted the things he had done to her, and especially grieved her absence from his life. Always, he remembered the good things about her, and those memories were the source of great joy and great sorrow simultaneously.

Inside the house Mike went and stood before Michael's closed door. Though he entered occasionally, it was usually only to dust the furniture. Each time he did, he found the air to be too heavy to breathe. Today he turned the knob, pushed the door open, and stood in the doorway without going fully into the room. For the most part, all his son's things were packed away upstairs. All that remained in the blue room was the crib, dresser, and a rocking chair sitting beside the window.

The day Michael died, Robin had called him, hysterical, saying he wasn't breathing. Mike beat the paramedics to the house, and this is where he found her, holding their dead baby in her arms, rocking him. A part of her died too that day, and for him, each day became a struggle to hold on to the one thing he had left, his wife. When Robin continued to slip farther and farther away from him, for Mike, the most alarming sense of resentment set in.

"God, forgive me for how much I hated You."

Mike had said it a million times, and deep down he knew he was forgiven, but anytime a memory such as this stirred him, he reminded the Lord of his regret. If only he had known Jesus then, Mike would have healed and been able to help his wife heal. Instead, he had battled God and lost.

Mike sat in his truck at the cemetery, debating whether or not he should leave. He was parked beside Robin's rental car. Since he had waited more than an hour before leaving home, he assumed she would be gone by the time he arrived. The fact that she was still out in the cemetery and it was getting so close to dark concerned him. Though he didn't want to interrupt her, he made his way to Mikey's graveside anyway to check on her.

When he was near enough to see her, he stood off in the distance and watched her. How many times had he done this very thing? After Mikey died, she came faithfully. It took some time for him to realize just how often, but after a week or two, he discovered she was going every day. Often, on his lunch break, he would drive out, knowing he would find her there. He never approached her, but he watched her, concerned that she may never make it back to him. It was after the first two months that he began falling to pieces along with her, never sure which was worse, losing his son or watching his wife come undone. From there forward he had felt as if he was falling down some giant hole with no bottom to it.

***

Robin caught sight of Mike and motioned for him. His hesitance as he walked toward her was obvious.

"I'm sorry. I thought you would be gone, or I would've never come."

She was sitting on the grass with her knees bent up to her chest, hugging her legs.

"It's okay. I didn't realize I would be here so long either."

He sat near but not too near her. "I feel guilty when I leave."

She turned to him and nodded. "That's exactly what I feel, like I'm leaving him here all alone. I can't make myself stand up." Tears sprang to her eyes, so she rubbed them away with the sleeve of her shirt.

Her son wasn't there in that grave but in heaven. This was just a place where his little body rested. Still, to stand up and walk away made her feel as if she were abandoning him.

After he died she had come to sit beside his grave nearly every day. Mike never knew. She would wait until he was gone to work, and with nothing at home to give her purpose anymore, she would drive out and spend hours on end. When she finally accepted the job at the car dealer, she reduced her trips to the weekends. It was a small step toward moving forward, or at least she had thought so at the time.

Mike said, "You and I are the only ones who can understand this grief. I know other parents grieve lost children, but I mean him, Michael. No one else can understand what it feels like to sit here by his grave, knowing we will never see him again." He reached out and rubbed his hand across her back. "I've been here so many times this past year and each time I wonder, will it ever stop hurting this bad? Today is the first day it doesn't hurt quite as much. I think maybe because you're here, and I know that you share this with me." With a sad smile, he looked at her. "Does that make sense?"

"Yes, I think it does."

He took her hand, lifted it to his lips, and kissed her knuckle. His voice broke as he said, "I'm so sorry I couldn't help you through it. I was never sure what to say or do or how to make it better for you."

"We both did the best we could with what we had at the time."

Without looking at him, she whispered, "I never napped. I can't for the life of me remember why I took a nap that day."

"Don't do that, Rob. It was never your fault."

"If I had been awake, I would've known something was wrong."

"If you had been awake, you would have been doing laundry or cleaning. You would have thought he was sleeping. He always slept well. You can't possibly blame yourself."

After a moment, he said, "Come to think of it, you were up, off and on during the night. That's why you took a nap."

"Why?" She couldn't remember.

"I don't know. You just couldn't sleep."

She would always wonder. How could she have been asleep while her baby needed her?

"I know I said a lot of horrible things when I was drinking, but I need you to know that I never blamed you. It was never you. I was angry at God." He reached for her and pulled her closer to him. "I'll never figure it out, why He took our son. Back then, I was convinced it was because of me, because of…"

When he looked away, she said, "Because of what?"

He shook his head and wouldn't look at her.

Though she sensed he wanted to say something more, she didn't press him.

When he remained quiet, she said, "This one place is where I stay stuck. I've tried and tried to get past it. I've found my way out of the darkness in so many areas, but this, this still envelops me. It's the one stitch I can't seem to unravel."

Mike nodded. "This was the beginning of my undoing, and my only way to reconcile it is to believe God is good, even when He doesn't show up and save a baby."

"I've finally come to believe that, too. But it's been a long time in coming." Chris's entrance into her life helped her to see that.

"I met with a counselor, and he gave me this one thing, this way of remembering that has helped. He showed me that I was clinging to Michael's death rather than the love I have for him. So now, I try to remember the good things, the sweet little baby he was. Like, I loved how he would rub my chest while he was nursing. It must have been soothing for him."

She was warmed by the memory of it. "Do you remember how his eyes would roll back in his head and he could barely stay awake long enough to finish?"

"Of course I remember. I was thinking about that just after you left."

Mike sat close, with no space between them, and draped his arm around her and rested his hand on her leg. He gave her a slight squeeze. "He sure was a good baby."

Robin nodded, knowing she was talking about her son with the one other person who knew him and loved him as she did.

"I'll have to pray about what you said, if I'm clinging to his life or death. It's probably a mixture of both." He sat for a moment and then said, "Truth is, I rarely allow myself to think of him because of the pain and regret his memory brings. I guess that's my answer."

A moment passed. Mike turned to face her. "Know what this is?"

The look on his face was so tender and sweet, tears sprang to her eyes again. "What?"

"A holy moment, like God is physically present here with us. I've known several such occasions since that night, but this is by far the best."

"I feel Him too. It's what we both needed."

They sat for a while longer in this way, together, reminiscing about their son. At one point Robin considered how the Lord had prompted her to make the trip in the first place. He knew it was exactly what she needed to begin to live again. Most likely, it was the same with Mike. Still, her future was a mystery to her, but she had no doubt that God had good planned for her and Mike, too. This would be a crucial step for both of them to finally heal.

They repeated their earlier goodbyes as Mike stood with Robin by her car. Before she could open the door, though, he placed his hand on the glass, preventing her from opening it.

"Can I have a hug?" His voice was soft.

"That's easy enough." She wrapped her arms around his waist and rested her head on his chest. It felt just like she knew it would. His heart was pounding hard and strong in her ear, something she found to be especially sweet. For as long as she could remember, she had affected him that way. The smell of him was familiar and triggered memories of who they used to be and how they once held to one another with no intention of ever letting go. To remember them – who they used to be – caused a stirring deep within her belly, something she could scarcely identify. If she allowed herself to give it a name, she would call it a distant longing for that lost love.

With Robin nestled in his arms, Mike squeezed her, pressed his lips to the top of her head, and gave her a long kiss.

Robin smiled at that, at the fact that he was doing so as if in secret. How many hundreds of times had he done that over the years? Being more than a foot taller than her, it was where he could most easily reach. Of all the moments they had shared this day, this one was by far the most precious.

***

The following morning, dressed early, Mike made the trip to Raleigh. He had spent most of the night awake, thinking of Robin and all that had transpired the day before. Finally, by sunrise, he had found himself sitting at the kitchen table drafting a letter, actually, many drafts of a letter, to her. She had said she was staying at the Ramada, so he had to assume it would be the one nearest the airport. He would try delivering it there.

He found her rental car in the parking lot as he had hoped and went inside the hotel. Mike approached the only clerk on duty.

"I need to drop this off for Robin McGarrett. She should be checking out this morning."

The clerk began typing. "I don't have a McGarrett registered," he said and offered no further help.

Mike's heart plummeted. He was sure the car was hers.

"What about Jacobs? She may be registered under Jacobs."

He typed again. "Yes, we have a Robin Jacobs."

Since the man didn't seem helpful, Mike towered over him and warned him. "Look, I'm leaving this here for her, and I'm holding you personally responsible for making sure she gets it. Do you understand?"

Eyes growing larger by the second, the clerk said, "Yes, sir. I'll hand it to her personally."

Mike sat in his truck and watched Robin exit the hotel with his letter in hand. After she loaded her bag into the trunk, she got in her car and opened the letter. She smiled; he was sure. When she pulled out of the parking lot, he sat there a minute longer, realizing if she found him watching her it might seem kind of creepy. At that, he could only laugh at himself and admit, it probably was pretty creepy.

***

Robin's flight was delayed, and the drive back to the inn was long. By the time she reached home, she was in no mood to field Emma's questions. After a brief summary of her trip, she headed down to Chris's cabin to think – and to read Mike's letter again.

Though it was mid-September, the weather was still unseasonably warm. In some parts of the state, there was a touch of fall color arriving, but at the lake it was still a ways away. Each year, she held on to every last trace of summer, dreading the changing of the seasons. Though fall was magnificent, another New England winter wasn't something she looked forward to with enthusiasm. Once the real cold set in, she would move back up to the main house with Emma, but for as long as she could, she would stay where she felt closest to God.

Robin sat on the porch and inspected the envelope again. It was addressed to Robin McGarrett. Since her arrival in New Hampshire, she had taken back her maiden name. Even prior to having divorce papers drawn up, she signed her name as Robin Jacobs since the sight of Mike's name in print was so devastating for her. Today, seeing Mike's name there was another reminder of how much had changed over the years. She was a lifetime away from that campfire and burnt marshmallow.

With a slight smile, she slid the single sheet of paper from the envelope and scanned his writing. How many letters had she read and re-read when he was overseas? During the two and a half years they were apart, they lived and loved through their letters. From telling the most trivial details of their day to sharing the deepest loneliness each was experiencing, both hung onto every word the other would write. His letters were all that got her through each deployment. She had them still, tucked away in a box at the bottom of the chest in the spare room, untouched for years.

> Dear Robin,
>
> Words can never express my gratitude. The fact that you forgive me is a reminder to me of God's grace. The fact that you felt you needed to be forgiven reminds me of your tenderness. After you left I realized that in all the arguing I did that you didn't owe me an apology, I never said these words to you – I forgive you. I always did. Just as I needed to hear you say those words, if what you need is to hear them, then I'll say them again. I forgive you.
>
> I know our early life together is now a lifetime away, but to sit and talk with you was proof that it actually did exist once. Sometimes, I wonder if things really were as I remember them to be. I ask myself, were the good years really that good? Now I know.
>
> What I've found most difficult is that the one person who was my best friend all those years was just gone one day. Even though we may no longer be friends in the normal sense of the word, while you were here I felt that I had my best friend back. I've missed simply talking to you.
>
> When I got home last night, I realized I left the food out, so there went my leftovers. Nothing about yesterday turned out as I expected, and I can honestly say, for someone who never much liked surprises, yesterday was a great day.
>
> I'm glad you are settled and happy where you are. You deserve all the happiness in the world. It's what I pray for you each and every day without fail.
>
> I hope you don't mind that I'm bringing this letter to you. So as much as I feel like a stalker, I'll try the airport Ramada and look for your car.
>
> Well, I have an hour drive ahead to find you, so I'll close.
>
> Thanks again and again.
>
> Mike

Robin had re-read the letter once on the plane and again this time. Because she knew him as well as she did, she knew he had agonized over every word. His letters from Afghanistan were frequent but brief. He wrote something to her nearly every day and would let them build into a few pages before sending them. So for him this was a fairly long letter.

She smiled and wondered if she should write in return.

154

TWENTY

A week passed after Robin's visit, and for the life of him, Mike couldn't get back into the normal groove of things. It was as if he walked around in a daze. Work was a good distraction, and the time he spent volunteering helped, but being at home caused him to recount their conversation over and over. For hours on end he would sit on the patio and imagine her sitting there, hearing in his heart the words she had spoken. Many nights, long into the night, he would sit and look at the empty chair where she had cried, and he prayed for her.

After spending the morning at his mother's place, mowing and working on odd jobs, Mike was heading home to mow his own yard. He still hadn't told his mother about Robin's visit and wasn't sure if he ever would. Somehow, that time together was so personal, it seemed nearly sacred to him. He didn't even want to open up the conversation with her. No telling what she would say, nothing encouraging, to be sure.

He pulled into the drive just far enough that his tail end was out of the road and stopped. At the mailbox he opened the door and stood frozen. There, on top of the stack was a letter from Robin. Even though there was no return address, he recognized her handwriting. He looked at it for a few seconds, unable to open it. With a broad smile on his face, he went back to the truck and drove on up to the house. He took the letter and sat on the porch.

> Dear Mike,
> Thank you for your thank you, but no thanks are necessary.

He smiled at her words. When he was overseas, he could usually expect some sort of silly opening. Though not at all prepared for it this time, it made his heart warm.

> Thank you for so graciously offering your forgiveness. I'm sure it's not often that people in our unusual circumstance force apologies on one another. Nothing has ever been usual for us.

Sorry about your burgers. It was the best I've had in some time. If I had known you cared so little about them, I would have smuggled them out in my pocket.

And I agree – it was nice to talk again as friends. I've missed that, too.

I wanted to tell you, I really am glad that you were able to get back on at the sheriff's department. For as long as I can recall, you've wanted to be a cop. I remember all the way back to ninth grade and the career fair. We all had to make a display of what we wanted to be. Yours was all about police work. I should know: I did most of your poster board, and you're very welcome.

Your letter was a pleasant surprise – not stalkerish at all.

Speaking of surprises, when I came home, Emma told me she'll be baptized next Sunday. I don't think I told you that she's been going to church with me for some time now. For as many years as I've been here, she has been closed off to the things of God. It wasn't until last summer that she agreed to go. She was saved in April but hasn't felt ready to be baptized yet. So pray for her.

Well, I should close now. We have weekend guests due soon, and I have some last-minute things to do. Things are slow now during the week, but weekends will still be busy.

Have a good week and stay safe.

Robin

For a moment he was taken back in time. That was exactly how she wrote when he was overseas, answering paragraph by paragraph. He scanned her letter again and found what he was looking for. One thing he was unable to get off his mind was the career fair. He tried to remember what she had done her display on but couldn't recall. After reading the letter through again, he was determined to figure it out.

Several days later, his mind was still occupied with the things she said. Her words tumbled over and over in his head. She even agreed it was nice to talk as friends. Certainly, he was overanalyzing it. Mostly, though, he kept wondering if she might welcome another letter.

Finally, at the one-week point, the question about the career fair began to bother him again. No matter how hard he tried, he couldn't remember what she wanted to be. He had racked his brain to try to recollect. Eventually he concluded he may have never known. That disturbed him even more. How could he have been with her so many years and not known or cared what she dreamed of becoming? Was he so caught up in his own dreams that he overlooked hers?

Once his hope for a football scholarship was shot, there was no money for college, so he joined the Marines. Besides serving his country, he knew it would give him money for his education. He planned to go to school when they moved back home from Pendleton, but once they were back in Whitley, he was able to get on as a deputy. Even without a degree, they hired him, a benefit to small town life and knowing the right people. Things seemed to fall into place for him, and she was right there beside him every step of the way.

He thought back with new appreciation. Robin was behind him at each stage of a hope or dream. Whether it was training for football, shipping out to war, or spending nights alone that first year he was on the job, she was always there rooting for him. But what did she want to do and be, and why did he never even try to find out?

Early Monday morning just after the sun had risen, Mike began to write.

> Hey, Rob –
> First, and most importantly, I think I would've noticed you smuggling the burgers out in your pocket. I'm a trained professional. I have an eye for that sort of thing. Actually, I have you to thank for my career. Without that poster board at the career fair, I most certainly would never have become the fine officer I am today. So I thank you, indeed.
> You know, I've been racking my brain this week trying to figure something out. During the career fair, what did you do your display on? What did you want to be? Sorry that I'm taking a slight turn toward the serious, but I have to say, I can't for the life of me remember. I think maybe I was so caught up in what I wanted to be that I never asked you. I know it's a little late, but I would really like to know.
> Speaking of surprises again, I'm so glad to hear about Emma. I may be able to top that one, though. My mom went to church with me Sunday. I have no idea why. She just showed up. You should have seen the looks on the faces in the church that morning. You know my mom; she wasn't fazed. She finished her cigarette on the porch and walked right in like she owned the place. It was weird and funny, but really nice, too. So pray for her.
> Glad to hear things are busy. That's a good thing, right?
> Will stay safe, and you do the same.
> Mike

***

Robin had spent the entire day with Emma but was glad to have a few minutes alone. It was Emma who had checked the mail that day, so when handing the letter from Mike to her, she wore a deep scowl on her face. Who could blame her really? What Emma had witnessed when Robin arrived all those years ago was bound to set her at odds with Mike for good. The pieces of Robin's heart had been scattered about. It was Emma who had begun to pick them up and help her to put her life back together again. Emma knew firsthand what Mike was capable of.

No matter Emma's feelings about it, upon receiving another envelope with his handwriting, Robin found she wanted nothing more than to hear from Mike. It was as he had implied in his first letter: you can't be best friends with someone so long without a tremendous gap emerging in their absence. He got her jokes and she got his. She shared a history with him she could never have with another living soul. When Emma handed the letter to her, she had tried to act as if it was no big deal.

Alone in her cabin, Robin started a fire and sat in Chris's chair to read the letter. The words, "Hey, Rob," caused her to stop reading altogether. She closed her eyes and fought back the urge to cry. There was a lump in her throat, and she swallowed hard to try to clear it. From early on that was his usual greeting. Even in the moment, she could hear his voice ringing in her head. "Hey, Rob." Finally, she continued on with his letter.

His trained eye – that was funny and caused her to giggle aloud. Then she came to his question about what she wanted to be back in ninth grade. Though he could have never known its impact, it caused her to weep. At no time was he caught up in himself. He included her in every aspect of his life. The truth was, and she could understand how he might have missed it, she wanted to be exactly what she was – his.

Robin moved to the edge of her seat and gazed into the fire, lost in the memories of who they once were.

From the moment they had begun dating, she wanted to be his wife and the mother of his children. No one ever believed they would stay together throughout school. She knew, though, and so did he. Within weeks of the campfire, they started talking about a future. At first her parents thought it a crush, one that would pass. It took at least two years before they became too worried, then worry became acceptance. When the two decided to marry at such a young age, no one, especially her parents, was surprised by it. They loved Mike; everyone did.

She read his question again, knowing she would never be able to respond to it. It was something too painful for both of them.

Robin spent all week thinking about Mike's letter, and though wanting to reply, she put it off for another week. It was similar to eating ice cream. At first you are enjoying it, until you get that pounding in your head – brain freeze. She had heart freeze. Certainly, she enjoyed his letters. Before he was ripped away from her, he was the foundation of her life and existence. While she now understood how unhealthy that was, it was a fact, so for him to be gone left a tremendous void in her life. Long before the night they had last seen each other, he was gone. Nearly at the first drink she had lost him, and she had missed him every moment since he became that stranger.

***

Mike sat alone in a booth at the diner staring at the full plate of food in front of him. For the first time in as long as he could remember, he found he had no appetite. Since he hadn't received a response from Robin in nearly three weeks, he had to assume their correspondence was over. In constant prayer, he thanked God for the one thoughtful letter she had sent. When viewing things in proper context, he could expect no more.

"You seem miles away."

He hadn't noticed her approach, so when Shelly slid into the booth across from him, Mike looked up at her and grimaced. Always uneasy in her presence, he opted not to respond. Newly divorced, she had made it a point to let him know on several occasions. It was obvious she had set her sights on him since every time he turned around she was there. Even at the gym, she had begun going at the same time he did, and while he tried to avoid her, she was everywhere.

"I was just leaving." He reached for the check, but when he did she placed her hand on his.

"Don't you ever get lonesome out there all alone?"

The way she looked at him conveyed her real intentions. In that moment he realized that she would show up at his house sooner or later if he failed to put a stop to this now. The last thing he needed was her out there with him alone. Although he trusted himself fine, he didn't trust her at all.

He thought of her birthday party all those years before. Though he never told Robin, it was his first time to drink, and that day he had drunk way more than he should have. By the time they got to the party, having been drinking since midday, he was three sheets to the wind. While not passing out drunk, he felt unlike himself. So when Shelly had come on to him and he responded as he had, it wasn't what it seemed to her. Shelly thought he was interested in her, but truthfully, the entire time he was with her, he was envisioning Robin. They had gone no further than kissing in all the years they had dated, so when tempted that way, combined with the effects of the alcohol, he lost himself in the moment. By nine o'clock he was throwing up, mainly due to regret over his actions and the fact that he might possibly lose Robin because of it.

Mike pulled his hand from beneath Shelly's. "As a matter of fact, I don't. I'm content just as I am. So let me be up front with you; I am not looking for a relationship."

With eyes narrowed, she bit at her lower lip and whispered, "Who said anything about a relationship?"

Her desperation was as sad as it was pathetic, but he had no intention of allowing a door of possibility to remain open. Mike leaned in to ensure no one would overhear. "I said no seventeen years ago, and the answer is still no."

He was referring to her proposition at the bonfire the night he had met Robin. What Shelly had suggested they do for seven minutes was downright filthy for kids that age.

Shelly stood. "Yeah, I guess there's no accounting for taste. How'd that work out for ya, Mike? Where's your precious Robin now?" A little louder, she said, "If you're still pining away for her after all she has done to you, then God help you."

While watching her leave, Mike realized how much he must have hurt her. Though not his intention, he knew he had to be firm and clear. An apology crossed his mind, but he suspected that if he acknowledged her at all, he would only be opening the door for more trouble. He considered her words, pining away, and admitted the truth of them. For years he had and for life he would. And what did she mean when she said after all Robin had done to him?

Once home, Mike went through the same routine he had over the past weeks. This time, though, instead of disappointment awaiting him, inside the mailbox was a letter from Robin. "Thank you, Lord," he whispered aloud. He felt like a kid again, like when they first began "going together" – that was what they had called it. Her parents wouldn't allow her to date or even call it dating until they were sixteen. He smiled at the recollection of those times, of how they had passed notes back and forth during school since her dad wouldn't allow her to have a phone. In the hallway, at lunch, constantly, they wrote to each other throughout the day, just short notes, ones describing how boring a class was or how much they missed each other. Did he appreciate those notes then the way he did now? Maybe not as much, but even back then he would feel a thrill of excitement when she slipped a folded sheet of paper into his hand.

He sped up the driveway and came to an abrupt stop. Without bothering to put his truck into park, Mike tore into the envelope. With the small sheet of paper in hand, his heart plummeted when he read the brief note.

Hey Mike –
  Still praying for your mom.
  Robin

He sat for several minutes staring at the one sentence. What did he expect from her? Without a doubt she had been more than gracious as it was. Did he really believe that something could begin again after all that had happened? Sure, he secretly hoped, but deep down he had known better. Robin's willingness to reply to his first letter was more kindness than he deserved. Still, no matter how he tried to frame it or put it into proper perspective or talk himself out of being disappointed, the simple truth was he was devastated.

After a minute more he forced himself to climb out of the truck and then made his way into the house. Mike slumped into a chair and sat. Evening came and still he sat. Without energy even to get up and turn on a light, he just sat with the Lord, seeking comfort. His prayers were more for his wife than for himself. "God give her a better life than I offered her."

TWENTY-ONE

Stir crazy, Robin volunteered to go to the market. It had been more than a month since she received Mike's second letter, and she was beginning to believe she wouldn't hear from him again. That's what was constantly on her mind all morning and something she wouldn't dare talk to Emma about. It kept coming to mind: Maybe he had found a way to move on. She hoped so for his sake. Maybe someone new had come into the picture. That thought stung, but ultimately, she had to know it would happen.

Mike was handsome enough as a young man, but now she found him even more so as he had matured. What was once smooth and soft young man's skin had become more weathered and creased. When he smiled, tiny lines formed in the corners of his eyes. There was wisdom in them and newfound tenderness. Something about his presence altogether seemed more confident. It struck her – it was godliness – that was what made him so much more attractive. He had become a good and godly man, and it flowed from him in words and actions. He was so broad and beautiful, how could any woman not be attracted to him? She knew how life worked in Whitley and was certain he must be the object of much affection. No matter what comfort or connection with her former life his letters had brought her, she had to let him go.

Though she had said it was over, so far for her it hadn't been. Maybe that was why the Lord was so heavy-handed with her about going to see him personally, to allow some healing. He needed to be set free as much as she did. She could see it in his eyes when they were together on the patio. Of course she would give him that.

While making the turn into the market, Robin's phone slid from the console and onto the passenger seat. Once parked, she stretched over the gear shift to reach for it when something caught her eye. There, between the console and passenger seat was an envelope. She wedged her hand between the two and caught the paper with the tips of her fingers and dragged it upward. It was her last letter to Mike.

When she had taken his letter to the post office, she had a bundle of mail from the inn and had tossed it all over onto the passenger seat. She failed to notice one missing envelope when she carried the stack in. With a heavy sigh she tried to put this in perspective. She had waited two weeks before writing

162

and then a week later she had sent a simple note telling him she was praying for his mom. For all he knew she had only sent the one note. That was why he had never written back.

She decided to skip the market for the time being and rushed over to the post office. From her console, Robin pulled a small piece of paper and scribbled,

> Thankfully, I'm a wild driver. My phone went flying when I made a turn just now, and when I reached for it, I found this letter. Sorry this is so late.
> Robin Andretti

At the post office Robin purchased a blank envelope and tucked the misplaced letter and note inside. She handed the envelope to the clerk and silently prayed, "Please don't let him think I simply ignored his letter."

Back in the car she felt a stinging sense of conviction. The way she had taken her letter with the mail from the inn that day was, in a way, a form of deception. In truth, she hadn't wanted Emma to know that she was communicating with Mike on a regular basis. Though she hadn't fully come to understand her motives in keeping it a secret, she had some inkling of an idea. In one way it was Emma's disapproval of Mike that prevented Robin from being open about it. Prior to her visiting him, Emma had done nothing but discourage it. Her bitterness toward Mike was understandable, and no matter what Robin had said about the need to see him face to face, Emma tried to dissuade her.

Robin felt just as convicted over keeping the secret from her parents. She talked to them weekly. At any point she could have mentioned it. Their reaction couldn't be good, so she had chosen to remain quiet.

Another truth she had to admit to herself, part of her hesitation, was that she didn't want to be one of those women, the type who gets knocked around and then when her man comes around full of apologies, she goes back for more of the same. While she knew the circumstances were different, still, she feared appearing that way. It was something she was trying to work through. Its name, as difficult as it was to admit, was pride.

The fact was, she enjoyed having Mike back in her life. She loved seeing his handwriting and being able to envision him sitting there, choosing every word so carefully. She wanted to know what was happening in his life, even if it meant he would soon share something as painful as falling in love again. That thought made Robin sigh at the finality that would bring. After all the years apart and all the grief and pain, they could be no more than friends, but she wanted that, and she hoped he did, too.

Later, while putting groceries away, she realized she would have to be honest with Emma. No matter how she reacted, Robin was determined to keep the lines of communication open with Mike, and Emma would have to try to understand. It would likely run its course and eventually dwindle anyway, so what was the harm?

***

Mike served at the church more often recently. During the spring and summer, he had spent his Saturdays there, maintaining the lawn and whatever else needed to be done. Since fall was fully upon them, not as much was required of him. Still, he went and did odd jobs that other people avoided – anything to keep him out of the house.

After his release from prison, he had gone to church that first Sunday, Robin's church. At the time he considered it hers since when they were younger, his only motive in going had been to be with her. Then when they returned home from Pendleton, he had gone while she was pregnant and while Mikey was still alive. After that, though, he found any and every excuse to stay away. Other than Christmas and Easter, he stayed home and watched ball or worked around the house.

That first day, walking back in after five years in prison, he wasn't sure what to expect. What he did know was that God was leading him there, and while he fought it at first, the prompting was too strong to ignore. To his amazement he was welcomed by most everyone. It was certainly a God thing. A man with his history of abuse, especially against a woman who had grown up in their church, could hardly expect much of a welcome. There, though, he found a new family and had grown to love them more and more over time.

This day, having finished at the church early, Mike went home. He made the drive out of town not looking forward to a lonesome afternoon at home. After all that time he had stopped waiting and hoping for anything more from Robin, and finally, he was at peace with it. God had given him that peace. So this time, opening his mailbox, there was no expectation. Maybe that was what made the sight of her letter so much sweeter. His hand trembled as he reached for it, something that made him smile at himself. Back at his truck, he lowered the tailgate and sat there to read it. It was chilly out, but he barely noticed with such warmth stirring inside. Based on the bulk of the envelope, he could tell it was no single page inside. He tore into it and first opened the small piece of paper.

Mike smiled as he read the note explaining the missing letter. And her signature, Robin Andretti, made him laugh out loud. For years he had called her that. When they were out together he drove, having feared her getting pulled over for speeding with him in the car. A deputy with a reckless driving wife, how embarrassing would that have been?

He pulled out the page and began.

Hey Mike -

An eye for that sort of thing? Really? So while you were busy stuffing your face with half a cow, you think you would notice? I hate to say I doubt your detective skills, but my memory is not all that bad. I've seen you eat. You go to a faraway place, you and your food.

With that comment, he rested the letter on his lap, threw his head back, and chuckled. She had always given him a hard time about how much he ate – everyone did. No matter how much grief she gave him, though, she often said how much she loved to cook for him and watch him eat. He missed her cooking. That thought prompted him to close his eyes and swallow hard. He missed everything about her. In his mind when he read her words, he could hear her voice which served only to make him miss her all the more.

He continued reading.

Finally! My work is acknowledged. Though I've had no reason to make a poster board lately, I'm confident I still have the gift. As for mine back then, it was nothing to write home about. Actually, Bobby Taylor went before me and went on and on. So I never did mine, and Mr. Howell never noticed, probably bored to tears. Somehow, I dodged the bullet. So now, I guess innkeeper would be the answer.

Speaking of surprises again and again – that is a huge surprise! Your mom, really? I have to say, "And me of little faith," though I shouldn't have been. When God begins to touch a life, amazing things happen. I'm so happy, and I hope she continues to go with you. We both know she's lived a hard life, so if anyone needs Jesus, your mom does. I'll be praying for her.

Thinking back, all I can say is that she was kind to me. Though you and everyone else found her so difficult, we got along well. I was glad about that. Somewhere beneath that hard exterior, I saw something others didn't see. Maybe she saw something in me, too.

Okay, the cigarette thing kills me. Well, at least she put it out first. That proves there's a God. I can still see her now, eating dinner with a cigarette burning in the ashtray. She would stop and take a puff then continue eating. How can you not find that funny?

Things here are slower, on the downhill slide into winter. It has rained a lot – too much. I've been cooped up day after day. These next few months will drag on and on. At least I have Thanksgiving and Christmas to look forward to. My parents will fly in for Christmas, but I suppose Emma and I will spend Thanksgiving alone. Or possibly, we will be joined by a handsome veterinarian who has wooed and pursued Emma until she's finally on the verge of breaking. Will keep you posted.

Have a safe Halloween. I know that's when the crazies come out. Will you work that night?

Well, going to throw a log on the fire. Will be moving back up to the main house tomorrow. Too cold for a Southern girl.

Blessings to you!

Robin

He read it again and again. By the way she had asked questions, her letter opened the door for him to respond. In hers she was open and sweet and funny, everything she always was. He smiled. If nothing more ever came of this but a friendship restored, he would take it. This new whatever-it-was, was enough.

TWENTY-TWO

When Emma handed Robin Mike's letter, she sighed and gave her a look. "Do you think this is wise?"

"I don't know about wise, but I like hearing from Mike."

Emma was quiet for a moment. "I know you share a long history, but..." She just stopped and sighed again.

"I admit, I'm conflicted, but this feels like having a piece of my old self back."

"Just be careful, sweetie." Emma was about to walk off but stopped. "I can't help but worry about you. I saw the aftermath of what happened before."

Robin stood and watched Emma go. She hadn't needed the reminder and could only shake her head that Emma had felt the need to bring it up. That wasn't this Mike.

She went into the dining room and sat at a table by the wall of windows. What had been an overcast and gloomy day was taking a brighter turn. Before she could get the letter open, Emma walked to the table and sat a cup of steaming coffee before her.

"I thought you might enjoy this with your letter."

"Thanks."

"I'm sorry for what I said. I will just have to trust that you know what you're doing. But you can't fault me for caring, for worrying."

"I know you care. I'm glad you care."

Emma patted her cheek and left her alone to read.

> Dear Ms. Andretti,
>
> Half a cow? Whatever. It was two and a half burgers. The last one didn't count since there was no bun.
>
> I still don't cook much, and I'm so overdone with diner food. You know us cops: we do eat a lot of donuts, but what does the Good Book say? "Cop does not live by donut alone." I may be paraphrasing a bit.
>
> Okay, so you never did your presentation, but you still didn't remind me what it was about. Being an innkeeper now doesn't count. That's new news. Still, tell me more about that. What do

167

your days look like, summer and winter? And what did you mean you're moving back to the main house?

About my mom, so far not so good news. She hooked up with some guy and hasn't been back again. That's typical. I don't press her.

I was always surprised at the way she was with you. She was different, and of course she saw something special in you – everyone did. When everyone else, including me, judged her, you accepted her. That had to have meant something to her. I should have learned from you, and maybe things would've been better between her and me.

I can hardly believe that Thanksgiving is a week and a half away. The year will be over before we know it. It's turned out to be an exceptional year, though.

Robin stopped to take a sip of her coffee. His next questions were about the weather and how cold natured she was. Robin smiled when he said it was an exceptional year. It was for her, too. He didn't mention what he would do for Thanksgiving, so she speculated. In years past his mom had never had dinner at her house. While they were together, Mike had come to her house. From fifteen on they were together every year for Thanksgiving dinner. That first year was a hard year for him, the year his father went to prison.

Halloween was crazy for sure. I requested off work so I could serve at the church. I worked the caramel apple table, which come to find out wasn't the best assignment for someone with my appetite. Miss Allen said next year I can't work a food table. Know how you would always say, "You're gonna be sick, eating all that"? Well, it finally happened. I was so sick at my stomach that night and even through lunch the next day. In hindsight, I've determined eating seven caramel apples wasn't such a good idea. I wrote myself a reminder for next year. (Now is where you say, "I told you so.")

Remember to tell me about the move to the main house. Where were you before? A cabin, I guess?

Okay, Southern girl, stay warm and dry, and write back when you get a chance.

And Rob, I'm glad you wrote. Honestly, I thought maybe you were sending me a message by not sending me a message. If it ever gets to that point for you, please just say so. An empty mailbox is worse than knowing up front.

Blessings right back at ya,

Mike

Robin decided this was his best letter yet. He was open and funny, while in his prior letters she sensed his restraint, as if he feared saying the wrong thing. This time, he wrote as an old friend and didn't tiptoe around old subjects. She felt as if she were glowing, radiating sunshine right there in the dining room. His letters made her feel the same feelings as when they had written back and forth during his deployments. While reading them she rode the waves of the ocean, soaring high one minute, and at times his words took her heart to the very depths of despair.

Once she finished her coffee in her afterglow, she went into the kitchen for another cup and found Emma there.

"How was your letter?"

"It was sweet and kinda funny."

"Are you sure you know what you're doing?" Her tone was not disapproving, rather, more protective than anything.

"Not at all."

Robin took her letter and tucked it into her coat pocket. After bundling up she slipped her hat on and went down to the dock. No matter how cold it was, if it wasn't raining, she went there to pray. Besides the cabin, it was the place she felt closest to God. Each morning, while watching the sun come up, even if only from the warmth of the kitchen window, she was reminded of His faithfulness. Something she discovered, a revelation from Him that amazed her still, was that all that time she had felt so compelled to sit before the water and watch the sunrise, it was actually the Spirit drawing her back to Him. At night when she ran, it was the water she ran to. He is the Living Water. He was calling her to the depths with Him.

In the mornings only the sun could cause the shadows of the night to flee. He was the Son she looked for. Somehow, her physical world and what she ran toward was ever symbolic of her deepest spiritual longings. It was always Him. With eyes open to how relentlessly He pursued her, she had fallen helplessly and entirely in love with Him. Jesus was her love story, only she had missed it for the first thirty years of her life. Astonished He could love her so much and even more so that she was able to love Him with such a feeble heart, she looked out at the water and whispered, "I love because You first loved me."

The dock swayed with the current as Robin read Mike's letter again. Something in it disturbed her, and the more she read it the more troubled she became. She finally had to admit that she was jealous. There he was, living his life at her church in her home, and she was far away in practically the coldest place on earth. He was eating caramel apples until he was sick, and she had missed another fall festival. It was his home and his town, but it was no longer hers.

She knew she could never go back, not with the way things had ended there. The things they had said about her caused her cheeks to flush in humiliation still. Since no one knew of his history of abuse, that final night left the town dumbfounded. Her parents got her out of town without anyone seeing how battered and broken she was. It had been easier to run away than to stay and fight.

Within a few months she realized she had nothing there to go back to except Michael's grave, so she simply stayed in New Hampshire. It wasn't what she chose, rather where she landed, like a tornado had picked her up and flung her hundreds of miles away. She was the victim of a storm that destroyed her home and left her no place to return, a misplaced object.

Later that evening, Robin sat in the gathering room before the fireplace. Emma had gone up to bed, and the house was quiet. It was then she decided to answer Mike's letter.

She began first to reply to his "cop does not live by donut alone" statement until the word donut leapt off the page. Robin wondered why she hadn't noticed before. Did he think of its implications when he mentioned donuts? Something unusual and unsettling happened within her. There was a stirring inside she hadn't felt in many years, a longing for him unlike anything she had experienced since he was overseas. She set the paper aside, unable to continue on.

It would be days before she could finish. When she finally did, Robin took the letter to the post office and took great care as it slid into the blue box. No more mishaps with her letters.

TWENTY-THREE

It was Thanksgiving Day, and Mike was home alone. Although he had been invited to the homes of several families from church, he couldn't bring himself to go. A guy he met with regularly, a vet from Ft. Bragg, had invited him to his mother's house, too. That wouldn't be comfortable for him either. Instead, Mike would do what he had done the year before, sit around and watch football. He at least had a turkey sandwich, but that was the extent of his holiday festivities. Without family the day didn't mean so much. His brother had gone with his girlfriend to visit her family. Who knew where his mom was?

Unable to keep his mind on any game, he went and got Robin's letter out of his bedroom and sat in the recliner to read it again. The wait had been excruciating, but when it finally came he was amazed by its length and content. She was her but a totally different her, and he found he was so proud of the woman she had become. The things she said were so deep and meaningful. She had become a better version of herself without him. It was obvious: he had held her back all those years. Now, when looking back at the entirety of their lives together, it really was all about him. She was unable to remember what she wanted to be, likely because the focus was on him: what he wanted and what he dreamed of becoming. How could he have been so selfish?

> Dear Apple Glutton,
> Even as I write, I'm still laughing about the apples. Seriously, seven?
> I'll have to admit your "Cop does not live by donut alone" was good, actually, really funny. Good stand-up material, but don't quit your day job.
> Since I've seen you recently, I have to believe you are being fed and relatively well. I almost feel sorry for you, but not quite. I really believe in you. You can follow a recipe. Start at the top and work your way down. It's kind of satisfying to eat a meal you've prepared for yourself, one that doesn't come from a box. I can hardly imagine, though, that you could be tired of the diner's food. From what I remember, their food was good.

My presentation – hmm, I can't recall, but if it helps, I really don't want to be an innkeeper, well, maybe half and half. What I really would like is to become a counselor of some sort. I've been taking classes to try to finish my degree. I will someday, though I may be ninety-seven by then. But hey, old people can counsel, too.

I had a friend, Chris. He was here at the inn last year and helped me work through some difficult things. Although he passed away last year at this time, he left a lasting imprint on my life. It was he who led me back to God and toward forgiveness. Something he taught me will be part of how I help others.

During one of our first conversations, he talked about mending the veil. Though the veil was torn when Christ died, allowing us access to God, some people spend their lives trying to mend the veil so they don't have to see Him. In my case I did so stitch by stitch. Michael was among the first I suppose, then the things that happened between us. Though I once was open to God, as a result of all the pain, I shut Him out of my life. I want to work with people like that and help them to unmend the veil the way Chris helped me, stitch by stitch.

Some people when they are saved later on in life come right in and install a zipper. Some of this, the Lord has revealed to me through talking with Emma. When she was saved, she had complete access to God, but instead of seeking Him, immediately she began to hide from Him. There are things from her past that keep her from opening up to and trusting Jesus. I know the reality of being stuck there, which makes me think maybe God has me here for this very reason, for her. Just so you know, she's making progress, and not because of anything I'm doing but what He's doing through me. So that's what I want to be when I grow up, a counselor – I think.

What do my days look like? Now, they're dull and uneventful. I drink a lot of coffee and wonder why I'm jittery. We sometimes get online and look at warm beaches and swear we're going, though we probably never will. I have a women's group that meets on Tuesday evenings. That, I love. They are a great group of women, even if they do talk funny.

Summer here is fun and busy. We stay at full capacity through June, July, and early August. There are kids everywhere. I like that. Each and every day is different. I would think it's like your job in a way since you encounter different people and situations every day. There's nothing repetitive during the summer, which makes up for the drudgery of winter.

My move to the main house – no big news. I was staying in a cabin, but once colder weather arrived, I knew I couldn't survive by hauling in tons of firewood. I'm not exactly the lumberjack type. I still lean toward the girly side.

Hmm, some new guy? We will pray for your mom anyway. No, don't press her. You know that would only push her away. Give it time. I have to believe that seeing the change in you has to make her think twice about God. I saw the difference. I'm sure she does, too. Just love her. Lost people act lost. While I know how frustrated you get about the choices she makes, the simple truth is, she's just looking for Jesus. She doesn't know it, but that's the "thing" she keeps searching for. Let's just pray and pray. That's not the only thing we can do; it's the most powerful thing we can do. "The prayer of a righteous man is powerful and effective." You're a righteous man. Pray!

The vet is on schedule for T'giving. I can hardly wait to see Emma that day. Already, she's flittering around like a school girl. He's a widower with four grown children and ten grandchildren. I know I'm putting the cart before the horse when I say this, but I would sure like to see her fall for him.

The fall festival sounded fun. I miss those. I was at every one from the time I was a little girl until we moved to California.

What you said about if the time comes that we should stop writing – I would let you know. I would never just leave you hanging. I ask that you do the same. I realize there will come a time when someone special will enter your life, and when that happens, I would think she would feel uncomfortable with this. So we will keep that in mind.

I hope you have a wonderful Thanksgiving. Don't eat so much; you'll be sick. Haha.

With His love,
Robin

Mike sighed. When he had read the letter for the first time, his heart soared with every line, with every word even, until he got to the end. There will come a time... Though she didn't say as much on her side, when she assumed he would find someone special, she was likely preparing him for when she did. He could read between the lines and see she was setting the stage for that possibility. It nearly killed him to consider it, but had that not been his prayer for her, to find someone? Mike never entered the church without going to the altar and pleading for her happiness. She had been a tremendous wife to him, and someday she should have the opportunity to be a wife again and hopefully a mother. There might come a time for her but never for him.

Mike took her letter, went into the kitchen, and pulled some paper from the drawer.

Dear Counselor,

I asked you to share details of your life, and you did that. Thank you, and thank you for being my friend still.

Yes, I am being fed, just not as well. I eat out too much, and I know that's not good for me. I'm working out a lot and stay hungry 24/7. The new pastor at church, Tim, has been working out with me. We meet after work every night and even hit the gym some Saturdays. I'm pushing him, and in doing that, end up pushing myself, too. It relieves stress and clears my head after a long day. All that to say: that's the reason I'm the size I am. I've grown out of most of my clothes and had to – gulp, go shopping. It was dreadful, so traumatic, in fact, that I can hardly talk about it.

I've tried to cook a few times, and it turned out okay. Honestly, though, I just don't like it much; plus, I end up with too much food for just me, which means I eat too much.

This counselor thing, wow! I'm amazed at you. So why haven't you told me about school before now? Are you actually going, or are you doing it online? And what does it matter how old you are when you finish, as long as you finish? Rob – I'm really so proud of you. After reading your letter, I realize how much I held you back. I'm sorry about that, more so than I can express. Now, you seem to be able to fly.

I've wondered about the guy I saw there. He must have been Chris. I'm sorry you lost such a good friend, and I'm thankful for how much he helped you. His words are wise.

I installed the zipper. I've been thinking about this unmending the veil thing since reading your letter. In prison (and I'm sorry if this is too uncomfortable a subject for you) I really sought hard after God. Maybe it was my military background, but I had no trouble calling Him Lord. I got that, and a heart of obedience came without much effort. But there was one area where I simply could never connect, or maybe a better word is relate to Him. I could hardly see Him as my Father. I brought too much baggage, I guess.

Did it ever cross your mind that I was in the same prison as my dad? That's why my mom never came to visit. She couldn't bring herself to. I never saw him, but I thought about him often. I began to pray for him, and eventually, I learned to forgive him for how he treated my mom and Trevor and me. Now I can say with hindsight and the use of your terminology, the veil had been unmended. You can't imagine the freedom I feel. It began to reshape me. Now, I joyfully call God my Father. I needed one my whole life, and after all these years, He is mine.

Pursue this dream of counseling. Don't let it go. I'll pray for you.

I can hardly imagine you as a major coffee drinker. You never used to drink it at all. Hot chocolate – that I can see. Do you still have a sweet tooth? I do.

What are the warm places you dream about?

Tell me more about your women's study. What are you studying? Do you lead it? I ask for a reason. Tim has asked me to lead a men's group on Wednesday nights. So far, I haven't said yes. I feel way too inadequate. I can't imagine he would even ask me. I can't imagine anyone would come. They all know…

I just got this mental image of you in a red flannel shirt chopping wood. Ha! Funny. You are very girly indeed, but that isn't a bad thing.

Your insight about my mom is right on. I can see how broken she is now. When I remember how my dad knocked her around and then just up and left her, I feel a deeper level of compassion for her than I ever did. Occasionally, I remember a little more about her from when I was younger, like really young. There was a time when she was tender. It has been a really long time, though. You know, like she was with Mikey, she was like that with Trevor and me. It's in there somewhere.

How are things going with the vet? Any love connection as of yet? This is T'giving Day, so by the time you receive this, you can tell me how dinner went. Tell me the menu, too. I'll live vicariously through your stomach. I decided not to do the big dinner thing this year.

You said something about there coming a time… If that happens with you, please let me know. It's my greatest prayer that you find happiness. And I understand that, at that point, there will be no place for me in your life. I'm more than grateful for this friendship you're offering me. I certainly don't deserve it, and will never take it for granted. So for as long as you are willing, I would like to continue writing.

Love,
Mike

***

Robin stood on the dock shivering. It was barely above forty, and she was foolish to be standing out in the gusty wind. Rain was on the way, which would certainly add to the gloominess of the day. The day was not only overcast and dark, it was plain sad. Mike's letter was tucked in her coat pocket, and having read it so many times, she had no need to read it again to recall the sadness of it. Did he realize how poignant it was? His openness and sincerity gave her greater insight into the new man he had become, and along with that insight, came a longing to know him more.

Taken off guard by his story of his father, she grieved again for him, just as she had all those years ago. They had been together just over two years when his father killed a man during a bar fight and was sentenced to life in prison. He was an alcoholic, an abuser, and a womanizer. He had been brutal to Mike's mom and to both boys. Finally, he left when Trevor was ten and Mike was twelve. From that time on Mike was mostly in charge of Trevor as their mom began an endless pursuit of men. At fourteen Mike went to work at his uncle's feed store and continued to work there until he left for the Marines.

His story was sad, the early one and then what happened to them after Michael, but in between the two stories, he thought he had made it out of the turmoil and chaos. So did she.

Robin braced herself against the cold and made the trip back to the house. All the way up the stairs, she thought of how he had said he felt inadequate to lead a class. Then he had said, "They all know." She wondered what that must feel like for him. What was it like to live in such a small town where everyone knows something so ugly about you? Sure, she had experienced a small taste of it, but she had fled. Mike, though, was able to go back after prison and carve out a new life for himself in spite of it all.

Because she knew the human heart and how the enemy tries to make you second guess your every move, especially in matters of service, she was certain his struggle was a great one. So her prayer for him was that God would give him wisdom and courage to do what He called him to do, if that was indeed His call to lead the class.

She stopped and turned back to face the water. Tears stung her eyes as she imagined him alone on Thanksgiving Day. While she, Emma, and Stan had laughed and ate until their bellies hurt, Mike was there alone, in their home.

This wasn't the first stirring, but it was the most intense and painful of her heart's longing to go home. No matter what she felt, how could she? There was something about that town that felt so alienating now.

Later that evening, Robin began a note that would take her but a moment.

> Dear Inadequate,
> You are inadequate for the task. When we are weak, He is strong. What does He say? Has He told you to lead this class? If

so, what is the verse He used to speak to you? If He has given you one to stand on, then don't doubt – do.

Your friend still and always,
Robin

***

Mike read Robin's brief note and was amazed at the simplicity of it. He had heard and he did know.

Dear Robin,

You sound just like a counselor. Yes, I am inadequate, but He isn't. Thank you for the reminder. He says so. Without doubt, He has told me to feed His sheep. What a humbling thought.

Pray for me.
Mike

TWENTY-FOUR

The day after her note, Mike received another envelope. He sat in his patrol car, having just eaten lunch, and read it again, planning his responses. He found that the more they wrote the more he missed her. Seems it should be the other way around. Somehow, though, as she shared her daily life through her letters, he was jealous that he wasn't able to see those things in person, that he was unable to live them with her. He knew the details of her life would always be secondhand. Even so, it was enough.

For as long as he had known her, she was spiritual. Now, though, she was such a godly woman. It was as if she had taken all the things she knew in her head before and moved them down into her heart. It was application. She had applied her lifetime of church to life and hearts, and because of it she would make a great counselor.

Still, in her letters she was as funny, maybe more so, than she ever was. When he read her words, he knew exactly where to apply sarcasm and teasing. Then when her tone turned to one of tenderness, he could hear her sweet voice saying the words. She turned him into a big pile of mush, and oddly enough, he didn't mind one bit.

> Dear Mike,
> I didn't realize you had a new preacher. What happened to Brother Billy? Tell me more about Tim. I think it's cool that you are working out together. Is he as into it as you are, or are you forcing him?
> Me, I try my best to avoid that kind of exercise. I have a gym allergy. I like to walk and bike and other outdoorsy things when it's warm. No gym for me, thanks.
> Shopping? What have you done with Mike?
> I should have been a fly on the wall while you were cooking. Yes, you can grill – well established, but I would like to see you make a casserole. Now that I think about it, what do you take to covered-dish dinners? Are you one of those show-up-empty-handed guys, or a store-bought-cookie guy?
> I'm taking online courses. I only take two per semester, which is plenty. I just started in January, so I have forever to go.

Mike – what you said, you never held me back, never. I was content as things were. Yes, now there's something new, but you never stood in the way of it. It simply wasn't my desire then. As for flying, I don't know about that. It still seems like a faraway dream, a place I'm not sure I'll ever reach.

Thank you for sharing your story with me. You have never talked much about your dad, but when you did, I knew how much it hurt you. I'm so grateful to God for your healing and forgiveness. You are free!

I'm glad for you that you've found your Father. Because my dad was so great that wasn't an area where I struggled as much. Who knows, maybe I did in some ways. Now that I think about it, because I did have such a good dad, I didn't feel as much of a need for God as Father. It was merely a title. Over the course of this year, though, I have found Him to be the Father who took me into His lap and consoled me. Hey! We have the same Father!

It did cross my mind about your dad being there, and I did wonder if the two of you ever saw each other. Have you seen him since you've been out? I suppose that would be hard to do. Your forgiveness may begin to reshape him, too.

Thank you for your prayers, and I will continue to pursue this. Honestly, I'm not sure if I'm supposed to be a formal counselor, or maybe it'll be something I use as ministry at church. I'm open to His leading. I think of the verse in Isaiah that says, "Whether you turn to the right or the left, your ears will hear a voice behind you, saying, 'This is the way; walk in it.' " I'm beginning to hear God more and more, and I understand His leading in a way I never used to. So finally, I feel safe in following as I feel led. I try not to stress about what's up ahead.

Coffee? Yes, and too much of it. I don't know, I tried a cup one day and thought, "Hey, is this what I've been missing all these years?" So now, I'm trying to make up for lost time. I do switch to decaf later in the day; but still, I drink it and drink it until my eyes are floating.

Do I still have a sweet tooth? Absolutely! I try not to bake much because I'll eat until I'm sick. (I know - the hypocrisy of it.) When we have guests, we have sweets and pastries for breakfast, and I find it difficult to say no. I try to stick with proteins since I know that sweets make me feel as if I'm running on empty by ten.

The places I dream about are anywhere warm and sandy. Maybe someday I'll come there to the beach. We used to go to Carolina Beach on vacation when I was a little girl. I have no idea why we stopped, but I can't recall going after I was about nine.

My women's study is still going strong. We meet here because we have so much room, but no, I don't lead it. We've recently done a study on Jonah and just began one about contentment. Since I replied already about your study, I simply can't wait to hear what you decide. Keep me posted. The ones who are supposed to be there will come. You can't allow those whispers to prevent you from obeying.

While I don't own a red flannel shirt, I can see how the image in your head would make you laugh until you cry.

Your mom and Michael, that was sweet. You're right. She was different when she held him. Maybe she could look back and see you before things got so bad between her and your dad. There is something special inside of her, but I doubt she believes that. I think your dad may have stolen that from her.

The vet? What a difference a dinner makes. If you can imagine, they were like teenagers together. Emma let down her guard and enjoyed the day. He is a really nice man, and he makes her laugh and compliments her in sweet ways while she blushes like a school girl. I want this for her. She deserves it more than she knows.

Dinner was just okay: turkey was dry, dressing gooey, potatoes lumpy, and sweet potatoes not-so-sweet. I hope that helps your envy. It wasn't at all true, but maybe that will help. Why? Why didn't you go somewhere for a big dinner? I know how the ladies at church operate, so you could have. It made me sad to think you were all alone for Thanksgiving. Each and every holiday, knowing you're alone, I've grieved for you. Have I said too much?

Mike, before I loved you, I liked you. There will always be a place in my life for you. While I can't imagine what that will look like in the time to come, you'll always be my friend. Our history is too long to undo. These letters have reminded me of why I like you. So thank you for being my friend, too. And you shouldn't take me for granted because I did your poster board, which we all know led to your lucrative career.

I should go now. Maybe I should start typing these letters. I may be getting carpal tunnel. Have a good week.

Love,

Rob

Another day later, the day Mike mailed an especially painful letter to Robin, he received a package from her and could hardly imagine what was in it. He tore into the brown paper and found a box filled with chocolate chip cookies, his favorite. She used to send them to him when he was in Afghanistan, and by the time they arrived the chocolate had melted and reformed many times. Then, it was like having a little piece of home to hang onto. In a way, standing there looking at those cookies, he felt the same way, as if he had a small part of his old life there in his hand.

Why had she done such a thing for him? Was she missing him at all the way he was missing her? He knew better, but still his mind pondered the question. What he knew was, if he hadn't loved her before, he would love her now. With every letter he fell in love with her all over again.

***

After recently sending Mike a care package of cookies, Robin had begun to question the decision. Was she somehow setting up expectations for more than was available to them? The gesture was similar to when she was waiting for him during his deployments, too similar.

More than anything, she wondered what in the world she was doing. Mike being back in her life, at least her long-distance life, felt right. That's what bothered her most. For the moment they were acting as casual friends, but was that possible going forward? Their feelings ran too deep to believe this would be enough for either of them. To have more, though, would mean one or the other would have to move. Mike wouldn't be able to be a cop if he relocated. What would he do in that case, work some retail job? There wasn't much open to a man with no degree and a criminal record.

That led Robin to consider moving back – a thought that shut her down in an instant. For the next few days she did nothing but question her sanity for even corresponding with Mike as a friend. All she knew to do was pray. When she felt most overwhelmed, a verse would come to mind about asking for wisdom. She didn't want to be tossed back and forth in a wave of unbelief. She had to believe God would give her the wisdom to know what to do when the time came.

The day Mike's letter arrived, she knew it was too soon to contain anything about the cookies. She would have to wait to see what he thought of them. Hopefully, they would fare better shipped to North Carolina than overseas. Emma was out with Stan for the evening, and Robin had held onto his letter so she could read it in private. The more they wrote, the more intimate the letters felt. Anyone else who might read them would never see them as intimate, but they were becoming so much more personal that she wanted to cherish them without someone looking on.

It was already December, and they had been writing since mid-September. Though old fashioned, writing back and forth was like having a tiny piece of her past in her hands. Phone calls or texts would never feel the same. She was no closer to knowing what might happen with them in the future, but she did know one thing, she wasn't willing to stop their communications. It meant the world to her to know what was going on in his life.

She went up early to her bedroom, got into bed, and opened the envelope.

> Dear Robin,
>
> This is not a reply to the letter I have just received. I'll reply to that next. This is something different, something I've felt led to say for a few weeks now. I refuse to run from it anymore since I know I owe you some explanation for my actions, as weak as it may seem.
>
> A few months before coming home from my second tour, a friend of mine was killed. He was the one guy I trusted most. You can't imagine the things we saw there, the unforgivable things we did. We were kinda holding each other up, keeping each other going.
>
> Just that morning we were discussing all the things we wanted to do when we got home, and by lunch, he was lying dead next to me. It could have been me. Often, I wondered why it wasn't.
>
> For the remainder of my tour, I spent every waking moment in fear of not coming home to you. Every mission I went on, everywhere I went, it was in the forefront of my mind. I became convinced that something would happen at the last minute and I'd be killed. I would lie in bed at night and wonder who would take care of you if I never came home.
>
> Once I came home, I couldn't get my mind straight. My brain never shut down, and I wasn't sleeping most nights. No matter how hard I tried, I could never seem to get back to who I was before. You got pregnant and we moved back home, so it gave me something to focus on besides the mess that was going on in my head. I did everything in my power to pretend I was okay, but I was far from okay.
>
> Then Mikey died. You know, when he was a tiny baby, probably just a week or two old, I sat with him one night rocking. I was looking at him and realized he would bind us together for life. I'm not exactly sure why I felt as if I needed that so badly, but I did. Now that I think of it, I suppose it was due to the turmoil in my parents' marriage.
>
> Early on after he died, we really clung to each other. Then that stopped, and you seemed so far away. I became more and more fearful and angry. Eventually, anger began to consume me. Like I told you when you were here, I was angry at God, never at you. It has taken me years to figure this out, but you were the only God I had ever seen. So I lashed out at Him through you.

He knows this and is my witness; I'm so sorry, both to you and to Him.

Once you went to work, I think that's when I really lost it. I remember a moment when it occurred to me: Michael no longer bound us together. You were working, so it was only a matter of time before you left me, too. That was when I started pressuring you to have another baby. I have foggy recollections of how I forced myself on you. I raped you. Forgive me! Please forgive me for how I hurt you and how, instead of being your protector, I became the perpetrator. I wasn't thinking clearly at all. I was so much worse than when I came home from war. I was lost and knew I was the reason our lives were falling apart.

When I first started drinking, it seemed to take the edge off, to quiet the noise in my head. What I didn't anticipate, though, was how it would begin to overtake me. I became angrier when I drank but was unbearably agitated when I didn't. The more I tried to drown out what I was feeling, the more I felt as if I were drowning. I lost myself somewhere along the way. Then I lost you. Even before that final night, I knew I had lost you. I could see it in your eyes every time you looked at me. You were disgusted by me and disappointed in me. Even then, I could hardly blame you. That afternoon when I went to the pharmacy to get something for my shoulder, the pharmacist saw me there and gave me your prescription. I went crazy. I left my shift without even calling out and went straight to the bar, and well, you know the rest better than I do.

Dear God, I am so sorry!!

Robin, that night was surreal. After all I had done to you, you loved me enough to stay with me. You told me Jesus would forgive me if I would ask Him. I do remember that part and what happened after. You held me when I was certain I was dying. I nearly killed you – and what you did was purely in self-defense whether you accept that or not – still, you led me to Jesus. I asked Him to come into my life while I was in the ambulance, and I've never been the same since.

So many guys have come home messed up. That's why I want to help them, to keep them from becoming what I became. Brother Billy came to see me soon after I got to prison. After we talked he arranged for someone nearer to the prison to come out and talk to me once a week. It was a good start for me to begin to understand what was happening in my head. The greatest healing, though, came through God's Word. There's a verse in the Psalms that I now hold as my very own. "He sent forth His word and healed them." That's what happened: He sent forth His Word and healed me.

Now, I talk with men who are messed-up like I was. I can't do much, but I can lead them to the Healer.

I apologize for laying such a heavy load on you. It has never been my intention to justify my actions in any way. Instead, I know I've been prompted by the Lord these months we've been writing. I tried to be as thoughtful as possible with how I've written this. The last thing I want is to drag your mind back to such dark days. I was the cause of them, and I know it. Forgive me, Rob.

With all my love,
Michael Sr.

By his signature he was reminding himself and her that he would always be Michael's father. Sometimes she had to remind herself she was still a mom, even though she had no child to mother. His death could in no way take her title away. Apparently, it was the same with Mike. He probably needed to see proof of Michael's existence occasionally, and by his own name he could remember. Tears dripped onto the sheets of paper.

"Lord, how could I not have known how sick he was? Why didn't I get him help?"

After reading his letter, she knew one thing more than she did before: she had failed him. She wasn't to blame for the violence that came, but she should have gotten him some help. Even broken in her own way after Michael, she had the presence of mind to know her husband needed help. It kept coming back to her how her unwillingness for people to know was what kept her from telling.

That night she didn't sleep well, and when she did she dreamed of Mike. The next morning, Robin remained in a fog for hours. Memories of his final homecoming floated along with her throughout the hours of the day. It was her most vivid dream from the night before. They were in the large auditorium. Mike, along with all the others returning home, stood at strict attention. When he was finally released, he ran to her and circled his arms around her, lifting her off the ground. When he did, she wrapped her legs around his waist and clung to him, as he would later say, like a monkey. From that moment on he never put her back down. He even stooped over to grab his bags with her still clinging to him.

At the time there was no way she could know how their lives would disintegrate over the next few years. That moment, with Mike home and never to deploy again, she had thought it was the beginning of the rest of their lives. Instead, it was the beginning of the end.

TWENTY-FIVE

The following day, after reading Mike's letter, Robin went to Chris's cabin and started a fire. Once settled in, she began to pen what she knew would be her most difficult letter to date.

Dearest Michael Sr.,

I'm rocked to my soul by your letter. I knew something wasn't right, and yet I did nothing to help you. I wanted you to be okay, so I think maybe I buried my head in the sand. Early on I had no idea you were going through such turmoil – not to that degree. I thought it was what was to be expected from war. Mike, why didn't you talk to me?

I have an admission of my own. After Michael died, even before my milk dried up, I went on birth control pills. I believed I would never love another baby the way I loved him. I was terrified of the thought of getting pregnant again. I didn't want to forget him and move on. I only wanted him. When you began to talk about having another child, I was scared to tell you. You had become so explosive that I feared your reaction, so I hid it from you. I'm sorry that I deceived you in that way. Now, thinking back to how you would get your hopes up each month, I regret allowing you that false hope. It was wrong and cruel, no matter my motives. You can't imagine the guilt I've carried over the years for doing that to you.

And in case you haven't finally realized, Michael will bind us together for life. You will always be the father of my son.

I understand your anger at God. I felt the same, only my anger was expressed by rejecting Him, by not allowing Him access to my heart anymore. Just as you were, I've been healed of that, and I love, love, love the verse you shared. I'll own it as well. He did send forth His word and heal me, too.

I was never disgusted or disappointed with you. While I was disappointed at how our lives turned out, deep inside, I held on to my memories of the real you. When you weren't drinking, I could still see you and longed for things to be the way they were in the early days.

The things that happened that terrible night will always haunt us. I don't doubt that. I think, though, what matters is what we do with the memories when they come. The whispers still come. Now, when they do, I call out to Jesus. What He can and will do in and through us both because of this can affect lives in immeasurable ways. I'm so proud of you that you're working with others who are struggling. I didn't mention it before, but I've attended a support group for family members of those with PTSD. Who knows, maybe God will someday lead me to counsel with people who are hurting as I once did. I want to help them do better with it than I did.

This is indeed a heavy load, but shared, it's something we can both withstand. Now I ask you to never apologize again. When you do, after having received my forgiveness, you're saying you don't trust my ability to forgive. I can forgive because I'm forgiven.

With a heart full of love,
Michael's Mom

P.S. Okay, I know how morbid this will sound even before I write it. Will you please take a photo of Michael's grave and send it to me? Not being able to go there is the worst part of living so far away.

When Robin took her letter to the front desk, she found another from Mike waiting for her. She smiled and held it up to her nose. Why, she wasn't exactly sure. Did she expect perfume? All she could do was giggle when she found Emma staring at her from the dining room door.

"Are you falling back in love with him?"

"I'm realizing that I may have never fallen out."

Emma's expression held concern. "What will you do about this?"

"I don't know. Right now, I just want to love him this way."

Alone, sitting out on the back porch, Robin tore into Mike's latest letter.

Hey Rob –

Brother Billy retired two years ago, before I got back. Tim is a great guy and has really turned this place around. There's a new excitement that I can hardly believe. It's nothing like you remember. Obviously, he knew part of the story. Gossip line is still working well here, and we still know each other's business. But Tim welcomed me as if I were anyone else.

I've never tried to cook a casserole, and I don't plan on it. I think I would lose my man card if I did that. I'll stick with grilling meat and baking potatoes in the microwave. That's what real men do. With head hung low, I admit I'm a store-bought-cookie guy. Then, once I'm there I eat the homemade stuff. Kids eat my cookies, so it all works out.

Speaking of cookies – you are the greatest! I just got them this morning and have eaten half of them already. Not feeling sick at all, so no lectures. I don't know what possessed you to do that, but whatever it was, keep it up. I never tire of chocolate chip, though I do remember you make a rockin' oatmeal raisin, too. Really, I'm merely doing my part. I know how you like to bake, and since you said you eat too many when you do, I'm willing to take one for the team. I'll eat them. (Sigh)

Tell me more about the classes you're taking.

You mentioned your dad, and I have to tell you, you couldn't possibly know how much he meant to me, he and your mom. All those years, I felt so welcome there. It was the closest to a normal family I ever knew. Exactly! You do have great parents. After all that happened I won't even allow myself to consider what they think of me. I hope someday you'll share with them how much they meant to me and maybe even how much I've changed. Do they even know you're writing to me? They're coming for Christmas, right?

I've thought about going to see my dad. I just haven't worked up the nerve yet. Trevor has seen him and says he really is a different guy. Good thing for the McGarrett men they don't serve booze in the big house.

Robin chuckled at his words. Some things about him never changed, and she was glad that his sense of humor was one of them. From the very beginning he made her laugh.

She continued on.

Someday? To the beach here? That would be something. If you ever do, would you mind if I met you there? Maybe we could have lunch or dinner. I'm not talking about a date or anything, so don't go getting your hopes up there, desperate girl. Just two friends eating dinner at the same place and time.

His words reminded her of Chris's. She wondered what Mike was really thinking when he asked that question, maybe the same sense of long lost love that she was? Was he trying to hide his true feelings, or could he possibly be content with having just a friendship restored? Why had she made that statement? Would she really go?

My men's study began last week. Rob, thanks for your words. Deep down, I knew I was supposed to do it, but I was scared. The whispers… I know exactly what you mean by that – hard to tune them out sometimes. You always know what to say, always have. How did you get so wise?

You mentioned me laughing until I cry. It doesn't take much for me to cry these days, which prompts me to ask something I've wondered for years now. You almost never cried. My mom cried a lot, just never when anyone was around. Were you like that? I know I made you cry with the whole Shelly thing. To see you cry that night nearly killed me. What I'm wondering is, when no one else was around, did you cry more?

Any more news on Emma and the vet? Does Emma still hate my guts? That was an odd lead-in, wasn't it? I can't help but wonder.

Thanks for the dishonest Thanksgiving recap. Why did I stay home? I couldn't imagine sitting at a table with someone else's family. I would feel out of place. So I stayed home. Yes, you said too much. You have to stop telling me things like you were grieving for me because when I answer you, I feel something – I don't know, stupid or, I would say vulnerable if I were a girl, but I'm not, so I'll go with weak. Please, never grieve for me. I do have joy and contentment that is surprising and surely from the Lord. Yes, holidays are hard, but I would rather be at our home alone than somewhere I don't belong.

Before I loved you, I liked you, too – I think. I don't know for sure; I loved you so quickly that I can't swear to it. I think I loved you when I saw your marshmallow burn up. You were looking at me, and there it went, up in flames. That would have been funny to me had I not been so nervous about talking to you. That night, I was determined you would be mine, no matter what it took. Did I ever tell you that? I might have been too much of a guy back then to admit it.

There will always be a place in my life for you, no matter what life looks like in the time to come, always.

These letters have reminded me why I like and love you. You are a funny, funny girl, and sometimes, when you aren't picking on me, you can be very sweet.

Please, no typing. It's much more personal this way.

Always,
Mike

Her response was immediate.

Dear Always Mike,

Tim sounds great. Glad to know you have a friend like him.

I suppose real men, like you, should only grill and use the microwave. Since I remember you like chili, which is a relatively manly thing to cook, I'm including a recipe in with this letter. Just put it all in the slow cooker before work and when you come home, you'll have dinner waiting.

I'm certain your cookies are gone by now. Maybe I'll send you some more soon. And my, how selfless of you to offer to eat my cookies and keep me from over-indulging. You are a real team player.

This semester, I'm taking physics and history. Not so bad. Next year, I am considering taking more than two.

You'll have to let me know if you decide to go to see your dad. I'm sure he would love to see you.

The beach – with the weather here now, it sounds like a wonderful dream. If I ever do make it there to the beach, a buddy-old-pal dinner would be nice. Thank you for offering.

I'm glad your group went well. I don't know that I would call me wise, just learning.

I never did cry much and am not sure why, just wasn't me. This past year, I've cried a lot. I think I needed it. I spent too many years with things bottled up inside me. Now, I feel lighter on my feet. Who knew tears weighed so much?

Emma and Stan are like two kids in love. It's just been a few weeks, but you would think they have known each other for years. Recently, I asked if maybe they were moving a bit too fast, and she informed me that they're on an accelerated calendar. She said, "Honey, at this age, you can't afford a long courtship." I take that to mean they're already talking about a future together.

Does she hate you? No. She was worried at first and maybe still. I don't talk about it much with her.

Glad to hear you have joy and contentment. I told you: that's the subject of my current Bible study, so I'm working on contentment myself.

I understand what you mean about feeling out of place if you went to someone else's house. I'm just sorry you were alone. That's all.

No, you never told me you made up your mind that first night. I wish you would have. That would have been a sweet memory to carry all these years. I'll treasure it now, though.

Notice: I'm writing by hand and not typing.

Always too,
Robin

P.S. Decided to make cookies tonight, so I'll send with the letter tomorrow. Hope you enjoy. I ate three when they first came out of the oven.

***

After reading her letter, Mike noticed Robin left out any mention of her parents. He could hardly blame them for hating him. If he had to guess, he would suspect they didn't even know about the letters, and he understood why she would keep it from them. In a way it clarified something for him. If she were feeling something deeper than friendship, she would have at least told her mom. More than once, he reminded himself that friendship was enough. Before September he had no hope of that even.

The day before, Tim had cornered him at the gym, trying to get him to open up. Mike had only briefly mentioned that they were writing, and for the most part, Tim never asked questions. Yesterday, though, he had pursued the subject more than Mike appreciated. Tim's concern was that maybe this would prevent them both from moving on. Mike wondered if he was indeed preventing Robin from moving on. That wasn't the case on his part since he had no desire for any other woman but her, but the idea that he might somehow keep her from meeting someone who would love and cherish her in a way he would never be able to again, made him feel selfish. Wasn't it his selfishness that was exposed when they first began writing? Had he not overlooked what she wanted and what was best for her when they were together, focusing solely on himself? No longer that same man, Mike wanted more for Robin than he wanted for himself, a fact that would require something of him, a level of selflessness he wasn't so sure he possessed. After doing things the wrong way while with her, for once, he wanted to put her first.

The thought that maybe he was preventing her future happiness plagued him. He had prayed all morning about it. Should he leave her alone in the hopes that the right man would come along? While he tried to begin a letter to her, he found his heart was too heavy even to write. He threw away what he had so far and called Tim instead. They met down at the church and prayed together at the altar.

Once he arrived home, he felt better able to do what needed to be done, still sad, but able.

Dear Robin,

I've been thinking about this and praying hard about it. I'm at a loss here – and worried. Are we doing the right thing? This friendship means the world to me. My fear is that it'll somehow prevent you from moving on. That's been what I've asked God most for you, to find someone who will love you. I don't want to interfere with that, and if I stay in the picture it may never happen. For once, I want to do what's best for you.

I received your letter, and as much as I want to reply, I think maybe I shouldn't. I'll wait until I hear back from you. Think this over. Pray about it. If you think we should stop this now, I'll go along with whatever you want.

A thousand times thank you for the cookies. They're almost as good as choco-chip. You are a gifted cookie-making little elf.

Mike

P.S. I'll send you the photo you asked for. I can understand why you need it. Those years I was away that was one of the most difficult aspects, not being able to go there and sit with my boy.

***

Robin sat staring at the blank piece of paper in front of her. Should she? Before she could talk herself out of it, she scribbled out a few words, sealed the envelope, and drove it directly to the post office. Afterwards, she had some last minute Christmas shopping to do. Emma was leaving to go to upstate New York with Stan to visit his daughter and her family. Robin's parents canceled after Emma had already made plans. Though Emma insisted on staying home with her, Robin wouldn't hear of her canceling the trip. This turn of events would leave Robin all alone for Christmas.

Had she just made the biggest mistake of her life? Even if it was, she knew it was too late to change her mind. What was done was done.

***

Mike mailed the letter and the following day found he regretted it. What Tim had said was constantly on his mind, though, and now, he feared writing it down instead of talking it out was a mistake. All day at work, he tossed around the idea of calling her. By the time he came home, he was settled that he should.

The last thing Mike wanted to happen happened. Emma answered.

"Hi, Emma. This is Mike. Is Robin around?"

"She's not here right now."

Her tone was cool and he hated to ask. "Would you mind asking her to call me?"

"I'll let her know you called." Emma hung up without saying goodbye.

Mike held the phone for a few seconds before tossing it onto the kitchen table. That was obviously a mistake.

For the next few hours he waited for Robin to call, but she never did.

***

Mike found a letter from Robin in the mailbox and knew it was too soon to be a response to his. Still, when she never returned his call, he had to expect the worst when he did hear back. He slid his finger underneath the seal and pulled out the small note. He read the words again and again, certain they couldn't possibly mean what they said.

> Dear Mr. Solo,
> What are your plans for Christmas?
> Is it too last minute? Call me.
> Solo Too

He whispered, "Is this real, Lord?" and read her note again and laughed out loud. This was real; she had even included her number.

His hands were trembling, so it took him two tries to get the number right.

***

Robin was sitting in front of the fireplace, curled up under a blanket. When she saw the 919 area code, she inhaled and held her breath for a second.

"Hello."

"Hey, Rob."

192

"I guess you got my note?" Her heart was racing. Suddenly, she felt thirteen again, sitting there grinning and chewing on her thumbnail.

"Yeah, I got your note, and I'm not doing anything for Christmas."

"My parents have to stay in Tucson for some work thing of my dad's, and Emma is going out of town. I was wondering if maybe you would like to come here and spend Christmas with me?"

"There's nothing I would like more."

"I was thinking maybe the day before Christmas Eve. Would that work?"

"Yes. I don't think it'll be a problem." He paused. "I'll pay someone to take my shift if I have to."

That last part made her smile.

"So, okay then. You're coming."

Her stomach was flipping and flopping, and she wondered if he could sense the goofy smile on her face.

"This will be my first holiday with…" Mike stopped. "This will be the best Christmas I've had in a very long time."

"I'm looking forward to it." She was. And she suspected what caused him to stop midsentence before. It would be his first holiday with family. It had already crossed her mind many times since writing the note, the fact that this Christmas, Mike would be with family.

On their next phone call, Mike gave Robin his flight information and said, "I, um, sent a letter the same day I received your note. I'm not sure if I should tell you to forget it or to think about it still."

She paused and thought, his tone giving her reason to wonder. "Why, what did it say?"

"Just read it. I'm sorry if it seems silly."

Emma was calling her from the top floor.

"Hey, I have to run for now, should I call you back to discuss this?"

"No, that's okay. That's what I had called to talk to you about the other night, but we can talk when I get there."

"You called?"

"Yeah. Emma said she would tell you I called."

Robin became quiet.

"I don't blame her, Rob. Don't be mad at her."

"I'm sorry. I would have called you back. You know that, right?"

"I do now," Mike said.

"I'll talk to her, but you have my cell number now. Call me here anytime."

"Okay."

They got off the phone and Robin went straight upstairs, hardly able to believe Emma would do that.

In her doorway, Robin paused and watched as Emma was tucking shoes into a front compartment of her suitcase.

Emma turned. "I may need a bigger suitcase." She laughed.

Robin never even broke a smile. "Why didn't you tell me that Mike called?"

"Because I'm terrified to see what's happening."

"You had no right to screen my calls. I'm not a child, and you don't get to make my decisions for me."

Emma looked away. "I'm afraid you'll leave."

Without softening even a little, no matter Emma's pitiful expression, Robin said, "I'm not leaving. I'm not moving back to Whitley. But that's not even the point. You had no right to keep it from me. He thought I just ignored his call. I can only imagine how that made him feel."

"I don't care what Mike thinks. I don't care what Mike feels. I just want him to leave you alone."

Robin stood there staring at Emma. "This isn't your call, Emma."

"Someone needs to look out for you. I saw what he did to you, and I know it wasn't the first time."

"That's not who he is now."

"How do you know that?"

"Because I see who he is now. Every word he writes, every emotion he pours out, I see the new him – not even the old Mike I married. I see the man God has made him into." She sighed, thoughts of his letter coming to mind. "Emma, not only was Mike's mind broken from war and from losing our son, he was lost – like you were. He didn't have God then, but he does now. If you don't believe God can restore what was once so broken, then you don't know God at all. You don't know grace or mercy or the fact that nothing is impossible with God. Just look at me if you want to see proof."

She turned on her heel and left Emma's room. Once alone in her room, Robin took out Mike's stack of letters and began to sift through them. From the first word until his last, she could see him, the real him. There wasn't one ounce of fear of him that remained. Just as God had healed her brokenness, He had healed Mike's, too.

The following morning, Robin was at the front door with Emma while Stan was loading her bags.

Emma said, "I'm sorry I didn't tell you. I'm sorry I'm still so afraid." She began to cry. "I'm sorry I don't see God like you do. I'm sorry for a thousand things."

Robin wrapped her arms around Emma. "I forgive you. You go and have a good time. Don't you worry about this." She held Emma out to see her face. "Do you hear me? We are fine, you and me. I love that you love me this much."

Emma moved back in and squeezed Robin tight. "I do love you that much. But I promise to love you better than that from now on. I want for you what you want." She paused. "Even if that's Mike."

Two days later, only four days before Mike was to arrive, Robin received the note he must have been talking about. He asked if they were doing the right thing and said he was worried that their friendship might prevent her from moving on. Those two statements were enough to disturb her, but what he said about wanting her to find someone who would love her – that was what caused her chest to feel so heavy.

Obviously, he was thinking of moving on. Maybe there was someone he was interested in already. Finally, it registered with her: saying he wanted her to find someone to love her was his way of saying that wasn't him. He was trying to set her straight, to lessen her expectations. This was a crushing blow. All her deliberations over whether or not they might have a future together meant nothing in light of this.

After reading his letter, she saw how foolish it was to have invited him. Why had he agreed to come? She had known it was a mistake. The entire relationship was a mistake. Where could it lead, after all? With no reason to ponder the subject any longer, she picked up the phone and dialed.

***

At the diner with Tim, Mike reached for his vibrating phone. When he saw that it was Robin's number, he grinned. "Hello."

He hadn't slept the night before and was running on sheer adrenaline. In front of Tim he tried to act casual that Robin was calling and stood to walk out.

"Hey. Are you at lunch where you can talk for a minute?"

"I sure am, " he said as he walked out onto the sidewalk.

"You don't have to come." Her tone was abrupt.

Mike leaned against his patrol car, exhaled, and closed his eyes. All along he had feared it was too good to be true.

"I already have my ticket," he whispered.

"Maybe this isn't a good idea after all."

He wasn't about to argue with her. If she had changed her mind and didn't want him to come, he would cancel his flight. Then it occurred to him. "Did you receive my note?"

"I did."

"And?"

"And maybe this is a mistake. You don't have to worry about me holding on, or missing out, or whatever you think I might be doing."

He detected a hint of hurt feelings. Since he had known her as long as he had, of course he knew the you-have-hurt-my-feelings-but-I-will-pretend-I-don't-care voice.

"What do you think I meant by what I said?"

"I'm not sure, maybe that I need to move on because you are. Don't worry, I can do that. If I had known you were feeling this way, I never would have invited you, and if you were feeling this way, you never should have said you would come."

He grinned at how she had read way more into his words than he intended, but that was exactly what he often did when she wrote.

"I meant precisely what I said. I just don't want to prevent your happiness, nothing about me moving on."

He was glaring through the window at Tim.

"I'm a guy. There's nothing deeper or hidden in my message – believe me. I said something simple, and I meant it exactly like I wrote it."

She tried to speak, but he interrupted. "It was a dumb thought that someone planted in my head. Forget it. I don't want to stop writing to you. I don't want to cancel my flight. I have my ticket, and nothing will stop me from getting on that plane. If you aren't there to meet me, I'll rent a car and drive to the inn. If you aren't at the inn when I arrive, I'll sit out in the freezing cold until you get there.

"So now, I'm going to hang up the phone before you have a chance to tell me no. I'm coming, and I'm so excited I can hardly see straight. See you in four days at noon. Bake me some cookies. Bye." He hung up the phone.

Now, he wasn't going to allow anything to get in the way, especially some stupid note that he never should have sent.

Back inside the diner Mike sat across from Tim. "Really, you get paid to help people?"

"What?" Tim shrugged.

TWENTY-SIX

Since they hadn't spoken after the day he assured Robin he was coming, Mike walked through the terminal of the Concord airport uncertain of what to expect. He had no way of knowing if she would be there, but that didn't matter. If not, he would go to her and straighten things out. That stupid note! Why had he sent it? Certainly, he had learned a great lesson about doubt. Things were going along so well and then doubt crept in, which in turn gave her reason to doubt. From his point of view, the note expressed his concern for her. Obviously, his message was unclear, and she had taken it as some means of escape on his part, which was the craziest thing in the world. If she only knew how desperately he loved her still. Several times he had considered calling her but feared a conversation may give her some reason to tell him not to come. He wasn't willing to risk that.

With all of these thoughts rolling around in his head, in an instant, all deliberations faded. In his field of vision, about fifty yards ahead, was the answer to all his wonderings over the past few hours. Robin was there, smiling at him. Nothing mattered but that now. Her hair was down, with the ends curled and draped over her right shoulder. Literally, the sight of her took his breath away and he felt suddenly winded.

He picked up the pace as he moved toward her, nearly knocking people over in his path. When he drew close enough, he chuckled to see her move her thumb to chew on her nail. It was something she did when she was nervous or excited. Likely, it was a little of both. What most captured his attention, other than how beautiful she looked, was the way she smiled at him.

He stopped in front of her, wondering if it would be okay to hug her. Even as he wondered, she reached up on her tiptoes to slide her arms around his neck. This was what he had longed for most over the years, to feel her in his arms again. He stooped down and slid his arms around her waist. When he stood, he lifted her off the ground and squeezed her hard, then sighed in sheer contentment of the moment.

"You're here," he whispered.

"Of course I'm here."

Robin leaned back enough to see his face. "What was the deal with that note?"

He sat her back down, shaking his head. "Doubt, and I'm so sorry I even sent it. I never meant to hurt your feelings or make you doubt me." He reached for her hand. "That's the last thing I ever want to do."

"Do you still feel that way, that this is a mistake," Robin said.

"Not at all. I never did. I just feared for you." Mike lowered his head and rested it on hers. "Can we forget the stupid note?"

"We can. And just for the record, I've thought about it a lot. I don't know exactly what this is, but I don't feel as if it's a mistake either."

"I'm so glad to hear you say that."

When he circled his arms around her, she closed her eyes and slipped her arms around his waist, nestling into him. His fears of the past few days slipped away. Nothing about holding her was a mistake. How could he have ever thought that? For as long as she would allow him to be a part of her life, he would be. It would have to be her who pushed him away.

Robin took a step back. "Are you ready?"

He stood there looking at her, not sure what she had just asked. Finally, he whispered, "You look so beautiful." He touched her hair, mesmerized by the sight of her standing there. "Have you always been this beautiful?"

She grinned and blushed at that and kept standing there staring just as he was.

People all around them kept passing by but both stood lost in the moment. They had seen each other twice since their marriage had ended, but this was entirely different. Mike was beginning to have hope for more. If that weren't possible, why else would she have asked him to come?

Robin was the first to come to her senses. "Do you have bags to collect?"

"Yes," Mike said, trying to clear his head.

"You travel heavy."

"I come bearing gifts."

She smiled up at him. "Good. I've been a very good girl this year."

He slid his arm around her shoulder as they walked. "So I've heard."

"Who told you?"

Mike noticed, when she wrapped her arm around his waist, how she tucked her thumb into his belt loop, something she had done a million times in years past. Such a trivial detail brought with it unexpected comfort and familiarity. With her snuggled against him as they maneuvered through the mass of Christmas travelers, they were as good as alone together.

All the way to baggage claim they talked as if they had only seen each other yesterday. Mike found himself continually amazed and intentionally and prayerfully grateful to be with her. Over and over he gave thanks in his heart, sometimes even shouting at the top of his spirit in gratitude. Since waking up in the hospital, he knew nothing would ever stop his heart from loving her, but he could never have anticipated how much more he would someday. Astounded by this intense, patient devotion he felt toward her, he realized, it was a love only God could give him. It was the love God constantly extended toward him.

At the inn, once Mike was settled into his room, he came back downstairs with a stack of gifts and found Robin waiting in the main lobby area.

"Where's your tree?"

"I haven't gotten one yet."

"You? You're crazy about Christmas."

"I was thinking we could go get one together," she said. "Then we can decorate and have hot cocoa."

"I like that idea." His words were soft. The thought of it brought back a flood of memories of past Christmases together. She was like a kid when it came to decorating the tree.

"I'm glad you saved it for us to do together."

It would be the first family Christmas he had known in six years. While he visited his mother the afternoon of the previous Christmas, and Trevor came too, it didn't feel right to him. Robin was his family, and only she could make the day complete.

"Me, too." She pointed toward the parlor. "We will set it up in there if you want to take the gifts on in."

Once in the parlor he spotted a stack of gifts near the fireplace and decided to place his alongside them. When he got nearer, he realized they were all for him. Though he didn't care what was in them, to know she had gone out and picked things out for him caused tears to form in his eyes. He chuckled aloud, knowing if she caught him misty-eyed he would never hear the end of it, so he blinked them away.

Scattered around the room were boxes of ornaments and lights, but none of them were theirs. The attic at home was full of decorations and ornaments, ones they had collected over the years, even as teenagers. Each year he had taken her to pick out new ornaments to put on a tree in her bedroom at her parents' home. She was preparing for the day when they would have a tree of their own. When the memory brought to mind what he had lost, a knot formed in his throat, and his tears returned. This time, however, he was unable to blink them away, so he rubbed his face when he heard her come in and stand behind him.

"This feels right, doesn't it?" she said.

He nodded, hardly able to trust his voice to answer. When she moved near to where he stood, he wrapped his arms around her and held her to him. After a minute more he finally whispered, "Nothing has felt more right."

Bundled up to brace against the cold, they walked the lot looking for just the right tree. The temperatures were now below freezing, something Mike would never get used to. He was a Southern boy all right. To watch Robin, as cold natured as she was, shiver and dance around trying to stay warm was worth the cold, though. She couldn't be any cuter.

This was a serious event for her. She had definite standards and Mike was intent on making her happy. Where one tree was the perfect height, it was too scraggly on one side. If one was the right width, it was too short. He walked with her in the cold, realizing the little things in life are truly the most important. There wasn't a thing in the world he would rather be doing than searching for the perfect tree with her. Finally, happening upon the elusive flawless tree, they tied it down on Emma's Subaru and headed back to the inn.

With the tree indoors and in its holder, Mike started a fire while Robin went to make them cocoa. When she returned, he took the cup and sipped. "This is the real deal. I haven't had cocoa like this in years."

Everything about the afternoon felt like old times to Mike. Robin was her usual excited Christmas self. More than anything, he just watched her. At the moment they were on their fifth strand of lights as Robin went round and round the tree tucking and hiding the strands while he handed her the lights.

Mike finally stopped. "I'm starving! I skipped lunch."

"Why didn't you tell me? I'll go in and make us something."

"Why don't we go out to dinner instead? We can eat here tomorrow."

"I thought you were sick of eating out. After your poor poor-me routine, I planned to cook for you."

"I'm sick of diner and fast food. We can go out for a real dinner, like a steak."

"That would be nice." She glanced down at her sweater and jeans. "Do you mean like a go-get-nice-clothes-on kind of dinner?"

"You look great as you are. I'll grab a different shirt."

After freshening up, Mike met Robin on the stairwell on her way down from the third floor. His room was on the second. He leaned against the thick wooden banister and waited as she descended the last few steps. They walked down the last flight together, both grinning over the prospect of the evening to come.

"You look nice. Your pinstripes match your eyes," she said. "You really have been shopping."

"You look more than nice. I've hardly been able to take my eyes off of you all day."

"I would try to seem surprised by that, but you've been pretty obvious."

"I'm sure I have." He hesitated a second. "This is odd, huh?"

She nodded. "It is."

"But you're okay with it, right? No regrets that I came?"

"No regrets at all. You being here makes this feel like Christmas."

"Yeah, I've thought the same about you."

On the way to the steakhouse, the conversation remained light and Mike sensed she was at ease. He drove as he always had, and while riding and talking with no distraction of the radio, he listened as she chattered away about various things. He thought back and wondered if he had ever listened to her as he did then, hanging onto every word. With this new whatever they were sharing, he tried to catch any glimpse into her heart that he could. Although he had known her over seventeen years, now, his greatest desire was to know her more.

Once while she was describing some of the more colorful characters around town, he casually reached over and took her hand. He glanced at her. "Do you mind?"

"No." She looked at his hand holding hers. "I've missed holding your hand."

He rubbed the palm of her hand with his thumb and could only apologize. "I'm sorry I haven't been around to do this."

"Me, too."

The mood shifted, and Mike sensed they were both lost in regret. When they arrived and he shifted into park, he tried lightening the mood a little. "I'm starving!"

"Are you that hungry?"

"About to keel over."

"Why didn't you tell me? I would have made you some lunch before going out for a tree."

Mike grinned a lopsided grin. "I couldn't have eaten a bite then. Now, I'm feeling a bit less nervous."

She grinned back at him. "You were nervous?"

"Weren't you?"

"Yes." She hesitated before asking, "This wasn't a mistake, was it, like you said in that note?"

"No. This was no mistake."

***

Back at the inn as they trimmed the tree, Robin watched Mike as he placed the ornaments where she directed. For the first time in many years, she found no need for a ladder since he was easily able to place the star atop the tree without even standing on tiptoes.

"You're a nice helper."

"I just do what I'm told. So what's next?"

"I was thinking a movie."

He moved closer to her. "I've missed you, missed this. This is when you're happiest, getting ready for Christmas." He slid his hand behind her neck and pulled her into him.

With a soft sigh she leaned her head against his chest. She could hear his heart beating hard and strong. "I've missed you, too. I don't think I realized just how much until today."

She buried her face into the fabric of his shirt. Tears were burning her eyes and her face felt flush. Inside, there was a tangled mixture of excitement at being held by him, along with an alarming sense of how right it felt. Her own heart was beating clear up into her throat, and the rhythm blended with what she was hearing in his chest. Just as he had done at the cemetery, she felt him press his lips to the top of her head and kiss her. And just as he had then, he did so discreetly today, as if not wanting her to know. She smiled at that.

"Does this scare you?"

Robin nodded and without looking up, whispered, "A little." Then, after thinking it through, she said, "A lot."

"No need to be scared. We'll take things slowly." He lifted her chin. "I will never give you a reason to be scared again – never. You say back off, I'm back. You say draw near, I'll be here."

Her truest desire was to move in closer and kiss him, so much so that she found she had to take a step back to keep from it.

Mike smiled at her. "So, what movie?"

***

They watched two Christmas movies. By the end of the second, Mike could only sigh. Both were stories of miracles and love, which gave him impossible and irrational hope. At one point when Robin was engrossed in the story, he closed his eyes, wondering what in the world he was doing, fearing this was all just a set-up for a fall. How could it be anything but? Every moment he sat in total amazement that he was wide awake, not dreaming. How many dreams had he dreamt where he was with her this way? Over the years, probably hundreds. It was real this time, so in his heart he prayed, God, You are so good to me when we both know I don't deserve it.

When the last film ended, it was eleven o'clock, so they agree to go to bed so they could get up early and make the most of the day. They walked together up the stairs. Upon reaching the second floor, Mike took her hand, preventing her from continuing up the next flight of stairs.

"Rob…" He rested his forehead on hers. "This has been the best Christmas Eve eve I've ever had."

"Me, too."

"I know you felt uncomfortable earlier. I'm sorry I made you feel that way. We're friends, and that can be enough for me if that's all you want. You've been my best friend for as long as I can remember, and you always will be."

"You'll always be my best friend, too. Right now, beyond that, I don't know what to think."

"Don't think. That's when people get into trouble."

To let her go and watch her continue on up to her room had been difficult for him. In a strange place in a strange bed, he found it nearly impossible to sleep. Or maybe it was the knowledge that the love of his life was in a room sleeping just one level above him. Even early into the morning hours, he found his mind full of memories. He could close his eyes and see exactly what she looked like sleeping. More than anything he could think of, he wished he was there curled around her as they used to sleep.

"Lord, other than salvation and forgiveness, I think this may be the best gift You have ever given me. Well, and Mikey. Thank you for this. I still can't figure You out. I suppose I never will, but I do know this: You are beyond good to me."

TWENTY-SEVEN

When he heard a light tapping on his door, Mike lifted his head and blinked, trying to clear the fog from his mind. The clock read nine twenty.

"Hey, sleepyhead, you're missing the day."

Groggy still since he had only slept a couple of hours, he said, "I'm up. Sorry."

Robin peeked in. "Breakfast is ready, so hurry on down.

"Give me five minutes."

He found her in the dining room setting plates onto a table near the window. It was the first time he noticed it had snowed the night before. "Amazing!"

"We'll have a white Christmas. Have you ever had one before?"

"A dusting maybe but nothing like this. I checked the weather forecast before I came. This wasn't even on the radar."

"A happy surprise," she said. "We can get out and play today."

"I can't imagine anything better than that."

Mike sat across from Robin and, just as he had done at dinner, took her hand and gave thanks for the food. Both times he could see how it surprised her. The man he was years ago would never have done that. Only she had blessed the food before a meal back then. More than anything, he wanted her to see he had become the man he should have been all along. That thought caused the sting of regret to surface. He had gotten so much wrong that it caused him to wonder why she had stayed as long as she did.

"Are you okay? Do you want something else to eat?" Robin said.

"Absolutely not. Sorry, I just got lost there for a minute."

Before him sat his favorite breakfast, a heaping plate of bacon, eggs, and hash browns. On another small plate was toast with butter. She had set out little containers of various jellies.

"You're a great hostess."

"I should be. I do it enough."

"Why not in the winter? I would imagine people would come in droves to see a sight like this."

The lake did look spectacular surrounded by snow. From where they sat he could see clear across the water to the other side. Pine trees were draped with snow, a perfect picture, as if he had opened the largest Christmas card ever and propped it up beside the table.

"Emma never has winter guests. She says she needs to recharge, and I don't blame her. The spring through fall months are crazy. I didn't know this until I came here to live, but she doesn't have to rent out at all."

"Really?"

"Oh, she's loaded. You know, not like Rockefeller kind of rich but enough to simply live here in a place like this and not need an income."

"Hmm, I had no idea."

It was the grandest home Mike had ever been in and reminded him of how little he had to offer Robin.

"You must like living here."

"Yes, I suppose. It's been good for me these past years."

It was clear they were about to head down the road leading to the past, so he made no comment. The last thing he wanted was for her to remember who he once was. To change the course of the conversation, he said, "So, what did you get me in there?"

"I'm not telling."

"Will we keep tradition and open one tonight?"

"Of course." She pushed her plate aside and smiled as he reached for it and scraped the rest of her eggs onto his plate. "So, what did you get me?"

"A puppy."

Robin giggled. "We may have a problem then."

When she laughed, the warmth of it settle into his chest. Unexpected hope mingled with the warmth of her laughter, and he found it to be an emotionally charged combination. He fought to refocus his thoughts.

"Was there anything you wanted?" he said. "I almost called and asked, but I didn't think you would tell me."

"I've already gotten what I wanted."

Something about her expression as she said that caused his heart to beat faster. "What's that?"

"Being together. I couldn't stand the thought of you spending another Christmas alone."

"I feel the exact same." He paused. "Rob?"

"Huh?"

"I hope you made me cookies."

She laughed at that and pointed to his plate. "Finish your breakfast."

***

Their day together, Robin decided, proved to be even more fun than decorating the tree. They played out in the snow, built a snowman, bundled up in the afternoon and went out for a walk, and even ventured out to see the lights around town. The worst part of the day was how it passed by in such a blur.

After dinner they sat in the parlor by the Christmas tree and each exchanged one gift. Robin tore into the package and found a set of three coffee mugs: one said *Hope*, one *Faith*, and the other *Believe*.

"I love them. I'm a big coffee drinker, don't ya know?"

"I've heard that rumor. I thought we could use them in the morning."

Mike went next. When he opened the box and found his cookies, he jumped up, grabbed the "Hope" and "Faith" mugs, and started out of the room.

"Where are you going?"

He never stopped walking. "To get milk. Where else?"

When he returned with two mugs filled to the brim, he sat and handed Robin hers.

"You'll never top this gift." He dunked a cookie into the milk and put the whole thing in his mouth then held the box out to her. "I suppose I can spare one," he said with crumbs tumbling out of his mouth.

Robin took the cookie and dunked hers just as he had. Inside, her heart was brimming over with joy. For the past few years at Christmastime, she had never felt as if she belonged. While she loved Emma and Emma loved her, she wasn't home. Even the two years her parents had come to visit, she felt unusually alone. Now she realized, what she had been missing was Mike. He was her husband, and she would likely always feel his absence.

He set his tin of cookies aside and just sat looking at her for a moment. The atmosphere around them had taken a sudden turn. The fire had died to a low crackle and the lights were dim. Robin returned his gaze, knowing where the night was taking them.

Finally, he reached out, grabbed both of her ankles, and slid her nearer to him.

"Why did you invite me here?"

She stared into his penetrating eyes. *Longing* was the word that echoed in her head. In his eyes she could see it, and longing was the only way she could describe what was churning within her. She longed to be his again.

"I didn't want you to be alone for Christmas."

Mike reached out and touched her cheek. "Is that the only reason?" He slid his other hand behind her back and drew her a little closer.

At his nearness she swallowed hard and found that gazing into his eyes was a mistake, for she became lost in them. She shook her head no. "I wanted to be with you for Christmas. I needed to be with you." Her voice was barely a whisper.

He slid his hand behind her neck and pulled her nearer still. "I'm about two inches away from crossing the line of this friendship."

Mesmerized by the melody of his words, she could only stare at his lips. His breath smelled sweet like cookies, prompting her to say, "Draw nearer."

His kiss was soft and intentional as he cupped her face with both hands. After a minute he moved back and rested his forehead on hers. "There's been no one else – not ever. Since junior year, I haven't touched anyone else. It's always only been you."

With her arms still looped around his neck, Robin moved in to kiss him. She broke contact for a second as she whispered, "And there's always only been you."

What began as something tender and deliberate took a turn and became an intense, enflamed moment. His grip around her was so tight, Robin could barely breathe. He kissed her face and her neck as he whispered again and again how much he loved her. His whiskers were rough and scraped the smooth skin of her neck. How she had missed the feel of his face pressed against hers and his lips on her neck. She was lost in him just as she had always been.

The ringing of the phone was something they at first ignored. After the third ring, he gripped her by the shoulders and pushed her away from him. "You better get that."

Robin grinned, cheeks flushing as she stood and moved from the room.

***

Breathless long after Robin had left the room, Mike found he was barely able to regain his composure. Since arriving, he had wanted to kiss her. When given the opportunity, at the onset, it was his only intention. Once she responded as she had, though, his only thought was of making love to her. No doubt that was exactly where they were heading. Their circumstances were such, though, that he knew it would be a mistake.

Being with her, as they just were, was what he had dreamed of most since he had lost her. Not just to make love to her, but to hold her and be held. There was a moment when he had touched her cheek and she looked into his eyes and sighed. That was what he felt too, a sigh of relief, a sigh that he was holding her as he used to, a sigh that, for the first time in so many years his lips were touching hers.

He needed fresh air, so he went outside to wait for her on the back porch. Although the temperature was in the low twenties and he wore no coat, he still found himself overheated. His heart was pounding at the mere thought of her lips on his and the way she had dug her fingers into the skin of his neck. Several times, she had whispered, "I need you." He could still hear her soft words in his mind.

Mike drew in a deep breath, grabbed onto the railing of the porch, and prayed, "Lord, I want her more than I've ever wanted anything in my life. But I know things are too uncertain between us. While in my heart she's still my wife, and I believe in Your eyes she is, we're no longer even married. I can't allow myself to be with her like this. Not when she's not mine. I need You to give me strength, or I may make the biggest mistake and end up losing her again. Please don't let me lose her."

***

While on the phone with her parents, Robin watched Mike go outside, glad he did since she had allowed her parents to believe she was alone. Many times she had tried to work up the courage to tell them, but she never did. They had suffered too much heartbreak and upheaval in their lives after what had happened, and because of that, it wasn't at all likely they would understand her spending time with him.

During the call, she caught a chill, and from that point on, she wasn't herself. It was warm in the house, but for some reason she still shivered. She supposed it was nerves after her encounter with Mike and still found her heart racing at the mere memory of it. The feel of being in his arms had caused her to forget all her uncertainty. Her desire for him was unexpected, as if an explosion had happened in her heart. Even at that moment, the recollection of his warm hands on her face caused another shiver.

***

Mike turned at the sound of Robin opening the door.

"What are you doing out there?"

"Cooling down," he said as he stepped back indoors. He smiled down at her and reached out to rub his cold hands up and down on her arms. "I want you to know that was never my intention in coming here. Up until a few minutes ago, I never even thought about trying to get you into bed. I promise you."

"I don't think that."

Mike chuckled. "I'm thinking about it now for sure." He paused and reached for her hand. His heart was pounding still, and she looked so beautiful standing there looking up at him all wide-eyed. But he knew better than to allow things to go any further. "Tell me, can you honestly say you know where we stand?"

"No, not at all."

"As long as you have any uncertainty, I don't think we should go in that direction."

Robin rested her head on Mike's chest. "I agree."

"I couldn't be with you that way and then get on a plane and go home as if it never happened. When it does happen," he corrected himself, "if it does happen, it has to be forever. Agreed?"

She nodded.

When Robin shivered, he said, "Are you okay?" He lifted her chin to look up at him. "You're pale."

"I don't know. I'm not feeling well."

"Let's get you upstairs to bed." Mike chuckled again. "You know what I mean, to sleep. I'll come back down and take care of the fire and turn out the lights."

He walked up the first flight of stairs with her and continued up the second flight. What concerned him most was that she went from looking fine to white as a sheet in a matter of a few minutes. He wondered if the phone call had anything to do with it.

"Is everything okay? That phone call?"

When they reached her bedroom, she went and plopped down on the side of the bed.

"Oh, that was just my parents." With another shiver she reached for her quilt. "While we were talking, I got a chill. I hope I'm not coming down with something."

"Hey, the guy at the tree farm," he said.

"Oh, no!" She groaned.

While they were tying the tree onto the car, the man who had helped them was obviously sick because he complained and hacked and coughed in their direction the entire time.

"I'm not coughing, though."

He pressed his hand to her forehead. "You're warm. Do you have anything you can take?"

Without sitting up, she pointed to the bathroom. "Medicine cabinet, and there are paper cups under the sink."

When Mike returned, he held out the pills. "Here, sit up to take this."

She did and then rolled over onto her side and pulled the quilt up to her chin.

Mike sat on the side of the bed and looked around, wishing things were different. Everything in sight, all her belongings, were unfamiliar to him, which reminded him that he was an outsider now. Even though he had known and loved her for more than half the years he had been alive, here he wasn't a part of her world. He was a visitor, and in that moment he felt like a stranger. In the entire room all he recognized where the photos sitting on her bedside table, the one of Mikey's grave he had recently sent and the other a photo of him and Mikey. He reached for it and studied it, hardly able to believe she had kept a photo with him in it. It was taken on the front porch not long before their son had died. Of all the pictures of Mikey alone, why had she brought this one? He sat it back down as an unusual wave of emotion washed over him, and he was reminded of the worst truth of his life; his family was gone. He still felt like a dad and husband, yet he had no family. Nothing was more tragic to him than the loss of his wife and son.

He reached for her and stroked her hair. "Can I get you anything else?"

"No, I think I just need some rest. I'm sorry to cut the evening short."

"Probably safest. I'm sorry you feel bad, though." He stood to go. "Will you come get me if you need anything?"

"Yes," she said, barely mumbling the words.

Mike leaned back down and kissed her on the forehead. "Good night, sweetheart." When she didn't answer, he realized she was already drifting off to sleep. "I love you," he whispered.

"Love you, too," she whispered back.

He just stood there, staring at her, hoping that was still true.

TWENTY-EIGHT

Just after seven the next morning, Mike made his way up to Robin's room. He had been up for two hours, and every minute of it he had wondered if she was okay. He tapped on her bedroom door. "Robin, are you awake?" When he cracked the door open, he found her wrapped up in her quilt and shivering.

"I'm so sick. I've been throwing up most of the night."

At her bedside he pressed his hand to her forehead. "You're burning up. Why didn't you come get me?"

"I couldn't," she said through chattering teeth. "I felt too bad to even make it down the steps."

"Oh, baby." He kissed the top of her head. "I'll get you some more ibuprofen."

She slept off and on for hours, and he stayed there by her side the entire time. At one point when her temperature reached 103°, he suggested they go to the emergency room, but she refused, assuring him she would sleep it off.

There was a small TV sitting on her dresser, so Mike watched with the sound muted throughout the morning and past lunch, knowing there was nowhere else he would rather be than with her.

***

Throughout the morning, each time she had awoken, Robin found Mike there, sitting next to her in the bed. Most times, he was holding her hand or rubbing her head. She apologized for ruining their Christmas, but each time he shushed her. Next thing she knew, she was drifting off again. At least the vomiting had ended. Her last episode was just after he had come in that morning. All the while she had hovered over the toilet, he hovered over her, holding her hair back, whispering how sorry he was that she was sick. His tenderness toward her was a reminder of years past, when she was so sick early in her pregnancy. Those times, too, he stood with her and held her hair. Because that memory brought with it the best of them, she found herself

211

crying, yet unable to tell him what had caused her to. It would only hurt him to remind him of all they had lost.

At three that afternoon Robin awoke again to find Mike gone. When she heard the sound of him throwing up, she scrambled from the bed. She found him kneeling in front of the toilet heaving, so she reached for a washcloth, wet it, and pressed it against his forehead.

He waved his arm. "Go get back in bed."

"I'm okay. Let me help you." She ran her hand along his back.

For several minutes he was sick, and for a brief moment, she was reminded of the many times he vomited that way after drinking, especially when he first started going out after work. Robin pushed past the painful memory and prayed for him instead. It was what she did when the whispers came. She reminded herself, this wasn't that Mike. That man was dead and gone.

Finally, coming to a point where no more would come up, Mike fell back against the wall, took the cloth from her, and wiped his mouth.

"Merry Christmas. Can you wrap up a toothbrush?"

She laughed at that as she reached into the drawer for a new one. "Merry Christmas."

They shared the sink as they brushed their teeth and then made their way back to the bed. After taking ibuprofen with a shared cup, they climbed under two quilts and shivered together. He dragged her to him, wrapped himself around her, and within seconds, they were both drifting off to sleep.

The evening wore on like this with Robin feeling better first. She was far from well, but at least her fever had broken. Because she knew he must be starving, she slipped from the bed and made her way down the two dreaded flights of steps. She made him dry toast and opened a can of soda, and then she dragged herself back up the stairs. Back in her bedroom, she sat on his side of the bed and rubbed his forehead.

"Do you think you can eat something?"

His eyes were heavy as he peeked one eye open. "Are you better?"

"Yes, some."

He reached for her hand and pulled it to his cheek. "I don't like being a visitor."

At first she wasn't sure what he meant but then concluded he must wish he was at home in his own bedroom and could hardly blame him. It was miserable to be sick while traveling.

"Can you eat?"

"No, but thanks for bringing me something." He rolled over and went back to sleep.

212

It was the next morning before either was able to be up and around for long, having lost all of Christmas Day in bed. Robin stayed in her room to shower while Mike went downstairs to clean up. By the time she was dressed, she found him waiting in the parlor for her, sitting on the floor, leaning against the same chair he had on Christmas Eve.

"Merry day-after-Christmas."

Mike reached for her hand and pulled her toward him. "Is this our do-over?"

"I suppose it is." She sat next to him, noticing how pale he was still. "How will you travel today?"

"I'll be okay, but should I stay until you're better? I don't like the idea of leaving you alone while you are so weak."

"I'll be okay, too. You need to get back to work. I know this was last minute to begin with."

He squeezed her hand. "You're still pale."

"You are, too."

"I need to eat something and get some strength back. I'm not sure I can stomach anything, though," he said.

"I have some biscuits in the freezer. Let's start with that."

They had a small breakfast together and went back to the parlor to open gifts. Time was against them and both felt rushed. It wasn't at all what either had expected their Christmas together to be.

He gave her the first gift. "I hope this is okay."

Inside, she found CDs, something that made her smile. He used to make them for her when they were dating. "You made me CDs?"

"Not like before. These are all my favorite Christians songs. And there's a gift card to download music. I was thinking it would be something we could share. When you find something new you like, you can let me know, and I'll download it, too."

"Thank you for this. I like the idea of sharing music."

While she didn't say so, she was surprised. Mike had been a rock fan and could hardly tolerate what he called her Jesus music. This was an interesting new side of him.

When all the gifts were opened, both sat for a moment without speaking. With shirts – including her new red flannel one, socks, and books scattered about, there was also a new air of sadness that filled the room. Their time together had come to an end, and neither was ready for it.

Mike gazed out the window. "I'll call a taxi. I don't want you to get out in this weather."

"No, I'll take you."

"Please, it's cold out, and the roads are slick. I would rather say goodbye here. It will only be more difficult at the airport. On top of that I'll worry about you driving home, so please."

She sat there without arguing. It was hard letting him go. Now, she had to wonder what their relationship might look like going forward. After the closeness they had shared during their illness the day before and, she recalled with cheeks flushing, their kiss on Christmas Eve, was a simple friendship even possible anymore? What else was there for them, though? They lived eight hundred miles apart, and neither could afford to visit often enough to maintain a relationship.

"Your silence scares me." Mike reached for her and tucked her hair behind her ear. "Talk to me."

"I don't know where we go from here."

"Where do you want to go?"

"I'm not sure," Robin said.

He looked away.

Robin looked away too, hardly able to stand the look of sadness on his face. "I think for now we should leave things as they are."

There were no other options as far as she could see.

"That's what we'll do then," he said with forced enthusiasm.

Mike looked up at the grandfather clock and sighed. "It's time to get things packed up. Will you get me the number for a cab?"

She nodded, unable to speak for fear of crying.

Robin watched as Mike moved up the stairs to go pack, his sadness obvious in the way his shoulders slumped. It was reminiscent of the day he had come when Chris was there. She found it difficult to believe that soon after Mike's visit, she had told Chris that she had no intention of ever going back. In a way that was still her intention. But her feelings for Mike were altogether different now. Even though she wasn't sure about their way back, she had to believe there must be a way. How could they not with a love that could endure so much?

Mike's bags were by the front door and the cab was pulling into the lot of the inn. Robin stood there looking at him, wanting to say something that might reassure him over their future, but her thoughts were still so tangled that she didn't dare.

He pulled her to him and chuckled. "If I have to be sick, doing it with you is my first choice."

She grinned. "Me, too."

"Thank you for inviting me."

"Thank you for coming."

Her face was buried in his coat, and the thought of seeing him walk out that door was tearing at her heart. A small part of her wanted to beg him to stay, but then the whispers came and she had no strength to fight them. *It's too late*, were the words that echoed in her mind. How could they ever piece back together any sort of a life?

His words were soft and his voice cracked as he spoke. "This is even harder than I thought it would be."

She nodded.

The horn sounded again. He leaned down, kissed her cheek, and hovered there. "Stay inside where it's warm."

"Will you call me when you get home?"

"Of course I will." He reached for his bag.

Robin ignored his instructions, walked with him to the front door, and stepped out onto the porch. Mike walked on toward the cab, still so obviously ill that she wondered how he would make the trip. He seemed so weak.

It reminded her of the year before, standing on that very porch watching him leave. Then, he was completely broken, and for them both it was a final goodbye. This year, with him looking so weak, it felt as if she were watching an instant replay. Her heart was heavy knowing she wouldn't see him again for a long time. Though she was uncertain about a future, she was certain she wanted him to stay. She was certain she loved him. Reminiscent of that day the year before, her heart was tearing in two.

After he loaded his bag into the trunk, Mike jogged back up to where she was standing.

"I have to say this, Rob, to put it out there on the table. I want to come here, to be closer to you. I'll sell the house and come."

Robin looked away. "I don't know."

"I'm not pressuring you. I just wanted you to know I will. All you have to do is say the word, and I'll come."

"Can we give it some time?" she said.

"Of course." Mike took her into his arms and whispered, "You don't have to say anything, but I need you to know how much I love you, how much I will always love you." He sighed. "I promise, after this, we go back to being friends, no more love talk. But I had to say it."

Every word he spoke echoed her own heart. She kissed his cheek. "I love you right back."

The horn blasted again, so Mike turned to leave. For a final moment he stood by the open car door and held his hand out. It wasn't a wave exactly, just his hand extended. She did the same.

TWENTY-NINE

Emma had been home since the day after New Year's Day. Other than the worst cough she had ever had, Robin was feeling like herself again. All was back to normal at the inn, or what had become her new normal. She talked to Mike most days, and though she was no closer to defining their relationship, for the time being, it didn't seem to matter to either of them as long as they were able to stay in touch. January proceeded this way and then into February. Along with phone conversations, they wrote still, just not as often.

Stan had become a part of most of their evenings, so when he wasn't there that night, Robin wondered. Dinner progressed with no mention of him, but Emma's silence on the matter spoke volumes.

"So, where is Stan?" Robin watched Emma's face and was certain she winced.

"I don't know. I suppose he's home."

"Is everything okay?"

"Sure," Emma said with a smile. "Everything is just fine."

Robin knew better. "Did something happen between you?"

Emma set her fork down and shrugged her shoulders. "You know, things like this run their course. We had fun. What else can I say?"

"So it's over?"

"Yes." Emma stood, lifting her plate as she did so. "Don't worry. It's no big deal."

With no more said on the matter, she walked into the kitchen and left Robin sitting, holding her fork mid-bite.

Less than an hour later, Stan stood knocking at the door. Fortunately, Robin was the one to answer since Emma was upstairs soaking in the tub. Poor guy was standing there with flowers in hand, his nose and plump cheeks rosy from the brisk winter wind.

"Emma's up taking a bath right now. Would you like to wait."

"No, I better not. She asked me not to come. I just wanted to drop these off." He handed the bouquet of roses to Robin.

With flowers in hand, she stared at him for a moment. He was such a tender man, never more so than he seemed tonight. "I will tell her you stopped by."

He only nodded.

When he turned to go, Robin said, "Stan."

He looked back, eyes heavy with sadness.

"Don't give up on her. I have no doubt she cares about you."

"Oh, I don't plan to. I've known all along that woman would be a hard one to corral. I've been after her for nearly a decade now. I've got it in me to wait."

She smiled at that. "I'll try to talk some sense into her."

"You do that. In the meantime, expect a lot of flowers." He paused a moment. "I love her. I've loved her ever since I laid eyes on her."

"I can see that."

With a shiver and a wave he was off to his car.

Robin watched him go, determined to help them find a way back together. After that, for some time she sat alone beside the fire, praying for wisdom. More than anything, she wanted to see Emma love and be loved. It appeared, though, she would fight it to her own detriment.

When Emma never came back downstairs, Robin eventually went up to her room and found her there crying. She went and sat next to Emma on the bed.

"He loves you very much."

"I know."

"Then why are you doing this to him? I think you love him, too."

"Sometimes, people are just too different."

"What in the world are you talking about? You two have everything in common."

"He's such a good man."

"Yes, he is, and you're such an amazing woman. You belong together."

"There are things…" Emma trailed off as she looked away. "There are just some things that make it impossible. He'll find someone else."

"Are you kidding me? You're going to sit here and act like you don't care? I know you do."

Emma said nothing. After a quiet moment, she whispered, "Hummingbird, I really need some time alone."

Robin moved to the door and stopped there, then turned back to Emma. "What has you so bound?"

When Emma wouldn't look at her, Robin knew that she understood her meaning. They had discussed it before, but always Emma refused to tell her.

Emma said, "Choices. He deserves better."

Robin shook her head, frustrated over her friend's stubbornness. "I'm here when you're ready to talk."

"I know and thank you."

***

After work Mike had met Tim at the gym. When he got into his truck he noticed he had missed a call from Robin. He smiled. Since Christmas, he had done little but. Their relationship wasn't necessarily moving in a forward direction, but considering this time last year he had no hope of ever seeing her again, he would take what they had without complaint.

He dialed. When she answered, he said, "Hey, sorry I missed you. I've just left the gym."

"So you're driving then?"

"Yes."

"I wanted to talk to you about something. Why don't you call me when you get home."

Mike's stomach sank. "We can talk now."

"No, I'd rather talk when your home."

"You can't do this to me. Whatever it is, just say it."

"It's nothing bad, seriously. I didn't want to tell you in a letter, so I was going to when you were here. When we got sick and lost a day —"

"What? You're killing me." He sighed. "Look, I'll pull over if you want."

"I didn't mean to make it this big of a deal."

He pulled into a parking lot and stopped. "I'm parked in front of the library. I'm listening." He got out and went to lean against the hood of his truck, expecting the worst.

"It's something I should have told you when I was there. Honestly, I don't know why I didn't. It's about the divorce."

"Don't." Mike closed his eyes and bowed his head. "I don't want to talk about that. The day I signed those papers was one of the worst days of my life."

"I have the papers you signed, but I never filed them."

Mike's head snapped up. "What?"

"I never signed them. I couldn't."

He just stood there looking at his wedding band.

"Are you there?" Robin said.

"Yeah, I'm here, trying to figure out what to say."

"Say what you're thinking. I know it's a shock."

"I don't know if you want to know what I'm thinking."

"I do. Tell me."

"I'm thinking what I've been thinking since I left there. I think there's a chance for us. I think you're crazy for ever even talking to me again, but for whatever reason you are. You said you loved me while I was there. You haven't filed the divorce papers. All that tells me I should hold out hope for us to be together again."

Robin was quiet.

"If I'm off base, then tell me what this means."

"I don't know what it all means. I just thought you should know."

"You're my wife. I want to be with you. Let me come there. I said I wouldn't pressure you, and I won't. I'll get a place until we make some decisions, but being eight hundred miles apart will never allow us to see if there's a chance for us."

"Mike…"

When she became quiet, he said, "I know you're scared. I can hardly blame you. I'll tell you anything you want to know. I swear to you." Mike paused and closed his eyes. "I swear I'm not all mixed up in the head – not anymore. I don't always sleep well. Sometimes my mind just races and won't shut down, but it's not bad stuff I'm thinking about. And I never - ever have the urge to drink. It never even crosses my mind. I still cry a lot. I'm not sure that'll ever go away. It seems to be my release valve. But I'm okay now. I wouldn't lie to you."

"I'm not scared of you, Mike, not ever now. It's not that."

"Tell me what's still holding you back, then. Is it that last year? We've never really discussed it. Let's do that. Yell at me. Tell me how much I destroyed our lives. Do whatever you need to do, baby. Let's just get it out there."

"I don't need to revisit the past."

"So what then?"

"Honestly, I don't know. I just keep bumping up against a wall, and I don't understand it. Since you were here, I've been praying about it."

Mike said, "I have one question: Do you love me? I mean, like, are you still in love with me?"

"Yes."

"Then that's all I need to know. I will wait as long as you need. Rob, that final year, my greatest fear was losing you. I was so afraid you would leave me that I just kept hanging on tighter and tighter until I nearly crushed you. Now, you are sitting in my open palm. If you want me, I'm yours. There will never be a day that I'm not."

She began to cry.

"I'm so sorry. I didn't mean to make you cry."

"It's okay. I'm not upset."

"What are you then?"

"Relieved that you know. Relieved that you're willing to wait."

"Of course I will wait." Mike sighed. "You take all the time you need." He looked at his open palm. "And if you decide this isn't want you want, then I will let you go without a struggle. I will sign new papers. I will do anything you want me to do."

"For right now, I'm just asking for some time to figure this out."

"You have it."

Once they hung up, Mike shook his head. Nothing about that was expected. He laughed out loud at the fact that she was still his wife, then sunk to his knees at the goodness of God.

***

Weeks passed, and still Emma refused to speak to Stan. He called Robin often, and she sensed he was at the point of giving up. How could she blame him? With surprising determination he had wooed and pursued Emma without shame: calling, sending letters and flowers, and often stopping by unannounced, but his efforts were all in vain. Eventually, Robin began to feel sorry for him and to even hope, at least for his sake anyway, that Stan would stop the pursuit.

That thought made Robin stop in her tracks. Mike had been just a patient as Stan and still she held him at arm's length. The same wall kept giving her the same sense of hesitation. While she wouldn't dare tell Mike, at least she had come to better understand what the wall was constructed of: her fears, though never of him. She feared telling her parents. She feared Mike giving up his job and regretting it. For him to move to New Hampshire didn't sit well with her, especially since she had never felt as if she belonged there in the first place. That had led her to consider them moving somewhere else altogether, which presented them with the same problem of where Mike would work and her too, for that matter. At least at the inn she had a source of income.

She sighed. It all seemed too much to sort through and kept her thoughts tangled, so she ignored it as much as possible. In the meantime she and Mike spoke each day, sometimes more than once. The longer this went on, the more she knew she would have to make a decision. Never once had Mike pressured her. Instead, he simply ended every phone call by telling her that he loved her. She said the same. Deep down, Robin knew it would only be a matter of time until she agreed for him to come. Every time, though, that she thought of that for more than a minute or two, a heavy sense of angst settled in her chest and she had to push the thought away. In many ways she was acting like Emma, irrational, allowing old ghosts to keep her bound.

By all appearances winter was winding down. It was April and though all had not yet thawed, Robin watched as Emma kept herself deep in busyness, preparing guest rooms and planning menus. It was just a ruse to keep her mind and heart occupied.

One day, having had enough of the sulking and secrecy, Robin cornered Emma in the kitchen. "He's about to give up. Don't you care?"

"Of course I care."

"Why then? Why do you keep pushing him away? He loves you."

Emma walked over to the stool beside the island and tossed the cookbook onto the counter. "He doesn't know the real me."

"What do you mean?"

"I have a past I'm ashamed of, something I regret."

The memory of pulling that trigger came to Robin's mind. "We all have things we regret. That doesn't have to keep you so isolated."

"I thought I could keep it from him, but I can't. If I had stayed with him, I would have had to tell him things I'm not prepared to. It's just easier this way. I don't want him to think less of me."

"That would never happen. Stan loves you enough to keep up this pursuit. Surely you see that, how much he loves you."

Since Emma had accepted the Lord, they often spoke about her past. Robin knew something deep and deceptive had her utterly twisted in knots. Although she prayed about it time and time again, asking for insight, none came. Robin had explained the mending of the veil to her, and at times, Emma seemed likely to open up. Whatever it was, it would prevent her happiness and future with Stan if something wasn't resolved.

Robin walked over to her and took her by the hand. "What things are you talking about?"

Emma patted the stool next to her. "Hummingbird, you don't know the worst of me, either."

She sat. By the look on Emma's face, Robin realized for the first time how serious it must be, but still her heart was firm. "There's nothing I could find out about you that would change how I feel. I love you."

"Don't be so sure," Emma said.

"You realize, you'll never be free as long as you keep this inside? You can tell me anything."

Emma looked away and stared out the window. "After my fiancé died I found out I was pregnant. Early on it seemed like a gift, like a part of him I could hold onto, but then once the baby was born, I fell apart." She looked at Robin and sighed. "Now I guess you would call it post-partum depression, but back then, I had no idea what was going on. I thought it was just me, that I couldn't be a good mother. I cried every time the baby cried. I couldn't care for her. I was such a mess and could barely get through a day myself, let alone raise a baby.

"So I made the decision to give her up for adoption."

Robin put her arms around Emma. "You did what was best for your baby at the time. That's selfless."

"After a few months my mind began to clear." Emma shook her head. "I regretted what I had done, but it was too late. I still regret that decision more than any other thing in my life. If I could go back and do it all differently, I would."

"Now, you're afraid to tell Stan?"

Emma nodded and began to cry.

"He'll love you anyway."

"What about you?"

"Of course I love you. Nothing could ever change that."

Emma took Robin's hand and gave it a slight squeeze. "I gave my baby girl to my best friend since she couldn't have children of her own."

Robin sat frozen for a moment, trying to allow Emma's words to sink in. Her mom was Emma's best friend.

"I was that baby?"

"Yes."

Emma sat, waiting for some sort of reaction. Though Robin knew she needed to say something, instead, she sat still and quiet, trying to process Emma's revelation. All of a sudden, when looking back, her life was different – in many ways a lie.

For Emma's sake she said, "You made sure I had a very good home."

"I knew you would."

Still, Robin was hardly able to wrap her mind around it. Biologically, her mom wasn't her mom and her dad wasn't her dad. All those questions like, "Do I get my eyes from you or my nose from him?" she would ask her parents. How difficult that must have been for them, and all that time she had no idea whatsoever.

"Who was my father? What was his name?"

"Robert."

It was easy to connect the dots. "Robin? Is that where my name came from?"

"Yes." Emma touched her stomach and smiled. "When you would move, it felt like the fluttering of little wings. One day I called you Robin, and it just stuck. It was close to Robert, so I felt as if it would honor his memory."

"Hummingbird, where did that come from?"

Emma waved her hand. "Oh, there was no significance to that. When I would visit, you were such a busy little girl; one day I called you that and never stopped. The only thing I asked of your mother was to name you Robin. Well, that and that she not tell you about me. She hated being dishonest, but I made her swear.

"I think you should go and talk to them. They were willing to be open with you. I should have never put them in the position to keep it from you. Please don't blame them."

The rest of the day went by in a blur. Robin talked to Mike but didn't mentioned the adoption. It was hard enough to sort through in her own mind, let alone try to express her feelings aloud. Her flight to Tucson was scheduled for the next day, and until she spoke with her parents, she thought it best not to tell him.

Emma was gone to talk to Stan, leaving Robin alone with her thoughts. Her mind was still reeling after Emma's revelation. Although she tried to pretend she wasn't affected, she was. She didn't like that she was kept in the dark. That's what bothered her most. Since Emma had asked her parents not to tell, she could hardly fault them. Now that she knew they couldn't have a child biologically, she would have to guess they would have agreed to anything to get a baby. So that left Emma to blame, but honestly, after hearing her story, Robin couldn't find it in her heart to be angry with her either. Actually, because she had witnessed the life of self-imposed punishment Emma had lived, she knew Emma had been punished enough.

All these emotions stirring within had no outlet and only added to her already congested state of mind. Robin was at a loss. She prayed but heard nothing in return. She prayed over the conversation with her parents. She prayed not to look at Emma in a negative light. Her prayers were pouring out from a wounded heart, but all she heard was silence.

She prayed about Mike, about how to proceed in their relationship since every time she had talked to him recently she felt a heightening sense of confusion. Nothing was right anymore.

THIRTY

From the time she arrived in Tucson until this moment, Robin had wondered how to bring up the subject of the adoption. Her parents had taken her out for lunch, but a public place wasn't at all fitting for the conversation. Now, back at her parents' place, Robin was still dreading the conversation ahead. By this point she wished she didn't know. Ignorance had been bliss.

She put her suitcase in what they called her room, but even as she sat on the bed and looked around, it was all so foreign to her. Many of her things were in that room, things her parents had brought from Whitley, but this wasn't her room. No stuffed animals or photos could recreate the memories she had back in her old room. This wasn't her home. Even though her parents lived there, she would never have that sense of going home that most adult kids would feel when visiting their parents. She hadn't felt that since the storm tossed her to New Hampshire, which was why she seldom visited her folks.

"You okay?" Her mom was standing in the doorway.

"I feel out of sorts today."

"Anything you want to talk about?"

Robin nodded. "Yeah, that's why I'm here, but I would like to talk to you and Daddy together."

Once Robin was seated with her parents at the dining room table, she said, "Before I say anything at all, I want you to know how much I love you both."

Her mother's expression fell, and Robin had a sense that her mom knew what was coming.

"Emma told me about the adoption."

Bill reached over and took Robin's hand. "That means nothing. You're my kid – always have been."

"I know that, Daddy."

Robin looked at her mom. "Are you okay?"

Linda nodded. "I wanted to tell you, but I promised her."

"I know. I understand."

"You were this little unexpected gift. When she said I could have you…" Tears filled Linda's eyes. "I could hardly believe it was true. From the moment I scooped you up into my arms, you have been my heartbeat."

"I don't doubt that, Mama." Robin moved from her seat and went to hug her mother. "I only came so we could talk in person. I'm not upset with you."

How could Robin be angry with parents who had loved her so well? Her life growing up had been ideal with both a father and a mother. Had Emma kept her, she would have been raised without a father. Robin wouldn't have missed being a daddy's girl for the world.

Robin spent three days at her parents' home but left more unsettled than when she arrived. While on the way to the airport with her dad, her mind was filled with wandering thoughts as her dad talked on the phone. Oddly enough, her unease had nothing to do with the adoption or the secrets surrounding it. It was more the fact that she realized there was nowhere she belonged anymore. Her parents had a new life in Tucson, one that seemed to make them happy but one where she had no place.

Someday, probably sooner rather than later if Stan had his way about it, he and Emma would marry. Where would that leave her? Although certain she would be welcome to stay on at the inn, could she live with the newly married couple and still feel as if she belonged? The thought of it seemed awkward. Newlyweds deserved privacy. Though running an inn allowed little room for privacy, strangers around was one thing, but a daughter who recently found out she was a daughter seemed beyond awkward. Who knew, maybe Emma would decide to give up the inn? So, if not the inn and not with her parents, where did she belong?

Even worse, here she was at thirty years old feeling hurt that she didn't belong at her parents' anymore. She was a grown woman and wasn't supposed to belong there. Something was off in general. Everything was bothering her, and that just wasn't like her.

At the airport Robin asked that her father drop her off at the departing flights lane rather than going in for a long goodbye. After going through a tearful goodbye with her mother at the house, her emotions could handle no more.

Bill reached into the trunk for Robin's suitcase. "Let me park and come wait with you."

"I'm fine, Daddy, really."

"Are you sure? This is some big news to process."

Robin was tempted to tell her dad about Mike. It was an opportune time since she could just blurt it out and run catch her flight. She chickened out, though.

"It is big, but nothing too big to handle." She paused. "You know how much I love you, right? And Mom?"

"I do know. Same here, kiddo. You'll always be my little girl." He hugged her. "I love you so much."

Once he finally let her go and got back in the car, she watched him as he drove away. The moment he was out of sight, Robin went straight to the airline counter and changed her flight. Instead of flying directly to Concord, she added a layover in Raleigh. Uncertain how it might help, all she knew was that a familiar face and sympathetic ear was what she felt she needed at the moment. She needed Mike.

With her new ticket in-hand, Robin sat on a hard plastic chair at her gate, pondering, at a loss as to how to make sense of her life. There was a new turmoil stirring within her. She prayed about it all throughout the morning, but peace never came. Since walking again with the Lord, there was a sustained peace she had experienced, even when perplexed or uncertain about things, but that peace was gone, and in its place were chaotic thoughts and unsettled feelings. She couldn't seem to find her way through the maze of unresolved emotions.

She deliberated between three states and three sources of confusion. In New Hampshire there would soon be no room for her at the inn. With a grin at her own play on words, she thought of Emma and Stan, and knew that, out of kindness, they would welcome her. Still, something about the thought of it unsettled her. In Tucson her parents' new life held no place for her. Worst of all options, in North Carolina her face was on a proverbial wanted poster. Now, she not only felt misplaced, she felt alone.

Disturbed by this lack of peace, she thought of Chris's words, how, when you experience chaos and turmoil, you must look for the ways you may have stepped away from the Lord. "Lord, I don't feel as if I've moved a step. Tell me what's going on. I'm so sad – like before." She heard nothing in response.

By late afternoon on Saturday, Robin was driving towards her old hometown. Just as she had the last time she visited Mike, as she passed through the town, she looked straight ahead and didn't make eye-contact with anyone on the sidewalk. Then, she had made it a point to go straight to Mike's, the cemetery, and leave town. This day, however, she was daring a stop.

Inside the bakery she was startled to see Mrs. Andrews, whose husband was Mike's football coach all throughout high school. Unsure how she might be received, Robin said, "Hi there, Mrs. Andrews."

"Robin." Ellen's voice was cool.

"I would like a dozen of the chocolate chip." Robin said, pointing to the case, trying not to make eye contact.

Ellen slung the case door aside and reached in with a paper tissue to grab half a dozen cookies. She dropped them in a white paper sack then repeated the process. When finished, she slung the door closed again. "That'll be two-fifty."

Robin handed her a five and noticed how her hand shook. Why had she come in? She knew better but somehow hoped things might be different after so many years.

Ellen accepted the cash and dropped the change on the counter. "You have some nerve."

Robin took the bag and turned to leave.

"He's rebuilding his life. Last thing he needs is for you to come 'round and mess that up. He's a good man, too good for his own good, I s'pose."

Without turning or responding, Robin walked through the door and inched like a lowly worm to her car. She drove around for a few minutes to clear her head and found a drive by of her childhood home was a huge mistake. It reminded her of her earlier reflections of the morning. Where did she belong? What was certain was that it wasn't there in that town. That fact led to deeper concerns.

What was she doing with Mike? He belonged there, nowhere else. Their only possibility of being together was for him to leave his home and his job. She had no doubt he was willing, but she was too uncertain about everything to ask him to do that. Her dilemma was becoming more and more complex. Doubt was creeping in, and she was beginning to question everything.

She called Mike, wondering if she had made a mistake in coming.

"Hello."

"What are you up to?" More specifically, she needed to find out where he was. She had already driven by the house and knew he wasn't at home.

"Cleaning up around the church." He chuckled. "Well, taking a break now. What are you up to? Still with your folks?"

"No. I'm just out running some errands. I stopped off and bought some cookies."

"What, not homemade?"

"Not today."

"Don't bother mailing them. Well, you can bother, a cookie is a cookie."

When she pulled into the parking lot of the church, Robin saw Mike sitting on the front steps. Just as he had the last time she came to town, he wore jeans and a white t-shirt. Even at such a distance, the sight of him caused her heart to flutter like a butterfly was trapped inside, bouncing around, trying to get out.

He still hadn't seen her, so sitting for a moment longer, she studied the white building. It was her church from the time she was born, well, from the time she came to live in Whitley. It was where she and Mike had married. Those very steps where he sat were the same ones they had run down after they were pronounced man and wife, being pelted by birdseed. That memory sent her over an emotional cliff, and she began to cry.

"Robin, are you crying?"

She sat for a moment without answering and watched him as he rubbed his chin. His head was bowed.

"Baby, tell me why you're crying?"

"I'm okay."

She wiped her eyes, grabbed the bag of cookies, and began to walk toward the church.

When Mike looked up and caught sight of her, he bounded off the steps, scooped her up in his arms, and spun her round and round.

When he lowered her to the ground, he said, "What are you doing here?"

"I was hoping to talk."

He took her hand and led her to the porch. "Were you crying just now? You never cry."

"Not all-out crying."

Robin knew she couldn't tell him the craziness that was going on in her head. After the expression on his face when he saw that she was there, it would be like pulling the rug out from beneath him if she told him of her reservations. That wasn't her intention in the trip at all.

"Not homemade," she said as she handed him the bag.

Mike reached in for a cookie and offered her one.

The blood rushed to her face when she thought of Mrs. Andrews. She shook her head. "None for me."

He dropped his cookie back in the bag and pulled her nearer. "What's wrong, Rob? Talk to me."

Robin leaned her head on his shoulder and sighed. "I just found out I was adopted. That's some big news, huh?"

He just sat there. With his arm wrapped around her shoulder, he gave her a little squeeze. "Wow."

"Emma is my biological mother."

"Humph! I didn't see that coming."

"Yeah, me neither."

"How do you feel about it?"

"I'm not exactly sure." She paused and thought. "I do feel like I don't know who I am now. Like I'm not who I once thought I was."

"Sure you are. You're no different today than you always were."

"You were there for most of my life. Looking back, did I miss something?"

"No, not at all. There's no way you could have known. I mean, I guess it was unusual how Emma treated you. Think about the elaborate birthday gifts and wedding gifts. She showered you with stuff as long as I knew you."

"True, but I didn't know that was unusual. I thought it was because she never had kids of her own." She shook her head. "You know what I mean – besides me."

They had talked for a while when finally he said, "You seem okay with this. So why were you crying?"

"I've been sad today. At my parents, I don't know, they are so far away, and I'm not part of their lives now. Nothing fits anymore."

"I get that."

When she said nothing more for some time, he turned to her. "Are you hungry? We can go grab a bite at the diner and talk."

The thought of that made her nauseous. "I don't think so."

"Does anything else sound good?"

"I don't want to go anywhere or see anyone. I don't belong here anymore, Mike."

"Of course you do. After so long away I know plenty of folks would be glad to see you."

"You're wrong!" She cut her eyes around at him. "You can't possibly know what it was like after…" Robin stopped. The last thing she wanted was to bring up the past. It was much too painful for them both.

"What?"

Her tone softened. "Once you were gone, things were different for me, my parents, too. The town became different."

He reached for her, rubbing his hand in circles on her back. "Different how? As far as I can tell, this town never, ever changes. Same people. Same day in and day out."

She realized he honestly had no idea what had happened and didn't have the heart to tell him. "Nothing, it doesn't matter now." She stood. "I think I need to head on back to Raleigh now. Thanks for talking to me, though."

Robin walked down the church steps, trying to drown out the cheers of onlookers as they tossed birdseed at her. The memory of it was so vivid, she had to blink repeatedly in order to stop seeing the people there lining the sidewalk. The recollection brought with it such heartbreak, she was uncertain if she could make it to the car without crying again. A phrase crossed her mind that caused her to pause there on the bottom step – and two shall become one. She turned and looked up at the church, and for the first time in many months, intentionally closed her heart off to what she feared God was telling her.

Mike jumped to his feet and followed her.

"Let me come with you. We can have dinner in Raleigh and talk some more."

"I don't think so. I need to go by and see Mikey. I think I want to do that alone."

Mike walked her to the car, put his arms around her, and held her close. He whispered something she couldn't make out, about it being good to see her. With the haze and confusion that was plaguing her mind, she couldn't seem to process what he was saying. More than anything, she just needed to get away from that church and out of that town as soon as she could.

***

Unable to believe that she was leaving already, Mike just stood there and watched her go. There was something different about her, something distant. When they were together at Christmas, he sensed her fear, in that they were getting closer and it scared her, or maybe she feared what she was feeling. This time, however, it wasn't the same. It was emotional distance. She was pulling away from him. Deep down in his spirit, he knew it was about to be over.

Mike tapped on the screen door of his mother's house and said, "Mama!"

When she never answered, he let himself in and found her in the back bedroom, vacuuming Trevor's old room.

"What are you doing here?"

"I need to talk to you."

"Sure thing."

She set the vacuum back upright and followed him into the kitchen.

"Looks good in here. Spring cleaning?"

"Sorta. I haven't smoked in three days. I gotta keep busy or I'll blow it."

"Hey, good for you." He grabbed her hand and squeezed. "I'm so proud of you."

Since Robin had said the things she had in her letters about his mother, he was making an effort to be more kind and loving toward her. Until recently, he hadn't realized how much he used to distance himself from her. Other than Trevor and him, she had no one, so it was important for them to reconnect.

"I think I might make it this time," she said with hope. "I tried last month but didn't make it past day two."

When Mike sat at the kitchen table, she joined him.

"What is it you want to talk about?"

"Once I was gone, what was it like for Robin here?"

Kathy looked away and shook her head. "It was tough on her. Everybody turned on her and her parents, too."

"What do you mean, 'turned on her'?"

"They blamed her for what happened."

"How could they possibly blame her?"

Mike shook his head. Had they not seen what he saw in the photographs? The images flooded his mind, reminding him how crazed he was that night and how close he had come to killing her.

Kathy looked at her son. "You were their star, Mike. In their eyes you could do no wrong. When they could think of no way to make sense of what happened, they made things up."

"Like what?"

"Rumors started going around that you caught her cheatin' and that you got into it with the man she was sleeping with. Said she shot you to protect him and that you took the blame just to save her from going to jail. They glorified you, as if you were some saint. They had to know you were out drinking several nights a week. If they knew, they sure never spread that around. Folks said all kinds of things but never bad about you. One night, while she was still at her parents' house, someone dumped trash all over the yard and painted nasty things on the garage. She left right after that."

Mike sat there rubbing the stubble on his chin. "I don't know what to say, Mama. I had no idea."

"People like a shooting star, not a falling one. They didn't want to believe you were the problem." She stood to get a cup of coffee. "Some people know the truth, though, 'cause when anyone said anything to me, I set 'em straight.

"Can you believe a town that knows so much about everyone doesn't know the truth about you?"

Mike hung his head and whispered, "It was all me."

"I know." She patted his hand and shook her head. "I should have said something. I suspected – no, I knew what was going on, but I didn't want to butt in. I saw the signs but said nothing. After that night I sure wished I had." She sat for a moment more. "I blame myself."

"Don't. There's no one to blame but me. I accept that." When his mother never responded, he said, "Robin was here today."

"She was here? Really, what for?"

"She just wanted to talk. Some things are going on. I tried to get her to go out to eat with me, but she said she didn't want to see anyone. No wonder she feels that way."

231

***

Back in her hotel room Robin ate fast food and watched TV. Mike had called twice, and both times, she had let it go to voicemail. Her time at Mikey's grave had been so emotionally draining that she didn't have anything left to draw from. Mike would ask questions and at that point, Robin had no answers. All she wanted to do was be gone from there. While at the cemetery, she had reconciled herself to the fact that she wouldn't be back. That was the last time she would look at that headstone with her son's name engraved on it. It was that understanding that had caused her to crumble, that and the memory of the look of pain on Mike's face when she had left him so soon.

Since Christmas, she had actually entertained the idea of Mike moving to New Hampshire. Many times she had prayed about it. Now, she knew it was for the best that he didn't. She was too uncertain about their future together for him to uproot his life. There was never a moment when she doubted her feelings for him. She loved him, but ultimately, she didn't see a way back for them. There were too many obstacles to overcome, too many bad memories.

Robin dialed Emma. When she answered, Robin said, "It's not too late, is it? Were you in the bed yet?"

"Not yet. I'm just slathering my face with cold cream."

Robin could only smile at that, at Emma's long nighttime ritual. No wonder her skin was so smooth in her fifties.

"How are things with Stan?"

"Going great. We're back on track."

"Do you think you'll marry? Is it too early for me to ask that?"

"I don't know, sweetie. I'm awfully set in my ways."

"If you do, will you keep the inn?"

"Of course I will. Why do you ask?"

"I'm wondering if you think it'll seem awkward with me there."

There was a long pause, so Robin said, "Forget I asked. If you marry –"

"You are wanted if that's what you're thinking. I'm just surprised you asked."

"I'm not sure what else I would do. I just want to go back to the way things were – I mean things after Chris not before."

"So your visit with Mike isn't going well?"

"It was fine. I didn't stay long. I'm in Raleigh now."

Emma sighed. "What's going on with you? You're not acting like yourself."

"Honestly, I don't know. Nothing seems right anymore. I don't think it's going to work out with Mike. I don't think I'm able to go back."

"You mean back there or back with Mike."

"Either. I just want to come home – you know what I mean, to the inn."

"This is your home, Hummingbird. Come home."

***

The next morning, standing outside of his truck, Mike looked up at the hotel building, wondering which room Robin was in. He had been sitting in the parking lot for more than an hour, waiting for it to be late enough to call. The night before had been agonizing, and he hadn't slept even a moment. When he decided to drive to Raleigh, by that point he knew what he would encounter there. The anticipation of it was maddening, but if it was what she wanted, to never hear from him again, he would comply with her wishes. There's nothing he wouldn't do for her, even if that meant walking away.

Finally, thinking it was late enough, he dialed her number.

Robin answered. "Hello."

"I'm here. Can we have breakfast?"

"I think that would be a good idea."

He closed his eyes. "I'll meet you across the street. Pancakes okay?"

"Sure."

He sighed, her tone exactly what he had expected.

Mike sat across from Robin in a booth, and they both ordered. She wasn't saying much, which only confirmed what he knew was coming. For some time they just sat, looking at each other.

"I talked to my mom last night. I never knew what it was like for you then. I'm so sorry, Rob."

She looked away. "That's over now."

"Because of me, you lost everything: your family, your home, everything you've ever known. It was all my doing, and I'm sorrier than I could ever possibly express."

Their food arrived, and for a moment both sat again in silence. Mike mostly picked at his food and noticed she did the same. It was a chilly morning, and she wore the Panthers hoodie he had given her for Christmas. Out of that thought flowed the memory of their kiss, still as fresh on his lips as Christmas Eve. It was a memory he forced from his mind, especially knowing there was no more hope.

Finally, Robin rested her fork on her plate, "Mike, I'm glad you came this morning. I think we should talk."

He pushed his plate away and waited for the inevitable. He felt sorry for her as she struggled for the right words, ones that would let him down as easily as possible. She had such a tender heart, and the last thing he wanted was for it to be so difficult for her.

"That note you sent, where you said this might be a mistake. I think maybe you were right."

Mike exhaled as if he had been punched in the gut. Unable to look at her, he hung his head and rubbed his forehead, reminding himself how grateful he was for the time he had with her and praying for strength to do what he knew was right. While his first inclination was to fight for her, to try to convince her to give them a chance, he wanted her to be happy. Since the day before, he could tell she wasn't, so he would have to let her go. He wanted to say something to reassure her, but words failed him.

"I'm sorry, Mike. I think this is best for us both."

He looked up at her. "It's not best for me, but if you feel it is for you, then I won't try to change your mind."

Robin looked away. "I'm still bumping up against that same wall. I can't get past it all."

"I don't blame you. How could you?"

With both hands extended palm side up, Mike leaned in. "I've held you here, knowing this was the likely outcome. All along I've said we will do this however you want. I just thank you for the past eight months. Thank you for forgiveness. Thank you for doing this in person so that I could see you one last time."

He stood, leaned down, and kissed the top of her head.

After tossing a twenty onto the table, Mike turned and walked out of the restaurant. Once in his truck, he leaned his head over the steering wheel and began to sob. He recalled the words of Job. "Lord, though You slay me, still I will trust You."

Though he had plenty of time to make it on time, Mike decided to skip church. He needed to be alone with the Lord. On his knees in the kitchen, the place where the final events of that last night had taken place, he prayed for Robin and for strength to live another day without her. Once, crying out, he said, "I don't even know what to ask. I'm so lost in my grief. Won't You please help me?"

After many hours of this, Mike heard the Lord speak as loudly and as clearly as he ever had. In that moment he caught a glimpse of what his future held, and he had to trust God's grace was sufficient to carry him through.

He took out several sheets of paper and began to write.

THIRTY-ONE

That afternoon, when Robin arrived home, she spoke to Emma for a brief moment and then went up to her room. She was numb, the way she used to feel before meeting with Chris, as if the door to her feelings had closed again. Though she prayed and prayed, the door remained shut. For the next few days, it seemed as if every prayer was bouncing off the ceiling and she couldn't sense God's presence as she had come to know over the past year, leaving her to try to face this new separation from Mike all alone.

It was springtime, and her days wore on and on, even while she remained engaged in a flurry of activity, cleaning and preparing for the onslaught of guests in the months to come. She kept to herself, trying to find relief. Often, she spent her mornings on the dock, wrapped up in a blanket, pleading for a breakthrough that never came.

By Friday afternoon she was at the breaking point. She sat on the steps and looked out at the water, too sad even to pray. Simply, she missed Mike. Their last morning together haunted her still, the look on his face ever in the forefront of her mind.

Emma came and sat next to her. "Letter for you. I hope it's good news." She paused. "You haven't been yourself since you've been back. Are we good?"

"Of course we're good. This isn't about you."

"What are you doing, Hummingbird?"

"What do you mean?"

"You've ended things with Mike. It's obvious."

"I just can't..." Robin looked away.

"Of all people, for me to say this surprises even me. You love him, so I don't understand why you're pushing him away."

Robin said nothing but only shook her head.

"What's holding you back?"

"I wish I knew for sure. I thinks it several things that make it all seem impossible."

"Like?"

"I can't bring myself to tell my parents. Can you imagine how they'll react?"

235

Emma nodded. "That's a tough one, but not impossible. They want what you want – like me."

"He doesn't belong here. There's nothing for him. He would have to give up doing what he loves to do what? With his past I bet he couldn't even get a security job. I can't go back to Whitley." She glanced at Emma. "You know how things ended there."

"Yeah, I do know how things ended, but that doesn't mean it'll be that way after all this time."

With the blood rushing to her cheeks, Robin said, "Oh, they haven't forgotten. Trust me."

Emma sat for a moment and finally reached for Robin's hand. "For one, and I hate to say this since it's an insult, but you're acting like me. You can't come back here and bury your head." Emma gave her hand a squeeze. "And two, that's your town. You grew up there. Maybe you need to stop fighting against your home and decide to fight for your home.

"Robin, you're a grown woman. If you want to make your marriage work, it's not your parents' business. It's not my business. It's yours. This is your life, and as your second mom, I won't allow you to throw it away here just because you're scared."

Robin allowed Emma's words to sink in. What she said about fighting for her home was one of the wisest statements she had heard since her bare-footed counselor. "When did you get so smart?"

With her arm draped around Robin's shoulder, Emma pulled her close. "Moms just know stuff like this. I'm a late starter, but I'm catching on."

Emma stood. "I'll leave you to your letter. Find me if you want to talk. I'm always here for you."

"I know that. I will."

Mike's handwriting on the envelope caused her to sigh. He had addressed it as Robin Jacobs. All the months before, he had written McGarrett – even before he knew the divorce was never finalized. This was the image of him letting go. That made her sad for him, for what that must have felt like for him to give her up as his wife. She pulled out the paper and waited. When writing before, she had been so eager to read every word he wrote. This time, however, she dreaded it. It would be painful, and she was so weary of the pain.

> My Sweet Robin,
> I'm sorry I was unable say more when we were together. Honestly, I couldn't trust myself to say the right thing, so I figured it was best not to say much at all.
> Even as I write this letter, I realize the selfishness of it, the one thing I've been most guilty of. I should say what I've said before,

that I want you to be able to move on. I can't. I do want you to
have a future and a husband who will cherish you and especially
to be a mom again. You were an incredible mom. But I have to
admit; I want to be your future. I want that man to be me. I want
a family with you again.

I have this vision of us, after overcoming such a horrendous
past, that we can help others. I can see it. I can see God using this
for good.

That morning you seemed conflicted, and part of me wants
to believe you may be uncertain of your decision. Just in case you
are, I will share what I read yesterday in my devotion. It's what
prompted this letter. In the Psalms, there's a verse that says, "…
with my God I can scale a wall." You said you're still bumping up
against a wall. I get this mental image of God carrying you to the
top of that wall if only you would allow Him. That's all you have
to do, just make it to the top. If the way down seems too far, it's
okay, just let go, and I'll catch you. I promise I'll catch you. I'm
here with both arms open.

Maybe your decision is firm. Maybe the wall is one you want
to remain. If that's the case, then send me divorce papers, and I
will sign them with no fight. I will give you anything you want
even if that's your freedom from me.

As for me, I have to make this declaration: no matter what
any court says, you are my wife and the mother of my only son.
The verse, "husband of but one wife," continually rings in my
head. I know that's what God is calling me to be – only yours. Not
just now but for life. No one but you. I made that commitment to
you all those years ago, and it stands today. No one but you, ever!
I will never be anything other than your husband. I will always
pray for you, seeking your happiness above my own. I love you.

Always,
Mike

Robin began to wail. She curled into a ball, rolled over onto the grass,
and wept as hard as she ever had. The past years away from him she had
existed in a walking, talking coma state. At least then there was less pain
because she had, in a sense, died to her former life. Over the past months,
though, allowing him to be a part of her life, her dormant heart had been
resurrected. It was alive and in the deepest anguish she had known since the
day they buried their son.

She had ended things with Mike based on fear, not what her heart felt for
him. Deep inside her spirit, though she had sworn she would never return to
that town, a tiny little seed was growing. Already, she had a sense that God
would call her back there, and quite simply, she had tried her best to ignore it.

Like a child might do, she had stood with fingers in her ears, warding off the instructions she didn't want to hear. Only now did she understand the extent of how she had ignored her heavenly Father. Over the past weeks there was that still, small voice that whispered, "…and two shall become one." It was a whisper she had disregarded.

Now it made sense why she had such an uneasy feeling every time she considered Mike moving to New Hampshire. The wall she was colliding with wasn't about being with Mike, it was about where they were supposed to be.

In the days to follow, Robin lived in complete and utter turmoil. She could find no peace in the thought of remaining in New England, nor could she find relief in the prospect of returning to North Carolina. One afternoon, she sat still before the Lord. There in her healing chair, she looked across at the empty chair. Aloud, she said to God, "It's pride – has been all along." Since the early hours of the morning, she had been contending with pride. To admit it was the hard part, but once she did, narrowing in on the many facets of it was fairly easy. Her truest fear in going back was that the truth was out; they, she and Mike, were not perfect after all.

It had all seemed so perfect, and somewhere along the way, she had begun to believe it, too. It was in protecting that lie that she had refused to admit something was wrong with Mike when he came home from Afghanistan. When he began to drink and subsequently to hit her, it was in order to protect the lie that she never told anyone. To suffer at his hand was a lesser consequence than to make public their failings.

The Lord revealed to her that, though she was in the spotlight all those years because of Mike, she had still felt invisible, and deep down she had known that. She was somehow absorbed in Mike's glory, a byproduct of his greatness. When she was his girlfriend, then his wife, that made her feel like somebody. It took all that had happened between them to strip her away from Mike so that she might be torn down completely and rebuilt. She had to discover who she was and Whose she was in Mike's absence. In her new walk with Jesus, He made it clear to her, she was somebody to Him. She – or they, didn't have to be perfect, and to strive for that would lead to destruction. Had that not been well-proven?

Only now was she seeing who God had created her to be. She would continue working toward her degree and help people like Chris did, people like her who struggle with past trauma and loss. In a sense she would carry on Chris's legacy. None of that would have likely happened without this time at the inn. If Mike had gotten help and she had never left, she would have remained wrapped-up in her husband and never found her Groom.

It was late Tuesday night and Robin was sitting in the parlor reading Chris's Bible. She sat in the same spot where Mike had sat at Christmas, where he had kissed her. With a smile she touched her fingertips to her lips. "...and two shall become one," echoed again in her mind.

Her mind was distracted from her reading. She had scanned the same words over and over and could hardly comprehend what she was reading. No matter how hard she tried, she was unable to move past them. Finally, beginning again, she allowed the words to drop into her heart as dew would settle onto early morning grass. The words she read, without question, were the very words of God, His assurance, His promise of protection.

> "The fear of man bringeth a snare: but whoso putteth his trust in the LORD shall be safe." (Proverbs 29:25)

Frozen in place, Robin sat staring at those words. The Lord was not only calling her to go home, He was promising her protection when she did. This was as clear as she had heard from Him in weeks. The reason why He had seemed so far away was that she had been running from Him again. That explained the turmoil. The chaos in her heart and mind stemmed from her refusal to obey. It was she who had moved – not God. A vivid flashback of what life felt like without Jesus near was enough to bring tears to her eyes. She would not – no she could not live life that way ever again. With determination, she pulled the fingers from the little girl's ears and said, "Speak, Lord, for your servant is listening."

With her heart blazing within, she rushed to the small desk in the corner, pulled out a sheet of paper, and began what would be her journey home. Afterward, she ran up to her room, rummaged through her boxes until she came to the one she was looking for. She took the small box from a larger one, opened it, and gazed with tear-filled eyes at her wedding band, recalling how one day, soon after she had arrived at the inn, she had been tempted to throw it into the water. Thankfully, something prevented her from going through with it. Unsure at the time what caused her hesitation, there was now no doubt.

Robin grinned as she whispered to Jesus, "You always knew."

The next morning, Robin mailed her letter to Mike. Just as they had lived and loved through the written word from teenagers to a newly married couple, and ultimately a separated one, it befitted their love story to reunite in the same way. His declaration was merely the beginning of the end of life apart. Her plan was to show up and surprise him, and in her mind she tried to imagine his reaction, what the look on his face might be. Many times since they parted that last morning – that was the face she would see when she thought of him, how devastated he was. Soon that would change. It was all she could think of while packing: wrapping her arms around him and telling him she was home forever.

Forever. That word brought with it memories of Christmas Eve, of how close they had come to making love. He had said, "When it does happen, if it does happen, it has to be forever." Robin now had no reservations; it would be forever.

Robin's plan was to spend time with Emma on Wednesday and then begin to pack up her car. She would leave Thursday around midday and stop for the night when she became too tired to drive. By the time Mike returned home from work on Friday, she would be waiting for him. For the first time in years, the idea of going home gave Robin a sense of indescribable peace.

THIRTY-TWO

After lunch the day her daughter was to leave her for good, Emma walked with Robin to her car. She was weepy, having been so all morning. Stan would be arriving soon. He was a good man, and she was so blessed to have him in her life. With Robin gone Emma would be ready to start a new life with him. If Robin had stayed, she wasn't so sure she would have allowed the relationship to get much more serious. Her devotion would have been to Robin first.

Finally, after serious misgivings over Mike, Emma no longer feared he would revert back to the man he had once been. She had to trust her daughter's judgment. She had to trust God with her. This was new, this trusting God business, but she was trying to get the hang of it.

"Becky and Tommy will be here soon. Don't worry," Emma reminded her as they walked. Robin had been fretting that she was leaving her with no help. "After finals they'll both be here. If things get too hectic, I'll hire someone for mornings to help with breakfast." She took Robin's face in her hands and said, "Hummingbird, I've got this. It's time for you to fly again."

"I know. I just worry about you, though. I love you."

"Sweet girl, I know you do, and I love you more."

Emma wrapped her arms around Robin and reveled in the fact that she had a daughter who loved her. All the shame and guilt she had carried over the years was lifted, and she felt freer than she had in over thirty years. The secrecy was finally over, and she could do the things for Robin that she had always wanted to do. After Robin and Mike returned from California, she wanted to buy them a house to give them a fresh start. Of course she insisted that Robin's parents make the arrangements, like they were paying for it. Emma wanted to give Robin everything she hadn't been able to over the years. Money meant nothing to her but Robin was everything.

"Listen, when you get there, it may be like starting over. If you need anything for the house, you let me know. I love that kind of thing. You know that. Let me help you. I'll fly down and we'll shop and decorate."

"I will."

"One more thing." Emma looked up at the house and then back at Robin. "What?"

"Someday, I want you to have this place. It could never mean to anyone else what it means to us. It's a special place, a place where you and I were both healed."

"I would be honored to take over someday. I like the thought of living here with Mike. He'll retire someday."

"So get in the car already."

Robin just stood there looking at her wide-eyed for a few seconds and then moved in to hug her. "I would've never made it without you." She whispered in her ear, "We're no longer damaged goods."

"No, Hummingbird. We're both free to fly."

***

It had become his adversary, so most days Mike passed by the mailbox without stopping. Often, by the time he would check the mail, several days' worth had piled up. This day, he passed by again and pulled on up to the house, but when he got out of the truck, he looked back down the gravel drive, knowing he needed to check for bills. That was all that came anymore, bills and sale papers. So, dragging himself along, dreading the feeling of disappointment he would find there, he made the trip down to the road. He knew he wouldn't hear back from her after his letter, and truthfully, he knew it was for the best that he didn't. It was time to let her go as he said he would. Someday, he would find a new normal. Different, though, after having lived with her in his life for a brief season and subsequently falling so much more deeply in love with her, it could never be as it was. He would live – but just barely.

When Mike opened the door to the mailbox, he found the stack was large, and rather than sort through it in route, he held the bundle at his side. He sighed. This, checking the mail, had become the saddest part of his week.

On the way back to the house, he wondered what she was doing. Their busy season was about to begin. Was she preparing for that? Every day at random times, he would wonder such things. At breakfast time he would wonder what she was eating. He wondered how many cups of coffee she would drink and if she would use the mugs he had given her for Christmas. Each morning he drank milk out of his Love mug that went with her set, regretting having kept it at all. Who needed the reminder, and why did he feel compelled to wash it every night just to have the same reminder the following morning?

Clearly, he admitted to himself and to the Lord, he was losing his mind over her, but it was beyond his ability to control. Robin was his every waking

242

thought, and while thinking of her was painful, not thinking of her caused him to live with an even deeper sense of emptiness. Even in solitary confinement, kept apart from the other prisoners for his safety, he hadn't felt as alone as he had since he saw her in Raleigh. Every man had a breaking point, and Mike was reaching his. Day after day, he waited for the Lord to give him even the slightest bit of relief, but so far it hadn't come.

Inside the house he tossed the pile onto the kitchen table and went in to change. He was going by his mother's before meeting Tim at the gym that evening. Prior to things ending with Robin, he and Tim had met earlier, right after they got off work. Since Mike had discovered that nights at home alone drove him even crazier, they agreed to change the schedule. Often, afterwards, they would eat dinner together or shoot hoops, any activity that would keep him out of the home his wife had made.

After a strenuous workout, Mike and Tim went to the diner. Mike choked down a few bites before pushing his plate away, something that only reminded him of his last morning with Robin. He sighed.

Tim rested his fork on his plate. "Have things been any different for you?"

"No, not really. These people here must be crazy." Mike took a drink of his coffee, wishing he hadn't picked up the stupid habit. "Same town, same people."

"So no one has treated you any differently since the truth came out?"

"Not at all."

"Maybe they're just forgiving."

Mike shrugged and then thought of Coach Andrews' wife and how she had all but chased him down the sidewalk the day after the article hit the paper. She told him how sorry she was for how she had treated Robin and that she wished she had known the truth before. He wasn't sure what had transpired between them the day Robin came to visit, but it must have been significant to them both. When he thought back to that day when he had offered Robin a cookie, there was something unusual about her expression. She seemed embarrassed or self-conscious or maybe a little of both. With this new insight he realized how hurt she must have been over whatever was said. Anything that would bring Robin to tears was a big thing.

Tim sighed, his expression somber. "I really am sorry about how things have turned out. I held out hope, I guess."

Mike sighed, too. "There for a while, I had hope, too. You were right about us. Thanks for not saying so."

"You have to know, I didn't want to be right. I was just trying to look out for you."

Tim sat for a moment stirring his coffee. Once he set his spoon aside, he looked at Mike. "With as many prayer concerns as I have in the church, you seem to stay at the top of my list, especially lately. I know this feels like the worst possible scenario, but I have a sense that God is up to something. It's just a feeling I can't shake."

Mike walked into his quiet house and went into the kitchen. With little enthusiasm he began to sort through the stack of mail, stopping when he came to a letter from Robin. His hands trembled as he ripped open the envelope and unfolded the page.

Sweet Michael Sr.,

When Mike saw his name written that way he gasped. He pulled out a chair and plopped down. Part of him feared reading on, feared hoping. For a moment he sat there, until finally, curiosity got the better of him.

> You had a declaration to make. I have a confession to make: when we first began writing, you asked me a question. I dodged it. You asked again. I said I forgot what I wanted to be back in ninth grade. I lied, but only because I wanted to spare you the pain of my answer. The truth is, all I ever wanted to be was your wife. I wanted to be by your side while you pursued your dreams. That was my dream. I wanted to have your children. Michael was my greatest joy. All those things are still true today! Thought you might want to know.
> You have my heart!
> Robin

With his breath caught in his chest and trembling hands, he read her words one more time – word by word. Robin wanted to be his wife. Written out plain as day, she said that she wanted to be his wife! He jumped from his chair, sending it flying behind him and crashing into the refrigerator. But then he froze in his tracks, his heart plummeting at the sight. Mike stood and stared at the floor just in front of the sink. How could he ever expect her to live there with him again? He would go to her there at the lake. They would build a new life together, one without constant reminders of the monster he once was.

Mike fumbled as he tried to dig his phone from his pocket and finally dialed her number.

***

Robin had been waiting for this call. Since hitting the road just after lunchtime, she had been watching the clock and waiting with excitement. This was much later than she had expected.

"Hi, babe," she said.

She sat for a few seconds, and when he said nothing, she said, "Mike?"

"I'm sorry."

"It's okay." For only a second more she listened until she was crying along with him, so much so that she had to pull over to the shoulder of the highway.

He pulled himself together enough to say, "I'm coming to fight for you."

"You don't have to fight for me. I'm yours already."

Robin rested her head on the steering wheel and waited. He was so choked up that on occasion he would apologize, but each time she assured him that she understood. She did understand. Part of her wanted to tell him she was on the way home, but more than anything, she wanted to see the look on his face when he found her there, ready to begin again. This wasn't a phone conversation.

"I'll give my notice tomorrow," he said.

"Mike, can we talk about the future tomorrow?"

"That's not the response I was hoping for. Are you still unsure?"

"Not at all. I know exactly what I want."

"Me?"

"Only you." She smiled at that, that phrase taking her back to the best of them.

Robin said, "Please don't take this the wrong way, but I have something I have to do, somewhere I have to be. I need to go now." If she didn't get back on the road, she would never make it home.

"Tell me again."

She could hear a trace of concern in his voice but knew he would understand tomorrow. "I want only you."

"That's enough then. We will talk about the future when you're ready."

"Tomorrow, Mike. I promise we will talk about it tomorrow."

"I love you, baby."

"I love you, too, Mike. With all my heart, I do."

***

Mike dropped his phone on the table. Of course he was disappointed, but it made sense that she would need some time. How could he expect her to jump back into a relationship after all those years apart? He would slow down and be patient with her while he waited. This wasn't about what he wanted or needed; it was about his wife and what was best for her. One thing was for certain, though, he wouldn't be waiting long distance.

With that in mind he went into his bedroom and began taking clothes out of the closet and piling them onto the bed. He would move close by and woo her and pursue her until she was ready to live together again. It didn't matter how long that took, as long as he knew that she loved him.

The following morning, and without any hesitation at all, Mike went into the sheriff's office and closed the door. He sat down across from his long-time friend and began.

"First of all, I want you to know how much I appreciate the way you fought to get me reinstated. I didn't deserve this second chance. Second, I consider you a great friend, and I'll miss you, but the bottom line is, I have a chance with Robin, and I'm going to take it."

It was settled. He was going after his wife.

THIRTY-THREE

Finally in sight of her little yellow house, Robin could only smile to herself. In the past weeks since her ponderings over where she belonged, at last she knew without doubt. It was less about where she was as it was with whom. She belonged with Mike. No matter what had happened in the past, he was her husband. No matter the humiliation that would certainly come, she belonged at home – with him. After the journey God had taken her on over the past two years, she found Him to be trustworthy, so if He said to go home, then home was the safest place to be. She had to believe He would deal with all things that came against her.

The morning she had left, Robin copied some of Mike's letters, especially the one where he had opened up about what things were like when he came home from war, and she mailed them to her parents. She apologized for having kept their relationship a secret and tried her best to help them see the new man he had become, not changed, but new. She explained how God had orchestrated their restoration over the months of writing. Now, she would have to trust that the Lord would soften their hearts toward Mike. It mattered to her that they accept him back as part of the family, but she also knew that if they refused to, it wouldn't change the reality of it. For her this was forever, so somehow they would have to learn to be around him without the bitterness they currently felt toward him.

On the front porch Robin opened the screen door and found the front door to be unlocked, which didn't surprise her since they had never felt the need. When she stepped inside the living room, the house seemed to welcome her home, envelop her in. Built in the late twenties, her home had charm that newer homes lacked. The room was warm and inviting, just the same as when she had left.

Straight across from the front entry was a large cased opening leading into her kitchen. From the moment she had laid eyes on the old-style farmhouse kitchen, she had fallen in love. It was what made her say yes to the home and where she had spent most of her time. She stepped through the doorway into the kitchen and found herself tumbling backward in time to the early days when they were so excited to be in their new home. Then with a flash, the splattering of Mike's blood came to mind.

Robin stood and stared at the place where her husband had once lain bleeding, trying to get the image out of her head. She refused to allow the past to rob her of her joy. With newfound courage, she went to the exact spot and dropped to her knees.

"Forget the former things. See, I do a new thing." It was one of her favorite verses from Isaiah. Again and again she spoke the words until the horrific image faded.

She knelt there, determined to fight for her home. If she had to drop to her knees in every room of her home in the days to come, she would. She would do battle like the enemy had never seen of her before. Nothing would stop her. With God by her side, she was there to reclaim her marriage and home.

Robin stood again and sighed, knowing she would need that verse often in the days to come since memories would certainly flood her mind and the accuser would certainly accuse. For the first time in her life, she was truly prepared for battle.

On the way to her bedroom, she paused and touched Michael's closed door. She drew a heart with her fingertip and rested her head against the frame. "I still miss you, baby."

Unable to open the door, not ready for that step yet, Robin moved on to her bedroom where she found the bed littered with clothes and only a narrow space where Mike must have slept the night before. She smiled at the realization – he was coming for her.

Robin looked at her watch and noted she had an hour or so before he came home, so she first began putting his clothes away. Afterwards, she made trips to her car, unloading her belongings. When she lifted the last box from the trunk, she sighed. This was right.

In the hopes of surprising Mike with a home-cooked meal, Robin searched the refrigerator and cabinets but found little to make for dinner. It had been her plan that she would have it waiting for him when he arrived home. After all his belly-aching about having to eat out, she wanted to surprise him with a real sit-down-at-the-table meal. When that plan fell through, she glanced over at the box of donuts on the table, knowing Mike would appreciate them even more than a meal.

It was nearly five o'clock when she heard the familiar sound of his truck grinding to a halt. For the first time in years, she no longer felt like a misplaced object. As a matter of fact, she was perfectly placed, at home waiting for her husband.

***

Mike threw his truck into park. Before it was fully stopped, he jumped from the cab and walked over to Robin's car. The trunk was open and empty, so he closed it. Could this be what it seemed? He stood still for a second before looking back up at the house. Was it at all possible he would walk through that door and find his wife had returned to him?

Breathless already, he jogged toward the steps and found her waiting just inside the screen door. Her smile was sweet and her eyes sparkled with her surprise. At that moment there was no doubt; she was home for good. His heart was pounding at the sight of her standing there, and he had a difficult time catching his breath.

"Honey, I'm home," she whispered.

He tugged so hard that he nearly pulled the screen door off the hinges. Once inside, he circled his arms around her and lifted her from the floor. For the longest time, he could only hold her, face buried in the soft curve of her neck. Finally, wanting her to know he would give up anything, everything, for her, he said, "I was coming there to be with you. I know it's painful for you here. We don't have to stay. As long as you're with me, it doesn't matter where we are."

"Home – I want to be here at home with you. I don't care what anyone thinks. Honestly, that was a big part of what kept me away these past months. Deep down I knew I could have no life without you, but I was afraid. None of that matters now. The Lord said to go home, so I'm home."

He walked with her farther into the living room, making no move to set her down. She had wrapped her legs around him and linked her feet. It reminded him of the day he had come home from his second tour, her wrapped around him like a monkey.

All he could do was smile as he walked into the kitchen with her. "I quit my job today."

"You did? You might want to call and sort that out. I'm a poor woman with no means to support you."

"I'll call."

Such tremendous, nearly unbearable emotion washed over him as he whispered, "Baby, I can't believe you're here. I can't believe you would love me again."

With her home and in his arms, after so many years apart, he was whole again, like a missing piece of him was restored.

"I'm here, and it's forever." Just before pressing her lips to his, she looked into his eyes. "I love you. I never stopped, not one minute; I promise you."

Similar to when he kissed her on Christmas Eve, it was as if an explosion occurred within him. Then, though, he had felt the need to maintain some kind of restraint. Today he felt no such need. All he could think of as he walked with her into the bedroom was making love to her. It had been seven long years. He needed her, and just as by the fire that night, she needed him as much. She whispered it again and again as she clung to him, her fingers digging into the skin of his neck.

Then it came, not a whisper but a roar from the past. How could he make love to her for the first time on a bed where he had hurt her the way he had? He became sick at his stomach at the mere thought of it. He stopped kissing her and set her down.

"What?"

There was no way to explain his hesitation without bringing the past to mind, so he suggested, "Let's pack a bag and head out to the beach. You told me you daydream about being there. Let me take you. We can make it in a couple of hours." He paused. "Unless you're tired of traveling."

"No, not at all. The beach sounds wonderful." She giggled. "We never had a real honeymoon. I think we deserve that."

"Me, too."

With a broad smile, he lifted her hand and looked at the ring on her finger. It was the first he had noticed she was wearing it again. He brought it to his lips and kissed it. "Hi, Robin McGarrett."

Robin slid her hands behind his neck and pulled his face to hers, then leaned in to kiss him.

The feel of her lips on his drove him wild. He wanted her more than he ever had but still the roaring sounded.

"Rob…"

He was trying to avoid her lips so that he could even finish a sentence. "You've gotta know how much I want you."

"And I want you," Robin said as she trailed a kiss along his cheek and to his ear.

Her tone was playful and flirty, and he could tell she wasn't picking up on his hesitation. Finally, he grasped her shoulders and moved her back so that he could look her in the eye. "Not here. Not now." Mike looked toward the bed. "Somewhere else for the first time. Okay?"

Robin followed his eyes and whispered, "Oh." She moved in to hug him. "I deserve a honeymoon anyway."

"You sure do."

They ransacked the bedroom as they packed, grabbed the box of donuts, and rushed to the car.

THIRTY-FOUR

After checking into their room, Robin watched with a grin as Mike pretended to carry their luggage into the elevator nonchalantly. His expression held no urgency, but she knew better. All along the drive, he was like a teenager again. Each time they stopped at a light he would kiss her, more than once long enough that the car behind them had to blow their horn. Once the elevator doors were closed, however, he dropped the bags, grabbed her, and lifted her off the floor. It was exactly what she expected.

"Still want me?"

His sudden action caused her heart to pound hard against her chest and her stomach fluttered. She was looking into his eyes, and the desire she found there caused her breath to catch in her throat.

"I want you," she whispered.

He moved his lips to her ear and said, "I will only make love to you when I hear those words."

She understood his meaning, actually felt his remorse permeate his words.

When the doors opened, he grabbed the bags, and together they practically ran for their room. Inside, he threw the bags, lifted her once again from the floor, and laid her with great care on the bed. He kissed her face and her neck and her face again. All the while, he told her over and over he loved her and that he would never let her go again.

Robin was grabbing at the hem of his t-shirt when she felt him remove her hand. Then he moved his hand beneath her shirt and traced his fingers along the skin below her belly button. She realized he was touching her stretch marks from Michael. When he lifted her shirt to look at them, she considered that he hadn't seen such physical evidence of his son in many years. The pained expression in his eyes caused tears to spring to hers.

"If I could take these away, would you let me?"

"No, of course not."

She slid her fingers beneath his and felt the small lines that spanned from hipbone to hipbone. Though she thought she had made it through without them, in her final week and a half of pregnancy, they had begun to appear.

Mike wrapped his hand around her fingers and slid them beneath his t-shirt. "I want you to be able to look at me without regret or guilt. This is

251

part of me now." He leaned down and whispered in her ear, "This is when I became a new man, when Jesus came into my life."

Every ounce of passion drained from her. Robin realized, by his preparing her this way, what she was about to see would be painful. How had she never thought of it? Of course he was scarred. He had to look at them each and every day and was forced to remember that his wife had tried to kill him.

Robin watched as Mike moved from the bed and stood before her. She sat up and tried to brace herself. When he slipped his shirt over his head, she could see two distinct bullet holes and several long surgical scars. Because of the scarring, the hair was patchy, unable to grow on the damaged tissue. It was worse than she could have prepared herself for. All she could do was press her face into his stomach and cry.

He put one hand behind her head and with the other he rubbed her back. "Robin…"

Unable to do anything but, she continued to weep. Finally, she choked out, "How did we get to that place?"

Mike sat down next to her. "Because of me. I took us there."

"No. I should have gotten you help." She put her arms around him and clung to him. "I'm so sorry. I wanted to believe you would be okay."

He moved her back to look at him. "Rob, I should have told you back then, but I was so messed up over it." He stopped.

"What?"

"I almost told you the day you first came to visit, when we sat by Mikey's grave together, but it's heavy stuff, and I didn't want to upset you more than you already were."

"Tell me now."

"Back then, when Mikey first died, I was sure it was because of me, because of what I had done in Kandahar. We raided a village on faulty intel. We went in hot and people were killed." He paused and swallowed hard. "Innocent people, including some kids."

With a heavy sigh, Mike leaned up and rested his elbows on his knees. "I killed a kid and his mom. He probably wasn't older than ten. So after Mikey I was sure God took our son as payback for that. I know better now. That's not the God we serve. But back then, that's all I could believe.

"You were destroyed, and I felt responsible. When you drifted so far from me, I kept thinking if I could give you another baby it might help bring you back, make up for what I had done. I was terrified you would leave me, too. I knew I deserved to lose you, but I also knew I would never survive it." He bowed his head.

"Mike." She rubbed his back and rested her head on his shoulder. "I would have never left you. I was just so lost."

"Please forgive me for what I did to you those times after I hit you. I still dream about it, flashes of how I forced you to be with me." He broke down crying. "There's no way to justify what I did – none. I just wanted you to know it was some misguided attempt to give you back what I thought I had taken from you. It was never an attempt to hurt you."

Robin's voice was soft. "It's not at all what you remember."

By this point Mike was crying so hard that Robin found herself at a loss for what to say. His words took her back to that last year and how he would cry and beg her not to leave him.

Finally, she whispered, "I do forgive you. Thank you for helping me understand what you were going through. I didn't then, but I knew you needed help. I'm so sorry."

"Me, too, baby. Me, too."

Tears were pouring down her face, and she actually felt Mike's pain in the moment. At one point she recalled a question that Chris had once asked her. He wondered why she never cried over Mike. She easily cried over Michael, but he noticed her restraint when it came to Mike. It was true, and she had wondered the same thing in the time since Chris had asked her the question. There was something in that exact moment that held the answer, like something on the tip of her tongue that never came.

Eventually, they lay together in silence, Robin's mind whirling with many tangled thoughts. During the drive home, she had tried to brace herself for the many obstacles they would face as they learned to begin again, and already she found she was ill prepared for the anguish of it.

Determined to push through this moment, she propped herself up on her elbow and traced her fingers along the letters of Mike's tattoo. "What is it like to see my name on your arm every day?"

"Before today, a sad reminder of what I had lost. Now," he said with a broad grin, "a reminder of how much God loves me that He would actually allow you to be mine again."

She rubbed her hand across his stomach and bent down to kiss each distinct bullet hole. "What is it like to see this?"

"It's my reminder that God loves me so much that He went to great lengths to make me His. I wouldn't give these up any more than you would give up yours."

"Have you ever hated me because of them?"

Mike closed his eyes and whispered, "I could never hate you." He looked back at her and shook his head. "You just don't get it do you? Without the scars you very well might be dead right now." He choked up. "God used that night to save us both."

His words were true. That night had been brutal and terrifying, but in hindsight she knew God did save them both.

"Mike?"

"What, baby?"

"You know what verse rings over and over in my head?"

He leaned in and kissed her nose. "What verse?"

"'And two shall become one.' I don't ever want to be two again."

With a smile he wrapped her in his arms. "Me either."

She grinned up at him. "Enough tears and regret. I think it's about time for that honeymoon."

"I couldn't agree more." Mike leaned in and kissed her.

Robin considered the consequences, and with a touch of that old fear burning in her belly, she pressed her hand into Mike's chest. "We have no protection, and I'm not ready for another baby. I'm not scared, not like I was." She reconsidered that. "Okay, I'm scared a little, but I also think we should be alone for a while, just you and me."

"We'll be careful tonight and go get something tomorrow."

Unlike the explosive passion they experienced at that first kiss in the kitchen earlier, coming together again after so many years apart was instead tender and gentle. There was no way she could count the number of times Mike whispered that he loved her, and she never tired of hearing it.

He was overly conscious of his past sins against her as it showed in his occasional hesitance of perhaps moving too aggressively. At one point she grabbed his face and said, "Please, be here with me in the moment. All things are new. You have to believe that."

From that moment on Robin knew he was present and that his mind was set on nothing but her. He loved her well as two, once again, became one.

***

The breeze was blowing in off the ocean and along with it a slight mist sprayed his face. Mike could taste the salty water on his lips, and he reveled in the newness of the morning. He was standing in the presence of God Almighty as he worshiped in a way he never had. After spending the entire night wide awake, even long after his sweet bride had gone to sleep, he could hardly wait for the morning hours so that he could stand beside the water and pray.

Earlier, while watching the sun rise, he had considered the mighty works of God in his life. At one point he felt the Lord direct him to consider the ocean waves. After dwelling on them for some time, Mike whispered, "Lord, sometimes You are the wave." Had God not swept in and overtaken him as a wave would a small child?

"I thank You for being the Wave. I thank You for being my Dad. I thank you for saving me and for another chance at life. I thank you for stopping me that night, and I thank you for my precious wife."

In awe of the moment, Mike dropped to his knees. Arms still extended, offering all that he was, Mike worshiped his God.

He wasn't there much longer when he saw Robin walking through the sand, coming his way. She sat next to him and snuggled in close.

He draped his arm around her and kissed her cheek. "I'm sorry that you woke up alone. I meant to be back before you did."

"That's okay. I wouldn't have missed this for the world, watching you here before God."

Mike smiled. "He feels so close here, like I can reach out and touch Him."

"I know exactly what you mean. The water draws me in that way too"

They were quiet for a minute until Robin said, "I can see it now too, your vision of us helping others together. I knew there was something for me, some purpose, but it never came into focus until now."

"Honestly, when I'm talking to guys who are struggling, I don't know what I'm doing half the time, so I just listen. It seems to mean something to them, though, to see that I've found my way back. It gives them hope."

"I'm sure it does. Maybe I can talk to wives. They can see that we both made it through."

Mike nodded. "We didn't go through all of this for nothing. I'll help them anyway I can."

"Me, too," Robin said. "Since last year, when I really began facing our past and working toward healing, I carried so much guilt that I didn't seek help for us both. I feel less of that now. I can see it with more clarity. When you first came home, you weren't as bad, so I really thought you would get back into the groove of life. After Michael died, when you did fall apart, by then I was such a mess that I wasn't thinking rationally. At the time I didn't want people to know we were having problems, or at least I thought that was my fear. I think on a deeper level, I was afraid of losing you, of losing us. I'm still a work in progress here, and much of this is newer revelation. That's all I know for now."

He nodded. "There are so many layers to all of this, I think we will both understand more as we go along."

Robin said, "Yeah. I do know this: I fell apart because I hadn't been real with God up until then. I may have talked a good spiritual game, but the truth was, I was playing church all those years rather than being in an all-out pursuit of God. When you couldn't make me okay after Mikey and I refused to turn to God, I didn't stand a chance."

She looked up at him. "I keep thinking about what you said in your letter, about the wall and how God would get me to the top and you would catch me. It was such beautiful imagery, the idea of you catching me. I have that verse tucked in my Bible and read it a lot. What I've come to realize, though, is that none of this was the wall, not you or telling my parents or facing the people in Whitley. Those were just excuses I came up with on a conscious level. I knew yesterday when I came home. The wall is Michael's door. I know I still have to walk through it and deal with that before God. There's a deeper level of healing God wants for me than what I now have."

"I'll be here when you're ready."

"I may not be ready for some time more."

"You don't have to be. You'll know when it's time." He hugged her to him. "Still, as much as I'm able, I'll be there for you this time. Honestly, I'm not where I need to be either. I just keep pushing all that away. Maybe when you begin, you can share what you discover with me. I can be your first counseling client."

When she grinned up at him, he said, "I want you to stay in school. When fall comes, you should go full-time. Before you know it, you'll have your degree."

"You can get yours, too. You've always planned to."

He shook his head. "Not until you're done. We don't need that kind of pressure. There's time for me to go later. For now I plan to fully support you in this. This time, I'll be by your side as you pursue your dreams." Mike sighed. "I'm glad to know this is just the beginning of our story."

***

They had spent the entire week at the beach, much of it hidden away in their room. On Saturday morning they packed up to go home. Robin was ready. It felt right to go back and reclaim her home. A week alone at the beach, to become them again, had been what they needed. Mike had swapped his notice for a week of vacation time. Since he would have to be at work on Monday, they wanted to have the weekend at home together to get her settled back in.

Sunday morning, on the way to church, Robin reached for Mike's hand. "Can we go in last?"

He sighed at her words. "Sweetest bride," he said, "we can do anything in the whole wide world you want."

Once they were parked, she found she could barely breathe. This wasn't easy, returning after so many years away, especially with everyone knowing the ugliness of their past life. Someone, a man she didn't recognize, was walking toward the truck with a broad grin.

"I'm guessing that's Tim?

"It is." Mike squeezed Robin's hand. "Baby, I've got this." He pointed up and smiled. "He's got this. Trust us."

She only nodded, reached for the door handle, and stepped from the truck, trusting her husband and trusting God.

From that moment until she reached her seat, one person after another came up to her welcoming her home. Many said how much they had missed her or how they had been praying for her. It wasn't at all what she had expected. *Oh, me of little faith*, she thought.

They were seated and the music began. Mike leaned over and whispered, "You can't imagine the countless hours I've prayed at that altar. I prayed for your happiness, that God would give you a new life. Never once did I expect that it would be with me."

"It's always only you, Mike."

After the service Robin looked on as Mike was speaking with Miss Allen across the room. Tim took that opportunity to approach her and slip her a piece of paper.

"I think you'll want to read this."

She unfolded a newspaper clipping. There was a photo of Mike and beside it was written: In His Own Words. She scanned the article and realized it was his admission of guilt.

"I thought you should know. This was on the front page. Everyone has seen it by now."

"I can't believe he did this," Robin said.

Tim glanced over at Mike and smiled. "I don't think there's anything he wouldn't do for you, Robin."

She nodded. "I believe that, too. Does he know you're giving me this?"

"Not yet, but I'll tell him."

"When did he do this?"

"Right after you left the last time."

Robin scanned the room looking for Mike and found he was still talking with Miss Allen, who had him cornered and was likely recruiting him for whatever event was next at the church. The sight made her grin.

She turned back to Tim. "I'm so glad you've been here for him. Thank you for being his friend when he needed one most."

"I will always be here for him, for you, too."

Mike was walking toward them, so she tucked the paper into her Bible. Before he was in hearing distance, she wanted Tim to know: "I love him, and I forgive him."

"I can see that, and I can honestly say, I've never seen a man love a woman more."

When Mike was by her side, she grinned up at him. "Are you already jockeying for the caramel apple table?"

He reached for his stomach, feigning nausea. "Not funny."

The next morning, Robin opened her Bible to the place where she had tucked the newspaper article. Mike was gone to work already, and it was her first moment alone to read his words. She had mentioned the article, but Mike asked that she wait until he left before reading it.

With the page in hand, she looked at the photo of Mike, noting the maturity in his eyes. For as long as she had known him, there was a sparkle of mischief in them. In this photo, however, she found wisdom, something gained only through years of walking with God and by experiencing the suffering of loss.

The article told of his PTSD and how that only worsened after losing their son. He admitted to the drinking and how that led to ongoing abuse.

Robin sat looking at the article, scanning portions of it again and again. The fact that he had exposed the details of their last year together caused a pit to form in her stomach. After reading this she could look back on the day before at church and better understand her reception. All those years ago, it wasn't as if she had felt condemned by her church family. Many had called and tried to see her in the aftermath of what happened. Somehow, the rejection and judgment of the ignorant few had translated in her mind to seem like all. That was never the case.

THIRTY-FIVE

Robin was in the kitchen cleaning up the lunch dishes. Mike had come home to eat as he usually did. They were sliding into a comfortable routine together, something even better than they had known before. Even in the early stages of young love, it wasn't like it was now. The transformation was easy to understand. This was the first time that the Lord Jesus lived in the midst of them, a stark contrast to their former life.

They had been home from the beach for just over two weeks, and each day she found something to fill her time. Because she had been gone for so long, and with a man in charge of the house, she found plenty to keep her busy as she cleaned baseboards and scrubbed floors. Day after day she found the house was becoming hers again.

After finishing in the kitchen, she folded laundry and did a few other chores, ran to the market, and put groceries away. By late afternoon she had run out of things to keep her occupied. Her mind had been cluttered all day, and she found it difficult to focus on even the most mindless of tasks. Mike had even noticed how distracted she was during lunch. He was talking to her, but her mind was elsewhere.

Robin slid a chair out from the kitchen table and sat looking at Mikey's door. Since coming home, she had yet to go inside, but over the past few days she had felt the Lord drawing her in. Paralyzed, she sat for a few minutes more and prayed, "Lord, I don't think I can handle what's on the other side of that door."

"*My grace is sufficient for you*," echoed in her mind and heart.

"I love him so much still. Please make sure he knows."

Empowered by a strength not her own, Robin walked to the door and placed her hand on it then rested her head against the wood and sighed. "With my God I can scale a wall," she whispered.

Unexpected and sudden courage allowed her to reach for the knob and turn it. She swung the door open wide and stood in the doorway for a few minutes, finding it looked exactly as she had left it seven years before. Not one thing was different.

When she was able to lift her right foot, Robin moved it over the threshold of the doorway. Then she lifted the other, and from there it was a conscious and difficult process to walk over to Michael's crib. Once there, she stood looking at the empty mattress and smiled, remembering what her baby had looked like when she would find him awake and waiting for her. When he would see her, he would grin, drool running down the corner of his mouth and onto the sheet. With her eyes closed she touched the mattress, knowing that in those memories of him, she was clinging to love as Chris had suggested. It was something she had done only in talking about him, but this day she was living out her love for him.

Lost in the sweetness of her memories of her son, Robin turned and walked to the rocking chair. The moment she sat, she heard the slight squeak that was once so familiar. With each movement there was a tiny little squeak, back and forth creating different tones. Adrift in the motion and familiar little melody, she closed her eyes and held out her arms, rocking her baby in her heart. In her mind she could see his dark blue eyes peeking up at her as she nursed him and could feel his chubby little hand rubbing her chest. Michael was the sweetest gift, and for ten months she was the happiest mommy in the world. Without question she would rather have those ten months with the pain than to never have known such love.

There, sitting in Michael's room, she could hear Chris's words from the day when they had knelt together in his cabin. "The Psalmist said, 'The LORD is close to the brokenhearted and saves those who are crushed in spirit.' He was there, Robin. No matter what it felt like, He was there."

Just as Chris had suggested, she tried again to see God that day so long ago. With all her heart she knew He was there, no matter what her eyes could see. For the first time it occurred to her: that day she was held in the shadow of His wings. That was why she couldn't see Him. God was wrapped around her, just as she had wrapped herself around Michael. He was so close in fact that she couldn't see Him at all.

> *"I will take refuge in the shadow of your wings until the disaster has passed."* (Psalm 57:1)

There was something about that revelation that settled the matter. The one place she had remained so stuck, even after such strides in healing over so many other things, Robin was suddenly and unexpectedly released. Beyond her ability to comprehend at the moment, she knew it was something that would be transformative, the final stitch unraveled.

***

Mike stood in the doorway watching his wife. The look on Robin's face was tranquil and tender, her arms extended, cradling emptiness. She was rocking his son, and his heart broke at the sight of her empty arms. The moment brought to mind images of lifting his lifeless baby from them.

Of course the rest followed: memories of how broken and faraway she became and how he had fought to hold on. All that time, he was drowning, and as he had eventually come to understand, clinging to her was him gasping for breath. She was his lifeline.

Now, knowing something was stirring within her, something she wasn't yet prepared to discuss with him, he was determined to be there for her in the right way. To find her here in Mikey's room confirmed his suspicion. This time, he would walk through her grief with her and be there for her in a way he wasn't able before. He would help her scale the wall.

***

With her eyes closed still, Robin sensed Mike's presence.

He knelt before her chair and whispered, "Baby, are you all right?"

Her head was resting on the back of the rocker. Without opening her eyes, she smiled. "Yes, I'm all right."

"Are you rocking our baby?"

"I sure am."

"Should I give you a few more minutes alone?"

Robin lifted her head and smiled as she said, "Many are the plans in a person's heart, but it is the Lord's purpose that prevails."

"I don't know what you mean. Tell me what you need. I want to help you through this." He drew her hand to his lips, whispering, "Please don't pull away from me, not again."

She reached out and touched his cheek, her tummy fluttering at how deeply he affected her. He was so handsome and hardly seemed to know it. She could only blush as a flash of memory of their first night back together came to mind.

"You weren't as careful as you thought."

"What do you mean? What did I do?"

Robin guided his hand to her stomach. "I'm a few days late."

She watched as Mike lowered his head onto her lap. He was muttering what seemed to be prayers and then finally she heard him whisper, "My baby."

"I haven't taken a test," she said, "so maybe you shouldn't get your hopes up yet. But if I'm not, we can begin to try."

261

Mike scooped her out of the chair and began to twirl her around the room. In all the years of her grief, it was easy to lose sight of the fact that he had lost his son, too. All that time she was holding on to Michael's death, Mike was holding on to his love for him. He wanted to share that love with another child, and she had withheld that from him – never again.

The past few days of pondering and waiting for her cycle to begin, a million feelings and emotions had bombarded her. Certain that one time without protection couldn't have gotten her pregnant; she refused to believe it at first. But finally, even without a test, she knew. She felt it deep within her. Her immediate reaction had been one of paralyzing fear, but the verse she had quoted was what ultimately brought her peace. The Lord knew His timing. Just as with Michael, the Lord had determined this baby's time to be conceived. His purpose would prevail.

Mike stopped spinning. "Let's go get a test right now."

"I knew you would be excited."

"More than you could ever know. Are you? Are you scared?" He stopped and looked at her. "You said you weren't ready. I should have been more careful or waited to go to the store. I'm sorry."

The look of concern on his face reminded her how much he loved her. "Don't be sorry. I'm not scared, and I only thought I wasn't ready. I'm ready."

She pointed to the doorway. "I want to paint Michael's name there over the door and put wings beside it. And you know the verse that says, '…and they can no longer die; for they are like the angels.' I want to paint that under his name. This will be their room."

While she knew Michael wasn't an angel, the thought that he was there in heaven with and like the angels was a tremendous comfort to her. He was waiting there for her, and she would see him again someday.

"I think that's a beautiful idea."

He lowered her to the ground and pulled her close. "I don't deserve this. I don't deserve any of this."

"You do. You deserve all the happiness you're feeling right now. Please believe that." Robin looked at him and said, "Mike McGarrett, you're the kindest, gentlest…" She stopped and rested her head on his chest again, her eyes filled with tears and she could hardly go on. Finally, she said. "You are the godliest man I know, and I'm so thankful to be yours."

She thought of Chris for a moment. Mike had become so much like him. Since she had been home, she had discovered just how much Mike had been pouring himself into others, not only at the church but at Ft. Bragg with PTSD groups. His life without her unfolded and revealed a level of transformation in him that left her in awe. Someday, they would do exactly as he envisioned, work together to help others.

After dinner they drove to the same pharmacy where her birth control pills were purchased. The irony wasn't lost on either of them, yet neither mentioned it. Their new life together would be filled with such moments, ones that served as a reminder of how lives and a marriage without God at its center would inevitably become unbalanced. Both were filled with excitement, though, so all lingering memories faded. All that mattered to either of them was what the test might reveal.

Back at home they waited. Robin held the stick and Mike paced, while occasionally stopping, grabbing her face, and kissing her.

"It doesn't matter either way to me, as long as you're happy," he said.

She smiled when he began to pace again. "I'm happy no matter what."

It was then she looked down and saw the hazy lines beginning to form. "Uh, Mike?"

He stopped and only stared.

Tears welled up in her eyes as she looked up at him and nodded.

Mike grabbed her by the arms and pulled her into his embrace. "This is all I've wanted, my family back. I'll get it right this time, I promise you."

"I don't doubt that."

THIRTY-SIX

Robin stood alone on the dock, looking out at the water she used to consider her escape, when the painting that depicted this exact location came to mind. In the gathering room of the inn, hung over the fireplace, Chris's canvas was displayed as if it were some priceless work of art. That was how they saw it anyway. Painted his first week there, it was what he had captured after he saw her dive into the water for the first time. In his final days there, he had given it to her, explaining how he could never draw her into the scene. He said he had pondered the reason over the course of the summer and determined it was because she never belonged there to begin with. It was Robin's place to run, never her place to be. Chris's words were the first seeds planted that God would use to eventually draw her home.

When she felt the gentle swaying of the dock, Robin turned to find Mike walking her way. He moved up close behind her, slid his arms around her, and rubbed her swollen belly. At six months pregnant, they knew already they were to have a girl. Never before, while standing in that exact spot grieving and agonizing over what was once lost, could she have dared to believe such happiness would exist for her again.

They were at the inn for only a few days, and fortunately, it was in the midst of the season of fall colors. Emma and Stan had chosen the time for their wedding precisely for that reason. The main house was in a flurry of activity since the wedding and reception would be there the following day. Robin had snuck away from the chaos to step back in time and reflect on how far the Lord had actually brought her. There was a verse that followed her to the dock that day. David once asked, "Who am I, O Sovereign Lord, and what is my family, that you have brought me so far?" That was her question to the Lord that day. What a mess she used to be, but finally she was whole and complete.

"Do you think you would like to come here to live someday?" She had never mentioned that Emma planned to leave the inn to her.

"I'll come now if it's what you want."

"No, I mean when you retire. Could you see yourself here?"

"If I'm with you, I can see myself anywhere. But, yes, I think I can handle a hard life of boating and fishing."

"The winters are tough, though."

"I'll keep you warm, Southern girl."

She smiled and sighed and rubbed his hands resting on her stomach. "I'm content where we are for now."

"Me, too."

Mike glanced back up at the house. "What do you think it will be like with your parents?"

"I think it will be okay. Are you nervous?" She looked up at him. Clearly he was, and with good reason. Her dad could be a hard man.

Her parents had called her the day after reading her letter. Their tone gave away their reservations, but they said they supported her decision. Since that time, they only called her on her cell phone, and she suspected they did so to ensure they wouldn't accidently reach Mike if they called her at home. She knew it would take time. With her parents due in that evening, neither of them knew what to expect.

"I am nervous – not about your mom, but your dad is another story. He was like a dad to me. I hate that I've let him down."

"Don't be nervous. I'm with you."

"It'll be fine then."

When Mike turned to go, he said, "Are you coming back up soon?"

"I will be up in a while."

When he was gone, she walked to Chris's cabin. Emma hadn't put anyone in there for the weekend. Stan's four kids and their families were there, plus her parents, Tommy and Becky, and the two of them, so the house and many of the cabins were full. She and Mike were staying in her old room. While it crossed her mind to stay in the cabin during the visit, she decided it wouldn't be fitting. Though it was never spoken, she knew Chris's feelings for her ran deep. It was evident in the way he had looked at her, especially there at the end.

Robin sat in Chris's chair and recalled the many wise things he had said to her, and the way that, no matter what she felt, he directed her back to Jesus. Chris had been sent for her; the Lord had proven His mercy and lovingkindness by that very act. Though never suspecting what was to come, help was on the way in the form of a barefoot, selfless school teacher, who, while facing the end of his own life, poured into hers, giving her the chance to begin again.

***

This was the first moment that Mike caught Emma alone. She was in the kitchen when he came in from the dock. Up until this point, Robin was with them, and Mike didn't want to have this conversation with Emma with her there.

"Do you have a minute?"

Emma nodded. "I'll make a minute."

"We've never gotten a chance to talk since Robin came home."

"No need to. As long as she is happy."

"I need to tell you this: You can trust me with your daughter. I would never do anything to hurt her again."

"I know that, Mike."

"Mostly, I just want to say thank you for taking care of my wife." Tears filled his eyes. "Thank you for putting her back together again." As much as he tried not to, he began to cry.

Emma closed the space between them and wrapped her arms around him. "It was the best thing that's ever happened to me, having her here."

For a few seconds more, they stood in that quiet embrace. Mike needed this. His intention was to apologize individually to Robin's parents too. He owed each of them that much.

When she moved back, Emma said, "Enough of all that. You and I aren't who we used to be."

"No, thankfully we're not."

"Mike, I'm sorry I didn't tell her you called. At the time –"

"No need to apologize. I completely understand. I understood then."

She patted his cheek. "Glad to have cleared the air. Now just be good to my little hummingbird and all will go well with you."

Mike grinned. "I promise I will be."

An hour later, Mike stood at the door of the cabin, trying to work up the nerve to go in. When Robin was no longer on the dock, he suspected she was at the cabin since she had told him that was where she most often prayed. When he had reached the cabin, however, he stopped dead in his tracks when he read the name on the plaque above it: *Chris's Cabin*. It caused a tightening sensation in his chest, just like he used to feel before he would explode, and the hair on the back of his neck stood on end. He took a deep breath and exhaled. Now, here he stood, paralyzed at the front door, unsure of what he might find on the other side. Would his wife be grieving over her lost friend? Finally, he tapped on the door and cracked it open to find her sitting in a chair beside the fireplace. He remained outside when he spoke. "Emma needs you, a shoe emergency."

Robin nodded and smiled. "Most everything with her has been an emergency today."

"Yeah, I suppose it has." He wasn't smiling in return and made no move to enter.

She pointed to the chair across from her. "That's where Jesus healed me."

With hesitation he walked in and over to the chair. He rubbed the woven tapestry fabric and for the first time voiced his suspicion aloud. "Chris was in love with you. I saw how he looked at you that day."

"He never, ever made that known. Each and every time we talked, he simply listened and then led me back to God. He was kind and compassionate and helped so many people, including me. You can't imagine the hundreds of people at his funeral."

His eyes widened. "You went to his funeral?"

"Yes, I did."

"I didn't realize you were that close."

"I was with him when he died."

When Mike never responded to that, Robin said, "Well, I better get back up there."

"I'll be up in a while. I think I need a minute alone."

She moved to his side and rubbed his arm. "Are you okay?"

"I will be." His smile was half-hearted.

Robin kissed his cheek. "I love you."

"I love you more."

Once alone, Mike knelt in front of the chair and placed his hands on the seat where his wife would have sat, praying, "Thank You for what You did for her right here in this very spot. Thank you for the man you sent. I'm sorry I've been so jealous of him all this time. It's just that he knew her in such an intimate way, and I have no doubt he loved her. I suppose that's my fault, though. Had I not left her in the world alone, so broken and vulnerable, she would have had no need of him. I did, though. Lord, I give these feelings to You, knowing You'll take them away. I don't ever doubt her or her feelings for me, but I'm still jealous. I'm so afraid she loved him, too."

Mike reached the back steps of the main house just as it was getting dark. When he opened the screen door to the porch, he found Robin's dad sitting there in a wicker chair, glaring at him. "Mr. Jacobs," he said and nodded.

Bill stood and took two steps forward. "Mike." Without taking Mike's extended hand, he paused and looked at him dead in the eye. "After what happened I swore I would kill you if I ever got the chance."

Mike just stood there, waiting for whatever Bill might say or do. Whether it was a punch in the face or gut or if Bill just needed to unload on him verbally, Mike was prepared to take what he had coming.

"But after reading your letters, and later the article Robin sent, I've come to regret how I missed what should have been obvious." His voice broke as he tried to hold back tears. "You could've come to me, son. I would've gotten you some help."

Bill reached for Mike, grabbed his shoulder, and pulled him nearer, embracing him as if he were his own boy. "I would have done anything to have helped you. I'm sorry I missed it."

Mike stood in that embrace with tears stinging his eyes. Because he had never had much of a dad in the picture, Bill had been the closest thing he had known. Second only to Robin, Mike needed this relationship restored.

"I would like to think if I had it all to do over again, I would come to you, but I was so confused, and I didn't understand what was happening to me. I'm so sorry that I failed you. Sorry for everything I did and didn't do."

They spent nearly an hour together talking and sorting through the past few years. For Mike it was one of the final steps he needed to take in the healing process. The things he had done to this man's daughter required confession, and it was only right that he ask for his forgiveness. Soon, he would have a little girl of his own, and even with her yet to be born, the thought of any man hurting her the way he had hurt Robin was something that could easily send him over the edge.

Again, from Bill this time, forgiveness and grace was extended to him, demonstrating God's love in a way he hoped he would be able to exhibit to others. If there was ever a man whose life could be modeled, it was his father-in-law.

***

Later, sitting around the dinner table, Robin scanned the large crowd, amazed at the transformation from just one year ago. Emma was beaming with happiness, a miracle within itself. Becky and Tommy were unofficially engaged. Situations that had little hope of coming together just a year before suddenly were.

On the dock before, she thought back to something Chris had said on more than one occasion. He reminded her that they lived in a fallen world. All who sat around her at the moment had each lived in their own distinct fallen worlds and experienced pain in differing degrees. From her own standpoint, she lived in a world where her baby had been taken much too soon and where the man she loved had succumbed to mental illness and the violence that followed. Even prior to those tragedies, she was a young woman, a perfect example of fallen humanity, who sought human love and approval to the exclusion of God's.

Mike was hardly even given a chance with a father who had abused the entire family. It's a fallen world indeed when the words "Our Father who art in heaven" cause you to cringe because it contains the word "Father," a word synonymous with pain and fear. Mike recently shared with her that all those years he had attended church with her, he despised the word father. In hindsight he said it was what had kept him from God in the first place. Once he had come to know his heavenly Father, however, the word became a comfort, something sweet to his ears and to his heart.

Chris's fallen world consisted of losing his father at such a young age then losing his mother to alcohol soon after. He was left with no parents to care for him. His beginning was harsh enough, and his end came much too soon, the result of some aggressive mutation of cancer cells. None of it was fair.

Becky's need had been much the same as her own, the desire for human love. The giving of herself to a young man who had no intention of loving her or marrying her was proof that she, too, sought after a love that left her empty. Tommy wouldn't receive a particular gift because of it.

There was Emma who had hobbled in her own fallen world for more than three decades, longing for what she had lost, then longing even more for what she had given away. Because of her choice, she locked herself away in a world where shame and self-loathing bound and gagged her.

Robin's parents had not only experienced infertility, but along with the sweetness of an adopted baby girl, they were forced to carry the burden of the secret of her birth, stripping them of the light and joy that could have been theirs had the truth been revealed.

While each of them inhabited individual worlds of pain and suffering, resulting from consequences of personal choices, their own and those of others, it was the very same Lord who, in His unfathomable mercy stepped into each individual world with the offer of His grace. One Lord, yet to each He offered different elements of His character based on individual need in the initial wooing and pursuing of each of them. To Mike and Chris, they each needed the Father. With that position solidified in their hearts, He then journeyed with them, demonstrating new layers and levels of His nature, cultivating them into sound and godly men.

To her, in the beginning, He was first and most essentially her Wonderful Counselor since her need of healing and restoration prohibited further growth. Then eventually and most importantly, after a lifetime of pretending to follow Him, Jesus became her First Love and her God. It was that layer upon layer of intimate knowledge of Him that would ensure she could never again be shaken. She was His.

For Emma and Becky, He showed Himself as the Lord who hears and forgives, the One who replenishes that which is lost by filling that place of longing with His Spirit and love.

It wasn't lost on her. Almighty God was to each what they needed. Just as their worlds were unique and individual, He was just as unique and individual in His dealings with them. In and for all of them, His timing was precise, whether patient or expedient. His touch was as needed, ranging from tender to heavy-handed.

The commonality for all of them in the beginning was that, though He chose to rend the veil and offer direct access to Himself, they each set out on a course to mend it right back. In their pain, shame, and fear, rather than looking toward Him, the One who heals and restores, they began to stitch and mend that veil, or in some cases install a zipper, to close Him out. When she pondered why, Robin came to the conclusion, at least in her own situation, she wanted to try to maintain some kind of control in a world out of control. Ultimately, she wanted to be her own god, not trusting Him to be, which in turn had led to utter devastation and self-imposed separation from the Source of Life Himself. Was that not likely the case for them all, the desire to control and direct their own destiny? Praise God for unraveling the stitches in each and every person sitting around that festive table.

At bedtime Robin and Mike were alone in their room. Since they had spoken in the cabin, he hadn't been himself. As much as she hated that it bothered him about Chris, she could never regret Chris's friendship. He was her lifeline back to God.

All evening she had felt conviction in her spirit on a particular matter, so she sat beside Mike on the bed, prepared to tell him.

"I need to tell you something." When he nodded, she said, "Soon after I met Chris, he asked me to dinner, and I said yes. I suppose you could call it nothing less than a date. I'm sorry."

Mike stood and paced for a moment, and her first inclination was to fear his former fits of jealousy. Back and forth he moved, not saying a word, but there was no risk of the old Mike resurfacing. She could tell by the look on his face; it was different than the old Mike. So she sat, waiting for some reply. Tempted to try to explain further, she decided instead to let her words sink in and allow him to form whatever questions he might have.

Finally, he stood before her and looked her in the eye. "Did you love him as much as he loved you?"

"Before the end of the date, I knew my heart was still so full of you that I could never love another man that way. I never will."

He sat back down on the bed beside her and rested his elbows on his knees. "I hate that he knew you so much better than I did and that your relationship with him was so intimate."

The word intimate caused her to look away. "Mike…" She had thought about the kiss many times. "At the very end, just before he died, we kissed."

He exhaled, shook his head, and began to stand. Then he stopped and sat again.

"It wasn't that kind of kiss, not like you're thinking, but I would never keep it from you."

"I don't want to hear anymore."

They sat for several seconds without speaking.

"I did love him, but it was like family love. Will you believe that?"

"Yes. I know you would never lie to me."

"That's why I had to tell you. We were still married then, so I ask you to forgive me."

"At that point I had no claim on you."

"Yes, you did. I have always been only yours."

Mike slid his arm around Robin's shoulder and pulled her to him. With his other hand he scooped her legs up, dragged her onto his lap, and buried his face into the curve of her neck.

She was snuggled against him, finally free of the secret she had kept. Though she had been tempted to tell him on more than one occasion, she had decided it was better left unsaid. Once she realized how jealous he was of Chris, though, she knew it had become a matter of obedience on her part.

"Something he asked me once was why I never cried when I talked about you. I bawled over Michael but never over you. At the time I couldn't figure it out for the life of me. It wasn't until recently that I began to understand."

"Why?"

"After I came here, I thought that if I cried over you, it would somehow give you power over me still. So I bottled everything up and pushed that entire part of my life into the darkness. Now, I realize you can have all the power you want over me, because I trust what you will do with it. I trust you with all that I have."

"Rob, I will love you as God loves me. I will give myself for you. When I look back now, I know my focus was on me. No matter what you say, it was. That's not the husband I want to be from now on. You are second only to Him but always before me."

"I believe that."

She did without question. Since being back at home, they had the most beautiful marriage. Theirs was a redeemed marriage. It wasn't the "perfect" pretense marriage, rather, a solid, godly marriage, one built upon the foundation of God and supported by the understanding of how precious and rare it was. They had a new appreciation for one another that can only come by losing and finding again.

Once settled into bed, Mike curled himself around Robin. She was lying with her back to him, and he was rubbing his baby girl.

"Wherever you are, I belong. Before, when I was here with you, I felt like a visitor. I hated that I wasn't part of your life. I missed so much."

Robin recalled how he had mentioned something about being a visitor while still delirious with fever, and now his explanation gave her clearer insight.

"From now on you will be a part of every aspect of it."

"I know." He kissed her cheek.

"I'm sorry I've been so jealous of Chris. I promise you that I'm working on it. I guess it will just take time. Believe me, I know how much he helped you, and I'm so thankful he was here for you."

"I've tried to put myself in your position. In some ways I've been jealous of Tim and the role he has played in your life. He was there for you when I wasn't. You have a history with him that you don't have with me. Sounds silly, I know."

"Not silly at all. That's what I feel, too. It's like, we've always been a part of each other's history, but now there's this gap there."

"I know there's a gap, but just look at what God did within both of us during that time. He knew He could never be first in either of our lives as long as we put each other first. It's something I've come to terms with. He had to take me away from you in order to allow me to see Him. This may sound odd, but I don't regret that."

"I don't either. How could I regret a journey that's made me this new man I am?"

She rubbed his hand. "We just have to make sure there's never another gap."

"You can know that will never happen. I will never allow anything to come between us again."

Mike was silent for a moment and then said, "I've been giving it some thought, and I like Christa Grace after all."

"Are you sure?"

Never would she have pressured him into the name. It was important that he love whatever name they picked for their little girl. Up until that day she hadn't understood the depth of his jealousy of Chris, suspected maybe, but not to the extent he had demonstrated earlier. Had she known, she never would have suggested Christa.

"I'm certain."

After some time Mike became quiet, so as Robin began drifting in and out of sleep herself, she listened to his steady breathing. His long frame was wrapped around her. It was how he slept every night, and it gave her the greatest sense of security and comfort. Simply, she was content. She contemplated her earliest girlish expectations of some happily-ever-after life. That was a notion of fairy tales, not real life. What the Lord gives is contentment. Even when the world around is difficult or when friends die or illness comes, contentment is still a possibility. A lump formed in her throat at such a thought, but even if Mike were to be killed on the job or her baby girl taken in her sleep, God would still bring peace in spite of the pain.

Now, looking back, Robin understood that the path to contentment and peace was paved as a result of unmending the veil. Once every barrier in her heart intended to keep God away was removed, she could see and know and be in His presence as He had died to achieve. And in His presence, it was He who had begun the process of stitching. As if mending by hand, He had healed her broken heart and wounded spirit, weaving within her the promise of joy and contentment and peace that could never be stolen away by circumstance. She could never be shaken. In a world where no self-imposed veil remained, a woman could indeed live contentedly-ever-after.

ABOUT THE AUTHOR

As an author and speaker, Lisa has a fresh voice in the genre of women's Christian fiction. Because she did not grow up as an active believer, Lisa's journey to her current life of faith was one filled with bumps and bruises, a fact that allows her genuine empathy toward broken believers and the lost. More in the line of secular fiction, her characters are in process and deeply flawed, individuals most readers can identify with. Lisa doesn't shy away from the tough subjects but rather creatively explores elements of the human condition and all the junk that comes along with life and faith.

Connect with Lisa:
Web: lisaheatonbooks.com

Facebook: facebook.com/lisaheatonbooks/
Twitter: @LisaHeatonBooks
Instagram: @lisaheatonbooks